At the Earth's Core

When Abner Perry invents a vehicle that essentially drills through the earth, he takes it to his good friend (and independently wealthy man about town) David Innes. And what else can they do? Drill down into the earth, of course. What they find there isn't what we'd expect: it's an inner world called Pellicidar, a place where the sun neither sets nor rises – because what appears to be the sun is no sun at all, but the molten core of the earth. Pellucidar is a great fun fantasy world, full of dragons, apes, and reptiles and Weird Things. It's ruled by sorcerous royalty (the princess falls in love with Our Hero, of course) and of course our heroes end up hip-deep in dragons . . .

Pellucidar

When American explorer David Innes first discovered Pellucidar, he fell under the spell of the strange world, earning the respect of many, the undying hatred of a few, and the love of the beautiful Dian. Torn from the arms of Dian by trickery, Innes vows revenge and returns to the Inner World in his most exciting adventure to date. But David Innes appears in Pellucidar far from the land of his beloved and is forced to cross a fierce, unyielding world to reach her. Innes's epic journey through the many strange lands of Pellucidar, including the brilliantly conceived pendent moon and Land of Awful Shadow, and his heart-pounding encounters with prehistoric beasts and strange peoples ranks as one of the best adventures ever penned by Edgar Rice Burroughs.

Tanar of Pellucidar

Pellucidar – the hollow centre of the Earth, a land of savage men and prehistoric beasts – is the scene of this exciting novel.

In Pellucidar dwell the Buried People; here is the Land of Awful Shadow; here the terrible Korsars terrorise the oceans, while dinosaurs and sabretooth tigers terrorise the lands.

This is the story of Tanar, a young chief, and the cave girl Stellara, and of their struggle for survival against a myriad dangers.

Also By Edgar Rice Burroughs

Tarzan

Tarzan of the Apes (1912)
The Return of Tarzan (1913)
The Beasts of Tarzan (1914)
The Son of Tarzan (1914)
Tarzan and the Jewels of Opar (1916)
Jungle Tales of Tarzan (1916, 1917)
Tarzan the Untamed (1919, 1921)
Tarzan the Terrible (1921)
Tarzan and the Golden Lion (1922, 1923)
Tarzan and the Ant Men (1924)
Tarzan, Lord of the Jungle (1927, 1928)
Tarzan and the Lost Empire (1928)
Tarzan at the Earth's Core (1929)
Tarzan the Invincible (1930–1931)
Tarzan Triumphant (1931)
Tarzan and the City of Gold (1932)
Tarzan and the Lion Man (1933, 1934)
Tarzan and the Leopard Men (1935)
Tarzan's Quest (1935, 1936)
Tarzan the Magnificent (1936, 1937)
Tarzan and the Forbidden City (1938)
Tarzan and the Foreign Legion (1947)
Tarzan and the Madman (1964)
Tarzan and the Castaways (1965)
Tarzan and the Valley of Gold (1965) (authorized sequel by Fritz Leiber)

Martian Tales*

A Princess of Mars (1917) (aka Under The Moons Of Mars, 1912)
The Gods of Mars (1918)
The Warlord of Mars (1919)
Thuvia, Maid of Mars (1920)
The Chessmen of Mars (1922)
The Master Mind of Mars (1927)
A Fighting Man of Mars (1930)
Swords of Mars (1934)
Synthetic Men of Mars (1938)

Llana of Gathol (1948)
John Carter of Mars (1941)

Pellucidar

At the Earth's Core (1914)
Pellucidar (1923)
Tanar of Pellucidar (1928)
Back to the Stone Age (1937)
Land of Terror (1944)
Savage Pellucidar (1963)

Venus

Pirates of Venus (1934)
Lost on Venus (1935)
Carson of Venus (1939)
Escape on Venus (1946)
The Wizard of Venus (1970)

The Land That Time Forgot

The Land That Time Forgot (1918)
The People That Time Forgot (1918)
Out of Time's Abyss (1918)

Other Science Fiction

The Moon Maid (1926) (aka The Moon Men)
Beyond the Farthest Star (1941)
The Lost Continent (1916)
The Monster Men (1929)
The Resurrection of Jimber-Jaw (1937)

The Mucker

The Mucker (1914)
The Return of the Mucker (1916)
The Oakdale Affair (1917)

Jungle Adventure Novels

The Man-Eater (1915)
The Cave Girl (1925)
The Eternal Lover (1925) (aka The Eternal Savage)
Jungle Girl (1932) (aka Land of the Hidden Men)
The Lad and the Lion (1938)

*Not available as SF Gateway eBooks

The Pellucidar
SF GATEWAY OMNIBUS

AT THE EARTH'S CORE
PELLUCIDAR
TANAR OF PELLUCIDAR

Edgar Rice Burroughs

GOLLANCZ
LONDON

This omnibus copyright © Edgar Rice Burroughs, Inc. 2013
At the Earth's Core copyright © Edgar Rice Burroughs, Inc. 1914
Pellucidar copyright © Edgar Rice Burroughs, Inc. 1923
Tanar of Pellucidar copyright © Edgar Rice Burroughs, Inc. 1928
Introduction copyright © SFE Ltd 2013
All rights reserved

The right of Edgar Rice Burroughs to be identified as the author
of this work has been asserted by him in accordance with the
Copyright, Designs and Patents Act 1988.

First published in Great Britain in 2013 by Gollancz
An imprint of the Orion Publishing Group
Orion House, 5 Upper St Martin's Lane, London WC2H 9EA

An Hachette UK Company

A CIP catalogue record for this book is available
from the British Library

ISBN 978 0 575 12921 4

1 3 5 7 9 10 8 6 4 2

Typeset by Input Data Services Ltd, Bridgwater, Somerset

Printed and bound by CPI Group (UK) Ltd, Croydon, CR0 4YY

The Orion Publishing Group's policy is to use papers
that are natural, renewable and recyclable products and
made from wood grown in sustainable forests. The logging
and manufacturing processes are expected to conform to
the environmental regulations of the country of origin.

www.orionbooks.co.uk
www.gollancz.co.uk

CONTENTS

ENTER THE SF GATEWAY . . .

Towards the end of 2011, in conjunction with the celebration of fifty years of coherent, continuous science fiction and fantasy publishing, Gollancz launched the SF Gateway.

Over a decade after launching the landmark SF Masterworks series, we realised that the realities of commercial publishing are such that even the Masterworks could only ever scratch the surface of an author's career. Vast troves of classic SF & Fantasy were almost certainly destined never again to see print. Until very recently, this meant that anyone interested in reading any of those books would have been confined to scouring second-hand bookshops. The advent of digital publishing changed that paradigm for ever.

Embracing the future even as we honour the past, Gollancz launched the SF Gateway with a view to utilising the technology that now exists to make available, for the first time, the entire backlists of an incredibly wide range of classic and modern SF and fantasy authors. Our plan, at its simplest, was – and still is! – to use this technology to build on the success of the SF and Fantasy Masterworks series and to go even further.

The SF Gateway was designed to be the new home of classic Science Fiction & Fantasy – the most comprehensive electronic library of classic SFF titles ever assembled. The programme has been extremely well received and we've been very happy with the results. So happy, in fact, that we've decided to complete the circle and return a selection of our titles to print, in these omnibus editions.

We hope you enjoy this selection. And we hope that you'll want to explore more of the classic SF and fantasy we have available. These are wonderful books you're holding in your hand, but you'll find much, much more . . . through the SF Gateway.

www.sfgateway.com

INTRODUCTION

from The Encyclopedia of Science Fiction

Edgar Rice Burroughs (1875–1950) was a US writer whose early life was marked by numerous false starts and failures – at the time he began to write, at the age of 36, he was a pencil-sharpener salesman – but it would seem that the impulse to create the psychically charged Science-Fantasy dream-worlds that became his trademark territory was deep-set and powerful. Once he began to write, with a great rush of built-up energy, within two years he had initiated three of his four most important series. He never stopped.

Certainly the first of his published works has ever since its first appearance served as a successful escape from mid-life burdens and frustrations. *A Princess of Mars* (**1917**), which was originally published February–July 1912 in *All-Story* as "Under the Moons of Mars" as by Norman Bean, opens the long **Barsoom** sequence of novels set on Mars (Barsoom). (Many of Burroughs's novels appeared first in magazines; we are giving only first book publications here).The long array of **Barsoom** tales established that planet as a venue for dream-like and interminable Planetary Romance sagas in which sf and fantasy protocols mixed indiscriminately as an enabling pretext and human men were preternaturally strong, due to the manly intensity of their native Earth gravity. *The Gods of Mars* (**1918**) and *The Warlord of Mars* (**1919**) further recount the exploits of John Carter as he variously befriends and battles various green, yellow and black Martians without the law, and wins the hand of the red-skinned (and oviparous) princess Dejah Thoris. The standard of storytelling and invention is high in the **Barsoom** books, *Chessmen* and *Swords* being particularly fine; but it has always been difficult for some critics to accept the Planetary Romance as being, in any cognitive sense, sf. Although Carter's adventures take place on another planet, he incontrovertibly travels there by magical means, and Barsoom itself is inconsistent and scientifically implausible to modern eyes. It is clear, however, that Burroughs's immense popularity has nothing to do with conventional sf virtues, for it depends on storylines and venues as malleable as dreams, exotic and dangerous and unending.

The **Tarzan** saga is just as much sf (or non-sf) as the **Barsoom** series. Though clearly influenced by H. Rider Haggard, Burroughs did not attempt to imitate one of that writer's prime virtues: Haggard's effort to embed his tales in a vision of history, even though (to modern eyes) his work seems almost dementedly dated, certainly in its imperialist assumptions about race. Allan Quatermain's Africa, even though it is romantically exaggerated, can distress modern readers; but Tarzan's Africa is a cartoon, and must be accepted as being no more governed by the reality principle than Barsoom. *Tarzan of the Apes* (**1914**), the story of an English aristocrat's son raised in the jungle by "great apes" (of a non-existent species) as a kind of feral child, was immensely popular from the beginning, and Burroughs continued producing sequels to the end of his career. In most of them Tarzan has unashamedly fantastic adventures, some of which – discovering lost cities and live Dinosaurs, being reduced to 18 in (46 cm) in height, visiting the Earth's core – evoke the adventure tropes of Pulp sf.

Burroughs's third major series was the **Pellucidar** novels (see below); his fourth series, the **Venus** sequence – created much later in Burroughs's career – concerns the exploits of spaceman Carson Napier on Venus, and consists of *Pirates of Venus* (**1934**), *Lost on Venus* (**1935**), *Carson of Venus* (**1939**) and *Escape on Venus* (**1946**). These books are not as stirring and vivid as the **Barsoom** series. A posthumous story, "The Wizard of Venus", was published in *Tales of Three Planets* (**1964**) and subsequently as the title story of a separate paperback, *The Wizard of Venus* (**1970**). Two of the stories from *Tales of Three Planets*, "Beyond the Farthest Star" (January 1942 *Blue Book*) and the posthumous "Tangor Returns" (in *Tales of Three Planets* **1964**), form the opening of a fifth series which Burroughs abandoned. They are of particular sf interest because they are his only tales with an interstellar setting. The two stories were subsequently republished as a paperback entitled *Beyond the Farthest Star* (**1965**).

Of Burroughs's non-series tales, perhaps the finest is *The Land that Time Forgot* (**1924**; revised in three volumes under the original magazine titles: *The Land that Time Forgot* **1962**, *The People that Time Forgot* **1962** and *Out of Time's Abyss* **1962**), set in the lost world of Caspak near the South Pole, and cunningly presenting in literal form – for animals here metamorphose through evolutionary stages – the dictum that ontogeny recapitulates phylogeny. The book was loosely adapted into two films, *The Land That Time Forgot* (*1975*) and *The People That Time Forgot* (*1977*). Also of interest is *The Moon Maid* **1926**), which describes a civilization in the hollow interior of the Moon and a future Invasion of the Earth.

Among Burroughs's other books, those which can be claimed as sf include: *The Eternal Lover* (**1925**), a prehistoric adventure involving Time Travel featuring a character, Barney Custer, who reappears in the Ruritanian *The Mad King* (**1926**); *The Monster Men* (**1929**), a reworking of the

Frankenstein theme, which should not be confused with *The Man without a Soul* (**1922**), which is not fantasy or sf; *The Cave Girl* (**1925**), another prehistoric romance; *Jungle Girl* (**1932**), about a lost civilization in Cambodia; and *Beyond Thirty* (**1956**), a story set in the twenty-second century after the collapse of European civilization.

It cannot be claimed that Burroughs's works aim at literary polish, or that their merits are intellectual. His lovers and his critics agree on this. Nevertheless, because of their efficient narrative style, and because Burroughs had a genius for highly-energized literalizations of dream-worlds, they have endured. Tarzan is a figure with the iconic density of Sherlock Holmes or Dracula. His "rediscovery" during the 1960s was an astonishing publishing phenomenon, with the majority of his books being reprinted regularly. He had never been forgotten, however. Burroughs has probably had more imitators than any other sf writer, ranging from Otis Adelbert Kline in the 1930s to Kenneth Bulmer (writing as Alan Burt Akers) in the 1970s, with homages from much later writers like Terry Bisson in *Voyage to the Red Planet* (**1990**) and Hitoshi Yoshioka in *Nangun Kihei Taii John Carter* ["Southern Cavalry Captain John Carter"] (**2005**). Serious sf writers who owe a debt to Burroughs include Leigh Brackett, Ray Bradbury, Michael Moorcock and, above all, Philip José Farmer, whose **Lord Grandrith** and **Ancient Opar** novels are among the most enjoyable of latter-day Burroughs-inflected romances. Burroughs was posthumously inducted into the Science Fiction Hall of Fame in 2003. It was clear he belonged there.

Burroughs's third major series, the **Pellucidar** novels, takes its inspiration from the early nineteenth-century Hollow-Earth theory espoused by John Cleves Symmes, and first dramatized by the pseudonymous Adam Seaborn as *Symzonia* (**1820**). To modern eyes, this may well be the most congenial of Burroughs's locales: a secret world without time, where Dinosaurs and beast-men, hidden in their mazes and vast caverns, roam inside our planet. It is perhaps the perfect setting for a Planetary Romance. The first three volumes, here presented, are *At the Earth's Core* (**1922**), *Pellucidar* (**1923**) and *Tanar of Pellucidar* (**1930**); they capture the essence of the concept. A cross-over volume, *Tarzan at the Earth's Core* (**1930**), appeared next, and adds an innovative thrill to the proceedings (cross-over volumes of this sort were exceedingly scarce 80 years ago). This was followed by *Back to the Stone Age* (1937), *Land of Terror* (1944) and *Savage Pellucidar* (1941). Burroughs's genius at giving pleasure was never more perfectly realized than here, miles beneath our feet.

For a more detailed version of the above, see Edgar Rice Burroughs' author entry in *The Encyclopedia of Science Fiction*:

http://sf-encyclopedia.com/entry/burroughs_edgar_rice

Some terms above are capitalised when they would not normally be so rendered; this indicates that the terms represent discrete entries in *The Encyclopedia of Science Fiction*.

AT THE EARTH'S CORE

PROLOGUE

In the first place, please bear in mind that I do not expect you to believe this story. Nor could you wonder had you witnessed a recent experience of mine when, in the armour of blissful and stupendous ignorance, I gaily narrated the gist of it to a Fellow of the Royal Geological Society on the occasion of my last trip to London.

You would surely have thought that I had been detected in no less a heinous crime than the purloining of the Crown Jewels from the Tower, or putting poison in the coffee of His Majesty the King.

The erudite gentleman in whom I confided congealed before I was half through – it is all that saved him from exploding – and my dreams of an Honorary Fellowship, gold medals, and a niche in the Hall of Fame faded into the thin, cold air of his arctic atmosphere.

But I believe the story, and so would you, and so would the learned Fellow of the Royal Geological Society, had you and he heard it from the lips of the man who told it to me. Had you seen, as I did, the fire of truth in those grey eyes; had you felt the ring of sincerity in that quiet voice; had you realized the pathos of it all – you, too, would believe. You would not have needed the final ocular proof that I had – the weird rhamphorhynchus-like creature which he had brought back with him from the inner world.

I came upon him quite suddenly, and no less unexpectedly, upon the rim of the great Sahara Desert. He was standing before a goat-skin tent amidst a clump of date palms within a tiny oasis. Close by was an Arab douar of some eight or ten tents.

I had come down from the north to hunt lions. My party consisted of a dozen children of the desert – I was the only 'white' man. As we approached the little clump of verdure I saw the man come from his tent and with hand-shaded eyes peer intently at us. At sight of me he advanced rapidly to meet us.

'A white man!' he cried. 'May the good Lord be praised! I have been watching you for hours, hoping against hope that *this* time there would be a white man. Tell me the date. What year is it?'

And when I told him he staggered as though he had been struck full in the face, so that he was compelled to grasp my stirrup leather for support.

'It cannot be!' he cried after a moment. 'It cannot be! Tell me that you are mistaken, or that you are but joking.'

'I am telling you the truth, my friend,' I replied. 'Why should I deceive a stranger, or attempt to, in so simple a matter as the date?'

For some time he stood in silence, with bowed head.

'Ten years!' he murmured, at last. 'Ten years, and I thought that at the most it could be scarce more than one!'

That night he told me his story – the story that I give you here as nearly in his own words as I can recall them.

1

Towards the Eternal Fires

I was born in Connecticut about thirty years ago. My name is David Innes. My father was a wealthy mine-owner. When I was nineteen he died. All his property was to be mine when I had attained my majority – provided that I had devoted the two years intervening in close application to the great business I was to inherit.

I did my best to fulfil the last wishes of my parent – not because of the inheritance, but because I loved and honoured my father. For six months I toiled in the mines and in the counting-rooms, for I wished to know every minute detail of the business.

Then Perry interested me in his invention. He was an old fellow who had devoted the better part of a long life to the perfection of a mechanical subterranean prospector. As relaxation he studied palaeontology. I looked over his plans, listened to his arguments, inspected his working model, and then, convinced, I advanced the funds necessary to construct a full-sized, practical prospector.

I shall not go into the details of its construction – it lies out there in the desert now – about two miles from here. To-morrow you may care to ride out and see it. Roughly, it is a steel cylinder a hundred feet long, and jointed so that it may turn and twist through solid rock if need be. At one end is a mighty revolving drill operated by an engine which Perry said generated more power to the cubic inch than any other engine did to the cubic foot. I remember that he used to claim that that invention alone would make us fabulously wealthy – we were going to make the whole thing public after the successful issue of our first secret trial – but Perry never returned from that trial trip, and I only after ten years.

I recall as it were but yesterday the night of that momentous occasion upon which we were to test the practicability of that wondrous invention. It was near midnight when we repaired to the lofty tower in which Perry had constructed his 'iron mole,' as he was wont to call the thing. The great nose rested upon the bare earth of the floor. We passed through the doors into the outer jacket, secured them, and then passing on into the cabin, which contained the controlling mechanism within the inner tube, switched on the electric lights.

Perry looked to his generator; to the great tanks that held the life-giving chemicals with which he was to manufacture fresh air to replace that which we consumed in breathing; to his instruments for recording temperatures, speed, distance, and for examining the materials through which we were to pass.

He tested the steering device, and looked over the mighty cogs which transmitted its marvellous velocity to the giant drill at the nose of his strange craft.

Our seats, into which we strapped ourselves, were so arranged upon transverse bars that we would be upright whether the craft were plough-ing her way downward into the bowels of the earth, or running horizon-tally along some great seam of coal, or rising vertically towards the surface again.

At length all was ready. Perry bowed his head in prayer. For a moment we were silent, and then the old man's hand grasped the starting lever. There was a frightful roaring beneath us – the giant frame trembled and vibrated – there was a rush of sound as the loose earth passed up through the hollow space between the inner and outer jackets to be deposited in our wake. We were off.

The noise was deafening. The sensation was frightful. For a full minute neither of us could do aught but cling with the proverbial desperation of the drowning man to the handrails of our swinging seats. Then Perry glanced at the thermometer.

'Gad!' he cried, 'it cannot be possible – quick! What does the distance meter read?'

That and the speedometer were both on my side of the cabin, and as I turned to take a reading from the former I could see Perry muttering.

'Ten degrees rise – it cannot be possible!' and then I saw him tug franti-cally upon the steering wheel.

As I finally found the tiny needle in the dim light I translated Perry's ev-ident excitement, and my heart sank within me. But when I spoke I hid the fear which haunted me.

'It will be seven hundred feet, Perry,' I said, 'by the time you can turn her into the horizontal.'

'You'd better lend me a hand then, my boy,' he replied, 'for I cannot budge her out of the vertical alone. God give that our combined strength may be equal to the task, for else we are lost.'

I wormed my way to the old man's side with never a doubt but that the great wheel would yield on the instant to the power of my young and vig-orous muscles. Nor was my belief mere vanity, for always had my physique been the envy and despair of my fellows. And for that very reason it had waxed even greater than Nature had intended, since my natural pride in my great strength had led me to care for and develop my body and my muscles by every means within my power. What with boxing, football, and base-ball, I had been in training since childhood.

And so it was with the utmost confidence that I laid hold of the huge iron rim; but though I threw every ounce of my strength into it, my best effort was as unavailing as Perry's had been – the thing would not budge – the grim, insensate, horrible thing that was holding us upon the straight road to death!

At length I gave up the useless struggle, and without a word returned to my seat. There was no need for words – at least none that I could imagine, unless Perry desired to pray. And I was quite sure that he would, for he never left an opportunity neglected where he might sandwich in a prayer. He prayed when he arose in the morning, he prayed before he ate, he prayed when he had finished eating, and before he went to bed at night he prayed again. In between he often found excuses to pray, even when the provoca-tion seemed rather far-fetched to my worldly eyes; now that he was about to die I felt positive that I should witness a perfect orgy of prayer – if one may allude with such a simile to so solemn an act.

But to my astonishment I discovered that with death staring him in the face Abner Perry was transformed into a new being. From his lips there flowed – not prayer – but a clear and limpid stream of undiluted profan-ity, and it was all directed at that quietly stubborn piece of unyielding mechanism.

'I should think, Perry,' I chided, 'that a man of your professed religious-ness would rather be at his prayers than cursing in the presence of imminent death.'

'Death!' he cried. 'Death is it that appals you? That is nothing by compar-ison with the loss the world must suffer. Why, David, within this iron cylin-der we have demonstrated possibilities that science has scarce dreamed. We have harnessed a new principle, and with it animated a piece of steel with the power of ten thousand men. That two lives will be snuffed out is noth-ing to the world-calamity that entombs in the bowels of the earth the dis-coveries that I have made and proved in the successful construction of the thing that is now carrying us farther and farther towards the eternal central fires.'

I am frank to admit that for myself I was much more concerned with our own immediate future than with any problematical loss which the world might be about to suffer. The world was at least ignorant of its bereavement, while to me it was a real and terrible actuality.

'What can we do?' I asked, hiding my perturbation beneath the mask of a low and level voice.

'We may stop here, and die of asphyxiation when our atmosphere tanks are empty,' replied Perry, 'or we may continue on with the slight hope that we may later sufficiently deflect the prospector from the vertical to carry us along the arc of a great circle which must eventually return us to the surface. If we succeed in so doing before we reach the higher internal temperature we may even yet survive. There would seem to me to be about one chance in several million that we shall succeed – otherwise we shall die more quickly but no more surely than as though we sat supinely waiting for the torture of a slow and horrible death.'

I glanced at the thermometer. It registered 110 degrees. While we were talking the mighty iron mole had bored its way over a mile into the rock of the earth's crust.

'Let us continue on, then,' I replied. 'It should soon be over at this rate. You never intimated that the speed of this thing would be so high, Perry. Didn't you know it?'

'No,' he answered. 'I could not figure the speed exactly, for I had no instrument for measuring the mighty power of my generator. I reasoned, however, that we should make about five hundred yards an hour.'

'And we are making seven miles an hour,' I concluded for him, as I sat with my eyes upon the distance meter. 'How thick is the earth's crust, Perry?' I asked.

'There are almost as many conjectures as to that as there are geologists,' was his answer. 'One estimates it thirty miles, because the internal heat, increasing at the rate of about one degree to each sixty to seventy feet depth, would be sufficient to fuse the most refractory substances at that distance beneath the surface. Another finds that the phenomena of precession and nutation require that the earth, if not entirely solid, must at least have a shell not less than eight hundred to a thousand miles in thickness. So there you are. You may take your choice.'

'And if it should prove solid?' I asked.

'It will be all the same to us in the end, David,' replied Perry. 'At the best our oil fuel will suffice to carry us but three or four days, while our atmosphere cannot last to exceed three. Neither, then, is sufficient to bear us in safety through eight thousand miles of rock to the antipodes.'

'If the crust is of sufficient thickness we shall come to a final stop between six and seven hundred miles beneath the earth's surface; but during the last hundred and fifty miles of our journey we shall be corpses. Am I correct?' I asked.

'Quite correct, David. Are you frightened?'

'I do not know. It all has come so suddenly that I scarce believe that either of us realizes the real terrors of our position. I feel that I should be reduced to panic; but yet I am not. I imagine that the shock has been so great as to partially stun our sensibilities.'

Again I turned to the thermometer. The mercury was rising with less rapidity. It was now but 140 degrees, although we had penetrated to a depth of nearly four miles. I told Perry, and he smiled.

'We have shattered one theory at least,' was his only comment, and then he returned to his self-assumed occupation of fluently cursing the steering wheel. I once heard a pirate swear, but his best efforts would have seemed like those of a tyro alongside of Perry's masterful and scientific imprecations.

Once more I tried my hand at the wheel, but I might as well have essayed to swing the earth itself. At my suggestion Perry stopped the generator, and as we came to rest I again threw all my strength into a supreme effort to move the thing even a hair's breadth – but the results were as barren as when we had been travelling at top speed.

I shook my head sadly, and motioned to the starting lever. Perry pulled it towards him, and once again we were plunging downward towards eternity at the rate of seven miles an hour. I sat with my eyes glued to the thermometer and the distance meter. The mercury was rising very slowly now, though even at 145 degrees it was almost unbearable within the narrow confines of our metal prison.

About noon, or twelve hours after our start upon this unfortunate journey, we had bored to a depth of eighty-four miles, at which point the mercury registered 153 degrees F.

Perry was becoming more hopeful, although upon what meagre food he sustained his optimism I could not conjecture. From cursing he had turned to singing – I felt that the strain had at last affected his mind. For several hours, we had not spoken except as he asked me for the readings of the instruments from time to time, and I announced them. My thoughts were filled with vain regrets. I recalled numerous acts of my past life which I should have been glad to have had a few more years to live down. There was the affair in the Latin Commons at Andover when Calhoun and I had put gunpowder in the stove – and nearly killed one of the masters. And then – but what was the use? I was about to die and atone for all these things and several more. Already the heat was sufficient to give me a foretaste of the hereafter. A few more degrees and I felt that I should lose consciousness.

'What are the readings now, David?' Perry's voice broke in upon my sombre reflections.

'Ninety miles and 153 degrees,' I replied.

'Gad, but we've knocked that thirty-mile crust theory into a cocked hat!' he cried gleefully.

'Precious lot of good it will do us,' I growled back.

'But, my boy,' he continued, 'doesn't that temperature reading mean anything to you? Why it hasn't gone up in six miles. Think of it, son!'

'Yes, I'm thinking of it,' I answered; 'but what difference will it make when our air supply is exhausted whether the temperature is 153 degrees or

153,000? We'll be just as dead, and no one will know the difference, anyhow.' But I must admit that for some unaccountable reason the stationary temperature did renew my waning hope. What I hoped for I could not have explained, nor did I try. The very fact, as Perry took pains to explain, of the blasting of several very exact and learned scientific hypotheses made it apparent that we could not know what lay before us within the bowels of the earth, and so we might continue to hope for the best, at least until we were dead – when hope would no longer be essential to our happiness. It was very good and logical reasoning, and so I embraced it.

At one hundred miles the temperature had *dropped to 152½ degrees*! When I announced it Perry reached over and hugged me.

From then on until noon of the second day it continued to drop until it became as uncomfortably cold as it had been unbearably hot before. At a depth of two hundred and forty miles our nostrils were assailed by almost overpowering ammonia fumes, and the temperature had dropped to ten *below zero*! We suffered nearly two hours of this intense and bitter cold, until at about two hundred and forty-five miles from the surface of the earth we entered a stratum of solid ice, when the mercury quickly rose to 34 degrees. During the next three hours we passed through ten miles of ice, eventually emerging into another series of ammonia-impregnated strata, where the mercury again fell to 10 degrees below zero.

Slowly it rose once more until we were convinced that at last we were nearing the molten interior of the earth. At four hundred miles the temperature had reached 152 degrees. Feverishly I watched the thermometer. Slowly it rose. Perry had ceased singing and was at last praying.

Our hopes had received such a death-blow that the gradually increasing heat seemed to our distorted imaginations much greater than it really was. For another hour I saw that pitiless column of mercury rise and rise until at four hundred and ten miles it stood at 153 degrees. Now it was that we began to hang upon those readings in almost breathless anxiety.

One hundred and fifty-three degrees had been the maximum temperature above the ice stratum. Would it stop at this point again, or would it continue its merciless climb? We knew that there was no hope, and yet with the persistence of life itself we continued to hope against practical certainty.

Already the air-tanks were at low ebb – there was barely enough of the precious gases to sustain us for another twelve hours. But would we be alive to know or care? It seemed incredible.

At four hundred and twenty miles I took another reading.

'Perry!' I shouted. 'Perry, man! She's going down! She's going down! She's 152 degrees again.'

'Gad!' he cried. 'What can it mean? Can the earth be cold at the centre?'

'I do not know, Perry,' I answered; 'but thank God, if I am to die it shall not be by fire – that is all that I have feared. I can face the thought of any death but that.'

Down, down went the mercury until it stood as low as it had seven miles from the surface of the earth, and then of a sudden the realization broke upon us that death was very near. Perry was the first to discover it. I saw him fussing with the valves that regulate the air supply. And at the same time I experienced difficulty in breathing. My head felt dizzy – my limbs heavy.

I saw Perry crumple in his seat. He gave himself a shake and sat erect again. Then he turned towards me.

'Good-bye, David,' he said. 'I guess this is the end,' and then he smiled and closed his eyes.

'Good-bye, Perry, and good luck to you,' I answered, smiling back at him. But I fought off that awful lethargy. I was very young – I did not want to die.

For an hour I battled against the cruelly enveloping death that surrounded me upon all sides. At first I found that by climbing high into the framework above me I could find more of the precious, life-giving elements, and for a while these sustained me. It must have been an hour after Perry had succumbed that I at last came to the realization that I could no longer carry on this unequal struggle against the inevitable.

With my last flickering ray of consciousness I turned mechanically towards the distance meter. It stood at exactly five hundred miles from the earth's surface – and then of a sudden the huge thing that bore us came to a stop. The rattle of hurtling rock through the hollow jacket ceased. The wild racing of the giant drill betokened that it was running loose in air – and then another truth flashed upon me. The point of the prospector was *above* us. Slowly it dawned on me that since passing through the ice strata it had been above. We had turned in the ice and sped upward towards the earth's crust. Thank God! We were safe!

I put my nose to the intake pipe through which samples were to have been taken during the passage of the prospector through the earth, and my fondest hopes were realized – a flood of fresh air was pouring into the iron cabin. The reaction left me in a state of collapse, and I lost consciousness.

2

A Strange World

I was unconscious little more than an instant, for as I lunged forward from the crossbeam to which I had been clinging and fell with a crash to the floor of the cabin, the shock brought me to myself.

My first concern was with Perry. I was horrified at the thought that upon the very threshold of salvation he might be dead. Tearing open his shirt, I placed my ear to his breast. I could have cried with relief – his heart was beating quite regularly.

At the water tank I wetted my handkerchief, slapping it smartly across his forehead and face several times. In a moment I was rewarded by the raising of his lids. For a time he lay wide-eyed and quite uncomprehending. Then his scattered wits slowly forgathered, and he sat up sniffing the air with an expression of wonderment upon his face.

'Why, David,' he cried at last, 'it's air, as sure as I live. Why – why what does it mean? Where in the world are we? What has happened?'

'It means that we're back at the surface all right, Perry,' I cried; 'but where, I don't know. I haven't opened her up yet. Been too busy reviving you. Lord, man, but you had a close squeak!'

'You say we're back at the surface, David? How can that be? How long have I been unconscious?'

'Not long. We turned in the ice stratum. Don't you recall the sudden whirling of our seats? After that the drill was above us instead of below. We didn't notice it at the time; but I recall it now.'

'You mean to say that we turned back in the ice stratum, David? That is not possible. The prospector cannot turn unless its nose is deflected. If the nose were deflected from the outside – by some external force or resistance – the steering wheel within would have moved in response. The steering wheel has not budged, David, since we started. You know that.'

I did know it; but here we were with our drill racing in pure air, and copious volumes of it pouring into the cabin.

'We couldn't have turned in the ice stratum, Perry, I know as well as you,' I replied, 'but the fact remains that we did, for here we are this minute at the surface of the earth again, and I am going out to see just where.'

'Better wait till morning, David – it must be midnight now.'

I glanced at the chronometer.

'Half after twelve. We have been out seventy-two hours, so it must be midnight. Nevertheless I'm going to have a look at the blessed sky that I had given up all hope of ever seeing again,' and so saying I lifted the bars from the inner door, and swung it open. There was quite a quantity of loose material in the jacket, and this I had to remove with a shovel to get at the opposite door in the outer shell.

In a short time I had removed enough of the earth and rock to the floor of the cabin to expose the door beyond. Perry was directly behind me as I threw it open. The upper half was above the surface of the ground. With an expression of surprise I turned and looked at Perry – it was broad daylight without!

'Something seems to have gone wrong either with our calculations or the chronometer,' I said. Perry shook his head – there was a strange expression in his eyes.

'Let's have a look beyond that door, David,' he cried.

Together we stepped out to stand in silent contemplation of a landscape at once weird and beautiful. Before us a low and level shore stretched down to a silent sea. As far as the eye could reach the surface of the water was dotted with countless tiny isles – some of towering, barren, granite rock – others resplendent in gorgeous trappings of tropical vegetation, myriad-starred with the magnificent splendour of vivid blooms.

Behind us rose a dark and forbidding wood of giant arborescent ferns intermingled with the commoner types of a primeval tropical forest. Huge creepers depended in great loops from tree to tree, dense underbrush over-grew a tangled mass of fallen trunks and branches. Upon the outer verge we could see the same splendid colouring of countless blossoms that glorified the islands, but within the dense shadows all seemed dark and gloomy as the grave.

And upon all the noonday sun poured its torrid rays out of a cloudless sky.

'Where on earth can we be?' I asked, turning to Perry.

For some moments the old man did not reply. He stood with bowed head, buried in deep thought. But at last he spoke.

'David,' he said, 'I am not so sure that we are on earth.'

'What do you mean, Perry?' I cried. 'Do you think that we are dead, and that this is heaven?'

He smiled, and turning, pointed to the nose of the prospector protruding from the ground at our backs.

'But for that, David, I might believe that we were indeed come to the country beyond the Styx. The prospector renders that theory untenable – it certainly, could never have gone to heaven. However, I am willing to con-cede that we actually may be in another world from that which we have always known. If we are not *on* earth, there is every reason to believe that we may be *in* it.'

'We may have quartered through the earth's crust and come out upon some tropical island of the West Indies,' I suggested.

Again Perry shook his head.

'Let us wait and see, David,' he replied, 'and in the meantime suppose we do a bit of exploring up and down the coast – we may find a native who can enlighten us.'

As we walked along the beach Perry gazed long and earnestly across the water. Evidently he was wrestling with a mighty problem.

'David,' he said abruptly, 'do you perceive anything unusual about the horizon?'

As I looked I began to appreciate the reason for the strangeness of the landscape that had haunted me from the, first with an illusive suggestion of the bizarre and unnatural – *there was no horizon!* As far as the eye could reach out the sea continued, and upon its bosom floated tiny islands, those in the distance reduced to mere specks; but ever beyond them was the sea, until the impression became quite real that one was *looking up* at the most distant point that the eye could fathom – the distance was lost in the distance. That was all – there was no clear-cut horizontal line marking the dip of the globe below the line of vision.

'A great light is commencing to break on me,' continued Perry, taking out his watch. 'I believe that I have partially solved the riddle. It is now two o'clock. When we emerged from the prospector the sun was directly above us. Where is it now?'

I glanced up to find the great orb still motionless in the centre of the heavens. And such a sun! I had scarcely noticed it before. Fully thrice the size of the sun I had known throughout my life, and apparently so near that the sight of it carried the conviction that one might almost reach up and touch it.

'My God, Perry, where are we?' I exclaimed. 'This thing is beginning to get on my nerves.'

'I think that I may state quite positively, David,' he commenced, 'that we are – ' but he got no farther. From behind us in the vicinity of the prospector there came the most thunderous, awe-inspiring roar that ever had fallen upon my ears. With one accord we turned to discover the author of that fearsome noise.

Had I still retained the suspicion that we were on earth the sight that met my eyes would quite entirely have banished it. Emerging from the forest was a colossal beast which closely resembled a bear. It was fully as large as the largest elephant, and with great forepaws armed with huge claws. Its nose, or snout, depended nearly a foot below its lower jaw, much after the manner of a rudimentary trunk. The giant body was covered by a coat of thick, shaggy hair.

Roaring horribly it came towards us at a ponderous, shuffling trot. I turned towards Perry to suggest that it might be wise to seek other surroundings – the idea had evidently occurred to Perry previously, for he was already a hundred paces away, and with each second his prodigious bounds increased the distance. I had never guessed what latent speed possibilities the old gentleman possessed.

I saw that he was headed towards a little point of the forest which ran out towards the sea not far from where we had been standing, and as the mighty creature, the sight of which had galvanized him into such remarkable action, was forging steadily towards me I set off after Perry, though at a somewhat more decorous pace. It was evident that the massive beast pursuing us was not built for speed, so all that I considered necessary was to gain the trees sufficiently ahead of it to enable me to climb to the safety of some great branch before it came up.

Notwithstanding our danger I could not help but laugh at Perry's frantic capers as he essayed to gain the safety of the lower branches of the trees he now had reached. The stems were bare for a distance of some fifteen feet – at least on those trees which Perry attempted to ascend, for the suggestion of safety carried by the larger of the forest giants had evidently attracted him to them. A dozen times he scrambled up the trunks like a huge cat, only to fall back to the ground once more, and with each failure he cast a horrified glance over his shoulder at the oncoming brute, simultaneously emitting terror-stricken shrieks that awoke the echoes of the grim forest.

At length he spied a dangling creeper about the bigness of one's wrist, and when I reached the trees he was racing madly up it, hand over hand. He had almost reached the lowest branch of the tree from which the creeper depended when the thing parted beneath his weight and he fell sprawling at my feet.

The misfortune now was no longer amusing, for the beast was already too close to us for comfort. Seizing Perry by the shoulder I dragged him to his feet, and rushing to a smaller tree – one that he could easily encircle with his arms and legs – I hoisted him as far up as I could, and then left him to his fate, for a glance over my shoulder revealed the awful beast almost upon me.

It was the great size of the thing alone that saved me. Its enormous bulk rendered it too slow upon its feet to cope with the agility of my young muscles, and so I was enabled to dodge out of its way and run completely behind it before its slow wits could direct it in pursuit.

The few seconds of grace that this gave me found me safely lodged in the branches of a tree a few paces from that in which Perry had at last found a haven.

Did I say safely lodged? At the time I thought we were quite safe, and so did Perry. He was praying – raising his voice in thanksgiving at our deliverance – and had just completed a sort of paean of gratitude that the thing couldn't climb a tree when without warning it reared up beneath him on its enormous tail and hind feet, and reached those fearfully armed paws quite to the branch upon which he crouched.

The accompanying roar was all but drowned in Perry's scream of fright, and he came near tumbling headlong into the gaping jaws beneath him, so precipitate was his impetuous haste to vacate the dangerous limb. It was with a deep sigh of relief that I saw him gain a higher branch in safety.

And then the brute did that which froze us both anew with horror. Grasping the tree's stem with his powerful paws he dragged down with all the great weight of his huge bulk and all the irresistible force of those mighty muscles. Slowly, but surely, the stem began to bend towards him. Inch by inch he worked his paws upward as the tree leaned more and more from the perpendicular. Perry clung chattering in a panic of terror. Higher and higher into the bending and swaying tree he clambered. More and more rapidly was the tree-top inclining towards the ground.

I saw now why the great brute was armed with such enormous paws. The use that he was putting them to was precisely that for which nature had intended them. The sloth-like creature was herbivorous, and to feed that mighty carcase entire trees must be stripped of their foliage. The reason for its attacking us might easily be accounted for on the supposition of an ugly disposition such as that which the fierce and stupid rhinoceros of Africa possesses. But these were later reflections. At the moment I was too frantic with apprehension on Perry's behalf to consider aught other than a means to save him from the death that loomed so close.

Realizing that I could out-distance the clumsy brute in the open, I dropped from my leafy sanctuary intent only on distracting the thing's attention from Perry long enough to enable the old man to gain the safety of a larger tree. There were many close by which not even the terrific strength of that titanic monster could bend.

As I touched the ground I snatched a broken limb from the tangled mass that matted the jungle-like floor of the forest and, leaping unnoticed behind the shaggy back, dealt the brute a terrific blow. My plan worked like magic. From the previous slowness of the beast I had been led to look for no such marvellous agility as he now displayed. Releasing his hold upon the tree he dropped on all-fours and at the same time swung his great, wicked tail with a force that would have broken every bone in my body had it struck me; but, fortunately, I had turned to flee at the very instant that I felt my blow land upon the towering back.

As it started in pursuit of me I made the mistake of running along the edge of the forest rather than making for the open beach. In a moment I was knee-deep in rotting vegetation, and the awful thing behind me was gaining rapidly as I floundered and fell in my efforts to extricate myself.

A fallen log gave me an instant's advantage, for climbing upon it I leapt to another a few paces farther on, and in this way was able to keep clear of the mush that carpeted the surrounding ground. But the zigzag course that this necessitated was placing such a heavy handicap upon me that my pursuer was steadily gaining upon me.

Suddenly from behind I heard a tumult of howls and sharp, piercing barks

– much the sound that a pack of wolves raise when in full cry. Involuntarily I glanced backward to discover the origin of this new and menacing note, with the result that I missed my footing and went sprawling once more upon my face in the deep mush.

My mammoth enemy was so close by this time that I knew I must feel the weight of one of his terrible paws before I could rise, but to my surprise the blow did not fall upon me. The howling and snapping and barking of the new element which had been infused into the mêlée now seemed centred quite close behind me, and as I raised myself upon my hands and glanced around I saw what it was that had distracted the *dyryth*, as I afterwards learned the thing is called, from my trail.

It was surrounded by a pack of some hundred wolf-like creatures – wild dogs they seemed – that rushed growling and snapping in upon it from all sides, so that they sank their white fangs into the slow brute and were away again before it could reach them with its huge paws or sweeping tail.

But these were not all that my startled eyes perceived. Chattering and gibbering through the lower branches of the trees came a company of man-like creatures evidently urging on the dog pack. They were to all appearances strikingly similar in aspect to the negro of Africa. Their skins were very black, and their features much like those of the more pronounced negroid, type, except that the head receded more rapidly above the eyes, leaving little or no forehead. Their arms were rather longer and their legs shorter in proportion to the torso than in man, and later I noticed that their great toes protruded at right angles from their feet – because of their arboreal habits, I presume. Behind them trailed long, slender tails, which they used in climbing quite as much as they did either their hands or feet.

I had stumbled to my feet the moment that I discovered that the wolf-dogs were holding the dyryth at bay. At sight of me several of the savage creatures left off worrying the great brute to come slinking with bared fangs towards me, and as I turned to run towards the trees again to seek safety among the lower branches, I saw a number of the man-apes leaping and chattering in the foliage of the nearest tree.

Between them and the beasts behind me there was little choice, but at least there was a doubt as to the reception these grotesque parodies on humanity would accord me, while there was none as to the fate which awaited me beneath the grinning fangs of my fierce pursuers.

And so I raced on towards the trees, intending to pass beneath that which held the man-things and take refuge in another farther on; but the wolf-dogs were very close behind me – so close that I had despaired of escaping them, when one of the creatures in the trees above swung down head-foremost, his tail looped about a great limb, and grasping me beneath my armpits swung me in safety up among his fellows.

There they fell to examining me with the utmost excitement and curiosity. They picked at my clothing, my hair, and my flesh. They turned me about to see if I had a tail, and when they discovered that I was not so equipped they fell into roars of laughter. Their teeth were very large and white and even, except for the upper canines, which were a trifle longer than the others – protruding just a bit when the mouth was closed.

When they had examined me for a few moments one of them discovered that my clothing was not part of me, with the result that garment by garment they tore it from me amidst peals of the wildest laughter. Ape-like, they essayed to don the apparel themselves, but their ingenuity was not sufficient to the task and so they gave it up.

In the meantime I had been straining my eyes to catch a glimpse of Perry, but nowhere about could I see him, although the clump of trees in which he had first taken refuge was in full view. I was much exercised by the fear that something had befallen him, and though I called his name aloud several times there was no response.

Tired at last of playing with my clothing the creatures threw it to the ground, and catching me, one on either side, by an arm, started off at a most terrifying pace through the tree-tops. Never have I experienced such a journey before or since – even now I oftentimes awake from a deep sleep haunted by the horrid remembrance of that awful experience.

From tree to tree the agile creatures sprang like flying squirrels, while the cold sweat stood upon my brow as I glimpsed the depths beneath, into which a single misstep on the part of either of my bearers would hurl me. As they bore me along, my mind was occupied with a thousand bewildering thoughts. What had become of Perry? Would I ever see him again? What were the intentions of these half-human things into whose hands I had fallen? Were they inhabitants of the same world into which I had been born? No! It could not be. But yet where else? I had not left that earth – of that I was sure. Still neither could I reconcile the things which I had seen to a belief that I was still in the world of my birth. With a sigh I gave it up.

3

A Change of Masters

We must have travelled several miles through the dark and dismal wood when we came suddenly upon a dense village built high among the branches of the trees. As we approached it my escort broke into wild shouting which was immediately answered from within, and a minute later a swarm of creatures of the same strange race as those who had captured me poured out to meet us. Again I was the centre of a wildly chattering horde. I was pulled this way and that. Pinched, pounded, and thumped until I was black and blue, yet I do not think that their treatment was dictated by either cruelty or malice – I was a curiosity, a freak, a new plaything, and their childish minds required the added evidence of all their senses to back up the testimony of their eyes.

Presently they dragged me within the village, which consisted of several hundred rude shelters of boughs and leaves supported upon the branches of the trees. Between the huts, which sometimes formed crooked streets, were dead branches and the trunks of small trees which connected the huts upon one tree to those within adjoining trees; the whole network of huts and pathways forming an almost solid flooring a good fifty feet above the ground.

I wondered why these agile creatures required connecting bridges between the trees, but later, when I saw the motley aggregation of half-savage beasts which they kept within their village I realized the necessity for the pathways. There were a number of the same vicious wolf-dogs which we had left worrying the dyryth, and many goatlike animals whose distended udders explained the reason for their presence.

My guard halted before one of the huts, into which I was pushed; then two of the creatures squatted down before the entrance – to prevent my escape, doubtless. Though where I should have escaped to I certainly had not the remotest conception.

I had no more than entered the dark shadows of the interior than there fell upon my ears the tones of a familiar voice, in prayer.

'Perry!' I cried. 'Dear old Perry! Thank the Lord you are safe.'

'David! Can it be possible that you escaped?' And the old man stumbled towards me and threw his arms about me.

He had seen me fall before the dyryth, and then he had been seized by a number of the ape-creatures and borne through the tree-tops to their village. His captors had been as inquisitive as to his strange clothing as had mine, with the same result. As we looked at each other we could not help but laugh.

'With a tail, David,' remarked Perry, 'you would make a very handsome ape.'

'Maybe we can borrow a couple,' I rejoined. 'They seem to be quite the thing this season. I wonder what the creatures intend doing with us, Perry. They don't seem really savage. What do you suppose they can be? You were about to tell me where we are when that great hairy frigate bore down upon us – have you really any idea at all?'

'Yes, David,' he replied, 'I know precisely where we are. We have made a magnificent discovery, my boy! We have proved that the earth is hollow. We have passed entirely through its crust to the inner world.'

'Perry, you are mad!'

'Not at all, David. For two hundred and fifty miles our prospector bore us through the crust beneath our outer world. At that point it reached the centre of gravity of the five-hundred-mile-thick crust. Up to that point we had been descending – direction is, of course, merely relative. Then at the moment that our seats revolved – the thing that made you believe that we had turned about and were speeding upward – we passed the centre of gravity and, though we did not alter the direction of our progress, yet we were in reality moving upward – towards the surface of the inner world. Does not the strange fauna and flora which we have seen convince you that you are not in the world of your birth? And the horizon – could it present the strange aspect which we both noted unless we were indeed standing upon the inside surface of a sphere?'

'But the sun, Perry,' I urged. 'How in the world can the sun shine through five hundred miles of solid crust?'

'It is not the sun of the outer world that we see here. It is another sun – an entirely different sun – that casts its eternal noonday effulgence upon the face of the inner world. Look at it now, David, – if you can see it from the doorway of this hut – and you will see that it is still in the exact centre of the heavens. We have been here for many hours – yet it is still noon.

'And withal it is very simple, David. The earth was once a nebulous mass. It cooled, and as it cooled it shrank. At length a thin crust of solid matter formed upon its outer surface – a sort of shell; but within it was partially molten matter and highly expanded gases. As it continued to cool, what happened? Centrifugal force hurled the particles of the nebulous centre towards the crust as rapidly as they approached a solid state. You have seen the same principle practically applied in the modern cream separator. Presently there was only a small superheated core of gaseous matter remaining within a huge vacant interior left by the contraction of the cooling gases. The equal attraction of the solid crust from all directions maintained this luminous core in the exact centre of the hollow globe. What remains of it is the sun you saw to-day – a relatively tiny thing at the exact centre of the earth. Equally to every part of this inner world it diffuses its perpetual noonday light and torrid heat.

'This inner world must have cooled sufficiently to support animal life long ages after life appeared upon the outer crust, but that the same agencies were at work here is evident from the similar forms of both animal and vegetable creation which we have already seen. Take the great beast which attacked us, for example. Unquestionably a counterpart of the Megatherium of the post-Pliocene period of the outer crust, whose fossilized skeleton has been found in South America.'

'But the grotesque inhabitants of this forest?' I urged. 'Surely they have no counterpart in the earth's history.'

'Who can tell?' he rejoined. 'They may constitute the link between ape and man, all traces of which have been swallowed by the countless convulsions which have racked the outer crust, or they may be merely the result of evolution along slightly different lines – either is quite possible.'

Further speculation was interrupted by the appearance of several of our captors before the entrance of the hut. Two of them entered and dragged us forth. The perilous pathways and the surrounding trees were filled with the black ape-men, their females, and their young. There was not an ornament, a weapon, or a garment among the lot.

'Quite low in the scale of creation,' commented Perry.

'Quite high enough to play the deuce with us, though,' I replied. 'Now what do you suppose they intend doing with us?'

We were not long in learning. As on the occasion of our trip to the village we were seized by a couple of the powerful creatures and whirled away through the tree-tops, while about us and in our wake raced a chattering, gibbering, grinning horde of sleek, black ape-things.

Twice my bearers missed their footing, and my heart ceased beating as we plunged towards instant death among the tangled deadwood beneath. But on both occasions those lithe, powerful tails reached out and found sustaining branches, nor did either of the creatures loosen their grasp upon me. In fact, it seemed that the incidents were of no greater moment to them than would be the stubbing of one's toe at a street crossing in the outer world – they but laughed uproariously and sped on with me.

For some time they continued through the forest – how long I could not guess for I was learning, what was later borne very forcibly to my mind, that time ceases to be a factor the moment means for measuring it cease to exist. Our watches were gone, and we were living beneath a stationary sun. Already I was puzzled to compute the period of time which had elapsed since we broke through the crust of the inner world. It might be hours, or it might be days – who in the world could tell where it was always noon! By the sun, no time had elapsed – but my judgment told me that we must have been several hours in this strange world.

Presently the forest terminated, and we came out upon a level plain. A short distance before us rose a few low, rocky hills. Towards these our captors urged us, and after a short time led us through a narrow pass into a tiny, circular valley. Here they got down to work, and we were soon convinced that if we were not to die to make a Roman holiday, we were to die for some other purpose. The attitude of our captors altered immediately they entered the natural arena within the rocky hills. Their laughter ceased. Grim ferocity marked their bestial faces – bared fangs menaced us.

We were placed in the centre of the amphitheatre – the thousand creatures forming a great ring about us. Then a wolf-dog was brought – *hyaenodon*, Perry called it – and turned loose with us inside the circle. The thing's body was as large as that of a full-grown mastiff, its legs were short and powerful, and its jaws broad and strong. Dark, shaggy hair covered its back and sides, while its breast and belly were quite white. As it slunk towards us it presented a most formidable aspect with its upcurled lips baring its mighty fangs.

Perry was on his knees, praying. I stooped and picked up a small stone. At my movement the beast veered off a bit and commenced circling us. Evidently it had been a target for stones before. The ape-things were dancing up and down urging the brute on with savage cries, until at last, seeing that I did not throw, he charged us.

At Andover, and later at Yale, I had pitched on winning ball teams. My speed and control must both have been above the ordinary, for I made such a record during my senior year at college that overtures were made to me in behalf of one of the great major-league teams; but in the tightest pinch that ever had confronted me in the past I had never been in such need for control as now.

As I wound up for the delivery, I held my nerves and muscles under absolute command, though the grinning jaws were hurtling towards me at terrific speed. And then I let go, with every ounce of my weight and muscle and science back of that throw. The stone caught the *hyaenodon* full upon the end of the nose, and sent him bowling over upon his back.

At the same instant a chorus of shrieks and howls arose from the circle of spectators, so that for a moment I thought that the upsetting of their champion was the cause; but in this I soon saw that I was mistaken. As I looked, the ape-things broke in all directions towards the surrounding hills, and then I distinguished the real cause of their perturbation. Behind them, streaming through the pass which leads into the valley, came a swarm of hairy men – gorilla-like creatures armed with spears and hatchets, and bearing long, oval shields.

Like demons they set upon the ape-things, and before them the *hyaenodon*, which had now regained its senses and its feet, fled howling with fright. Past us swept the pursued and the pursuers, nor did the hairy ones accord us more than a passing glance until the arena had been emptied of its former occupants. Then they returned to us, and one who seemed to have authority among them directed that we be brought with them.

When we had passed out of the amphitheatre on to the great plain we saw a caravan of men and women – human beings like ourselves – and for the first time hope and relief filled my heart, until I could have cried out in the exuberance of my happiness. It is true that they were a half-naked, wild-appearing aggregation; but they at least were fashioned along the same lines as ourselves – there was nothing grotesque or horrible about them as about the other creatures in this strange, weird world.

But as we came closer, our hearts sank once more, for we discovered that the poor wretches were chained neck to neck in a long line, and that the gorilla-men were their guards. With little ceremony Perry and I were chained at the end of the line, and without further ado the interrupted march was resumed.

Up to this time the excitement had kept us both up; but now the tiresome monotony of the long march across the sun-baked plain brought on all the agonies consequent to long-denied sleep. On and on we stumbled beneath that hateful noonday sun. If we fell we were prodded with a sharp spear point. Our companions in chains did not stumble. They strode along proudly erect. Occasionally they would exchange words with one another in a monosyllabic language. They were a noble-appearing race with well-formed heads and perfect physiques. The men were heavily bearded, tall and muscular; the women, smaller and more gracefully moulded, with great masses of raven hair caught into loose knots upon their heads. The features of both sexes were well proportioned – there was not a face among them that would have been called even plain if judged by earthly standards. They wore no ornaments; but this I later learned was due to the fact that their captors had stripped them of everything of value. As garmenture, the women possessed a single robe of some light-coloured spotted hide, rather similar in appearance to a leopard's skin. This they wore either supported entirely about the waist by a leathern thong, so that it hung partially below the knee on one side, or possibly looped gracefully across one shoulder. Their feet were shod with skin sandals. The men wore loin cloths of the hide of some shaggy beast, long ends of which depended before and behind nearly to the ground. In some instances these ends were finished with the strong talons of the beast from which the hides had been taken.

Our guards, whom I already have described as gorilla-like men, were rather lighter in build than a gorilla, but even so they were indeed mighty creatures. Their arms and legs were proportioned more in conformity with human standards, but their entire bodies were covered with shaggy, brown hair, and their faces were quite as brutal as those of the few stuffed specimens of the gorilla which I had seen in the museums at home.

Their only redeeming feature lay in the development of the head above and back of the ears. In this respect they were not one whit less human than we. They were clothed in a sort of tunic of light cloth which reached to the knees. Beneath this they wore only a loin cloth of the same material, while their feet were shod with rather heavy sandals apparently made of the thick hide of some mammoth creature of this inner world.

Their arms and necks were encircled by many ornaments of metal – silver predominating – and on their tunics were sewn the heads of tiny reptiles in odd and rather artistic designs. They talked among themselves as they marched along on either side of us, but in a language which I perceived differed from that employed by our fellow-prisoners, When they addressed the latter they used what appeared to be a third language, and which I later learned is a mongrel tongue rather analogous to the pidgin-English of the Chinese coolie.

How far we marched I have no conception, nor had Perry. Both of us were asleep much of the time for hours before a halt was called – then we dropped in our tracks. I say 'for hours'; but how may one measure time where time does not exist!

When our march commenced the sun stood at zenith, when we halted our shadows still pointed toward nadir. Whether an instant or an eternity of earthly time elapsed who may say? That march may have occupied nine years and eleven months of the ten years that I spent in the inner world, or it may have been accomplished in the fraction of a second – I cannot tell. But this I do know, that since you have told me that ten years have elapsed since I departed from this earth I have lost all respect for time – I am commencing to doubt that such a thing exists other than in the weak, finite mind of man.

4

Dian the Beautiful

When our guards aroused us from sleep we were much refreshed. They gave us food. Strips of dried meat it was, but it put new life and strength into us, so that now we too marched with high-held heads, and took noble strides. At least I did, for I was young and proud; but poor Perry hated walking. On earth I had often seen him call a cab to travel a square – he was paying for it now, and his old legs wobbled so that I put my arm about him and half carried him through the balance of those frightful marches.

The country began to change at last, and we wound up out of the level plain through mighty mountains of virgin granite. The tropical verdure of the lowlands was replaced by hardier vegetation, but even here the effects of constant heat and light were apparent in the immensity of the trees and the profusion of foliage and blooms. Crystal streams roared through their rocky channels, fed by the perpetual snows which we could see far above us. Above the snow-capped heights hung masses of heavy clouds. It was these, Perry explained, which evidently served the double purpose of replenishing the melting snows and protecting them from the direct rays of the sun.

By this time we had picked up a smattering of the bastard language in which our guards addressed us, as well as making good headway in the rather charming tongue of our co-captives. Directly ahead of me in the chain-gang was a young woman. Three feet of chain linked us together in a forced companionship which I, at least, soon rejoiced in. For I found her a willing teacher, and from her I learned the language of her tribe, and much of the life and customs of the inner world – at least that part of it with which she was familiar.

She told me that she was called Dian the Beautiful, and that she belonged to the tribe of Amoz, which dwells in the cliffs above the Darel Az, or shallow sea.

'How came you here?' I asked her.

'I was running away from Jubal the Ugly One,' she answered, as though that was explanation quite sufficient.

'Who is Jubal the Ugly One?' I asked. 'And why did you run away from him?'

She looked at me in surprise.

'Why *does* a woman run away from a man?' She answered my question with another.

'They do not, where I come from,' I replied. 'Sometimes they run after them.'

But she could not understand. Nor could I get her to grasp the fact that I was of another world. She was quite as positive that creation was originated solely to produce her own kind and the world she lived in as are many of the outer world.

'But Jubal,' I insisted. 'Tell me about him, and why you ran away to be chained by the neck and scourged across the face of a world.'

'Jubal the Ugly One placed his trophy before my father's house. It was the head of a mighty *tandor*. It remained there and no greater trophy was placed beside it. So I knew that Jubal the Ugly One would come and take me as his mate. None other so powerful wished me, or they would have slain a mightier beast and thus have won me from Jubal. My father is not a mighty hunter. Once he was, but a *sadok* tossed him, and never again had he the full use of his right arm. My brother, Dacor the Strong One, had gone to the land of Sari to steal a mate for himself. Thus there was none, father, brother, or lover, to save me from Jubal the Ugly One, and I ran away and hid among the hills that skirt the land of Amoz. And there these Sagoths found me and made me captive.'

'What will they do with you?' I asked. 'Where are they taking us?'

Again she looked her incredulity.

'I can almost believe that you are of another world,' she said, 'for otherwise such ignorance were inexplicable. Do you really mean that you do not know that the Sagoths are the creatures of the Mahars – the mighty Mahars who think that they own Pellucidar and all that walks or grows upon its surface, or creeps or burrows beneath, or swims within its lakes and oceans, or flies through its air? Next you will be telling me that you never before heard of the Mahars!'

I was loath to do it, and further incur her scorn; but there was no alternative if I were to absorb knowledge, so I made a clean breast of my pitiful ignorance as to the mighty Mahars. She was shocked. But she did her very best to enlighten me, though much that she said was as Greek would have been to her. She described the Mahars largely by comparisons. In this way they were like unto *thipdars*, in that to the hairless *lidi*.

About all I gleaned of them was that they were quite hideous, had wings, and webbed feet; lived in cities built beneath the ground; could swim under water for great distances, and were very, very wise. The Sagoths were their weapon of offence and defence, and the races like herself were their hands and feet – they were the slaves and servants who did all the manual labour. The Mahars were the heads – the brains – of the inner world. I longed to see this wondrous race of supermen.

Perry learned the language with me. When we halted, as we occasionally did, though sometimes the halts seemed ages apart, he would join in the conversation, as would Ghak the Hairy One, he who was chained just ahead of Dian the Beautiful. Ahead of Ghak was Hooja the Sly One. He too, entered the conversation occasionally. Most of his remarks were directed towards Dian the Beautiful. It didn't take half an eye to see that he had developed a bad case; but the girl appeared totally oblivious to his thinly veiled advances. Did I say thinly veiled? There is a race of men in New Zealand, or Australia, I have forgotten which, who indicate their preference for the lady of their affections by banging her over the head with a bludgeon. By comparison with this method Hooja's love-making might be called thinly veiled. At first it caused me to blush violently although I have seen several Old Years out at Rectors and in other less fashionable places off Broadway, and in Vienna, and Hamburg.

But the girl! She was magnificent. It was easy to see that she considered herself as entirely above and apart from her present surroundings and company. She talked with me, and with Perry, and with the taciturn Ghak because we were respectful; but she couldn't even see Hooja the Sly One, much less hear him, and that made him furious. He tried to get one of the Sagoths to move the girl up ahead of him in the slave gang, but the fellow only poked him with his spear and told him that he had selected the girl for his own property – that he would buy her from the Mahars as soon as they reached Phutra. Phutra, it seemed, was the city of our destination.

After passing over the first chain of mountains we skirted a salt sea, upon whose bosom swam countless horrid things. Seal-like creatures there were with long necks stretching ten and more feet above their enormous bodies, and whose snake heads were split with gaping mouths bristling with countless fangs. There were huge tortoises too, paddling about among these other reptiles, which Perry said were Plesiosaurs of the Lias. I didn't question his veracity – they might have been most anything.

Dian told me they were *tandorazes*, or tandors of the sea, and that the other, and more fearsome reptiles, which occasionally rose from the deep to do battle with them, were *azdyryths*, or sea-dyryths. Perry called them Ichthyosaurs. They resembled a whale with the head of an alligator.

I had forgotten what little geology I had studied at school – about all that remained was an impression of horror that the illustrations of restored prehistoric monsters had made upon me, and a well-defined belief that any man with a pig's shank and a vivid imagination could 'restore' most any sort of Palaeolithic monster he saw fit, and take rank as a first-class palaeontologist. But when I saw these sleek, shiny carcasses shimmering in the sunlight as they emerged from the ocean, shaking their giant heads; when I saw the waters roll from their sinuous bodies in miniature waterfalls as they glided hither and thither, now upon the surface, now half submerged; as I saw them meet, open-mouthed, hissing and snorting, in their titanic and interminable warring, I realized how futile is man's poor, weak imagination by comparison with Nature's incredible genius.

And Perry! He was absolutely flabbergasted. He said so himself.

'David,' he remarked, after we had marched for a long time beside that awful sea. 'David, I used to teach geology, and I thought that I believed what I taught; but now I see that I did not believe it – that it is impossible for man to believe such things as these unless he sees them with his own eyes. We take things for granted, perhaps, because we are told them over and over again, and have no way of disproving them – like religions, for example; but we don't believe them, we only think we do. If you ever get back to the outer world you will find that the geologists and palaeontologists will be the first to set you down a liar, for they know that no such creatures as they restore ever existed. It is all right to *imagine* them as existing in an equally imaginary epoch – but now? Poof!'

At the next halt Hooja the Sly One managed to find enough slack chain to permit him to worm himself back quite close to Dian. We were all standing, and as he edged near the girl she turned her back upon him in such a truly earthly feminine manner that I could scarce repress a smile; but it was a short-lived smile for on the instant the Sly One's hand fell upon the girl's bare arm, jerking her roughly towards him.

I was not then familiar with the customs or social ethics which prevailed within Pellucidar; but even so I did not need the appealing look which the girl shot at me from her magnificent eyes to influence my subsequent act. What the Sly One's intention was I paused not to inquire; but instead, before he could lay hold of her with his other hand, I placed a right to the point of his jaw that felled him in his tracks.

A roar of approval went up from those of the other prisoners and the Sagoths who had witnessed the brief drama; not, as I later learned, because I had championed the girl, but for the neat and, to them, astounding method by which I had bested Hooja.

And the girl? At first she looked at me with wide, wondering eyes, and then she dropped her head, her face half averted, and a delicate flush suffused her cheek. For a moment she stood thus in silence, and then her head went high, and she turned her back upon me as she had upon Hooja. Some of the prisoners laughed, and I saw the face of Ghak the Hairy One go very black as he looked at me searchingly. And what I could see of Dian's cheek went suddenly from red to white.

Immediately after we resumed the march, and though I realized that in some way I had offended Dian the Beautiful I could not prevail upon her to talk with me that I might learn wherein I had erred – in fact I might quite as well have been addressing a sphinx for all the attention I got. At last my own foolish pride stepped in and prevented my making any further attempts, and thus a companionship that without my realizing it had come to mean a great deal to me was cut off. Thereafter I confined my conversation to Perry. Hooja did not renew his advances towards the girl, nor did he again venture near me.

Again the weary and apparently interminable marching became a perfect nightmare of horrors to me. The more firmly fixed became the realization that the girl's friendship had meant so much to me, the more I came to miss it; and the more impregnable the barrier of silly pride. But I was very young and would not ask Ghak for the explanation which I was sure he could give, and that might have made everything all right again.

On the march, or during halts, Dian refused consistently to notice me – when her eyes wandered in my direction she looked either over my head or directly through me. At last I became desperate, and determined to swallow my self-esteem, and again beg her to tell me how I had offended, and how I might make reparation. I made up my mind that I should do this at the next halt. We were approaching another range of mountains at the time, and when we reached them, instead of winding across them through some high-flung pass we entered a mighty natural tunnel – a series of labyrinthine grottos, dark as Erebus.

The guards had no torches or light of any description. In fact we had seen no artificial light or sign of fire since we had entered Pellucidar. In a land of perpetual noon there is no need of light above ground, yet I marvelled that they had no means of lighting their way through these dark, subterranean passages. So we crept along at snail's pace, with much stumbling and falling – the guards keeping up a sing-song chant ahead of us, interspersed with certain high notes which I found always indicated rough places and turns.

Halts were now more frequent, but I did not wish to speak to Dian until I could see from the expression of her face how she was receiving my apologies. At last a faint glow ahead forewarned us of the end of the tunnel, for which for one was devoutly thankful. Then at a sudden turn we emerged into the full light of the noonday sun.

But with it came a sudden realization of what meant to me a real catastrophe – Dian was gone, and with her a half-dozen other prisoners. The guards saw it too, and the ferocity of their rage was terrible to behold. Their awesome, bestial faces were contorted in the most diabolical expressions, as they accused each other of responsibility for the loss. Finally they fell upon us, beating us with their spear hafts and hatchets. They had already killed two near the head of the line, and were like to have finished the balance of us when their leader finally put a stop to the brutal slaughter. Never in all my life had I witnessed a more horrible exhibition of bestial rage – I thanked God that Dian had not been one of those left to endure it.

Of the twelve prisoners who had been chained ahead of me each alternate one had been freed commencing with Dian. Hooja was gone. Ghak remained. What could it mean? How had it been accomplished? The commander of the guards was investigating. Soon he discovered that the rude locks which had held the neckbands in place had been deftly picked.

'Hooja the Sly One,' murmured Ghak, who was now next to me in line. 'He has taken the girl that you would not have,' he continued, glancing at me.

'That I would not have!' I cried. 'What do you mean?'

He looked at me closely for a moment.

'I have doubted your story that you are from another world,' he said at last, 'but yet upon no other grounds could your ignorance of the ways of Pellucidar be explained. Do you really mean that you do not know that you offended the Beautiful One, and how?'

'I do not know, Ghak,' I replied.

'Then shall I tell you. When a man of Pellucidar intervenes between another man and the woman the other man would have, the woman belongs to the victor. Dian the Beautiful belongs to you. You should have claimed her or released her. Had you taken her hand, it would have indicated your desire to make her your mate, and had you raised her hand above her head and then dropped it, it would have meant that you did not wish her for a mate and that you released her from all obligation to you. By doing neither you have put upon her the greatest affront that a man may put upon a woman. Now she is your slave. No man will take her as mate, or may take her honourably, until he shall have overcome you in combat, and men do not choose slave women as their mates – at least not the men of Pellucidar.'

'I did not know, Ghak,' I cried. 'I did not know. Not for all Pellucidar would I have harmed Dian the Beautiful by word, or look, or act of mine. I do not want her as my slave. I do not want her as my—' But here I stopped. The vision of that sweet and innocent face floated before me amidst the soft mists of imagination, and where I had on the second believed that I clung only to the memory of a gentle friendship I had lost, yet now it seemed that it would have been disloyalty to her to have said that I did not want Dian the Beautiful as my mate. I had not thought of her except as a welcome friend in a strange, cruel world. Even now I did not think that I loved her.

I believe Ghak must have read the truth more in my expression than in my words, for presently he laid his hand upon my shoulder.

'Man of another world,' he said, 'I believe you. Lips may lie, but when the heart speaks through the eyes it tells only the truth. Your heart has spoken to me. I know now that you meant no affront to Dian the Beautiful. She is not of my tribe; but her mother is my sister. She does not know it – her mother was stolen by Dian's father, who came with many others of the tribe of Amoz to battle with us for our women – the most beautiful women of Pellucidar. Then was her father King of Amoz, and her mother was daughter of the King of Sari – to whose power I, his son, have succeeded. Dian is the daughter of kings, though her father is no longer king since the sadok tossed him and Jubal the Ugly One wrested his kingship from him. Because of her lineage the wrong you did her was greatly magnified in the eyes of all who saw it. She will never forgive you.'

I asked Ghak if there was not some way in which I could release the girl from the bondage and ignominy I had unwittingly placed upon her.

'If ever you find her, yes,' he answered. 'Merely to raise her hand above her head and drop it in the presence of others is sufficient to release her; but how may you ever find her, you who are doomed to a life of slavery yourself in the buried city of Phutra?'

'Is there no escape?' I asked.

'Hooja the Sly One escaped and took the others with him,' replied Ghak. 'But there are no more dark places on the way to Phutra, and once there it is not so easy – the Mahars are very wise. Even if one escaped from Phutra there are the thipdars – they would find you, and then—' the Hairy One shuddered. 'No, you will never escape the Mahars.'

It was a cheerful prospect. I asked Perry what he thought about it; but he only shrugged his shoulders and continued a long-winded prayer he had been at for some time. He was wont to say that the only redeeming feature of our captivity was the ample time it gave him for the improvisation of prayers – it was becoming an obsession with him. The Sagoths had begun to take notice of his habit of declaiming throughout entire marches. One of them asked him what he was saying – to whom he was talking. The question gave me an idea, so I answered quickly before Perry could say anything.

'Do not interrupt him,' I said. 'He is a very holy man in the world from which we come. He is speaking to spirits which you cannot see – do not interrupt him or they will spring out of the air upon you and rend you limb from limb – like that,' and I jumped towards the great brute with a loud 'boo!' that sent him stumbling backwards.

I took a long chance, I realized, but if we could make any capital out of Perry's harmless mania I wanted to make it while the making was prime. It worked splendidly. The Sagoths treated us both with marked respect during the balance of the journey, and then passed the word along to their masters, the Mahars.

Two marches after this episode we came to the city of Phutra. The entrance to it was marked by two lofty towers of granite, which guarded a flight of steps leading to the buried city. Sagoths were on guard here as well as at a hundred or more other towers scattered about over a large plain.

5

Slaves

As we descended the broad staircase which led to the main avenue of Phutra I caught my first sight of the dominant race of the inner world. Involuntarily I shrank back as one of the creatures approached to inspect us. A more hideous thing it would be impossible to imagine. The all-powerful Mahars of Pellucidar are great reptiles, some six or eight feet in length, with long narrow heads and great round eyes. Their beak-like mouths are lined with sharp, white fangs, and the backs of their huge, lizard bodies are serrated into bony ridges from their necks to the end of their long tails. Their feet are equipped with three webbed toes, while from the forefeet membranous wings, which are attached to their bodies just in front of the hind legs, protrude at an angle of forty-five degrees towards the rear, ending in sharp points several feet above their bodies.

I glanced at Perry as the thing passed me to inspect him. The old man was gazing at the horrid creature with wide, astonished eyes. When it passed on, he turned to me.

'A rhamphorhynchus of the Middle Oölitic, David,' he said, 'but, gad, how enormous! The largest remains we ever have discovered have never indicated a size greater than that attained by an ordinary crow.'

As we continued on through the main avenue of Phutra we saw many thousands of the creatures coming and going upon their daily duties. They paid but little attention to us. Phutra is laid out underground with a regularity that indicates remarkable engineering skill. It is hewn from solid limestone strata. The streets are broad and of a uniform height of twenty feet. At intervals tubes pierce the roof of this underground city, and by means of lenses and reflectors transmit the sunlight, softened and diffused, to dispel what would otherwise be Cimmerian darkness. In like manner air is introduced.

Perry and I were taken, with Ghak, to a large public building, where one of the Sagoths who had formed our guard explained to a Maharan official the circumstances surrounding our capture. The method of communication between these two was remarkable in that no spoken words were exchanged. They employed a species of sign language. As I was to learn later, the Mahars have no ears, nor any spoken language. Among themselves they communicate by means of what Perry says must be a sixth sense which is cognizant of a fourth dimension.

I never did quite grasp him, though he endeavoured to explain it to me upon numerous occasions. I suggested telepathy, but he said no, that it was not telepathy since they could only communicate when in each other's presence, nor could they talk with the Sagoths or the other inhabitants of Pellucidar by the same method they used to converse with one another.

'What they do,' said Perry, 'is to project their thoughts into the fourth dimension, when they become appreciable to the sixth sense of their listener. Do I make myself quite clear?'

'You do not, Perry,' I replied. He shook his head in despair, and returned to his work. They had set us to carrying a great accumulation of Maharan literature from one apartment to another, and there arranging it upon shelves. I suggested to Perry that we were in the public library of Phutra, but later, as he commenced to discover the key to their written language, he assured me that we were handling the ancient archives of the race.

During this period my thoughts were continually upon Dian the Beautiful. I was, of course, glad that she had escaped the Mahars, and the fate that had been suggested by the Sagoth who had threatened to purchase her upon our arrival at Phutra. I often wondered if the little party of fugitives had been overtaken by the guards who had returned to search for them. Sometimes I was not so sure but that I should have been more contented to know that Dian was here in Phutra, than to think of her at the mercy of Hooja the Sly One.

Ghak, Perry, and I often talked together of possible escape, but the Sarian was so steeped in his lifelong belief that no one could escape from the Mahars except by a miracle, that he was not much aid to us – his attitude was of one who waits for the miracle to come to him.

At my suggestion Perry and I fashioned some swords of scraps of iron which we discovered among some rubbish in the cells where we slept, for we were permitted almost unrestrained freedom of action within the limits of the building to which we had been assigned. So great were the number of slaves who waited upon the inhabitants of Phutra that none of us was apt to be overburdened with work, nor were our masters unkind to us.

We hid our new weapons beneath the skins which formed our beds, and then Perry conceived the idea of making bows and arrows – weapons apparently unknown within Pellucidar. Next came shields; but these I found it easier to steal from the walls of the outer guard-room of the building.

We had completed these arrangements for our protection after leaving Phutra when the Sagoths who had been sent to recapture the escaped prisoners returned with four of them, of whom Hooja was one. Dian and two others had eluded them. It so happened that Hooja was confined in the same building with us. He told Ghak that he had not seen Dian or the others after releasing them within the dark grotto. What had become of them he had not the faintest conception – they might be wandering yet, lost within the labyrinthine tunnel, if not dead from starvation.

I was now still further apprehensive as to the fate of Dian, and at this time, I imagine, came the first realization that my affection for the girl might be prompted by more than friendship. During my waking hours she was constantly the subject of my thoughts, and when I slept her dear face haunted my dreams. More than ever was I determined to escape the Mahars.

'Perry,' I confided to the old man, 'if I have to search every inch of this diminutive world I am going to find Dian the Beautiful and right the wrong I unintentionally did her.' That was the excuse I made for Perry's benefit.

'Diminutive world!' he scoffed. 'You don't know what you are talking about, my boy,' and then he showed me a map of Pellucidar which he had recently discovered among the manuscript he was arranging.

'Look,' he cried, pointing to it, 'this is evidently water, and all this land.' Do you notice the general configuration of the two areas? Where the oceans are upon the outer crust, is land here. These relatively small areas of ocean follow the general lines of the continents of the outer world.

'We know that the crust of the globe is 500 miles in thickness; then the inside diameter of Pellucidar must be 7,000 miles, and the superficial area 165,480,000 square miles. Three-fourths of this is land. Think of it! A land area of 124,110,000 square miles! Our own world contains but 53,000,000 square miles of land, the balance of its surface being covered by water. Just as we often compare nations by their relative land areas, so if we compare these two worlds in the same way we have the strange anomaly of a larger world within a smaller one!

'Where within vast Pellucidar would you search for your Dian? Without stars, or moon, or changing sun how could you find her even though you knew where she might be found?'

The proposition was a corker. It quite took my breath away; but I found that it left me all the more determined to attempt it.

'If Ghak will accompany us we may be able to do it,' I suggested.

Perry and I sought him out and put the question straight to him.

'Ghak,' I said, 'we are determined to escape from this bondage. Will you accompany us?'

'They will set the thipdars upon us,' he said, 'and then we shall be killed; but' – he hesitated – 'I would take the chance if I thought that I might possibly escape and return to my own people.'

'Could you find your way back to your own land?' asked Perry. 'And could you aid David in his search for Dian?'

'Yes.'

'But how,' persisted Perry, 'could you travel a strange country without heavenly bodies or a compass to guide you?'

Ghak didn't know what Perry meant by heavenly bodies or a compass, but he assured us that you might blindfold any man of Pellucidar and carry him to the farthermost corner of the world, yet he would be able to come directly to his own home again by the shortest route. He seemed surprised to think that we found anything wonderful in it. Perry said it must be some sort of homing instinct such as is possessed by certain breeds of earthly pigeons. I didn't know, of course, but it gave me an idea.

'Then Dian could have found her way directly to her own people?' I asked.

'Surely,' replied Ghak, 'unless some mighty beast of prey killed her.'

I was for making the attempted escape at once, but both Perry and Ghak counselled waiting for some propitious accident which would ensure us some small degree of success. I didn't see what accident could befall a whole community in a land of perpetual daylight where the inhabitants had no fixed habits of sleep. Why I am sure that some of the Mahars never sleep, while others may, at long intervals, crawl into the dark recesses beneath their dwellings and curl up in protracted slumber. Perry says that if a Mahar stays awake for three years he will make up all his lost sleep in a long year's snooze. That may be all true, but I never saw but three of them asleep, and it was the sight of these three that gave me a suggestion for our means of escape.

I had been searching about far below the levels that we slaves were supposed to frequent – possibly fifty feet beneath the main floor of the building – among a network of corridors and apartments, when I came suddenly upon three Mahars curled up upon a bed of skins. At first I thought they were dead, but later their regular breathing convinced me of my error. Like a flash the thought came to me of the marvellous opportunity these sleeping reptiles offered as a means of eluding the watchfulness of our captors and the Sagoth guards.

Hastening back to Perry where he pored over a musty pile of, to me, meaningless hieroglyphics, I explained my plan to him. To my surprise he was horrified.

'It would be murder, David,' he cried.

'Murder to kill a reptilian monster?' I asked in astonishment.

'Here they are not monsters, David,' he replied. 'Here they are the dominant race – we are the "monsters" – the lower orders. In Pellucidar evolution has progressed along different lines than upon the outer earth. There terrible convulsions of nature time and time again wiped out the existing species – but for this fact some monster of the Saurozoic epoch might rule to-day upon our own world. We see here what might well have occurred in our own history had conditions been what they have been here.

'Life within Pellucidar is far younger than upon the outer crust. Here man has but reached a stage analogous to the Stone Age of our own world's history, but for countless millions of years these reptiles have been progressing. Possibly it is the sixth sense which I am sure they possess that has given them an advantage over the other and more frightfully armed of their fellows; but this we may never know. They look upon us as we look upon the beasts of our fields, and I learn from their written records that other races of Mahars feed upon men – they keep them in great droves, as we keep cattle. They breed them most carefully, and when they are quite fat, they kill and eat them.'

I shuddered.

'What is there horrible about it, David?' the old man asked. 'They understand us no better than we understand the lower animals of our own world. Why, I have come across here very learned discussions of the question as to whether *gilaks*, that is men, have any means of communication. One writer claims that we do not even reason – that our every act is mechanical, or instinctive. The dominant race of Pellucidar, David, have not yet learned that men converse among themselves, or reason. Because we do not converse as they do it is beyond them to imagine that we converse at all. It is thus that we reason in relation to the brutes of our own world. They know that the Sagoths have a spoken language, but yet they cannot comprehend it, or how it manifests itself, since they have no auditory apparatus. They believe that the motions of the lips alone convey the meaning. That the Sagoths can communicate with us is incomprehensible to them.

'Yes, David,' he concluded, 'it would entail murder to carry out your plan.'

'Very well then, Perry,' I replied. 'I shall become a murderer.'

He got me to go over the plan again most carefully, and for some reason which was not at the time clear to me insisted upon a very careful description of the apartments and corridors I had just explored.

'I wonder, David,' he said at length, 'as you are determined to carry out your wild scheme, if we could not accomplish something of very real and lasting benefit for the human race of Pellucidar at the same time. Listen, I have learned much of a most surprising nature from these archives of the Mahars. That you may appreciate my plan I shall briefly outline the history of the race.

'Once the males were all-powerful, but ages ago the females, little by little, assumed the mastery. For other ages no noticeable change took place in the race of Mahars. It continued to progress under the intelligent and beneficent rule of the ladies. Science took vast strides. This was especially true of the sciences which we know as biology and eugenics. Finally a certain female scientist announced the fact that she had discovered a method whereby eggs might be fertilized by chemical means after they were laid – all true reptiles, you know, are hatched from eggs.

'What happened? Immediately the necessity for males ceased to exist – the race was no longer dependent upon them. More ages elapsed until at the present time we find a race consisting exclusively of females. But here is the point. The secret of this chemical formula is kept by a single race of Mahars. It is in the city of Phutra, and unless I am greatly in error I judge from your description of the vaults through which you passed to-day that it lies hidden in the cellar of this building.

'For two reasons they hide it away and guard it jealously. First, because upon it depends the very life of the race of Mahars, and second, owing to the fact that when it was public property, as at first, so many were experimenting with it that the danger of over-population became very grave.

'David, if we can escape, and at the same time take with us this great secret what will we not have accomplished for the human race within Pellucidar!'

The very thought of it fairly overpowered me. Why, we two would be the means of placing the men of the inner world in their rightful place among created things. Only the Sagoths would then stand between them and absolute supremacy, and I was not quite sure but that the Sagoths owed all their power to the greater intelligence of the Mahars – I could not believe that these gorilla-like beasts were the mental superiors of the human race of Pellucidar.

'Why, Perry,' I exclaimed, 'you and I may reclaim a whole world! Together we can lead the races of men out of the darkness of ignorance into the light of advancement and civilization. At one step we may carry them from the Age of Stone to the twentieth century. It's marvellous – absolutely marvellous just to think about it.'

'David,' said the old man, 'I believe that God sent us here for just that purpose – it shall be my life work to teach them His word – to lead them into the light of His mercy while we are training their hearts and hands in the ways of culture and civilization.'

'You are right, Perry,' I said, 'and while you are teaching them to pray I'll be teaching them to fight, and between us we'll make a race of men that will be an honour to us both.'

Ghak had entered the apartment some time before we concluded our conversation, and now he wanted to know what we were so excited about. Perry thought we had best not tell him too much, and so I only explained that I had a plan for escape. When I had outlined it to him, he seemed about as horror-struck as Perry had been; but for a different reason. The Hairy One only considered the horrible fate that would be ours were we discovered; but at last I prevailed upon him to accept my plan as the only feasible one, and when I had assured him that I would take all the responsibility for it were we captured, he accorded a reluctant assent.

6

The Beginning of Horror

Within Pellucidar one time is as good as another. There were no nights to mask our attempted escape. All must be done in broad daylight – all but the work I had to do in the apartment beneath the building. So we determined to put our plan to an immediate test lest the Mahars who made it possible should awake before I reached them; but we were doomed to disappointment, for no sooner had we reached the main floor of the building on our way to the pits beneath than we encountered hurrying bands of slaves being hastened under strong Sagoth guard out of the edifice to the avenue beyond.

Other Sagoths were darting hither and thither in search of other slaves, and the moment that we appeared we were pounced upon and hustled into the line of marching humans.

What the purpose or nature of the general exodus we did not know, but presently through the line of captives ran the rumour that two escaped slaves had been, recaptured – a man and a woman – and that we were marching to witness their punishment, for the man had killed a Sagoth of the detachment that had pursued and overtaken them.

At the intelligence my heart sprang to my throat, for I was sure that the two were of those who escaped in the dark grotto with Hooja the Sly One, and that Dian must be the woman. Ghak thought so, too, as did Perry.

'Is there naught that we may do to save her?' I asked Ghak.

'Naught,' he replied.

Along the crowded avenue we marched, the guards showing unusual cruelty towards us, as though we, too, had been implicated in the murder of their fellow. The occasion was to serve as an object-lesson to all other slaves of the danger and futility of attempted escape, and the fatal consequences of taking the life of a superior being, and so I imagine the Sagoths felt amply justified in making the entire proceeding as uncomfortable and painful to us as possible.

They jabbed us with their spears and struck at us with their hatchets at the least provocation, and at no provocation at all. It was a most uncomfortable half-hour that we spent before we were finally herded through a low entrance into a huge building the centre of which was given up to a good-sized arena. Benches surrounded this open space upon three sides, and along the fourth were heaped huge boulders which rose in receding tiers towards the roof.

At first I couldn't make out the purpose of this mighty pile of rock, unless it were intended as a rough and picturesque background for the scenes which were enacted in the arena before it, but presently, after the wooden benches had been pretty well filled by slaves and Sagoths, I discovered the purpose of the boulders, for then the Mahars began to file into the enclosure.

They marched directly across the arena towards the rocks upon the opposite side, where, spreading their bat-like wings, they rose above the high wall of the pit, settling down upon the boulders above. These were the reserved seats, the boxes of the elect.

Reptiles that they are, the rough surface of a great stone is to them as plush and upholstery to us. Here they lolled, blinking their hideous eyes, and doubtless conversing with one another in their sixth-sense fourth-dimension language.

For the first time I beheld their queen. She differed from the others in no feature that was appreciable to my earthly eyes; in fact, all Mahars look alike to me; but when she crossed the arena after the balance of her female subjects had found their boulders, she was preceded by a score of huge Sagoths, the largest I ever had seen, and on either side of her waddled a huge thipdar, while behind came another score of Sagoth guardsmen.

At the barrier the Sagoths clambered up the steep side with truly ape-like agility, while behind them the haughty queen rose upon her wings with her two frightful dragons close behind her, and settled down upon the largest boulder of them all in the exact centre of that side of the amphitheatre which is reserved for the dominant race. Here she squatted, a most repulsive and uninteresting queen; though doubtless quite as well assured of her beauty and divine right to rule as the proudest monarch of the outer world.

And then the music started – music without sound! The Mahars cannot hear, so the drums and fifes and horns of earthly bands are unknown among them. The 'band' consists of a score or more Mahars. It filed out in the centre of the arena where the creatures upon the rocks might see it, and there it performed for fifteen or twenty minutes.

Their technique consisted in waving their tails and moving their heads in a regular succession of measured movements, resulting in a cadence which evidently pleased the eye of the Mahar as the cadence of our own instrumental music pleases our ears. Sometimes the band took measured steps in unison to one side or the other, or backwards and again forward – it all seemed very silly and meaningless to me, but at the end of the first piece the Mahars upon the rocks showed the first indications of enthusiasm that I had seen displayed by the dominant race of Pellucidar. They beat their great wings up and down, and smote their rocky perches with their mighty tails until the ground shook. Then the band started another piece, and all was again as silent as the grave. That was one great beauty about Mahar music – if you didn't happen to like a piece that was being played all you had to do was shut your eyes.

When the band had exhausted its repertoire it took wing and settled upon rocks above and behind the queen. Then the business of the day was on. A man and woman were pushed into the arena by a couple of Sagoth guardsmen. I leaned far forward in my seat to scrutinize the female – hoping against hope that she might prove to be another than Dian the Beautiful. Her back was towards me for a while, and the sight of the great mass of raven hair piled high upon her head filled me with alarm.

Presently a door in one side of the arena wall was opened to admit a huge, shaggy, bull-like creature.

'A Bos,' whispered Perry, excitedly. 'His kind roamed the outer crust with the cave bear and the mammoth ages and ages ago. We have been carried back a million years, David, to the childhood of a planet – is it not wondrous?'

But I saw only the raven hair of a half-naked girl, and my heart stood still in dumb misery at the sight of her, nor had I any eyes for the wonders of natural history. But for Perry and Ghak I should have leaped to the floor of the arena and shared whatever fate lay in store for this priceless treasure of the Stone Age.

With the advent of the Bos – they call the thing a *thag* within Pellucidar – two spears were tossed into the arena at the feet of the prisoners. It seemed to me that a pea-shooter would have been as effective against the mighty monster as these pitiful weapons.

As the animal approached the two, bellowing and pawing the ground with the strength of many earthly bulls, another door directly beneath us was opened, and from it issued the most terrific roar that had ever fallen upon my outraged ears. I could not at first see the beast from which emanated this fearsome challenge, but the sound had the effect of bringing the two victims around with a sudden start, and then I saw the girl's face – she was not Dian! I could have wept for relief.

And now, as the two stood frozen in terror, I saw the author of that fearsome sound creeping stealthily into view. It was a huge tiger – such as hunted the great Bos through the jungles primeval when the world was young. In contour and markings it was not unlike the noblest of the Bengals of our own world, but as its dimensions were exaggerated to colossal proportions so too were its colourings exaggerated. Its vivid yellows fairly screamed aloud; its whites were as eiderdown; its blacks glossy as the finest anthracite coal, and its coat long and shaggy as a mountain goat. That it is a beautiful animal there is no gainsaying, but if its size and colours are magnified here within Pellucidar, so is the ferocity of its disposition. It is not the occasional member of its species that is a man-hunter – all are man-hunters; but they do not confine their foraging to man alone, for there is no flesh or fish within Pellucidar that they will not eat with relish in the constant efforts which they make to furnish their huge carcasses with sufficient sustenance to maintain their mighty thews.

Upon one side of the doomed pair the thag bellowed and advanced, and upon the other *tarag*, the frightful, crept towards them with gaping mouth and dripping fangs.

The man seized the spears, handing one of them to the woman. At the sound of the roaring of the tiger the bull's bellowing became a veritable frenzy of rageful noise. Never in my life had I heard such an infernal din as the two brutes made, and to think that it was all lost upon the hideous reptiles for whom the show was staged!

The thag was charging now from one side, and the tarag from the other.

The two puny things standing between them seemed already lost, but at the very moment that the beasts were upon them the man grasped his companion by the arm, and together they leaped to one side, while the frenzied creatures came together like locomotives in collision.

There ensued a royal battle which for sustained and frightful ferocity transcends the power of imagination or description. Time and again the colossal bull tossed the enormous tiger high into the air, but each time that the huge cat touched the ground he returned to the encounter with apparently undiminished strength, and seemingly increased ire.

For a while the man and woman busied themselves only with keeping out of the way of the two creatures, but finally I saw them separate and each creep stealthily towards one of the combatants. The tiger was now upon the bull's broad back, clinging to the huge neck with powerful fangs while its long, strong talons ripped the heavy hide into shreds and ribbons.

For a moment the bull stood bellowing and quivering with pain and rage, its cloven hoofs widespread its tail lashing viciously from side to side, and then, in a mad orgy of bucking, it went careening about the arena in frenzied attempt to unseat its rending rider. It was with difficulty that the girl avoided the first mad rush of the wounded animal.

All its efforts to rid itself of the tiger seemed futile, until in desperation it threw itself upon the ground, rolling over and over. A little of this so disconcerted the tiger, knocking its breath from it, I imagine, that it lost its hold, and then, quick as a cat, the great thag was up again and had buried those mighty horns deep in the tarag's abdomen, pinning him to the floor of the arena.

The great cat clawed at the shaggy head until eyes and ears were gone, and naught but a few strips of ragged, bloody flesh remained upon the skull. Yet through all the agony of that fearful punishment the thag still stood motionless pinning down his adversary, and then the man leaped in, seeing that the blind bull would be the least formidable enemy, and ran his spear through the tarag's heart.

As the animal's fierce clawing ceased, the bull raised his gory, sightless head, and with a horrid roar ran headlong across the arena. With great leaps and bounds he came, straight towards the arena wall directly beneath where we sat, and then accident carried him, in one of his mighty springs, completely over the barrier into the midst of the slaves and Sagoths just in front of us.

Swinging his bloody horns from side to side the beast cut a wide swath before him straight upward towards our seats. Before him slaves and gorillamen fought in mad stampede to escape the menace of the creature's death agonies, for such only could that frightful charge have been.

Forgetful of us, our guards joined in the general rush for the exits, many of which pierced the wall of the amphitheatre behind us. Perry, Ghak, and I became separated in the chaos which reigned for a few moments after the beast cleared the wall of the arena, each intent upon saving his own hide.

I ran to the right, passing several exits choked with the fear-mad mob that were battling to escape. One would have thought that an entire herd of thags was loose behind them, rather than a single blinded, dying beast; but such is the effect of panic upon a crowd.

7

Freedom

Once out of the direct path of the animal, fear of it left me, but another emotion as quickly gripped me – hope of escape that the demoralized condition of the guards made possible for the instant.

I thought of Perry, and but for the hope that I might better encompass his release if myself free I should have put the thought of freedom from me at once. As it was, I hastened on towards the right, searching for an exit towards which no Sagoths were fleeing, and at last I found it – a low, narrow aperture leading into a dark corridor.

Without thought of the possible consequences, I darted into the shadows of the tunnel, feeling my way along through the gloom for some distance. The noises of the amphitheatre had grown fainter and fainter until now all was as silent as the tomb about me. Faint light filtered from above through occasional ventilating and lighting tubes, but it was scarce sufficient to enable my human eyes to cope with the darkness, and so I was forced to move with extreme care, feeling my way along step by step with a hand upon the wall beside me.

Presently the light increased and a moment later, to my delight, I came upon a flight of steps leading upwards, at the top of which the brilliant light of the noonday sun shone through an opening in the ground.

Cautiously I crept up the stairway to the tunnel's end, and peering out saw the broad plain of Phutra before me. The numerous lofty granite towers which mark the several entrances to the subterranean city were all in front of me – behind, the plain stretched level and unbroken to the near-by foothills. I had come to the surface, then, beyond the city, and my chances for escape seemed much enhanced.

My first impulse was to await darkness before attempting to cross the plain, so deeply implanted are habits of thought; but of a sudden I recollected the perpetual noonday brilliance which envelops Pellucidar, and with a smile I stepped forth into the daylight.

Rank grass, waist high, grows upon the plains of Phutra – the gorgeous flowering grass of the inner world, each particular blade of which is tipped with a tiny, five-pointed blossom – brilliant little stars of varying colours that twinkle in the green foliage to add still another charm to the weird, yet lovely, landscape.

But then the only aspect which attracted me was the distant hills in which I hoped to find sanctuary, and so I hastened on, trampling the myriad beauties beneath my hurrying feet. Perry says that the force of gravity is less upon the surface of the inner world than upon that of the outer. He explained it all to me once, but I was never particularly brilliant in such matters and so most of it has escaped me. As I recall it the difference is due in some part to the counter-attraction of that portion of the earth's crust directly opposite the spot upon the face of Pellucidar at which one's calculations are being made. Be that as it may, it always seemed to me that I moved with greater speed and agility within Pellucidar than upon the outer surface – there was a certain airy lightness of step that was most pleasing and a feeling of bodily detachment which I can only compare with that occasionally experienced in dreams.

And as I crossed Phutra's flower-bespangled plain that time I seemed almost to fly, though how much of the sensation was due to Perry's suggestion and how much to actuality I am sure I do not know. The more I thought of Perry the less pleasure I took in my new-found freedom. There could be no liberty for me within Pellucidar unless the old man shared it with me, and only the hope that I might find some way to encompass his release kept me from turning back to Phutra.

Just how I was to help Perry I could scarce imagine, but I hoped that some fortuitous circumstances might solve the problem for me. It was quite evident, however, that little less than a miracle could aid me, for what could I accomplish in this strange world, naked and unarmed? It was even doubtful that I could retrace my steps to Phutra should I once pass beyond view of the plain, and even were that possible, what aid could I bring to Perry no matter how far I wandered?

The case looked more and more hopeless the longer I viewed it, yet with a stubborn persistency I forged ahead towards the foothills. Behind me no sign of pursuit developed, before me I saw no living thing. It was as though I moved through a dead and forgotten world.

I have no idea, of course, how long it took me to reach the limit of the plain, but at last I entered the foothills, following a pretty little cañon upward towards the mountains. Beside me frolicked a laughing brooklet, hurrying upon its noisy way down to the silent sea. In its quieter pools I discovered many small fish, of four- or five-pound weight I should imagine. In appearance, except as to size and colour, they were not unlike the whale of our own seas. As I watched them playing about I discovered, not only that they suckled their young, but that at intervals they rose to the surface to breathe as well as to feed upon certain grasses and a strange scarlet lichen which grew upon the rocks just above the water-line.

It was this last habit that gave me the opportunity I craved to capture one of these herbivorous cetaceans – that is what Perry calls them – and make as good a meal as one can on raw, warm-blooded fish; but I had become rather used, by this time, to the eating of food in its natural state, though I still balked on the eyes and entrails, much to the amusement of Ghak, to whom I always passed these delicacies.

Crouching beside the brook, I waited until one of the diminutive whales rose to nibble at the long grasses which overhung the water, and then, like the best of prey that man really is, I sprang upon my victim, appeasing my hunger while he yet wriggled to escape.

Then I drank from the clear pool, and after washing my hands and face continued my flight. Above the source of the brook, I encountered a rugged climb to the summit of a long ridge. Beyond was a steep declivity to the shore of a placid, inland sea, upon the quiet surface of which lay several beautiful islands.

The view was charming in the extreme, and as no man or beast was to be seen that might threaten my new-found liberty, I slid over the edge of the bluff, and half sliding, half falling, dropped into the delightful valley, the very aspect of which seemed to offer a haven of peace and security.

The gently-sloping beach along which I walked was thickly strewn with strangely shaped, coloured shells, some empty, others still housing as varied a multitude of molluscs as ever might have drawn out their sluggish lives along the silent shores of the antediluvian seas of the outer crust. As I walked I could not but compare myself with the first man of that other world, so complete the solitude which surrounded me, so primal and untouched the virgin wonders and beauties of adolescent nature. I felt myself a second Adam wending my lonely way through the childhood of a world, searching for my Eve, and at the thought there rose before my mind's eye the exquisite outlines of a perfect face surmounted by a loose pile of wondrous, raven hair.

As I walked, my eyes were bent upon the beach, so that it was not until I had come quite upon it that I discovered that which shattered all my beautiful dream of solitude and safety and peace and primal overlordship. The thing was a hollowed log drawn up upon the sands, and in the bottom of it lay a crude paddle.

The rude shock of awakening to what doubtless might prove some new form of danger was still upon me when I heard a rattling of loose stones from the direction of the bluff, and turning my eyes in that direction I beheld the author of the disturbance, a great copper-coloured man, running rapidly towards me.

There was that in the haste with which he came which seemed quite sufficiently menacing, so that I did not need the added evidence of brandishing spear and scowling face to warn me that I was in no safe position, but whither to flee was indeed a momentous question.

The speed of the fellow seemed to preclude the possibility of escaping him upon the open beach. There was but a single alternative – the rude skiff – and with a celerity which equalled his, I pushed the thing into the sea and as it floated gave a final shove and clambered in over the end.

A cry of rage rose from the owner of the primitive craft, and an instant later his heavy, stone-tipped spear grazed my shoulder and buried itself in the bow of the boat beyond. Then I grasped the paddle, and with feverish haste urged the awkward, wobbly thing out upon the surface of the sea.

A glance over my shoulder showed me that the copper-coloured one had plunged in after me and was swimming rapidly in pursuit. His mighty strokes bade fair to close up the distance between us in short order, for at best I could make but slow progress with my unfamiliar craft, which nosed stubbornly in every direction but that which I desired to follow, so that fully half my energy was expended in turning its blunt prow back into the course.

I had covered some hundred yards from shore when it became evident that my pursuer must grasp the stern of the skiff within the next half-dozen strokes. In a frenzy of despair, I bent to that grandfather of all paddles in a hopeless effort to escape, and still the copper giant behind me gained and gained.

His hand was reaching upward for the stem when I saw a sleek, sinuous body shoot from the depths below. The man saw it too, and the look of terror that overspread his face assured me that I need have no further concern as to him, for the fear of certain death was in his look.

And then about him coiled the great, slimy folds of a hideous monster of that prehistoric deep – a mighty serpent of the sea, with fanged jaws, and darting, forked tongue, with bulging eyes, and bony protuberances upon head and snout that formed short, stout horns.

As I looked at that hopeless struggle my eyes met those of the doomed man, and I could have sworn that in his I saw an expression of hopeless appeal. But whether I did so or no there swept through me a sudden compassion for the fellow. He was indeed a brother-man, and that he might have killed me with pleasure had he caught me was forgotten in the extremity of his danger.

Unconsciously I had ceased paddling as the serpent rose to engage my pursuer, so now the skiff still drifted close beside the two. The monster seemed to be but playing with his victim before he closed his awful jaws upon him and dragged him down to his dark den beneath the surface to devour him The huge, snake-like body coiled and uncoiled about its prey. The hideous, gaping jaws snapped in the victim's face. The forked tongue, lightning-like, ran in and out upon the copper skin.

Nobly the giant battled for his life, beating with his stone hatchet against the bony armour that covered that frightful carcass; but for all the damage he inflicted he might as well have struck with his open palm.

At last I could endure no longer to sit supinely by while a fellow-man was dragged down to a horrible death by that repulsive reptile. Embedded in the prow of the skiff lay the spear that had been cast after me by him whom I suddenly desired to save. With a wrench I tore it loose, and standing upright in the wobbly log drove it with all the strength of my two arms straight into the gaping jaws of the hydrophidian.

With a loud hiss the creature abandoned its prey to turn upon me, but the spear, imbedded in its throat, prevented it from seizing me, though it came near to overturning the skiff in its mad efforts to reach me.

8

The Mahar Temple

The aborigine, apparently uninjured, climbed quickly into the skiff, and seizing the spear with me helped to hold off the infuriated creature. Blood from the wounded reptile was now crimsoning the waters about us, and soon from the weakening struggles it became evident that I had inflicted a death wound upon it. Presently its efforts to reach us ceased entirely, and with a few convulsive movements it turned upon its back quite dead.

And then there came to me a sudden realization of the predicament in which I had placed myself. I was entirely within the power of the savage man whose skiff I had stolen. Still clinging to the spear I looked into his face to find him scrutinizing me intently, and there we stood for some several minutes, each clinging tenaciously to the weapon the while we gazed in stupid wonderment at each other.

What was in his mind I do not know, but in my own was merely the question as to how soon the fellow would recommence hostilities.

Presently he spoke to me, but in a tongue which I was unable to translate. I shook my head in an effort to indicate my ignorance of his language, at the same time addressing him in the bastard tongue that the Sagoths use to converse with the human slaves of the Mahars.

To my delight he understood and answered me in the same jargon.

'What do you want of my spear?' he asked.

'Only to keep you from running it through me,' I replied.

'I would not do that,' he said, 'for you have just saved my life,' and with that he released his hold upon it and squatted down in the bottom of the skiff.

'Who are you?' he continued, 'and from what country do you come?'

I too sat down, laying the spear between us, and tried to explain how I came to Pellucidar, and where from, but it was as impossible for him to grasp or believe the strange tale I told him as I fear it is for you upon the outer crust to believe in the existence of the inner world.

To him it seemed quite ridiculous to imagine that there was another world far beneath his feet peopled by beings similar to himself, and he laughed uproariously the more he thought upon it. But it was ever thus. That which has never come within the scope of our really pitifully meagre world-experience cannot be – our finite minds cannot grasp that which may not exist in accordance with the conditions which obtain about us upon the outside of the insignificant grain of dust which wends its tiny way among the boulders of the universe – the speck of moist dirt we so proudly call the World.

So I gave it up and asked him about himself. He said he was a Mezop, and that his name was Ja.

'Who are the Mezops?' I asked. 'Where do they live?'

He looked at me in surprise.

'I might indeed believe that you were from another world,' he said, 'for who of Pellucidar could be so ignorant! The Mezops live upon the islands of the seas. In so far as I ever have heard no Mezop lives elsewhere, and no others than Mezops dwell upon the islands, but of course it may be different in other far-distant lands. I do not know. At any rate, in this sea, and those nearby, it is true that only people of my race inhabit the islands.

'We are fishermen, though we are great hunters as well, often going to the mainland in search of the game that is scarce upon all but the larger islands. And we are warriors also,' he added proudly. 'Even the Sagoths of the Mahars fear us. Once, when Pellucidar was young, the Sagoths were wont to capture us for slaves, as they do the other men of Pellucidar: it is handed down from father to son among us that this is so; but we fought so desperately and slew so many Sagoths, and those of us that were captured killed so many Mahars in their own cities, that at last they learned that it were

47

better to leave us alone; and later came the time that the Mahars became too indolent even to catch their own fish, except for amusement, and then they needed us to supply their wants, and so a truce was made between the races. Now they give us certain things which we are unable to produce in return for the fish that we catch, and the Mezops and the Mahars live in peace.

'The great ones even come to our islands. It is there, far from the prying eyes of their own Sagoths, that they practise their religious rites in the temples they have built there with our assistance. If you live among us you will doubtless see the manner of their worship, which is strange indeed, and most unpleasant for the poor slaves they bring to take part in it.'

As Ja talked, I had an excellent opportunity to inspect him more closely. He was a huge fellow, standing I should say six feet six or seven inches, well developed and of a coppery red not unlike that of the North American Indian, nor were his features dissimilar to theirs. He had the aquiline nose found among many of the higher tribes, the prominent cheek bones, and black hair and eyes, but his mouth and lips were better moulded. All in all, Ja was an impressive and handsome creature, and he talked well too, even in the miserable makeshift language we were compelled to use.

During our conversation Ja had taken the paddle and was propelling the skiff with vigorous strokes towards a large island that lay some half a mile from the mainland. The skill with which he handled his crude and awkward craft elicited my deepest admiration, since it had been so short a time before that I had made such pitiful work of it.

As we touched the pretty, level beach Ja leaped out and I followed him. Together we dragged the skiff far up into the bushes that grew beyond the sand.

'We must hide our canoes,' explained Ja, 'for the Mezops of Luana are always at war with us and would steal them if they found them.' He nodded towards an island farther out at sea, and at so great a distance that it seemed but a blur hanging in the distant sky. The upward curve of the surface of Pellucidar was constantly revealing the impossible to the surprised eyes of the outer-earthly. To see land and water curving upward in the distance until it seemed to stand on edge where it melted into the distant sky, and to feel that seas and mountains hung suspended directly above one's head, required such a complete reversal of the perceptive and reasoning faculties as almost to stupefy one.

No sooner had we hidden the canoe than Ja plunged into the jungle, presently emerging into a narrow but well-defined trail which wound hither and thither, much after the manner of the highways of all primitive folk, but there was one peculiarity about this Mezop trail which I was later to find distinguished them from all other trails that I ever have seen within or without the earth.

It would run on, plain and clear and well defined, to end suddenly in the midst of a tangle of matted jungle, then Ja would turn directly back in his tracks for a little distance, spring into a tree, climb through it to the other side, drop on to a fallen log, leap over a low bush, and alight once more upon a distinct trail which he would follow back for a short distance only, to turn directly about and retrace his steps until after a mile or less this new pathway ended as suddenly and mysteriously as the former section. Then he would pass again across some media which would reveal no spoor, to take up the broken thread of the trail beyond.

As the purpose of this remarkable avenue dawned upon me I could not but admire the native shrewdness of the ancient progenitor of the Mezops who hit upon this novel plan to throw his enemies from his track and delay or thwart them in their attempts to follow him to his deep-buried cities.

To you of the outer earth it might seem a slow and tortuous method of travelling through the jungle, but were you of Pellucidar you would realize that time is no factor where time does not exist. So labyrinthine are the windings of these trails, so varied the connecting links and the distances which one must retrace one's steps from the paths' ends to find them that a Mezop often reaches man's estate before he is familiar even with those which lead from his own city to the sea.

In fact three-fourths of the education of the young male Mezop consists in familiarizing himself with these jungle avenues, and the status of an adult is largely determined by the number of trails which he can follow upon his own island. The females never learn them, since from birth to death they never leave the clearing in which the village of their nativity is situated except they be taken to mate by a male from another village, or captured in war by the enemies of their tribe.

After proceeding through the jungle for what must have been upward of five miles we emerged suddenly into a large clearing in the exact centre of which stood as strange an appearing village as one might well imagine.

Large trees had been chopped down fifteen or twenty feet above the ground, and upon the tops of them spherical habitations of woven twigs, mud covered, had been built. Each ball-like house was surmounted by some manner of carven image, which Ja told me indicated the identity of the owner.

Horizontal slits, six inches high, and two or three feet wide, served to admit light and ventilation. The entrances to the houses were through small apertures in the bases of the trees and thence upward by rude ladders through the hollow trunks to the rooms above. The houses varied in size from two to several rooms. The largest that I entered was divided into two floors and eight apartments.

All about the village, between it and the jungle, lay beautifully cultivated fields in which the Mezops raised such cereals, fruits, and vegetables as they required. Women and children were working in these gardens as we crossed toward the village. At sight of Ja they saluted deferentially, but to me they paid not the slightest attention. Among them and about the outer verge of the cultivated area were many warriors. These too saluted Ja, by touching the points of their spears to the ground directly before them.

Ja conducted me to a large house in the centre of the village – the house with eight rooms – and taking me up into it gave me food and drink. There I met his mate, a comely girl with a nursing baby in her arms. Ja told her of how I had saved his life, and she was thereafter most kind and hospitable towards me, even permitting me to hold and amuse the tiny bundle of humanity whom Ja told me would one day rule the tribe, for Ja, it seemed, was the chief of the community.

We had eaten and rested, and I had slept, much to Ja's amusement, for it seemed that he seldom if ever did so, and then the red man proposed that I accompany him to the temple of the Mahars, which lay not far from his village.

'We are not supposed to visit it,' he said, 'but the great ones cannot hear, and if we keep well out of sight they need never know that we have been there. For my part I hate them and always have, but the other chieftains of the island think it best that we continue to maintain the amicable relations which exist between the two races; otherwise I should like nothing better than to lead my warriors amongst the hideous creatures and exterminate them – Pellucidar would be a better place to live were there none of them.'

I wholly concurred in Ja's belief, but it seemed that it might be a difficult matter to exterminate the dominant race of Pellucidar. Thus conversing we followed the intricate trail towards the temple, which we came upon in a small clearing surrounded by enormous trees similar to those which must have flourished upon the outer crust during the carboniferous age.

Here was a mighty temple of hewn rock built in the shape of a rough oval with rounded roof in which were several large openings. No doors or windows were visible in the sides of the structure, nor was there need of any, except one entrance for the slaves, since, as Ja explained, the Mahars flew to and from their place of ceremonial, entering and leaving the building by means of the apertures in the roof.

'But,' added Ja, 'there is an entrance near the base of which even the Mahars know nothing. Come!' and he led me across the clearing and about the end to a pile of loose rock which lay against the foot of the wall. Here he removed a couple of large boulders, revealing a small opening which led straight within the building, or so it seemed, though as I entered after Ja I discovered myself in a narrow place of extreme darkness.

'We are within the outer wall,' said Ja. 'It is hollow. Follow me closely.'

The red man groped ahead a few paces and then began to ascend a primitive ladder, similar to that which leads from the ground to the upper stories of his house. We ascended for some forty feet, when the interior of the space between the walls commenced to grow lighter, and presently we came opposite an opening in the inner wall which gave us an unobstructed view of the entire interior of the temple.

The lower floor was an enormous tank of clear water in which numerous hideous Mahars swam lazily up and down. Artificial islands of granite rock dotted this artificial sea, and upon several of them I saw men and women like myself.

'What are the human beings doing here?' I asked.

'Wait and you shall see,' replied Ja. 'They are to take a leading part in the ceremonies which will follow the advent of the queen. You may be thankful that you are not upon the same side of the wall as they.'

Scarcely had he spoken than we heard a great fluttering of wings above, and a moment later a long procession of the frightful reptiles of Pellucidar winged slowly and majestically through the large central opening in the roof and circled in stately manner above the temple.

There were several Mahars first, and then at least twenty awe-inspiring pterodactyls – thipdars, they are called within Pellucidar. Behind these came the queen, flanked by other thipdars, as she had been when she entered the amphitheatre at Phutra.

Three times they wheeled about the interior of the oval chamber, to settle finally upon the damp, cold boulders that fringe the outer edge of the pool. In the centre of one side the largest rock was reserved for the queen, and here she took her place surrounded by her terrible guard.

All lay quiet for several minutes after settling to their places. One might have imagined them in silent prayer. The poor slaves upon the diminutive islands watched the horrid creatures with wide eyes. The men, for the most part, stood erect and stately, with folded arms, awaiting their doom; but the women and children clung to one another, hiding behind the males. They are a noble-looking race, these cave-men of Pellucidar, and if our progenitors were as they, the human race of the outer crust has deteriorated rather than improved with the march of ages. All they lack is opportunity. We have opportunity, and little else.

Now the queen moved. She raised her ugly head, looking about; then very slowly she crawled to the edge of her throne and slid noiselessly into the water. Up and down the long tank she swam, turning at the ends as you have seen captive seals turn in their tiny tanks, turning upon their backs and diving below the surface.

Nearer and nearer to the island she came, until at last she remained at rest before the largest, which was directly opposite her throne. Raising her hideous head from the water she fixed her great, round eyes upon the slaves. They were fat and sleek, for they had been brought from a distant Mahar city where human beings are kept in droves, and bred and fattened as we breed and fatten beef cattle.

The queen fixed her gaze upon a plump young maiden. Her victim tried to turn away, hiding her face in her hands and kneeling behind a woman; but the reptile, with unblinking eyes, stared on with such fixity that I could have sworn her vision penetrated the woman and the girl's arms to reach at last the very centre of her brain.

Slowly the reptile's head commenced to move to and fro, but the eyes never ceased to bore towards the frightened girl, and then the victim responded. She turned wide, fear-haunted eyes towards the Mahar queen, slowly she rose to her feet, and then as though dragged by some unseen power she moved as one in a trance straight towards the reptile, her glassy eyes fixed upon those of her captor.

To the water's edge she came, nor did she even pause, but stepped into the shallows beside the little island. On she moved towards the Mahar, who now slowly retreated as though leading her victim on. The water rose to the girl's knees, and still she advanced, chained by that clammy eye. Now the water was at her waist; now her armpits. Her fellows upon the island looked on in horror, helpless to avert her doom, in which they saw a forecast of their own.

The Mahar sank now till only the long, upper bill and eyes were exposed above the surface of the water, and the girl had advanced until the end of that repulsive beak was but an inch or two from her face, her horror-filled eyes riveted upon those of the reptile.

Now the water passed above the girl's mouth and nose – her eyes and forehead all that showed – yet still she walked on after the retreating Mahar. The queen's head slowly disappeared beneath the surface and after it went the eyes of her victim – only a slow ripple widened toward the shores to mark where the two vanished.

For a time all was silence within the temple. The slaves were motionless in terror. The Mahars watched the surface of the water for the reappearance of their queen, and presently at one end of the tank her head rose slowly into view. She was backing towards the surface, her eyes fixed before her as they had been when she dragged the helpless girl to her doom.

And then to my utter amazement I saw the forehead and eyes of the maiden come slowly out of the depths, following the gaze of the reptile just as when she had disappeared beneath the surface. On and on came the girl until she stood in water that reached barely to her knees, and though she had been beneath the surface sufficient time to have drowned her thrice over, there was no indication other than her dripping hair and glistening body that she had been submerged at all.

Again and again the queen led the girl into the depths and out again, until the uncanny weirdness of the thing got on my nerves, so that I could have leaped into the tank to the child's rescue had I not taken a firm hold of myself.

Once they were below much longer than usual, and when they came to the surface I was horrified to see that one of the girl's arms was gone – gnawed completely off at the shoulder but the poor thing gave no indication of realizing pain, only the horror in her set eyes seemed intensified.

The next time they appeared the other arm was gone, and then the breasts, and then a part of the face – it was awful. The poor creatures on the islands awaiting their fate tried to cover their eyes with their hands to hide the fearful sight, but now I saw that they too were under the hypnotic spell of the reptiles, so that they could only crouch in terror with their eyes fixed upon the terrible thing that was transpiring before them.

Finally the queen was under much longer than ever before, and when she rose she came alone and swam sleepily towards her boulder. The moment she mounted it seemed to be the signal for the other Mahars to enter the tank, and then commenced, upon a larger scale, a repetition of the uncanny performance through which the queen had led her victim.

Only the women and children fell prey to the Mahars – they being the weakest and most tender – and when they had satisfied their appetite for human flesh, some of them devouring two and three of the slaves, there were only a score of full-grown men left, and I thought that for some reason these were to be spared, but such was far from the case, for as the last Mahar crawled to her rock the queen's thipdars darted into the air, circled the temple once, and then, hissing like steam engines, swooped down upon the remaining slaves.

There was no hypnotism here – just the plain, brutal ferocity of the beast of prey tearing, rending, and gulping its meat, but at that it was less horrible than the uncanny method of the Mahars. By the time the thipdars had disposed of the last of the slaves the Mahars were all asleep upon their rocks, and a moment later the great pterodactyls swung back to their posts beside the queen, and themselves dropped into slumber.

'I thought the Mahars seldom, if ever, slept,' I said to Ja.

'They do many things in this temple which they do not do elsewhere,' he replied. 'The Mahars of Phutra are not supposed to eat human flesh, yet slaves are brought here by thousands and almost always you will find Mahars on hand to consume them. I imagine that they do not bring their Sagoths here because they are ashamed of the practice, which is supposed to obtain only among the least advanced of their race; but I would wager my canoe against a broken paddle that there is no Mahar but eats human flesh whenever she can get it.'

'Why should they object to eating human flesh,' I asked, 'if it is true that they look upon us as lower animals?'

'It is not because they consider us their equals that they are supposed to look with abhorrence upon those who eat our flesh,' replied Ja; 'it is merely that we are warm-blooded animals. They would not think of eating the meat of a thag, which we consider such a delicacy, any more than I would think of eating a snake. As a matter of fact it is difficult to explain just why this sentiment should exist among them.'

'I wonder if they left a single victim,' I remarked leaning far out of the opening in the rocky wall to inspect the temple better. Directly below me the water lapped the very side of the wall, there being a break in the boulders at this point, as there was at several other places about the side of the temple.

My hands were resting upon a small piece of granite which formed a part of the wall, and all my weight upon it proved too much for it. It slipped and I lunged forward. There was nothing to grasp to save myself and I plunged head foremost into the water below.

Fortunately the tank was deep at this point, and I suffered no injury from the fall, but as I was rising to the surface my mind filled with the horrors of my position as I thought of the terrible doom which awaited me the moment the eyes of the reptiles fell upon the creature that had disturbed their slumber.

As long as I could I remained beneath the surface, swimming rapidly in the direction of the islands that I might prolong my life to the utmost. At last I was forced to rise for air, and as I cast a terrified glance in the direction of the Mahars and the thipdars I was almost stunned to see that not a single one remained upon the rocks where I had last seen them, nor as I searched the temple with my eyes could I discern any within it.

For a moment I was puzzled to account for the thing, until I realized that the reptiles, being deaf, could not have been disturbed by the noise my body made when it hit the water, and that as there is no such thing as time within Pellucidar there was no telling how long I had been beneath the surface. It was a difficult thing to attempt to figure out by earthly standards – this matter of elapsed time – but when I set myself to it I began to realize that I might have been submerged a second or a month or not at all. You have no conception of the strange contradictions and impossibilities which arise when all methods of measuring time, as we know them upon earth, are non-existent.

I was about to congratulate myself upon the miracle which had saved me for the moment, when the memory of the hypnotic powers of the Mahars filled me with apprehension lest they be practising their uncanny art upon me, to the end that I merely imagined that I was alone in the temple. At the thought cold sweat broke out upon me from every pore, and as I crawled from the water on to one of the tiny islands I was trembling like a leaf – you cannot imagine the awful horror which even the simple thought of the repulsive Mahars of Pellucidar induces in the human mind, and to feel that you are in their power – that they are crawling, slimy and abhorrent, to drag you down beneath the waters and devour you! It is frightful.

But they did not come, and at last I came to the conclusion that I was indeed alone within the temple. How long I should be alone was the next question to assail me as I swam frantically about once more in search of a means to escape.

Several times I called to Ja, but he must have left after I tumbled into the tank, for I received no response to my cries. Doubtless he had felt as certain of my doom when he saw me topple from our hiding place as I had, and lest he too should be discovered had hastened from the temple and back to his village.

I knew that there must be some entrance to the building beside the doorways in the roof, for it did not seem reasonable to believe that the thousands of slaves which were brought here to feed the Mahars the human flesh they craved would all be carried through the air, and so I continued my search until at last it was rewarded by the discovery of several loose granite blocks in the masonry at one end of the temple.

A little effort proved sufficient to dislodge enough of these stones to permit me to crawl through into the clearing, and a moment later I had scurried across the intervening space to the dense jungle beyond.

Here I sank panting and trembling upon the matted grasses beneath the giant trees, for I felt that I had escaped from the grinning fangs of death out of the depths of my own grave. Whatever dangers lay hidden in this island jungle, there could be none so fearsome as those which I had just escaped. I knew that I could meet death bravely enough if it came in the form of some familiar beast or man – anything other than the hideous and uncanny Mahars.

9

The Face of Death

I must have fallen asleep from exhaustion. When I awoke I was very hungry, and after busying myself searching for fruit for a while, I set off through the jungle to find the beach. I knew that the island was not so large but that I could easily find the sea if I did but move in a straight line, but there came the difficulty as there was no way in which I could direct my course and hold it, the sun, of course, being always directly above my head, and the trees so thickly set that I could see no distant object which might serve to guide me in a straight line.

As it was, I must have walked for a great distance, since I ate four times and slept twice before I reached the sea; but at last I did so, and my pleasure at the sight of it was greatly enhanced by the chance discovery of a hidden canoe among the bushes through which I had stumbled just prior to coming upon the beach.

I can tell you that it did not take me long to pull that awkward craft down to the water and shove it far out from shore. My experience with Ja had taught me that if I were to steal another canoe I must be quick about it and get far beyond the owner's reach as soon as possible.

I must have come out upon the opposite side of the island from that at which Ja and I had entered it, for the mainland was nowhere in sight. For a long time I paddled around the shore, though well out, before I saw the mainland in the distance. At the sight of it I lost no time in directing my course towards it, for I had long since made up my mind to return to Phutra and give myself up that I might be once more with Perry and Ghak the Hairy One.

I felt that I was a fool ever to have attempted to escape alone, especially in view of the fact that our plans were already well formulated to make a break for freedom together. Of course I realized that the chances of the success of our proposed venture were slim indeed, but I knew that I never could enjoy freedom without Perry so long as the old man lived, and I had learned that the probability that I might find means from without to rescue him was less than slight.

Had Perry been dead, I should gladly have pitted my strength and wit against the savage and primordial world in which I found myself. I could have lived in seclusion within some rocky cave until I had found the means to outfit myself with the crude weapons of the Stone Age, and then set out in search of her whose image had now become the constant companion of my waking hours, and the central and beloved figure of my dreams.

But, to the best of my knowledge, Perry still lived and it was my duty and wish to be again with him, that we might share the dangers and vicissitudes of the strange world we had discovered. And Ghak, too; the great, shaggy man had found a place in the hearts of us both, for he was indeed every inch a man and king. Uncouth, perhaps, and brutal, too, if judged too harshly by the standards of effete twentieth-century civilization, but withal noble, dignified, chivalrous, and lovable.

Chance carried me to the very beach upon which I had discovered Ja's canoe, and a short time later I was scrambling up the steep bank to retrace my steps from the plain of Phutra. But my troubles came when I entered the cañon beyond the summit, for here I found that several of them centred at the point where I crossed the divide, and which one I had traversed to reach the pass I could not for the life of me remember.

It was all a matter of chance and so I set off down that which seemed the easiest going, and in this I made the same mistake that many of us do in selecting the path along which we shall follow out the course of our lives, and again learned that it is not always best to follow the line of least resistance.

By the time I had eaten eight meals and slept twice I was convinced that I was upon the wrong trail, for between Phutra and the inland sea I had not slept at all, and had eaten but once. To retrace my steps to the summit of the divide and explore another cañon seemed the only solution of my problem, but a sudden widening and levelness of the cañon just before me seemed to suggest that it was about to open into a level country, and with the lure of discovery strong upon me I decided to proceed but a short distance further before I turned back.

The next turn of the cañon brought me to its mouth, and before me I saw a narrow plain leading down to an ocean. At my right the side of the cañon continued to the water's edge, the valley lying to my left, and the foot of it running gradually into the sea, where it formed a broad level beach.

Clumps of strange trees dotted the landscape here and there almost to the water, and rank grass and ferns grew between. From the nature of the vegetation I was convinced that the land between the ocean and the foothills was swampy, though directly before me it seemed dry enough all the way to the sandy strip along which the restless waters advanced and retreated.

Curiosity prompted me to walk down to the beach, for the scene was very beautiful. As I passed along beside the deep and tangled vegetation of the swamp I thought that I saw a movement of the ferns at my left, but though I stopped a moment to look it was not repeated, and if anything lay hid there my eyes could not penetrate the dense foliage to discern it.

Presently I stood upon the beach looking out over the wide and lonely sea across whose forbidding bosom no human being had yet ventured, to discover what strange and mysterious lands lay beyond, or what its invisible islands held of riches, wonders, or adventure. What savage races, what fierce and formidable beasts were this very instant watching the lapping of the waves upon its farther shore! How far did it extend? Perry had told me that the seas of Pellucidar were small in comparison with those of the outer crust, but even so this great ocean might stretch its broad expanse for thousands of miles. For countless ages it had rolled up and down its countless miles of shore, and yet to-day it remained all unknown beyond the tiny strip that was visible from its beaches.

The fascination of speculation was strong upon me. It was as though I had been carried back to the birth of time of our own outer world to look upon its lands and seas before man had traversed either. Here was a new world, all untouched. It called to me to explore it. I was dreaming of the excitement and adventure which lay before us could Perry and I but escape the Mahars, when something, a slight noise I imagine, drew my attention behind me.

As I turned, romance, adventure, and discovery in the abstract took wing before the terrible embodiment of all three in concrete form that I beheld advancing upon me.

A huge, slimy amphibian it was, with toad-like body and the mighty jaws of an alligator. Its immense carcass must have weighed tons, and yet it moved swiftly and silently towards me. Upon one hand was the bluff that ran from the cañon to the sea, on the other the fearsome swamp from which the creature had sneaked upon me, behind lay the mighty untracked sea, and before me in the centre of the narrow way that led to safety stood this huge mountain of terrible and menacing flesh.

A single glance at the thing was sufficient to assure me that I was facing one of those long-extinct, prehistoric creatures whose fossilized remains are found within the outer crust as far back as the Triassic formation, a gigantic labyrinthodon. And there I was, unarmed, and with the exception of a loin cloth as naked as I had come into the world. I could imagine how my first ancestor felt that distant, prehistoric morn that he encountered for the first time the terrifying progenitor of the thing that had me cornered now beside the restless, mysterious sea.

Unquestionably he had escaped, or I should not have been within Pellucidar or elsewhere, and I wished at that moment that he had handed down to me, with the various attributes that I presume I have inherited from him, the specific application of the instinct of self-preservation which saved him from the fate which loomed so close before me to-day.

To seek escape in the swamp or in the ocean would have been similar to jumping into a den of lions to escape one upon the outside. The sea and swamp both were doubtless alive with these mighty, carnivorous amphibians, and if not, the individual that menaced me could pursue me into either the sea or the swamp with equal facility.

There seemed nothing to do but stand supinely and await my end. I thought of Perry – how he would wonder what had become of me. I thought of my friends of the outer world, and of how they all would go on living their lives in total ignorance of the strange and terrible fate that had overtaken me, or unguessing the weird surroundings which had witnessed the last frightful agony of my extinction. And with these thoughts came a realization of how unimportant to the life and happiness of the world is the existence of any one of us. We may be snuffed out without an instant's warning, and for a brief day our friends speak of us with subdued voices. The following morning, while the first worm is busily engaged in testing the construction of our coffin, they are teeing up for the first hole to suffer more acute sorrow over a sliced ball than they did over our, to us, untimely demise.

The labyrinthodon was coming more slowly now. He seemed to realize that escape for me was impossible, and I could have sworn that his huge, fanged jaws grinned in pleasurable appreciation of my predicament, or was it in anticipation of the juicy morsel which would so soon be pulp between those formidable teeth?

He was about fifty feet from me when I heard a voice calling to me from the direction of the bluff at my left. I looked and could have shouted in delight at the sight that met my eyes, for there stood Ja, waving frantically to me, and urging me to run for it to the cliff's base.

I had no idea that I should escape the monster that had marked me for his breakfast, but at least I should not die alone. Human eyes would watch my end. It was cold comfort I presume, but yet I derived some slight peace of mind from the contemplation of it.

To run seemed ridiculous, especially towards that steep and unscalable cliff, and yet I did so, and as I ran I saw Ja, agile as a monkey, crawl down the precipitous face of the rocks, clinging to small projections and the tough creepers that had found root-hold here and there.

The labyrinthodon evidently thought that Ja was coming to double his portion of human flesh, so he was in no haste to pursue me to the cliff and frighten away this other titbit. Instead he merely trotted along behind me.

As I approached the foot of the cliff I saw what Ja intended doing, but I doubted if the thing would prove successful. He had come down to within twenty feet of the bottom, and there, clinging with one hand to a small ledge, and with his feet resting precariously upon tiny bushes that grew from the solid face of the rock, he lowered the point of his long spear until it hung some six feet above the ground.

To clamber up that slim shaft without dragging Ja down and precipitating both to the same doom from which the copper-coloured one was attempting to save me seemed utterly impossible, and as I came near the spear I told Ja so, and that I could not risk him to try to save myself.

But he insisted that he knew what he was doing and was in no danger himself.

'The danger is still yours,' he called, 'for unless you move much more rapidly than you are now, the *sithic* will be upon you and drag you back before even you are halfway up the spear – he can rear up and reach you with ease anywhere below where I stand.'

Well, Ja should know his own business, I thought, and so I grasped the spear and clambered up towards the red man as rapidly as I could – being so far removed from my simian ancestors as I am. I imagine the slow-witted sithic, as Ja called him, suddenly realized our intentions and that he was quite likely to lose all his meal instead of having it doubled as he had hoped.

When he saw me clambering up that spear he let out a hiss that fairly shook the ground, and came charging after me at a terrific rate. I had reached the top of the spear by this time, or almost; another six inches would give me a hold on Ja's hand, when I felt a sudden wrench from below, and glancing fearfully downward saw the mighty jaws of the monster close on the sharp point of the weapon.

I made a frantic effort to reach Ja's hand, the sithic gave a tremendous tug that came near to jerking Ja from his frail hold on the surface of the rock, the spear slipped from his fingers, and still clinging to it I plunged feet foremost towards my executioner.

At the instant that he felt the spear come away from Ja's hand the creature must have opened his huge jaws to catch me, for when I came down, still clinging to the butt end of the weapon, the point yet rested in his mouth, and the result was that the sharpened end transfixed his lower jaw.

With the pain he snapped his mouth close. I fell upon his snout, lost my hold upon the spear, rolled the length of his face and head, across his short neck on to his broad back and from there to the ground.

Scarce had I touched the earth than I was upon my feet, dashing madly for the path by which I had entered this horrible valley. A glance over my shoulder showed me the sithic engaged in pawing at the spear stuck through his lower jaw, and so busily engaged did he remain in this occupation that I had gained the safety of the cliff-top before he was ready to take up the pursuit. When he did not discover me in sight within the valley he dashed, hissing, into the rank vegetation of the swamp, and that was the last I saw of him.

10

Phutra Again

I hastened to the cliff-edge above Ja and helped him to a secure footing. He would not listen to any thanks for his attempt to save me, which had come so near miscarrying.

'I had given you up for lost when you tumbled into the Mahar temple,' he said, 'for not even I could save you from their clutches, and you may imagine my surprise when on seeing a canoe dragged up upon the beach of the mainland I discovered your own footprints in the sand beside it.

'I immediately set out in search of you, knowing as I did that you must be entirely unarmed and defenceless against the many dangers which lurk upon the mainland both in the form of savage beasts and reptiles, and men as well. I had no difficulty in tracking you to this point. It is well that I arrived when I did.'

'But why did you do it?' I asked, puzzled at this show of friendship on the part of a man of another world and a different race and colour.

'You saved my life,' he replied; 'from that moment it became my duty to protect and befriend you. I would have been no true Mezop had I evaded my plain duty; but it was a pleasure in this instance, for I like you. I wish that you would come and live with me. You shall become a member of my tribe. Among us there is the best of hunting and fishing, and you shall have, to choose a mate from, the most beautiful girls of Pellucidar. Will you come?'

I told him about Perry then, and Dian the Beautiful, and how my duty was to them first. Afterward I should return and visit him – if I could ever find his island.

'Oh, that is easy, my friend,' he said. 'You need merely to come to the foot of the highest peak of the Mountains of the Clouds. There you will find a river which flows into the Lural Az. Directly opposite the mouth of the river you will see three large islands far out, so far that they are barely discernible, the one to the extreme left as you face them from the mouth of the river is Anoroc, where I rule the tribe of Anoroc.'

'But how am I to find the Mountains of the Clouds?' I asked.

'Men say that they are visible from half Pellucidar,' he replied.

'How large is Pellucidar?' I asked, wondering what sort of theory these primitive men had concerning the form and substance of their world.

'The Mahars say it is round, like the inside of a tola shell,' he answered, 'but that is ridiculous, since, were it true, we should fall back were we to travel far in any direction, and all the waters of Pellucidar would run to one spot and drown us. No, Pellucidar is quite flat and extends no man knows how far in all directions. At the edges, so my ancestors have reported and handed down to me, is a great wall that prevents the earth and waters from escaping over into the burning sea whereon Pellucidar floats; but I never have been so far from Anoroc as to have seen this wall with my own eyes. However, it is quite reasonable to believe that this is true, whereas there is no reason at all in the foolish belief of the Mahars. According to them Pellucidarians who live upon the opposite side walk always with their heads pointed downward!' and Ja laughed uproariously at the very thought.

It was plain to see that the human folk of this inner world had not advanced far in learning, and the thought that the ugly Mahars had so outstripped them was a very pathetic one indeed. I wondered how many ages it would take to lift these people out of their ignorance even were it given to

Perry and I to attempt it. Possibly we would be killed for our pains as were those men of the outer world who dared challenge the dense ignorance and superstitions of the earth's younger days. But it was worth the effort if the opportunity ever presented itself.

And then it occurred to me that here was an opportunity – that I might make a small beginning upon Ja, who was my friend, and thus note the effect of my teaching upon a Pellucidarian.

'Ja,' I said, 'what would you say were I to tell you that in so far as the Mahar's theory of the shape of Pellucidar is concerned it is correct?'

'I would say,' he replied, 'that either you are a fool, or took me for one.'

'But, Ja,' I insisted, 'if their theory is incorrect how do you account for the fact that I was able to pass through the earth from the outer crust to Pellucidar. If your theory is correct all is a sea of flame beneath us, wherein no peoples could exist, and yet I come from a great world that is covered with human beings, and beasts, and birds, and fishes in mighty oceans.'

'You live upon the under side of Pellucidar, and walk always with your head pointed downward?' he scoffed. 'And were I to believe that, my friend, I should indeed be mad.'

I attempted to explain the force of gravity to him, and by the means of the dropped fruit to illustrate how impossible it would be for a body to fall off the earth under any circumstances. He listened so intently that I thought I had made an impression, and started the train of thought that would lead him to a partial understanding of the truth. But I was mistaken.

'Your own illustration,' he said finally, 'proves the falsity of your theory.' He dropped a fruit from his hand to the ground. 'See,' he said, 'without support even this tiny fruit falls until it strikes something that stops it. If Pellucidar were not supported upon the flaming sea it too would fall as the fruit falls – you have proven it yourself!' He had me that time – you could see it in his eye.

It seemed a hopeless job and I gave it up, temporarily at least, for when I contemplated the necessary explanation of our solar system and the universe I realized how futile it would be to attempt to picture to Ja or any other Pellucidarian the sun, the moon, the planets, and the countless stars. Those born within the inner world could no more conceive of such things than can we of the outer crust reduce to factors appreciable to our finite minds such terms as space and eternity.

'Well, Ja,' I laughed, 'whether we be walking with our feet up or down, here we are, and the question of greatest importance is not so much where we came from as where we are going now. For my part, I wish that you could guide me to Phutra, where I may give myself up to the Mahars once more that my friends and I may work out the plan of escape which the Sagoths interrupted when they gathered us together and drove us to the arena to witness the punishment of the slaves who killed the guardsman. I wish now that I had not left the arena, for by this time my friends and I might have made good our escape, whereas this delay may mean the wrecking of all our plans, which depended for their consummation upon the continued sleep of the three Mahars who lay in the pit beneath the building in which we were confined.'

'You would return to captivity?' cried Ja.

'My friends are there,' I replied, 'the only friends I have in Pellucidar, except yourself. What else may I do under the circumstances?'

He thought for a moment in silence. Then he shook his head sorrowfully.

'It is what a brave man and a good friend should do,' he said; 'yet it seems most foolish, for the Mahars will most certainly condemn you to death for running away, and so you will be accomplishing nothing for your friends by returning. Never in all my life have I heard of a prisoner returning to the Mahars of his own free will. There are but few who escape them, though some do, and these would rather die than be recaptured.'

'I see no other way, Ja,' I said, 'though I can assure you that I would rather go to Sheol after Perry than to Phutra. However, Perry is much too pious to make the probability at all great that I should ever be called upon to rescue him from the former locality.'

Ja asked me what Sheol was, and when I explained, as best I could, he said, 'You are speaking of Molop Az, the flaming sea upon which Pellucidar floats. All the dead who are buried in the ground go there. Piece by piece they are carried down to Molop Az by the little demons who dwell there. We know this because when graves are opened we find that the bodies have been partially or entirely borne off. That is why we of Anoroc place our dead in high trees where the birds may find them and bear them bit by bit to the Dead World above the Land of Awful Shadow. If we kill an enemy we place his body in the ground that it may go to Molop Az.'

As we talked we had been walking up the cañon, down which I had come to the great ocean and the sithic. Ja did his best to dissuade me from returning to Phutra, but when he saw that I was determined to do so, he consented to guide me to a point from which I could see the plain where lay the city. To my surprise the distance was but short from the beach where I had again met Ja. It was evident that I had spent much time following the windings of a tortuous cañon, while just beyond the ridge lay the city of Phutra, near to which I must have come several times.

As we topped the ridge and saw the granite gate towers dotting the flowered plain at our feet, Ja made a final effort to persuade me to abandon my mad purpose and return with him to Anoroc, but I was firm in my resolve, and at last he bid me goodbye, assured in his own mind that he was looking upon me for the last time.

I was sorry to part with Ja, for I had come to like him very much indeed. With his hidden city upon the island of Anoroc as a base, and his savage warriors as escort, Perry and I could have accomplished much in the line of exploration, and I hoped that were we successful in our effort to escape we might return to Anoroc later.

There was, however, one great thing to be accomplished first – at least it was *the* great thing to me – the finding of Dian the Beautiful. I wanted to make amends for the affront I had put upon her in my ignorance, and I wanted to – well, I wanted to see her again, and to be with her.

Down the hillside I made my way into the gorgeous field of flowers, and then across the rolling land towards the shadowless columns that guard the ways to buried Phutra. A quarter of a mile from the nearest entrance I was discovered by the Sagoth guard, and in an instant four of the gorilla-men were dashing towards me.

Though they brandished their long spears and yelled like wild Indians I paid not the slightest attention to them, walking quietly towards them as though unaware of their existence. My manner had the effect upon them that I had hoped, and as we came quite near together they ceased their savage shouting. It was evident that they had expected me to turn and flee at sight of them, thus presenting that which they most enjoyed – a moving human target at which to cast their spears.

'What do you here?' shouted one, and then, as he recognized me, 'Ho! It is the slave who claims to be from another world – he who escaped when the thag ran amuck within the amphitheatre. But why do you return, having once made good your escape?'

'I did not "escape,"' I replied. 'I but ran away to avoid the thag, as did others, and coming into a long passage I became confused and lost my way in the foothills beyond Phutra. Only now have I found my way back.'

'And you come of your free will back to Phutra!' exclaimed one of the guardsmen.

'Where else might I go?' I asked. 'I am a stranger within Pellucidar and know no other where than Phutra. Why should I not desire to be in Phutra? Am I not well fed and well treated? Am I not happy? What better lot could man desire?'

The Sagoths scratched their heads. This was a new one on them, and so being stupid brutes they took me to their masters, whom they felt would be better fitted to solve the riddle of my return, for riddle they still considered it.

I had spoken to the Sagoths as I had for the purpose of throwing them off the scent of my purposed attempt at escape. If they thought that I was so satisfied with my lot within Phutra that I would voluntarily return when I had once had so excellent an opportunity to escape, they would never for an instant imagine that I could be occupied in arranging another escape immediately upon my return to the city.

So they led me before a slimy Mahar who clung to a slimy rock within the large room that was the thing's office. With cold, reptilian eyes the creature seemed to bore through the thin veneer of my deceit and read my inmost thoughts. It heeded the story which the Sagoths told of my return to Phutra, watching the gorilla-men's lips and fingers during the recital. Then it questioned me through one of the Sagoths.

'You say that you returned to Phutra of your own free will, because you think yourself better off here than elsewhere? Do you not know that you may be the next chosen to give up your life in the interests of the wonderful scientific investigations that our learned ones are continually occupied with?'

I hadn't heard of anything of that nature, but I thought best not to admit it.

'I could be in no more danger here,' I said, 'than naked and unarmed in the savage jungles or upon the lonely plains of Pellucidar. I was fortunate, I think, to return to Phutra at all. As it was I barely escaped death within the jaws of a huge sithic. No, I am sure that I am safer in the hands of intelligent creatures such as rule Phutra. At least such would be the case in my own world, where human beings like myself rule supreme. There the higher races of man extend protection and hospitality to the stranger within their gates and being a stranger here I naturally assumed that a like courtesy would be accorded me.'

The Mahar looked at me in silence for some time after I ceased speaking and the Sagoth had translated my words to his master. The creature seemed deep in thought. Presently he communicated some message to the Sagoth. The latter turned, and motioning me to follow him, left the presence of the reptile. Behind and on either side of me marched the balance of the guard.

'What are they going to do with me?' I asked the fellow at my right.

'You are to appear before the learned ones, who will question you regarding this strange world from which you say you come.'

After a moment's silence he turned to me again.

'Do you happen to know,' he asked, 'what the Mahars do to slaves who lie to them?'

'No,' I replied, 'nor does it interest me, as I have no intention of lying to the Mahars.'

'Then be careful that you don't repeat the impossible tale you told Sol-to-to just now – another world, indeed, where human beings rule!' he concluded in fine scorn.

'But it is the truth,' I insisted. 'From where else, then, did I come? I am not of Pellucidar. Anyone with half an eye could see that.'

'It is your misfortune, then,' he remarked dryly, 'that you may not be judged by one with but half an eye.'

'What will they do with me,' I asked, 'if they do not have a mind to believe me?'

'You may be sentenced to the arena, or go to the pits to be used in research work by the learned ones,' he replied.

'And what will they do with me there?' I persisted.

'No one knows except the Mahars and those who go to the pits with them, but as the latter never return, their knowledge does them but little good. It is said that the learned ones cut up their subjects while they are yet alive, thus learning many useful things. However, I should not imagine that it would prove very useful to him who was being cut up; but, of course, this is all but conjecture. The chances are that ere long you will know much more about it than I,' and he grinned as he spoke. The Sagoths have a well-developed sense of humour.

'And suppose it is the arena,' I continued. 'What then?'

'You saw the two who met the tarag and the thag the time that you escaped?' he said.

'Yes.'

'Your end in the arena would be similar to what was intended for them,' he explained, 'though, of course, the same kinds of animals might not be employed.'

'It is sure death in either event?' I asked.

'What becomes of those who go below with the learned ones I do not know, nor does any other,' he replied; 'but those who go to the arena may come out alive and thus regain their liberty, as did the two whom you saw.'

'They gained their liberty? And how?'

'It is the custom of the Mahars to liberate those who remain alive within the arena after the beasts depart or are killed. Thus it happened that several mighty warriors from far distant lands, whom we have captured on our slave raids, have battled the brutes turned in upon them and slain them, thereby winning their freedom. In the instance which you witnessed, the beasts killed each other, but the result was the same – the man and woman were liberated, furnished with weapons, and started on their homeward journey. Upon the left shoulder of each a mark was burned – the mark of the Mahars – which will for ever protect these two from slaving parties.'

'There is a slender chance for me, then, if I be sent to the arena, and none at all if the learned ones drag me to the pits?'

'You are quite right,' he replied; 'but do not felicitate yourself too quickly should you be sent to the arena, for there is scarce one in a thousand who comes out alive.'

To my surprise they returned me to the same building in which I had been confined with Perry and Ghak before my escape. At the doorway I was turned over to the guards there.

'He will doubtless be called before the investigators shortly,' said he who had brought me back, 'so have him in readiness.'

The guards in whose hands I now found myself, upon hearing that I had returned of my own volition to Phutra evidently felt that it would be safe to give me liberty within the building as had been the custom before I had escaped, and so I was told to return to whatever duty had been mine formerly.

My first act was to hunt up Perry, whom I found poring as usual over the great tomes that he was supposed to be merely dusting and re-arranging upon new shelves.

As I entered the room he glanced up and nodded pleasantly to me, only to resume his work as though I had never been away at all. I was both astonished and hurt at his indifference. And to think that I was risking death to return to him purely from a sense of duty and affection!

'Why, Perry!' I exclaimed, 'haven't you a word for me after my long absence?'

'Long absence!' he repeated in evident astonishment. 'What do you mean?'

'Are you crazy, Perry? Do you mean to say that you have not missed me since that time we were separated by the charging thag within the arena?'

'"That time,"' he repeated. 'Why, man, I have but just returned from the arena! You reached here almost as soon as I. Had you been much later I should indeed have been worried, and as it is I had intended asking you about how you escaped the beast as soon as I had completed the translation of this most interesting passage.'

'Perry, you *are* mad,' I exclaimed. 'Why, the Lord only knows how long I have been away. I have been to other lands, discovered a new race of humans within Pellucidar, seen the Mahars at their worship in their hidden temple, and barely escaped with my life from them and from a great labyrinthodon that I met afterwards, following my long and tedious wanderings across an unknown world. I must have been away for months, Perry, and now you barely look up from your work when I return and insist that we have been separated but a moment. Is that any way to treat a friend? I'm surprised at you, Perry, and if I'd thought for a moment that you cared no more for me than this I should not have returned to chance death at the hands of the Mahars for your sake.'

The old man looked at me for a long time before he spoke. There was a puzzled expression upon his wrinkled face, and a look of hurt sorrow in his eyes.

'David, my boy,' he said, 'how could you for a moment doubt my love for you? There is something strange here that I cannot understand. I know that I am not mad, and I am equally sure that you are not; but how in the world are we to account for the strange hallucinations that each of us seems to harbour relative to the passage of time since last we saw each other. You are positive that months have gone by, while to me it seems equally certain that not more than an hour ago I sat beside you in the amphitheatre. Can it be that both of us are right and at the same time both are wrong? First tell me what time it is, and then, may be, I can solve our problem. Do you catch my meaning?'

I did, and said so.

'Yes,' continued the old man, 'we are both right. To me, bent over my book here, there has been no lapse of time. I have done little or nothing to waste my energies and so have required neither food nor sleep, but you, on the contrary, have walked and fought and wasted strength and tissue which must needs be rebuilt by nutriment and food, and so, having eaten and slept many times since last you saw me, you naturally measure the lapse of time, largely by these acts. As a matter of fact, David, I am rapidly coming to the conviction that there is no such thing as time – surely there can be no time here within Pellucidar, where there are no means for measuring or recording time. Why, the Mahars themselves take no account of such a thing as time. I find here in all their literary works but a single tense, the present. There seems to be neither past nor future with them. Of course it is impossible for our outer, earthly minds to grasp such a condition, but our recent experiences seem to demonstrate its existence.'

It was too big a subject for me, and I said so, but Perry seemed to enjoy nothing better than speculating upon it, and after listening with interest to my account of the adventures through which I had passed, he returned once more to the subject, which he was enlarging upon with considerable fluency when he was interrupted by the entrance of a Sagoth.

'Come!' commanded the intruder, beckoning to me. 'The investigators would speak with you.'

'Good-bye, Perry!' I said, clasping the old man's hand. 'There may be nothing but the present and no such thing as time, but I feel that I am about to take a trip into the hereafter from which I shall never return. If you and Ghak should manage to escape I want you to promise me that you will find Dian the Beautiful, and tell her that with my last words I asked her forgiveness for the unintentional affront I put upon her, and that my one wish was to be spared long enough to right the wrong that I had done her.'

Tears came to Perry's eyes.

'I cannot believe but that you will return, David,' he said. 'It would be awful to think of living out the balance of my life without you among these hateful and repulsive creatures. If you are taken away I shall never escape, for I feel that I am as well off here as I should be anywhere within this buried world. Good-bye, my boy, good-bye!' And then his old voice faltered and broke, and as he hid his face in his hands the Sagoth guardsman grasped me roughly by the shoulder and hustled me from the chamber.

11

Four Dead Mahars

A moment later I was standing before a dozen Mahars – the official investigators of Phutra. They asked me many questions, through a Sagoth interpreter. I answered them all truthfully. They seemed particularly interested in my account of the outer earth and the strange vehicle which had brought Perry and I to Pellucidar. I thought that I had convinced them, and after they had sat in silence for a long time following my examination, I expected to be ordered to return to my quarters.

During this apparent silence they were debating through the medium of strange, unspoken language the merits of my tale. At last the head of the tribunal communicated the result of their conference to the officer in charge of the Sagoth guard.

'Come,' he said to me, 'you are sentenced to the experimental pits for having dared to insult the intelligence of the mighty ones with the ridiculous tale you have had the temerity to unfold to them.'

'Do you mean that they do not believe me?' I asked, totally astonished.

'Believe you!' he laughed. 'Do you mean to say that you expected anyone to believe so impossible a lie?'

It was hopeless, and so I walked in silence beside my guard down through dark corridors and runways towards my awful doom. At a low level we came upon a number of lighted chambers in which we saw many Mahars engaged in various occupations. To one of these chambers my guard escorted me, and before leaving they chained me to a side wall. There were other humans similarly chained. Upon a long table lay a victim even as I was ushered into the room. Several Mahars stood about the poor creature holding him down so that he could not move. Another, grasping a sharp knife with her three-toed fore-foot, was laying open the victim's chest and abdomen. No anaesthetic had been administered and the shrieks and groans of the tortured man were terrible to hear. This, indeed, was vivisection with a vengeance. Cold sweat broke out upon me as I realized that soon my turn would come. And to think that where there was no such thing as time I might easily imagine that my suffering was enduring for months before death finally released me!

The Mahars had paid not the slightest attention to me as I had been brought into the room. So deeply immersed were they in their work that I am sure they did not even know that the Sagoths had entered with me. The door was close by. Would that I could reach it! But those heavy chains precluded any such possibility. I looked about for some means of escape from my bonds. Upon the floor between me and the Mahars lay a tiny surgical instrument which one of them must have dropped. It looked not unlike a button-hook, but was much smaller, and its point was sharpened. A hundred times in my boyhood days had I picked locks with a button-hook. Could I but reach that little bit of polished steel I might yet effect at least a temporary escape.

Crawling to the limit of my chain, I found that by reaching one hand as far out as I could my fingers still fell an inch short of the coveted instrument. It was tantalizing! Stretch every fibre of my being as I would, I could not quite make it.

At last I turned about and extended one foot towards the object. My heart came to my throat! I could just touch the thing! But suppose that in my effort to drag it towards me I should accidentally shove it still farther away and thus entirely out of reach! Cold sweats broke out upon me from every pore. Slowly and cautiously I made the effort. My toes dropped upon the cold metal. Gradually I worked it towards me until I felt that it was within reach of my hand and a moment later I had turned about and the precious thing was in my grasp.

Assiduously I fell to work upon the Mahar lock that held my chain. It was pitifully simple. A child might have picked it, and a moment later I was free. The Mahars were now evidently completing their work at the table. One already turned away and was examining other victims, evidently with the intention of selecting the next subject.

Those at the table had their backs towards me. But for the creature walking towards us I might have escaped that moment. Slowly the thing approached me, when its attention was attracted by a huge slave chained a few yards to my right. Here the reptile stopped and commenced to go over the poor devil carefully, and as it did so its back turned towards me for an instant, and in that instant I gave two mighty leaps that carried me out of the chamber into the corridor beyond, down which I raced with all the speed I could command.

Where I was, or whither I was going, I knew not. My only thought was to place as much distance as possible between me and that frightful chamber of torture.

Presently I reduced my speed to a brisk walk, and later realizing the danger of running into some new predicament, were I not careful, I moved still more slowly and cautiously. After a time I came to a passage that seemed in some mysterious way familiar to me, and presently, chancing to glance within a chamber which led from the corridor, I saw three Mahars curled up in slumber upon a bed of skins. I could have shouted aloud in joy and relief. It was the same corridor and the same Mahars that I had intended to have led so important a role in our escape from Phutra. Providence had indeed been kind to me, for the reptiles still slept.

My one great danger now lay in returning to the upper levels in search of Perry and Ghak, but there was nothing else to be done, and so I hastened upward. When I came to the frequented portions of the building I found a large burden of skins in a corner and these I lifted to my head, carrying them in such a way that ends and corners fell down about my shoulders completely hiding my face. Thus disguised I found Perry and Ghak together in the chamber where we had been wont to eat and sleep.

Both were glad to see me, it is needless to say, though of course they had known nothing of the fate that had been meted out to me by my judges. It was decided that no time should now be lost before attempting to put our plan of escape to the test, as I could not hope to remain hidden from the Sagoths long, nor could I for ever carry that bale of skins about upon my head without arousing suspicion. However, it seemed likely that it would carry me once more safely through the crowded passages and chambers of the upper levels, and so I set out with Perry and Ghak – the stench of the ill-cured pelts fairly choking me.

Together we repaired to the first tier of corridors beneath the main floor of the building, and here Perry and Ghak halted to await me. The buildings are cut out of the solid limestone formation. There is nothing at all remarkable about their architecture. The rooms are sometimes rectangular, sometimes circular, and again oval in shape – the corridors which connect them are narrow and not always straight. The chambers are lighted by diffused sunlight reflected through tubes similar to those by which the avenues are lighted – the lower tiers of chambers, the darker. Most of the corridors are entirely unlighted. The Mahars can see quite well in semi-darkness.

Down to the main floor we encountered many Mahars, Sagoths, and slaves; but no attention was paid to us as we had become a part of the domestic life of the building. There was but a single entrance leading from the place into the avenue, and this was well guarded by Sagoths; this doorway alone were we forbidden to pass. It is true that we were not supposed to enter the deeper corridors and apartments except on special occasions, when we were instructed to do so; but as we were considered a lower order without intelligence there was little reason to fear that we could accomplish any harm by so doing, and so we were not hindered as we entered the corridor which led below.

Wrapped in a skin I carried three swords, and the two bows, and the arrows which Perry and I had fashioned. As many slaves bore skin-wrapped burdens to and fro my load attracted no comment. Where I left Ghak and Perry there were no other creatures in sight, and so I withdrew one sword from the package, and leaving the balance of the weapons with Perry, started on alone towards the lower levels.

Having come to the apartment in which the three Mahars slept, I entered silently on tip-toe, forgetting that the creatures were without the sense of hearing. With a quick thrust through the heart I disposed of the first, but my second thrust was not so fortunate, so that before I could kill the next of my victims it had hurled itself against the third, who sprang quickly up, facing me with wide distended jaws. But fighting is not the occupation which the race of Mahars loves, and when the thing saw that I already had dispatched two of its companions, and that my sword was red with their blood, it made a dash to escape me. But I was too quick for it, and so, half hopping, half flying, it scurried down another corridor with me close upon its heels.

Its escape meant the utter ruin of our plan, and, in all probability, my instant death. This thought lent wings to my feet; but even at my best I could do no more than hold my own with the leaping thing before me.

Of a sudden it turned into an apartment on the right of the corridor, and an instant later as I rushed in I found myself facing two of the Mahars. The one who had been there when we entered had been occupied with a number of metal vessels, into which had been put powders and liquids as I judged from the array of flasks standing about upon the bench where it had been working. In an instant I realized what I had stumbled upon. It was the very room for the finding of which Perry had given me minute directions. It was the buried chamber in which was hidden the Great Secret of the race of Mahars. And on the bench beside the flasks lay the skin-bound book which held the only copy of the thing I was to have sought, after dispatching the three Mahars in their sleep.

There was no exit from the room other than the doorway in which I now stood facing the two frightful reptiles. Cornered, I knew that they would fight like demons, and they were well equipped to fight, if fight they must. Together they launched themselves upon me, and though I ran one of them through the heart on the instant, the other fastened its gleaming fangs about my sword arm above the elbow, and then with her sharp talons commenced to rake me about the body, evidently intent upon disembowelling me. I saw that it was useless to hope that I might release my arm from that powerful, vice-like grip which seemed to be severing my arm from my body. The pain I suffered was intense, but it only served to spur me to greater efforts to overcome my antagonist.

Back and forth across the floor we struggled – the Mahar dealing me terrific, cutting blows with her fore-feet, while I attempted to protect my body with my left hand, at the same time watching for an opportunity to transfer my blade from my now useless sword-hand to its rapidly weakening mate. At last I was successful, and with what seemed to me my last ounce of strength I ran the blade through the ugly body of my foe.

Soundless, as it had fought, it died, and though weak from pain and loss of blood, it was with an emotion of triumphant pride that I stepped across its convulsively stiffening corpse to snatch up the most potent secret of a world. A single glance assured me it was the very thing that Perry had described to me.

And as I grasped it did I think of what it meant to the human race of Pellucidar – did there flash through my mind the thought that countless generations of my own kind yet unborn would have reason to worship me for the thing that I had accomplished for them? Did I? I did not. I thought of a beautiful oval face, gazing out of limpid eyes, through a waving mass of jet-black hair. I thought of red, red lips, God-made for kissing. And of a sudden, apropos of nothing, standing there alone in the secret chamber of the Mahars of Pellucidar, I realized that I loved Dian the Beautiful.

12

Pursuit

For an instant I stood there thinking of her, and then, with a sigh, I tucked the book in the thong that supported my loin cloth, and turned to leave the apartment. At the bottom of the corridor which leads aloft from the lower chambers I whistled in accordance with the pre-arranged signal, which was to announce to Perry and Ghak that I had been successful. A moment later they stood beside me, and to my surprise I saw that Hooja the Sly One accompanied them.

'He joined us.' explained Perry, 'and would not be denied. The fellow is a fox. He scents escape, and rather than be thwarted of our chance now I told him that I would bring him to you, and let you decide whether he might accompany us.'

I had no love for Hooja, and no confidence in him. I was sure that if he thought it would profit him he would betray us; but I saw no way out of it now, and the fact that I had killed four Mahars instead of only the three I had expected to, made it possible to include the fellow in our scheme of escape.

'Very well,' I said, 'you may come with us, Hooja; but at the first intimation of treachery I shall run my sword through you. Do you understand?'

He said that he did.

Some time later we had removed the skins from the four Mahars and so succeeded in crawling inside of them ourselves that there seemed an excellent chance for us to pass unnoticed from Phutra. It was not an easy thing to fasten the hides together where we had split them along the belly to remove them from their carcasses, but by remaining out until the others had all been sewed in with my help, and then leaving an aperture in the breast of Perry's skin through which he could pass his hands to sew me up, we were enabled to accomplish our design to really much better purpose than I had hoped. We managed to keep the heads erect by passing our swords up through the necks, and by the same means were enabled to move them about in a life-like manner. We had our greatest difficulty with the webbed feet, but even that problem was finally solved, so that when we moved about we did so quite naturally. Tiny holes punctured in the baggy throats into which our heads were thrust permitted us to see well enough to guide our progress.

Thus we started up towards the main floor of the building. Ghak headed the strange procession, then came Perry, followed by Hooja, while I brought up the rear, after admonishing Hooja that I had so arranged my sword that I could thrust it through the head of my disguise into his vitals were he to show any indication of faltering.

As the noise of hurrying feet warned me that we were entering the busy corridors of the main level, my heart came up into my mouth. It is with no sense of shame that I admit that I was frightened – never before in my life, nor since, did I experience any such agony of soul-searing fear and suspense as enveloped me. If it be possible to sweat blood, I sweated it then.

Slowly, after the manner of locomotion habitual to the Mahars, when they are not using their wings, we crept through throngs of busy slaves, Sagoths, and Mahars. After what seemed an eternity we reached the outer door which leads into the main avenue of Phutra. Many Sagoths loitered near the opening. They glanced at Ghak as he padded between them. Then Perry passed, and then Hooja. Now it was my turn, and then in a sudden fit of freezing terror I realized that the warm blood from my wounded arm was trickling down through the dead foot of the Mahar skin I wore and leaving its tell-tale mark upon the pavement, for I saw a Sagoth call a companion's attention to it.

The guard stepped before me and pointing to my bleeding foot spoke to me in the sign language which these two races employ as a means of communication. Even had I known what he was saying I could not have replied with the dead thing that covered me. I once had seen a great Mahar freeze a presumptuous Sagoth with a look. It seemed my only hope, and so I tried it. Stopping in my tracks I moved my sword so that it made the dead head appear to turn inquiring eyes upon the gorilla-man. For a long moment I stood perfectly still eyeing the fellow with those dead eyes. Then I lowered the head and started slowly on. For a moment all hung in the balance, but before I touched him the guard stepped to one side, and I passed on out into the avenue.

On we went up the broad street, but now we were safe, for the very numbers of our enemies that surrounded us on all sides. Fortunately there was a great concourse of Mahars repairing to the shallow lake which lies a mile or more from the city. They go there to indulge their amphibian proclivities in diving for small fish, and enjoying the cool depths of the water. It is a fresh-water lake, shallow, and free from the larger reptiles which make the use of the great seas of Pellucidar impossible for any but their own kind.

In the thick of the crowd we passed up the steps and out on to the plain. For some distance Ghak remained with the stream that was travelling towards the lake, but finally, at the bottom of a little gully, he halted, and there we remained until all had passed and we were alone. Then, still in our disguises, we set off directly away from Phutra.

The heat of the vertical rays of the sun was fast making our horrible prisons unbearable, so that after passing a low divide, and entering a sheltering forest, we finally discarded the Mahar skins that had brought us thus far in safety.

I shall not weary you with the details of that bitter and galling flight. How we travelled at a dogged run until we dropped in our tracks. How we were beset by strange and terrible beasts. How we barely escaped the cruel fangs of lions and tigers the size of which would dwarf into pitiful insignificance the greatest felines of the outer world.

On and on we raced, our one thought to put as much distance between ourselves and Phutra as possible. Ghak was leading us to his own land – the land of Sari. No sign of pursuit had developed, and yet we were sure that somewhere behind us relentless Sagoths were dogging our tracks. Ghak said they never failed to hunt down their quarry until they had captured it or themselves been turned back by a superior force.

Our only hope, he said, lay in reaching his tribe, which was quite strong enough in their mountain fastness to beat off any number of Sagoths.

And at last, after what seemed months, and may, I now realize, have been years, we came in sight of the dun escarpment which buttressed the foothills of Sari. At almost the same instant, Hooja, who looked ever quite as much behind as before, announced that he could see a body of men far behind us topping a low ridge in our wake. It was the long-expected pursuit.

I asked Ghak if we could make Sari in time to escape them.

'We may,' he replied, 'but you will find that the Sagoths can move with incredible swiftness, and as they are almost tireless they are doubtless much fresher than we. Then—' He paused, glancing at Perry.

I knew what he meant. The old man was nearly exhausted. For much of the period of our flight either Ghak or I had half supported him on the march. With such a handicap, less fleet pursuers than the Sagoths might easily overtake us before we could scale the rugged heights which confronted us.

'You and Hooja go on ahead,' I said. 'Perry and I will make it if we are able. We cannot travel as rapidly as you two, and there is no reason why all should be lost because of that. It can't be helped – we have simply to face it.'

'I will not desert a companion,' was Ghak's simple reply. I hadn't known that this great, hairy, primeval man had any such nobility of character stowed away inside him. I had always liked him, but now to my liking was added honour and respect; yes, and love.

But still I urged him to go on ahead, insisting that if he could reach his people he might be able to bring out a sufficient force to drive off the Sagoths and rescue Perry and myself.

No, he wouldn't leave us, and that was all there was to it, but he suggested that Hooja might hurry on and warn the Sarians of the king's danger. It didn't require much urging to start Hooja – the naked idea was enough to send him leaping on ahead of us into the foothills which we now had reached.

Perry realized that he was jeopardizing Ghak's life and mine, and the old fellow fairly begged us to go on without him, although I knew that he was suffering a perfect anguish of terror at the thought of falling into the hands of the Sagoths. Ghak finally solved the problem, in part, by lifting Perry in his powerful arms and carrying him. While the act cut down Ghak's speed he still could travel faster thus than when half supporting the stumbling old man.

13

The Sly One

The Sagoths were gaining on us rapidly, for once they had sighted us they had greatly increased their speed. On and on we stumbled up the narrow cañon that Ghak had chosen to approach the heights of Sari. On either side rose precipitous cliffs of gorgeous, parti-coloured rock, while beneath our feet a thick, mountain grass formed a soft and noiseless carpet. Since we had entered the cañon we had had no glimpse of our pursuers, and I was commencing to hope that they had lost our trail and that we would reach the now rapidly nearing cliffs in time to scale them before we should be overtaken.

Ahead we neither saw nor heard any sign which might betoken the success of Hooja's mission. By now he should have reached the outposts of the Sarians, and we should at least hear the savage cries of the tribesmen as they swarmed to arms in answer to their king's appeal for succour. In another moment the frowning cliffs ahead should be black with primeval warriors. But nothing of the kind happened – as a matter of fact the Sly One had betrayed us. At the moment that we expected to see Sarian spearmen charging to our relief at Hooja's back, the craven traitor was sneaking around the outskirts of the nearest Sarian village, that he might come up from the other side when it was too late to save us, claiming that he had become lost among the mountains.

Hooja still harboured ill-will against me because of the blow I had struck in Dian's protection, and his malevolent spirit was equal to sacrificing us all that he might be revenged upon me.

As we drew nearer the barrier cliffs and no sign of rescuing Sarians appeared Ghak became both angry and alarmed, and presently as the sounds of rapidly approaching pursuit fell upon our ears, he called to me over his shoulder that we were lost.

A backward glance gave me a glimpse of the first of the Sagoths at the far end of a considerable straight stretch of cañon through which we had just passed, and then a sudden turning shut the ugly creature from my view; but the loud howl of triumphant rage which rose behind us was evidence that the gorilla-man had sighted us.

Again the cañon veered sharply to the left, but to the right another branch ran on at a lesser deviation from the general direction, so that it appeared more like the main cañon than the left-hand branch. The Sagoths were now not over two hundred and fifty yards behind us, and I saw that it was hopeless for us to expect to escape other than by a ruse. There was a bare chance of saving Ghak and Perry, and as I reached the branching of the cañon I took the chance.

Pausing there I waited until the foremost Sagoth hove in sight. Ghak and Perry had disappeared round a bend in the left-hand cañon, and as the Sagoth's savage yell announced that he had seen me I turned and fled up the right-hand branch. My ruse was successful, and the entire party of man-hunters raced headlong after me up one cañon while Ghak bore Perry to safety up the other.

Running had never been my particular athletic forte, and now when my very life depended upon fleetness of foot I cannot say that I ran any better than on the occasions when my pitiful baseball running had called down upon my head the spectators' raucous and reproachful cries of 'Ice waggon,' and 'Call a cab.'

The Sagoths were gaining on me rapidly. There was one in particular, fleeter than his fellows, who was perilously close. The cañon had become but a rocky slit, rising roughly at a steep angle towards what seemed a pass between two abutting peaks. What lay beyond I could not even guess – possibly a sheer drop of hundreds of feet into the corresponding valley upon the other side. Could it be that I had plunged into a cul-de-sac?

Realizing that I could not hope to out-distance the Sagoths to the top of the cañon I had determined to risk all in an attempt to check them temporarily, and to this end had unslung my rudely-made bow and plucked an arrow from the skin quiver which hung behind my shoulder. As I fitted the shaft with my right hand I stopped and wheeled towards the gorilla-man.

In the world of my birth I never had drawn a shaft, but since our escape from Phutra I had kept the party supplied with small game by means of my arrows, and so, through necessity, had developed a fair degree of accuracy. During our flight from Phutra I had restrung my bow with a piece of heavy gut taken from a huge tiger which Ghak and I had worried and finally dispatched with arrows, spear, and sword. The hard wood of the bow was extremely tough, and this, with the strength and elasticity of my new string, gave me unwonted confidence in my weapon.

Never had I greater need of steady nerves than then – never were my nerves and muscles under better control. I sighted as carefully and deliberately as though at a straw target. The Sagoth had never before seen a bow and arrow, but of a sudden it must have swept over his dull intellect that the thing I held towards him was some sort of engine of destruction, for he, too, came to a halt, simultaneously swinging his hatchet for a throw. It is one of the many methods in which they employ this weapon, and the accuracy of aim which they achieve, even under the most unfavourable circumstances, is little short of miraculous.

My shaft was drawn back its full length – my eye had centred its sharp point upon the left breast of my adversary; and then he launched his hatchet and I released my arrow. At the instant that our missiles flew I leaped to one side, but the Sagoth sprang forward to follow up his attack with a spear thrust. I felt the swish of the hatchet as it grazed my head, and at the same instant my shaft pierced the Sagoth's savage heart, and with a single groan he lunged almost at my feet – stone dead.

Close behind him were two more – fifty yards perhaps – but the distance gave me time to snatch up the dead guardsman's shield, for the close call his hatchet had just given me had borne in upon me the urgent need I had for one. Those which I had purloined at Phutra we had not been able to bring along because their size precluded our concealing them within the skins of the Mahars which had brought us safely from the city.

With the shield slipped well up on my left arm I let fly another arrow, which brought down a second Sagoth, and then as his fellow's hatchet sped towards me I caught it upon the shield, and fitted another shaft for him; but he did not wait to receive it. Instead, he turned and retreated towards the main body of gorilla-men. Evidently he had seen enough of me for the moment.

Once more I took up my flight, nor were the Sagoths apparently over-anxious to press their pursuit so closely as before. Unmolested I reached the top of the cañon, where I found a sheer drop of two or three hundred feet to the bottom of a rocky chasm; but on the left a narrow ledge rounded the shoulder of the overhanging cliff. Along this I advanced, and at a sudden turning, a few yards beyond the cañon's end, the path widened, and at my left I saw the opening to a large cave. Before, the ledge continued until it passed from sight about another projecting buttress of the mountain.

Here, I felt, I could defy an army, for but a single foeman could advance upon me at a time, nor could he know that I was awaiting him until he came full upon me around the corner of the turn. About me lay scattered stones crumbled from the cliff above. They were of various sizes and shapes, but enough were of handy dimensions for use as ammunition in lieu of my precious arrows. Gathering a number of stones into a little pile beside the mouth of the cave, I waited the advance of the Sagoths.

As I stood there, tense and silent, listening for the first faint sound that should announce the approach of my enemies, a slight noise from within the cave's black depths attracted my attention. It might have been produced by the moving of the great body of some huge beast rising from the rocky floor of its lair. At almost the same instant I thought that I caught the scraping of hide sandals upon the ledge beyond the turn. For the next few seconds my attention was considerably divided.

And then from the inky blackness at my right I saw two flaming eyes glaring into mine. They were on a level that was over two feet above my head. It is true that the beast who owned them might be standing upon a ledge within the cave, or that it might be rearing up upon its hind-legs; but I had seen enough of the monsters of Pellucidar to know that I might be facing some new and frightful titan whose dimensions and ferocity eclipsed those of any I had seen before.

Whatever it was, it was coming slowly towards the entrance of the cave, and now, deep and forbidding, it uttered a low and ominous growl. I waited no longer to dispute possession of the ledge with the thing which owned that voice. The noise had not been loud – I doubt if the Sagoths heard it at all – but the suggestion of latent possibilities behind it was such that I knew it could only emanate from a gigantic and ferocious beast.

As I backed along the ledge I soon was past the mouth of the cave, where I no longer could see those fearful, flaming eyes, but an instant later I caught sight of the fiendish face of a Sagoth as it was warily advanced beyond the cliff's turn on the far side of the cave's mouth. As the fellow saw me he leaped along the ledge in pursuit, and after him came as many of his companions as could crowd upon each other's heels. At the same time the beast emerged from the cave, so that he and the Sagoths came face to face upon that narrow ledge.

The thing was an enormous cave bear, rearing its colossal bulk fully eight feet at the shoulder, while from the tip of its nose to the end of its stubby tail it was fully twelve feet in length. As it sighted the Sagoths it emitted a most frightful roar, and with open mouth charged full upon them. With a cry of terror the foremost gorilla-man turned to escape, but behind him he ran full upon his onrushing companions.

The horror of the following seconds is indescribable. The Sagoth nearest the cave bear, finding his escape blocked, turned and leaped deliberately to an awful death upon the jagged rocks three hundred feet below. Then those giant jaws reached out and gathered in the next – there was a sickening sound of crunching bones, and the mangled corpse was dropped over the cliff's edge. Nor did the mighty beast even pause in his steady advance along the ledge.

Shrieking Sagoths were now leaping madly over the precipice to escape him, and the last I saw he rounded the turn still pursuing the demoralized remnant of the man-hunters. For a long time I could hear the horrid roaring of the brute intermingled with the screams and shrieks of his victims, until finally the awful sounds dwindled and disappeared in the distance.

Later I learned from Ghak, who had finally come to his tribesmen and returned with a party to rescue me, that the *ryth*, as it is called, pursued the Sagoths until it had exterminated the entire band. Ghak was, of course, positive that I had fallen prey to the terrible creature, which, within Pellucidar, is truly the king of beasts.

Not caring to venture back into the cañon, where I might fall prey either to the cave bear or the Sagoths, I continued on along the ledge, believing that by following around the mountain I could reach the land of Sari from another direction. But I evidently became confused by the twisting and turning of the cañons and gullies, for I did not come to the land of Sari then, nor for a long time thereafter.

14

The Garden of Eden

With no heavenly guide, it is little wonder that I became confused and lost in the labyrinthine maze of those mighty hills. What, in reality, I did was to pass entirely through them and come out above the valley upon the farther side. I know that I wandered for a long time, until tired and hungry I came upon a small cave in the face of the limestone formation which had taken the place of the granite farther back.

The cave which took my fancy lay half-way up the precipitous side of a lofty cliff. The way to it was such that I knew no extremely formidable beast could frequent it, nor was it large enough to make a comfortable habitat for any but the smaller mammals or reptiles. Yet it was with the utmost caution that I crawled within its dark interior.

Here I found a rather large chamber, lighted by a narrow cleft in the rock above which let the sunlight filter in in sufficient quantities partially to dispel the utter darkness which I had expected. The cave was entirely empty, nor were there any signs of its having been recently occupied. The opening was comparatively small, so that after considerable effort I was able to lug up a boulder from the valley below which entirely blocked it.

Then I returned again to the valley for an armful of grasses and on this trip was fortunate enough to knock over an *orthopi*, the diminutive horse of Pellucidar, a little animal about the size of a fox-terrier, which abounds in all parts of the inner world. Thus, with food and bedding I returned to my lair, where after a meal of raw meat, to which I had now become quite accustomed, I dragged the boulder before the entrance and curled myself upon a bed of grasses – a naked, primeval, cave man, as savagely primitive as my prehistoric progenitors.

I awoke rested but hungry, and pushing the boulder aside crawled out upon the little rocky shelf which was my front porch. Before me spread a small but beautiful valley, through the centre of which a clear and sparkling river wound its way down to an inland sea, the blue waters of which were just visible between the two mountain ranges which embraced this little paradise. The sides of the opposite hills were green with verdure, for a great forest clothed them to the foot of the red and yellow and copper-green of the towering crags which formed their summit. The valley itself was carpeted with a luxuriant grass, while here and there patches of wild flowers made great splashes of vivid colour against the prevailing green.

Dotted over the face of the valley were little clusters of palmlike trees – three or four together as a rule. Beneath these stood antelope, while others grazed in the open, or wandered gracefully to a nearby ford to drink. There were several species of this beautiful animal, the most magnificent some-what resembling the giant eland of Africa, except that their spiral horns form a complete curve backward over their ears and then forward again beneath them, ending in sharp and formidable points some two feet before the face and above the eyes. In size they remind one of a pure-bred Hereford bull, yet they are very agile and fast. The broad yellow bands that stripe the dark roan of their coats made me take them for zebra when I first saw them. All in all, they are handsome animals, and added the finishing touch to the strange and lovely landscape that spread before my new home.

I had determined to make the cave my headquarters, and with it as a base make a systematic exploration of the surrounding country in search of the land of Sari. First I devoured the remainder of the carcass of the orthopi I had killed before my last sleep. Then I hid the Great Secret in a deep niche at the back of my cave, rolled the boulder before my front door, and with bow, arrows, sword, and shield scrambled down into the peaceful valley.

The grazing herds moved to one side as I passed through them, the little orthopi evincing the greatest wariness and galloping to safest distances. All the animals stopped feeding as I approached, and after moving to what they considered a safe distance stood contemplating me with serious eyes and upcocked ears. Once one of the old bull antelopes of the striped species low-ered his head and bellowed angrily – even taking a few steps in my direc-tion, so that I thought he meant to charge; but after I had passed he resumed feeding as though nothing had disturbed him.

Near the lower end of the valley I passed a number of tapirs, and across the river saw a great sadok, the enormous double-horned progenitor of the modern rhinoceros. At the valley's end the cliffs upon the left run out into the sea, so that to pass around them, as I desired to do, it was necessary to scale them in search of a ledge along which I might continue my jour-ney. Some fifty feet from the base I came upon a projection which formed a natural path along the face of the cliff, and this I followed out over the sea towards the cliff's end.

Here the ledge inclined rapidly upward towards the top of the cliffs – the stratum which formed it evidently having been forced up at this steep angle when the mountains behind it were born. As I climbed carefully up the ascent my attention suddenly was attracted aloft by the sound of strange hissing, and what resembled the flapping of wings.

And at the first glance there broke upon my horrified vision the most frightful thing I had ever seen within Pellucidar. It was a giant dragon such as is pictured in the legends and fairy tales of earth folk. Its huge body must have measured forty feet in length, while the bat-like wings that supported it in mid-air had a spread of fully thirty. Its gaping jaws were armed with long, sharp teeth, and its claws equipped with horrible talons.

The hissing noise which had first attracted my attention was issuing from its throat, and seemed to be directed at something beyond and below me which I could not see. The ledge upon which I stood terminated abruptly a few paces farther on, and as I reached the end I saw the cause of the reptile's agitation.

Some time in the past ages an earthquake had produced a fault at this point, so that beyond the spot where I stood the strata had slipped down a matter of twenty feet. The result was that the continuation of my ledge lay twenty feet below me, where it ended as abruptly as did the end upon which I stood.

And here, evidently halted in flight by this insurmountable break in the ledge, stood the object of the creature's attack – a girl cowering upon the narrow platform, her face buried in her arms, as though to shut out the sight of the frightful death which hovered just above her.

The dragon was circling lower, and seemed about to dart in upon its prey. There was no time to be lost, scarce an instant in which to weigh the possible chances that I had against the awfully armed creature; but the sight of that frightened girl below me called out to all that was best in me, and the instinct for protection of the other sex, which nearly must have equalled the instinct of self-preservation in primeval man, drew me to the girl's side like an irresistible magnet.

Almost thoughtless of the consequences, I leaped from the end of the ledge upon which I stood for the tiny shelf twenty feet below. At the same instant the dragon darted in towards the girl, but my sudden advent upon the scene must have startled him, for he veered to one side, and then rose above us once more.

The noise I made as I landed beside her convinced the girl that her end had come, for she thought that I was the dragon; but finally when no cruel fangs closed upon her she raised her eyes in astonishment. As they fell upon me the expression that came into them would be difficult to describe; but her feelings could scarcely have been one whit more complicated than my own – for the wide eyes that looked into mine were those of Dian the Beautiful.

'Dian!' I cried. 'Dian! Thank God that I came in time.'

'You?' she whispered, and then she hid her face again; nor could I tell whether she were glad or angry that I had come.

Once more the dragon was sweeping towards us, and so rapidly that I had no time to unsling my bow. All that I could do was to snatch up a rock, and hurl it at the thing's hideous face. Again my aim was true, and with a hiss of pain and rage the reptile wheeled once more and soared away.

Quickly I fitted an arrow now that I might be ready at the next attack, and as I did so I looked down at the girl, so that I surprised her in a surreptitious glance which she was stealing at me; but immediately she again covered her face with her hands.

'Look at me, Dian,' I pleaded. 'Are you not glad to see me?'

She looked straight into my eyes.

'I hate you,' she said, and then, as I was about to beg for a fair hearing she pointed over my shoulder. 'The thipdar comes,' she said, and I turned again to meet the reptile.

So this was a thipdar. I might have known it. The cruel bloodhound of the Mahars. The long-extinct pterodactyl of the outer world. But this time I met it with a weapon it never had faced before. I had selected my longest arrow, and with all my strength had bent the bow until the very tip of the shaft rested upon the thumb of my left hand, and then as the great creature darted towards us I let drive straight for that tough breast.

Hissing like the escape valve of a steam engine, the mighty creature fell turning and twisting into the sea below, my arrow buried completely in its carcass. I turned towards the girl. She was looking past me. It was evident that she had seen the thipdar die.

'Dian,' I said, 'won't you tell me that you are not sorry that I have found you?'

'I hate you,' was her only reply; but I imagined that there was less vehemence in it than before – yet it might have been but my imagination.

'Why do you hate me, Dian?' I asked, but she did not answer me.

'What are you doing here?' I asked, 'and what has happened to you since Hooja freed you from the Sagoths?'

At first I thought that she was going to ignore me entirely, but finally she thought better of it.

'I was again running away from Jubal the Ugly One,' she said. 'After I escaped from the Sagoths I made my way alone back to my own land; but on account of Jubal I did not dare enter the villages or let any of my friends know that I had returned for fear that Jubal might find it out. By watching for a long time I found that my brother had not yet returned, and so I continued to live in a cave beside a valley which my race seldom frequents, awaiting the time that he should come back and free me from Jubal.

'But at last one of Jubal's hunters saw me as I was creeping towards my father's cave to see if my brother had yet returned and he gave the alarm and Jubal set out after me. He has been pursuing me across many lands. He cannot be far behind me now. When he comes he will kill you and carry me back to his cave. He is a terrible man. I have gone as far as I can go, and there is no escape,' and she looked hopelessly up at the continuation of the ledge twenty feet above us.

'But he shall not have me,' she suddenly cried, with great vehemence. 'The sea is there' – she pointed over the edge of the cliff – 'and the sea shall have me rather than Jubal.'

'But I have you now, Dian,' I cried; 'nor shall Jubal nor any other have you, for you are mine,' and I seized her hand, nor did I lift it above her head and let it fall in token of release.

She had risen to her feet, and was looking straight into my eyes with level gaze.

'I do not believe you,' she said, 'for if you meant it you would have done this when the others were present to witness it – then I should truly have been your mate; now there is no one to see you do it, for you know that without witnesses your act does not bind you to me,' and she withdrew her hand from mine and turned away.

I tried to convince her that I was sincere, but she simply couldn't forget the humiliation that I had put upon her on that other occasion.

'If you mean all that you say you will have ample chance to prove it,' she said, 'if Jubal does not catch and kill you. I am in your power, and the treatment you accord me will be the best proof of your intentions towards me. I am not your mate, and again I tell you that I hate you, and that I should be glad if I never saw you again.'

Dian certainly was candid. There was no gainsaying that. In fact I found candour and directness to be quite a marked characteristic of the cave men of Pellucidar. Finally I suggested that we make some attempt to gain my cave, where we might escape the searching Jubal, for I am free to admit that I had no considerable desire to meet the formidable and ferocious creature, of whose mighty prowess Dian had told me when I first met her. He it was who, armed with a puny knife, had met and killed a cave bear in a hand-to-hand struggle. It was Jubal who could cast his spear entirely through the armoured carcass of the sadok at fifty paces. It was he who had crushed the skull of a charging dyryth with a single blow of his war club. No, I was not pining to meet the Ugly One – and it was quite certain that I should not go out and hunt for him; but the matter was taken out of my hands very quickly, as is often the way, and I did meet Jubal the Ugly One face to face.

This is how it happened. I had led Dian back along the ledge the way she had come, searching for a path that would lead us to the top of the cliff, for I knew that we could then cross over to the edge of my own little valley, where I felt certain we should find a means of ingress from the cliff-top. As we proceeded along the ledge I gave Dian minute directions for finding my cave against the chance of something happening to me. I knew that she would be quite safely hidden away from pursuit once she gained the shelter of my lair, and the valley would afford her ample means of sustenance.

Also, I was very much piqued by her treatment of me. My heart was sad and heavy, and I wanted to make her feel badly by suggesting that something terrible might happen to me – that I might, in fact, be killed. But it didn't work worth a cent, at least as far as I could perceive. Dian simply shrugged those magnificent shoulders of hers, and murmured something to the effect that one was not rid of trouble so easily as that.

For a while I kept still. I was utterly squelched. And to think that I had twice protected her from attack – the last time risking my life to save hers. It was incredible that even a daughter of the Stone Age could be so ungrateful – so heartless; but maybe her heart partook of the qualities of her epoch.

Presently we found a rift in the cliff, which had been widened and extended by the action of water draining through it from the plateau above. It gave us a rather rough climb to the summit, but finally we stood upon the level mesa which stretched back for several miles to the main mountain range. Behind us lay the broad inland sea, curving upward in the horizonless distance to merge into the blue of the sky, so that for all the world it looked as though the sea lapped back to arch completely over us and disappear beyond the distant mountains at our backs – the weird and uncanny aspect of the seascapes of Pellucidar balk description.

At our right lay a dense forest, but to the left the country was open and clear to the plateau's farther verge. It was in this direction that our way led, and we had turned to resume our journey when Dian touched my arm. I turned to her, thinking that she was about to make peace overtures; but I was mistaken.

'Jubal,' she said, and nodded towards the forest.

I looked, and there, emerging from the dense wood, came a perfect whale of a man. He must have been seven feet tall, and proportioned accordingly. He still was too far off to distinguish his features.

'Run,' I said to Dian. 'I can engage him until you get a good start. Maybe I can hold him until you have gotten entirely away,' and then, without a backward glance, I advanced to meet the Ugly One. I had hoped that Dian would have a kind word to say to me before she went, for she must have known that I was going to my death for her sake; but she never even so much as bid me good-bye, and it was with a heavy heart that I strode through the flower-bespangled grass to my doom.

When I had come close enough to Jubal to distinguish his features I understood how it was that he had earned the sobriquet of Ugly One. Apparently some fearful beast had ripped away one entire side of his face. The eye was gone, the nose, and all the flesh, so that his jaws and all his teeth were exposed and grinning through the horrible scar.

Formerly he may have been as good to look upon as the others of his handsome race, and it may be that the terrible result of this encounter had tended to sour an already strong and brutal character. However this may be, it is quite certain that he was not a pretty sight, and now that his features, or what remained of them, were distorted in rage at the sight of Dian with another male, he was indeed most terrible to see – and much more terrible to meet.

He had broken into a run now, and as he advanced he raised his mighty spear, while I halted and fitting an arrow to my bow took as steady aim as I could. I was somewhat longer than usual, for I must confess that the sight of this awful man had wrought upon my nerves to such an extent that my knees were anything but steady. What chance had I against this mighty warrior for whom even the fiercest cave bear had no terrors! Could I hope to best one who slaughtered the sadok and the dyryth single-handed! I shuddered; but, in fairness to myself, my fear was more for Dian than for my own fate.

And then the great brute launched his massive, stone-tipped spear, and I raised my shield to break the force of its terrific velocity. The impact hurled me to my knees, but the shield had deflected the missile and I was un-scathed. Jubal was rushing upon me now with the only remaining weapon that he carried – a murderous-looking knife. He was too close for a careful bowshot, but I let drive at him as he came, without taking aim. My arrow pierced the fleshy part of his thigh, inflicting a painful but not disabling wound. And then he was upon me.

My agility saved me for the instant. I ducked beneath his raised arm, and when he wheeled to come at me again he found a sword's point in his face. And a moment later he felt an inch or two of it in the muscles of his knife arm, so that thereafter he went more warily.

It was a duel of strategy now – the great, hairy man manoeuvring to get inside my guard where he could bring those giant thews to play, while my wits were directed to the task of keeping him at arm's length. Thrice he rushed me, and thrice I caught his knife blow upon my shield. Each time my sword found his body – once penetrating to his lung. He was covered with blood by this time and the internal haemorrhage induced paroxysms of coughing that brought the red stream through the hideous mouth and nose, covering his face and breast with bloody froth. He was a most unlovely spectacle, but he was far from dead.

As the duel continued I began to gain confidence, for, to be perfectly candid, I had not expected to survive the first rush of that monstrous engine of ungoverned rage and hatred. And I think that Jubal, from utter contempt of me, began to change to a feeling of respect, and then in his primitive mind there evidently loomed the thought that perhaps at last he had met his master, and was facing his end.

At any rate it is only upon this hypothesis that I can account for his next act which was in the nature of a last resort – a sort of forlorn hope which could only have been born of the belief that if he did not kill me quickly I should kill him. It happened on the occasion of his fourth charge, when, instead of striking me with his knife, he dropped that weapon, and seizing my sword blade in both his hands wrenched the weapon from my grasp as easily as from a babe.

Flinging it far to one side he stood motionless for just an instant glaring into my face with such a horrid leer of malignant triumph as to almost un-nerve me – then he sprang for me with his bare hands. But it was Jubal's day to learn new methods of warfare. For the first time he had seen a bow and arrows, never before that duel had he beheld a sword, and now he learned what a man who knows may do with his bare fists.

As he came for me, like a great bear, I ducked again beneath his out-stretched arm, and as I came up planted as clean a blow upon his jaw as ever you have seen. Down went that great mountain of flesh sprawling upon the ground. He was so surprised and dazed that he lay there for several seconds before he made any attempt to rise, and I stood over him with another dose ready when he should gain his knees.

Up he came at last, almost roaring in his rage and mortification; but he didn't stay up – I let him have a left fair on the point of the jaw that sent him tumbling over on his back. By this time I think Jubal had gone mad with hate, for no sane man would have come back for more as many times as he did. Time after time I bowled him over as fast as he could stagger up, until towards the last he lay longer on the ground between blows, and each time came up weaker than before.

He was bleeding very profusely now from the wounds in his lungs, and presently a terrific blow over the heart sent him reeling heavily to the ground, where he lay very still, and somehow I knew at once that Jubal the Ugly One would never get up again. But even as I looked upon that massive body lying there so grim and terrible in death I could not believe that I, single-handed, had bested this slayer of fearful beasts – this gigantic ogre of the Stone Age.

Picking up my sword I leaned upon it, looking down on the dead body of my foeman, and as I thought of the battle I had just fought and won a great idea was born in my brain – the outcome of this and the suggestion that Perry had made within the city of Phutra. If skill and science could render a comparative pygmy the master of this mighty brute, what could not the brute's fellows accomplish with the same skill and science. Why all Pelluci-dar would be at their feet – and I would be their king and Dian their queen.

Dian! A little wave of doubt swept over me. It was quite within the pos-sibilities of Dian to look down upon me even were I king. She was quite the most superior person I ever had met – with the most convincing way of letting you know that she was superior. Well, I could go to the cave, and tell her that I had killed Jubal, and then she might feel more kindly towards me, since I had freed her of her tormentor. I hoped that she had found the cave easily – it would be terrible had I lost her again, and I turned to gather up my shield and bow to hurry after her, when to my astonishment I found her standing not ten paces behind me.

'Girl!' I cried, 'what are you doing here? I thought that you had gone to the cave, as I told you to do.'

Up went her head, and the look that she gave me took all the majesty out of me, and left me feeling more like the palace janitor – if palaces have janitors.

'"As you told me to do!"' she cried, stamping her little foot. 'I do as I please. I am the daughter of a king, and, furthermore, I hate you.'

I was dumbfounded – this was my thanks for saving her from Jubal! I turned and looked at the corpse. 'May be that I saved you from a worse fate, old man,' I said, but I guess it was lost on Dian, for she never seemed to notice it at all.

'Let us go to my cave,' I said. 'I am tired and hungry.'

She followed along a pace behind me, neither of us speaking. I was too angry, and she evidently didn't care to converse with the lower orders. I was mad all the way through, as I had certainly felt that at least a word of thanks should have rewarded me, for I knew that even by her own standards I must have done a very wonderful thing to have killed the redoubtable Jubal in a hand-to-hand encounter.

We had no difficulty in finding my lair, and then I went down into the valley and bowled over a small antelope, which I dragged up the steep ascent to the ledge before the door. Here we ate in silence. Occasionally I glanced at her, thinking that the sight of her tearing at raw flesh with her hands and teeth like some wild animal would cause a revulsion of my sentiments towards her; but to my surprise I found that she ate quite as daintily as the most civilized woman of my acquaintance, and finally I found myself gazing in foolish rapture at the beauties of her strong, white teeth. Such is love.

After our repast we went down to the river together and bathed our hands and faces, and then after drinking our fill went back to the cave. Without a word I crawled into the farthest corner and, curling up, was soon asleep.

When I awoke I found Dian sitting in the doorway looking out across the valley. As I came out she moved to one side to let me pass, but she had no word for me. I wanted to hate her, but I couldn't. Every time I looked at her something came up in my throat, so that I nearly choked. I had never been in love before, but I did not need any aid in diagnosing my case – I certainly had it and had it bad. God, how I loved that beautiful, disdainful, tantalizing, prehistoric girl!

After we had eaten again I asked Dian if she intended returning to her tribe now that Jubal was dead, but she shook her head sadly, and said that she did not dare, for there was still Jubal's brother to be considered – his oldest brother.

'What has he to do with it? 'I asked. 'Does he too want you, or has the option on you become a family heirloom, to be passed on down from generation to generation? '

She was not quite sure as to what I meant.

It is probable,' she said, 'that they all will want revenge for the death of Jubal – there are seven of them – seven terrible men. Someone may have to kill them all, if I am to return to my people.'

It began to look as though I had assumed a contract much too large for me – about seven sizes, in fact.

'Had Jubal any cousins? 'I asked. It was just as well to know the worst at once.

'Yes,' replied Dian, 'but they don't count – they all have mates. Jubal's brothers have no mates because Jubal could get none for himself. He was so ugly that women ran away from him – some have even thrown themselves from the cliffs of Amoz into the Darel Az rather than mate with the Ugly One.'

'But what had that to do with his brothers? 'I asked.

'I forgot that you are not of Pellucidar,' said Dian, with a look of pity mixed with contempt, and the contempt seemed to be laid on a little thicker than the circumstance warranted – as though to make quite certain that I shouldn't overlook it. 'You see,' she continued, 'a younger brother may not take a mate until all his older brothers have done so, unless the older brother waives his prerogative, which Jubal would not do, knowing that as long as he kept them single they would be all the keener in aiding him to secure a mate.'

Noticing that Dian was becoming more communicative I began to entertain hopes that she might be warming up towards me a bit, although upon what slender thread I hung my hopes I soon discovered.

'As you dare not return to Amoz,' I ventured, 'what is to become of you, since you cannot be happy here with me, hating me as you do? '

'I shall have to put up with you,' she replied coldly, 'until you see fit to go elsewhere and leave me in peace, then I shall get along very well alone.'

I looked at her in utter amazement. It seemed incredible that even a prehistoric woman could be so cold and heartless and ungrateful. Then I arose.

'I shall leave you *now*,' I said haughtily. 'I have had quite enough of your ingratitude and your insults,' and then I turned and strode majestically down towards the valley. I had taken a hundred steps in absolute silence, and then Dian spoke.

'I hate you!' she shouted, and her voice broke – in rage, I thought.

I was absolutely miserable, but I hadn't gone far when I began to realize that I couldn't leave her alone there without protection, to hunt her own food amid the dangers of that savage world. She might hate me, and revile me, and heap indignity after indignity upon me, as she already had, until I should have hated her; but the pitiful fact remained that I loved her, and I couldn't leave her there alone.

The more I thought about it the madder I got, so that by the time I reached the valley I was furious, and the result of it was that I turned right around and went up that cliff again twice as fast as I had come down. I saw that Dian had left the ledge and gone within the cave, but I bolted right in after her. She was lying upon her face on the pile of grasses I had gathered for her bed. When she heard me enter she sprang to her feet like a tigress.

'I hate you!' she cried.

Coming from the brilliant light of the noonday sun into the semi-darkness of the cave I could not see her features, and I was rather glad, for I disliked to think of the hate that I should have read there.

I never said a word to her at first. I just strode across the cave and grasped her by the wrists, and when she struggled I put my arm around her so as to pinion her hands to her sides. She fought like a tigress, but I took my free hand and pushed her head back – I imagine that I had suddenly turned brute, that I had gone back a thousand million years, and was again a veritable cave man taking my mate by force – and then I kissed that beautiful mouth again and again.

'Dian,' I cried, shaking her roughly, 'I love you. Can't you understand that I love you? That I love you better than all else in this world or my own? That I am going to have you? That love like mine cannot be denied? '

I noticed that she lay very still in my arms now, and as my eyes became accustomed to the light I saw that she was smiling – a very contented, happy smile. I was thunderstruck. Then I realized that very gently, she was trying to disengage her arms, and I loosened my grip upon them so that she could do so. Slowly they came up and stole about my neck, and then she drew my lips down to hers once more and held them there for a long time. At last she spoke.

'Why didn't you do this at first, David? I have been waiting so long.'

'What!' I cried. 'You said that you hated me!'

'Did you expect me to run into your arms, and say that I loved you before I knew that you loved me?' she asked.

'But I have told you right along that I love you,' I said.

'Love speaks in acts,' she replied. 'You could have made your mouth say what you wished it to say, but just now when you came and took me in your arms your heart spoke to mine in the language that a woman's heart understands. What a silly man you are, David.'

'Then you haven't hated me at all, Dian?' I asked.

'I have loved you always,' she whispered, 'from the first moment that I saw you, although I did not know it until that time you struck down Hooja the Sly One, and then spurned me.'

'But I didn't spurn you, dear,' I cried. 'I didn't know your ways – I doubt if I do now. It seems incredible that you could have reviled me so, and yet have cared for me all the time.'

'You might have known,' she said, 'when I did not run away from you that it was not hate which chained me to you. While you were battling with Jubal I could have run to the edge of the forest, and when I had learned the outcome of the combat it would have been a simple thing to have eluded you and returned to my own people.'

'But Jubal's brothers – and cousins,' I reminded her, 'how about them?'

She smiled, and hid her face on my shoulder.

'I had to tell you *something*, David,' she whispered. 'I must needs have *some* excuse for remaining near you.'

'You little sinner!' I exclaimed. 'And you have caused me all this anguish for nothing!'

'I have suffered even more,' she answered simply, 'for I thought that you did not love me, and I was helpless. I couldn't come to you and demand that my love be returned, as you have just come to me. Just now when you went away hope went with you. I was wretched, terrified, miserable, and my heart was breaking. I wept, and I have not done that before since my mother died,' and now I saw that there was the moisture of tears about her eyes. It was near to making me cry myself when I thought of all that poor child had been through. Motherless and unprotected; hunted across a savage, primeval world by that hideous brute of a man; exposed to the attacks of the countless fearsome denizens of its mountains, its plains, and its jungles – it was a miracle that she had survived at all.

To me it was a revelation of the things my early forbears must have endured that the human race of the outer crust might survive. It made me very proud to think that I had won the love of such a woman. Of course she couldn't read or write; there was nothing cultured or refined about her as you judge culture and refinement; but she was the essence of all that is best in woman, for she was good, and brave, and noble, and virtuous. And she was all these things in spite of the fact that their observance entailed suffering, and danger, and possible death.

How much easier it would have been to have gone to Jubal in the first place! She would have been his lawful mate. She would have been queen in her own land – and it meant just as much to the cave woman to be a queen in the Stone Age as it does to the woman of to-day to be a queen now; it's all comparative glory any way you look at it, and if there were only half-naked savages on the outer crust to-day, you'd find that it would be considerable glory to be the wife of a Dahomey chief.

I couldn't help but compare Dian's action with that of a splendid young woman I had known in New York – I mean splendid to look at and to talk to. She had been head over heels in love with a chum of mine – a clean, manly chap – but she had married a broken-down, disreputable old debauchee because he was a count in some dinky little European principality that was not even accorded a distinctive colour on any map.

Yes, I was mighty proud of Dian.

After a time we decided to set out for Sari, as I was anxious to see Perry, and to know that all was right with him. I had told Dian about our plan of emancipating the human race of Pellucidar, and she was fairly wild over it. She said that if Dacor, her brother, would only return he could easily be king of Amoz, and that then he and Ghak could form an alliance. That would give us a flying start, for the Sarians and the Amozites were both very powerful tribes. Once they had been armed with swords, and bows and arrows, and trained in their use we were confident that they could overcome any tribe that seemed disinclined to join the great army of federated states with which we were planning to march upon the Mahars.

I explained the various destructive engines of war which Perry and I could construct after a little experimentation – gunpowder, rifles, cannon, and the like, and Dian would clap her little hands, and throw her arms about my neck, and tell me what a wonderful thing I was. She was beginning to think that I was omnipotent although I really hadn't done anything but talk – but that is the way with women when they love. Perry used to say that if a fellow was one-tenth as remarkable as his wife or mother thought him, he would have the world by the tail with a down-hill drag.

The first time we started for Sari I stepped into a nest of poisonous vipers before we reached the valley. A little fellow stung me on the ankle, and Dian made me come back to the cave. She said that I mustn't exercise, or it might prove fatal – if it had been a full-grown snake that struck me, she said, I wouldn't have moved a single pace from the nest – I'd have died in my tracks, so virulent is the poison. As it was I must have been laid up for quite a while, though Dian's poultices of herbs and leaves finally reduced the swelling and drew out the poison.

The episode proved most fortunate, however, as it gave me an idea which added a thousandfold to the value of my arrows as missiles of offence and defence. As soon as I was able to be about again I sought out some adult vipers of the species which had stung me, and having killed them, I extracted their virus, smearing it upon the tips of several arrows. Later I shot a hyaenodon with one of these, and though my arrow inflicted but a superficial flesh wound the beast crumpled in death almost immediately he was hit.

We now set out once more for the land of the Sarians, and it was with feelings of sincere regret that we bade good-bye to our beautiful Garden of Eden, in the comparative peace and harmony of which we had lived the happiest moments of our lives. How long we had been there I did not know, for, as I have told you, time had ceased to exist for me beneath that eternal noonday sun – it may have been an hour, or a month of earthly time; I do not know.

15

Back to Earth

We crossed the river and passed through the mountains beyond, and finally we came out upon a great level plain which stretched away as far as the eye could reach. I cannot tell you in what direction it stretched even if you would care to know, for all the while that I was within Pellucidar I never discovered any but local methods of indicating direction – there is no north, no south, no east, no west. *Up* is about the only direction which is well defined, and that, of course, is *down* to you of the outer crust. Since the sun neither rises nor sets there is no method of indicating direction beyond visible objects such as high mountains, forests, lakes, and seas.

The plain which lies beyond the white cliffs which flank the Darel Az upon the shore nearest the Mountains of the Clouds is about as near to direction as any Pellucidarian can come. If you happen not to have heard of the Darel Az, or the white cliffs, or the Mountains of the Clouds you feel that there is something lacking, and long for the good old understandable north-east or south-west of the outer world.

We had barely entered the great plain when we discovered two enormous animals approaching us from a great distance. So far were they that we could not distinguish what manner of beasts they might be, but as they came closer I saw that they were enormous quadrupeds, eighty or a hundred feet long, with tiny heads perched at the top of very long necks. Their heads must have been quite forty feet from the ground. The beasts moved very slowly – that is, their action was slow – but their strides covered such a great distance that in reality they travelled considerably faster than a man walks.

As they drew still nearer we discovered that upon the back of each sat a human being. Then Dian knew what they were, though she never before had seen one.

'They are lidis from the land of the Thorians,' she cried. 'Thoria lies at the outer verge of the Land of Awful Shadow. The Thorians alone of all races of Pellucidar ride the lidi, for nowhere else than beside the dark country are they found.'

'What is the Land of Awful Shadow?' I asked.

'It is the land which lies beneath the Dead World,' replied Dian: 'the Dead World which hangs for ever between the sun and Pellucidar above the Land of Awful Shadow. It is the Dead World which makes the great shadow upon this portion of Pellucidar.'

I did not fully understand what she meant, nor am I sure that I do yet, for I have never been to that part of Pellucidar from which the Dead World is visible; but Perry says that it is the moon of Pellucidar – a tiny planet within a planet – and that it revolves about the earth's axis coincidentally with the earth, and thus is always above the same spot within Pellucidar.

I remember that Perry was very much excited when I told him about this Dead World, for he seemed to think that it explained the hitherto inexplicable phenomena of nutation and the precession of the equinoxes.

When the two upon the lidis had come quite close to us we saw that one was a man and the other a woman. The former had held up his two hands, palms towards us, in sign of peace, and I had answered him in kind, when he suddenly gave a cry of astonishment and pleasure, and slipping from his enormous mount ran forward towards Dian, throwing his arms about her.

In an instant I was white with jealousy, but only for an instant; since Dian quickly drew the man towards me, telling him that I was David, her mate.

'And this is my brother, Dacor the Strong One, David,' she said to me.

It appeared that the woman was Dacor's mate. He had found none to his liking among the Sari, nor farther on until he had come to the land of the Thoria, and there he had found and fought for this very lovely Thorian maiden whom he was bringing back to his own people.

When they had heard our story and our plans they decided to accompany us to Sari, that Dacor and Ghak might come to an agreement relative to an alliance, as Dacor was quite as enthusiastic about the proposed annihilation of the Mahars and Sagoths as either Dian or I.

After a journey which was, for Pellucidar, quite uneventful, we came to the first of the Sarian villages, which consists of between one and two hundred artificial caves cut into the face of a great chalk cliff. Here to our immense delight we found both Perry and Ghak. The old man was quite overcome at sight of me for he had long since given me up as dead.

When I introduced Dian as my wife he didn't quite know what to say, but he afterwards remarked that with the pick of two worlds I could not have done better.

Ghak and Dacor reached a very amicable arrangement, and it was at a council of the head men of the various tribes of the Sari that the eventful form of government was tentatively agreed upon. Roughly, the various king- doms were to remain virtually independent, but there was to be one great overlord, or emperor. It was decided that I should be the first of the dynasty of the emperors of Pellucidar.

We set about teaching the women how to make bows and arrows and poison pouches. The young men hunted the vipers which provided the virus, and it was they who mined the iron ore, and fashioned the swords under Perry's direction. Rapidly the fever spread from one tribe to another until representatives from nations so far distant that the Sarians had never even heard of them came in to take the oath of allegiance which we required, and to learn the art of making the new weapons and using them.

We sent our young men out as instructors to every nation of the fed- eration, and the movement had reached colossal proportions before the Mahars discovered it. The first intimation they had was when three of their great slave caravans were annihilated in rapid succession. They could not comprehend that the lower orders had suddenly developed a power which rendered them really formidable.

In one of the skirmishes with slave caravans some of our Sarians took a number of Sagoth prisoners, and among them were two who had been members of the guards within the building where we had been confined at Phutra. They told us that the Mahars were frantic with rage when they discovered what had taken place in the cellars of the building. The Sag- oths knew that something very terrible had befallen their masters, but the Mahars had been most careful to see that no inkling of the true nature of their vital affliction reached beyond their own race. How long it would take for the race to become extinct it was impossible even to guess; but that this must eventually happen seemed inevitable.

The Mahars had offered fabulous rewards for the capture of any one of us alive, and at the same time had threatened to inflict the direst punishment upon whoever should harm us. The Sagoths could not understand these seemingly paradoxical instructions, though their purpose was quite evident to me. The Mahars wanted the Great Secret, and they knew that we alone could deliver it to them.

Perry's experiments in the manufacture of gunpowder and the fashion- ing of rifles had not progressed as rapidly as we had hoped – there was a whole lot about these two arts which Perry didn't know. We were both as- sured that the solution of these problems would advance the cause of civi- lization within Pellucidar thousands of years at a single stroke. Then there were various other arts and sciences which we wished to introduce, but our combined knowledge of them did not embrace the mechanical details which alone could render them of commercial, or practical, value.

'David,' said Perry, immediately after his latest failure to produce gunpowder that would even burn, 'one of us must return to the outer world and bring back the information we lack. Here we have all the labour and materials for reproducing anything that ever has been produced above – what we lack is knowledge. Let us go back and get that knowledge in the shape of books – then this world will indeed be at our feet.'

And so it was decided that I should return in the prospector, which still lay upon the edge of the forest at the point where we had first penetrated to the surface of the inner world. Dian would not listen to any arrangement for my going which did not include her, and I was not sorry that she wished to accompany me, for I wanted her to see my world, and I wanted my world to see her.

With a large force of men we marched to the great iron mole, which Perry soon had hoisted into position with its nose pointed back towards the outer crust. He went over all the machinery carefully. He replenished the air tanks, and manufactured oil for the engine. At last everything was ready, and we were about to set out when our pickets, a long, thin line of which had surrounded our camp at all times, reported that a great body of what appeared to be Sagoths and Mahars were approaching from the direction of Phutra.

Dian and I were ready to embark, but I was anxious to witness the first clash between two fair-sized armies of the opposing races of Pellucidar. I realized that this was to mark the historic beginning of a mighty struggle for possession of a world, and as the first emperor of Pellucidar I felt that it was not alone my duty, but my right, to be in the thick of that momentous struggle.

As the opposing army approached we saw that there were many Mahars with the Sagoth troops – an indication of the vast importance which the dominant race placed upon the outcome of this campaign, for it was not customary with them to take active part in the sorties which their creatures made for slaves – the only form of warfare which they waged upon the lower orders.

Ghak and Dacor were both with us, having come primarily to view the prospector. I placed Ghak with some of his Sarians on the right of our battle line. Dacor took the left, while I commanded the centre. Behind us I stationed a sufficient reserve under one of Ghak's head men. The Sagoths advanced steadily with menacing spears, and I let them come until they were within easy bowshot before I gave the word to fire.

At the first volley of poison-tipped arrows the front ranks of the gorilla-men crumpled to the ground; but those behind charged over the prostrate forms of their comrades in a wild, mad rush to be upon us with their spears. A second volley stopped them for an instant, and then my reserve sprang through the openings in the firing line to engage them with sword and shield.

The clumsy spears of the Sagoths were no match for the swords of the Sarian and Amozite, who turned the spear thrusts aside with their shields and leaped to close quarters with their lighter, handier weapons.

Ghak took his archers along the enemy's flank, and while the swordsmen engaged them in front, he poured volley after volley into their unprotected left. The Mahars did little real fighting, and were more in the way than otherwise, though occasionally one of them would fasten its powerful jaws upon the arm or leg of a Sarian.

The battle did not last a great while, for when Dacor and I led our men in upon the Sagoths' right with naked swords they were already so demoralized that they turned and fled before us. We pursued them for some time, taking many prisoners and recovering nearly a hundred slaves, among whom was Hooja the Sly One.

He told me that he had been captured while on his way to his own land; but that his life had been spared in hope that through him the Mahars would learn the whereabouts of their Great Secret. Ghak and I were inclined to think that the Sly One had been guiding this expedition to the land of Sari, where he thought that the book might be found in Perry's possession; but we had no proof of this and so we took him in and treated him as one of us, although none liked him. And how he rewarded my generosity you shall presently learn.

There were a number of Mahars among our prisoners, and so fearful were our own people of them that they would not approach them unless completely covered from the sight of the reptiles by a piece of skin. Even Dian shared the popular superstition regarding the evil effects of exposure to the eyes of angry Mahars, and though I laughed at her fears I was willing enough to humour them if it would relieve her apprehension in any degree, and so she sat apart from the prospector, near which the Mahars had been chained, while Perry and I again inspected every portion of the mechanism.

At last I took my place in the driving seat, and called to one of the men without to fetch Dian. It happened that Hooja stood quite close to the doorway of the prospector, so that it was he who, without my knowledge, went to bring her, but how he succeeded in accomplishing the fiendish thing he did I cannot guess, unless there were others in the plot to aid him. Nor can I believe that, since all my people were loyal to me and would have made short work of Hooja had he suggested the heartless scheme, even had he had time to acquaint another with it. It was all done so quickly that I may only believe that it was the result of sudden impulse, aided by a number of, to Hooja, fortuitous circumstances occurring at precisely the right moment.

All I know is that it was Hooja who brought Dian to the prospector, still wrapped from head to toe in the skin of an enormous cave lion which had covered her since the Mahar prisoners had been brought into camp. He deposited his burden in the seat beside me. I was all ready to get under way. The goodbyes had been said. Perry had grasped my hand in the last, long farewell. I closed and barred the outer and inner doors, took my seat again at the driving mechanism, and pulled the starting lever.

As before on that far-gone night that had witnessed our first trial of the iron monster, there was a frightful roaring beneath us – the giant frame trembled and vibrated – there was a rush of sound as the loose earth passed up through the hollow space between the inner and outer jackets to be deposited in our wake. Once more the thing was off.

But on the instant of departure I was nearly thrown from my seat by the sudden lurching of the prospector. At first I did not realize what had happened, but presently it dawned upon me that just before entering the crust the towering body had fallen through its supporting scaffolding, and that instead of entering the ground vertically we were plunging into it at a different angle. Where it would bring us out upon the upper crust I could not even conjecture. And then I turned to note the effect of this strange experience upon Dian. She still sat shrouded in the great skin.

'Come, come,' I cried, laughing, 'come out of your shell. No Mahar eyes can reach you here,' and I leaned over and snatched the lion skin from her. And then I shrank back upon my seat in utter horror.

The thing beneath the skin was not Dian – it was a hideous Mahar. Instantly I realized the trick that Hooja had played upon me, and the purpose of it. Rid of me for ever, as he doubtless thought, Dian would be at his mercy. Frantically I tore at the steering wheel in an effort to turn the prospector back towards Pellucidar; but, as on that other occasion, I could not budge the thing a hair.

It is needless to recount the horrors or the monotony of that journey. It varied but little from the former one which had brought us from the outer to the inner world. Because of the angle at which we had entered the ground the trip required nearly a day longer, and brought me out here upon the sands of the Sahara instead of in the United States as I had hoped.

For months I have been waiting here for a white man to come. I dared not leave the prospector for fear I should never be able to find it again – the shifting sands of the desert would soon cover it, and then my only hope of returning to my Dian and her Pellucidar would be gone for ever.

That I ever shall see her again seems but remotely possible, for how may I know upon what part of Pellucidar my return journey may terminate – and how, without a north or a south or an east or a west, may I hope ever to find

my way across that vast world to the tiny spot where my lost love lies grieving for me?

That is the story as David Innes told it to me in the goat-skin tent upon
the rim of the great Sahara Desert. The next day he took me out to see the
prospector – it was precisely as he had described it. So huge was it that it
could have been brought to this inaccessible part of the world by no means
of transportation that existed there – it could only have come in the way that
David Innes said it came – up through the crust of the earth from the inner
world of Pellucidar.

I spent a week with him, and then, abandoning my lion hunt, returned
directly to the coast and hurried to London, where I purchased a great quantity of stuff which he wished to take back to Pellucidar with him. There were
books, rifles, revolvers, ammunition, cameras, chemicals, telephones, telegraph instruments, wire, tools, and more books – books upon ever subject
under the sun. He said he wanted a library with which they could reproduce the wonders of the twentieth century in the Stone Age, and if quantity
counts for anything I got it for him.

I took the things back to Algeria myself, and accompanied them to the
end of the railroad; but from here I was recalled to America upon important
business. However, I was able to employ a very trustworthy man to take
charge of the caravan – the same guide, in fact, who had accompanied me
on the previous trip into the Sahara – and after writing a long letter to Innes,
in which I gave him my American address, I saw the expedition head south.

Among the other things which I sent to Innes was over five hundred miles
of double insulated wire of a very fine gauge. I had it packed on a special reel
at his suggestion, as it was his idea that he could fasten one end here before
he left and by paying it out through the end of the prospector lay a telegraph
line between the outer and inner worlds. In my letter I told him to be sure
to mark the terminus of the line very plainly with a high cairn, in case I was
not: able to reach him before he set out, so that I might easily find it and
communicate with him should he be so fortunate as to reach Pellucidar.

I received several letters from him after I returned to America – in fact
he took advantage of every northward-passing caravan to drop me word of
some sort. His last letter was written the day before he intended to depart.
Here it is:

MY DEAR FRIEND,
To-morrow I shall set out in quest of Pellucidar and Dian. That is if the
Arabs don't get me. They have been very nasty of late. I don't know the cause,
but on two occasions they have threatened my life. One, more friendly than
the rest, told me to-day that they intended attacking me to-night. It would

be unfortunate should anything of that sort happen now that I am so nearly ready to depart.

However, maybe I will be as well off, for the nearer the hour approaches, the slenderer my chances of success appear.

Here is the friendly Arab who is to take this letter north for me, so good-bye, and God bless you for your kindness to me.

The Arab tells me to hurry, for he sees a cloud of sand to the south – he thinks it is the party coming to murder me, and he doesn't want to be found with me. So good-bye again.

Yours,

DAVID INNES

A year later found me at the end of the railroad once more, headed for the spot where I had left Innes. My first disappointment was when I discovered that my old guide had died within a few weeks of my return, nor could I find any member of my former party who could lead me to the same spot.

For months I searched that scorching land, interviewing countless desert sheiks in the hope that at last I might find one who had heard of Innes and his wonderful iron mole. Constantly my eyes scanned the blinding waste of sand for the rocky cairn beneath which I was to find the wires leading to Pellucidar – but always was I unsuccessful.

And always do these awful questions harass me when I think of David Innes and his strange adventures.

Did the Arabs murder him, after all, just on the eve of his departure? Or, did he again turn the nose of his iron monster towards the inner world? Did he reach it, or lies he somewhere buried in the heart of the great crust? And if he did come again to Pellucidar was it to break through into the bottom of one of her great inland seas, or among some savage race far, far from the land of his heart's desire?

Does the answer lie somewhere upon the bosom of the broad Sahara, at the end of two tiny wires, hidden beneath a lost cairn? I wonder!

PELLUCIDAR

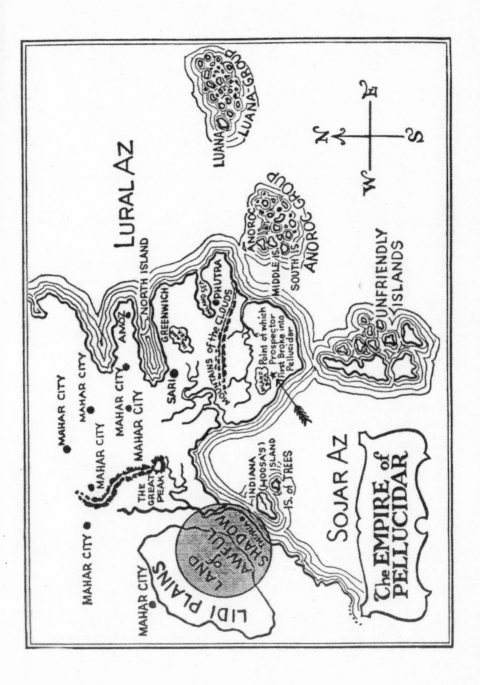

PROLOGUE

Several years had elapsed since I had found the opportunity to do any big-game hunting; for at last I had my plans almost perfected for a return to my old stamping-grounds in northern Africa, where in other days I had had excellent sport in pursuit of the king of beasts.

The date of my departure had been set; I was to leave in two weeks. No schoolboy counting the lagging hours that must pass before the beginning of 'long vacation' released him to the delirious joys of the summer camp could have been filled with greater impatience or keener anticipation.

And then came a letter that started me for Africa twelve days ahead of my schedule.

Often am I in receipt of letters from strangers who have found something in a story of mine to commend or to condemn. My interest in this department of my correspondence is ever fresh. I opened this particular letter with all the zest of pleasurable anticipation with which I had opened so many others. The post-mark (Algiers) had aroused my interest and curiosity, especially at this time, since it was Algiers that was presently to witness the termination of my coming sea voyage in search of sport and adventure.

Before the reading of that letter was completed lions and lion-hunting had fled my thoughts, and I was in a state of excitement bordering upon frenzy.

It – well, read it yourself, and see if you, too, do not find food for frantic conjecture, for tantalizing doubts, and for a great hope.

Here it is:

DEAR SIR: I think that I have run across one of the most remarkable coincidences in modern literature. But let me start at the beginning:

I am, by profession, a wanderer upon the face of the earth. I have no trade – nor any other occupation.

My father bequeathed me a competency; some remoter ancestor – a lust to roam. I have combined the two and invested them carefully and without extravagance.

I became interested in your story, *At the Earth's Core*, not so much because of the probability of the tale as of a great and abiding wonder that people should be paid real money for writing such impossible trash. You will pardon my candor, but it is necessary that you understand my mental attitude toward this particular story – that you may credit that which follows.

Shortly thereafter I started for the Sahara in search of a rather rare species of antelope that is to be found only occasionally within a limited area at a certain season of the year. My chase led me far from the haunts of man.

It was a fruitless search, however, in so far as antelope is concerned; but one night as I lay courting sleep at the edge of a little cluster of date-palms that surround an ancient well in the midst of the arid, shifting sands, I suddenly became conscious of a strange sound coming apparently from the earth beneath my head.

It was an intermittent ticking!

No reptile or insect with which I am familiar reproduces any such notes. I lay for an hour – listening intently.

At last my curiosity go the better of me. I arose, lighted my lamp and commenced to investigate.

My bedding lay upon a rug stretched directly upon the warm sand. The noise appeared to be coming from beneath the rug. I raised it, but found nothing – yet, at intervals, the sound continued.

I dug into the sand with the point of my hunting-knife. A few inches below the surface of the sand I encountered a solid substance that had the feel of wood beneath the sharp steel.

Excavating about it, I unearthed a small wooden box. From this receptacle issued the strange sound that I had heard.

How had it come here?

What did it contain?

In attempting to lift it from its burying place I discovered that it seemed to be held fast by means of a very small insulated cable running farther into the sand beneath it.

My first impulse was to drag the thing loose by main strength; but fortunately I thought better of this and fell to examining the box. I soon saw that it was covered by a hinged lid, which was held closed by a simple screwhook and eye.

It took but a moment to loosen this and raise the cover, when, to my utter astonishment, I discovered an ordinary telegraph instrument clicking away within.

'What in the world,' thought I, 'is this thing doing here?'

That it was a French military instrument was my first guess; but really there didn't seem much likelihood that this was the correct explanation, when one took into account the loneliness and remoteness of the spot.

As I sat gazing at my remarkable find, which was ticking and clicking away there in the silence of the desert night, trying to convey some message which I was unable to interpret, my eyes fell upon a bit of paper lying in the bottom of the box beside the instrument. I picked it up and examined it. Upon it were written but two letters:

D. I.

They meant nothing to me then. I was baffled.

Once, in an interval of silence upon the part of the receiving instrument, I moved the sending-key up and down a few times. Instantly the receiving mechanism commenced to work frantically.

I tried to recall something of the Morse Code, with which I had played as a little boy – but time had obliterated it from my memory. I became almost frantic as I let my imagination run riot among the possibilities for which this clicking instrument might stand.

Some poor devil at the unknown other end might be in dire need of succor. The very franticness of the instrument's wild clashing betokened something of the kind.

And there sat I, powerless to interpret, and so powerless to help!

It was then that the inspiration came to me. In a flash there leaped to my mind the closing paragraphs of the story I had read in the club at Algiers:

Does the answer lie somewhere upon the bosom of the broad Sahara, at the ends of two tiny wires, hidden beneath a lost cairn?

The idea seemed preposterous. Experience and intelligence combined to assure me that there could be no slightest grain of truth or possibility in your wild tale – it was fiction pure and simple.

And yet where *were* the other ends of those wires?

What was this instrument – ticking away here in the great Sahara – but a travesty upon the possible!

Would I have believed in it had I not seen it with my own eyes?

And the initials – D. I. – upon the slip of paper! David's initials were these – David Innes.

I smiled at my imaginings. I ridiculed the assumption that there was an inner world and that these wires led downward through the earth's crust to the surface of Pellucidar. And yet –

Well, I sat there all night, listening to that tantalizing clicking, now and then moving the sending-key just to let the other end know that the instrument had been discovered. In the morning, after carefully returning the box to its hole and covering it over with sand, I called my servants about me, snatched a hurried breakfast, mounted my horse, and started upon a forced march for Algiers.

I arrived here today. In writing you this letter I feel that I am making a fool of myself.

There is no David Innes.

There is no Dian the Beautiful.

There is no world within a world.

Pellucidar is but a realm of your imagination – nothing more.

But –

The incident of the finding of that buried telegraph instrument upon the lonely Sahara is little short of uncanny, in view of your story of the adventures of David Innes.

I have called it one of the most remarkable coincidences in modern fiction. I called it literature before, but – again pardon my candor – your story is not.

And now – why am I writing you?

Heaven knows, unless it is that the persistent clicking of that unfathomable enigma out there in the vast silences of the Sahara has so wrought upon my nerves that reason refuses longer to function sanely.

I cannot hear it now, yet I know that far away to the south, all alone beneath the sands, it is still pounding out its vain, frantic appeal.

It is maddening!

It is your fault – I want you to release me from it.

Cable me at once, at my expense, that there was no basis of fact for your story, *At the Earth's Core.*

Very respectfully yours,

COGDON NESTOR,
— and — Club,
Algiers.

June 1st,—.

Ten minutes after reading this letter I had cabled Mr. Nestor as follows: *Story true. Await me Algiers.*

As fast as train and boat would carry me, I sped toward my destination. For all those dragging days my mind was a whirl of mad conjecture, of frantic hope, of numbing fear.

The finding of the telegraph-instrument practically assured me that David Innes had driven Perry's iron mole back through the earth's crust to the buried world of Pellucidar; but what adventures had befallen him since his return?

Had he found Dian the Beautiful, his half-savage mate, safe among his friends, or had Hooja the Sly One succeeded in his nefarious schemes to abduct her?

Did Abner Perry, the lovable old inventor and paleontologist, still live?

Had the federated tribes of Pellucidar succeeded in overthrowing the mighty Mahars, the dominant race of reptilian monsters, and their fierce, gorilla-like soldiery, the savage Sagoths?

I must admit that I was in a state bordering upon nervous prostration when I entered the — and — Club, in Algiers, and inquired for Mr. Nestor. A moment later I was ushered into his presence, to find myself clasping hands with the sort of chap that the world holds only too few of.

He was a tall, smooth-faced man of about thirty, clean-cut, straight, and strong, and weather-tanned to the hue of a desert Arab. I liked him immensely from the first, and I hope that after our three months together in the desert country – three months not entirely lacking in adventure – he found that a man may be a writer of 'impossible trash" and yet have some redeeming qualities.

The day following my arrival at Algiers we left for the south, Nestor having made all arrangements in advance, guessing, as he naturally did, that I could be coming to Africa for but a single purpose – to hasten at once to the buried telegraph-instrument and wrest its secret from it.

In addition to our native servants, we took along an English telegraph-operator named Frank Downes. Nothing of interest enlivened our journey by rail and caravan till we came to the cluster of date-palms about the ancient well upon the rim of the Sahara.

It was the very spot at which I first had seen David Innes. If he had ever raised a cairn above the telegraph instrument no sign of it remained now. Had it not been for the chance that caused Cogdon Nestor to throw down his sleeping rug directly over the hidden instrument, it might still be clicking there unheard – and this story still unwritten.

When we reached the spot and unearthed the little box the instrument was quiet, nor did repeated attempts upon the part of our telegrapher succeed in winning a response from the other end of the line. After several days of futile endeavor to raise Pellucidar, we had begun to despair. I was as positive that the other end of that little cable protruded through the surface of the inner world as I am that I sit here today in my study – when about midnight of the fourth day I was awakened by the sound of the instrument.

Leaping to my feet I grasped Downes roughly by the neck and dragged him out of his blankets. He didn't need to be told what caused my excitement, for the instant he was awake he, too, heard the long-hoped for click, and with a whoop of delight pounced upon the instrument.

Nestor was on his feet almost as soon as I. The three of us huddled about that little box as if our lives depended upon the message it had for us.

Downes interrupted the clicking with his sending-key. The noise of the receiver stopped instantly.

'Ask who it is, Downes,' I directed.

He did so, and while we awaited the Englishman's translation of the reply, I doubt if either Nestor or I breathed.

'He says he's David Innes,' said Downes. 'He wants to know who we are.'

'Tell him,' said I; 'and that we want to know how he is – and all that has befallen him since I last saw him.'

For two months I talked with David Innes almost every day, and as Downes translated, either Nestor or I took notes. From these, arranged in chronological order, I have set down the following account of the further adventures of David Innes at the earth's core, practically in his own words.

1

Lost on Pellucidar

The Arabs, of whom I wrote you at the end of my last letter (Innes began), and whom I thought to be enemies intent only upon murdering me, proved to be exceedingly friendly – they were searching for the very band of marauders that had threatened my existence. The huge rhamphorhynchus-like reptile that I had brought back with me from the inner world – the ugly Mahar that Hooja the Sly One had substituted for my dear Dian at the moment of my departure – filled them with wonder and with awe.

Nor less so did the mighty subterranean prospector which had carried me to Pellucidar and back again, and which lay out in the desert about two miles from my camp.

With their help I managed to get the unwieldy tons of its great bulk into a vertical position – the nose deep in a hole we had dug in the sand and the rest of it supported by the trunks of date-palms cut for the purpose.

It was a mighty engineering job with only wild Arabs and their wilder mounts to do the work of an electric crane – but finally it was completed, and I was ready for departure.

For some time I hesitated to take the Mahar back with me. She had been docile and quiet ever since she had discovered herself virtually a prisoner aboard the 'iron mole.' It had been, of course, impossible for me to communicate with her since she had no auditory organs and I no knowledge of her fourth-dimension, sixth-sense method of communication.

Naturally I am kind-hearted, and so I found it beyond me to leave even this hateful and repulsive thing alone in a strange and hostile world. The result was that when I entered the iron mole I took her with me.

That she knew that we were about to return to Pellucidar was evident, for immediately her manner changed from that of habitual gloom that had pervaded her, to an almost human expression of contentment and delight.

Our trip through the earth's crust was but a repetition of my two former journeys between the inner and the outer worlds. This time, however, I imagine that we must have maintained a more nearly perpendicular course, for we accomplished the journey in a few minutes' less time than upon the occasion of my first journey through the five-hundred-mile crust. Just a trifle less than seventy-two hours after our departure into the sands of the Sahara, we broke through the surface of Pellucidar.

Fortune once again favored me by the slightest of margins, for when I opened the door in the prospector's outer jacket I saw that we had missed coming up through the bottom of an ocean by but a few hundred yards.

The aspect of the surrounding country was entirely unfamiliar to me – I had no conception of precisely where I was upon the one hundred and twenty-four million square miles of Pellucidar's vast land surface.

The perpetual midday sun poured down its torrid rays from zenith, as it had done since the beginning of Pellucidarian time – as it would continue to do to the end of it. Before me, across the wide sea, the weird, horizonless seascape folded gently upward to meet the sky until it lost itself to view in the azure depths of distance far above the level of my eyes.

How strange it looked! How vastly different from the flat and puny area of the circumscribed vision of the dweller upon the outer crust!

I was lost. Though I wandered ceaselessly throughout a lifetime, I might never discover the whereabouts of my former friends of this strange and savage world. Never again might I see dear old Perry, nor Ghak the Hairy One, nor Dacor the Strong One, nor that other infinitely precious one – my sweet and noble mate, Dian the Beautiful!

But even so I was glad to tread once more the surface of Pellucidar. Mysterious and terrible, grotesque and savage though she is in many of her aspects, I can not but love her. Her very savagery appealed to me, for it is the savagery of unspoiled Nature.

The magnificence of her tropic beauties enthralled me. Her mighty land areas breathed unfettered freedom.

Her untracked oceans, whispering of virgin wonders unsullied by the eye of man, beckoned me out upon their restless bosoms.

Not for an instant did I regret the world of my nativity. I was in Pellucidar. I was *home*. And I was content.

As I stood dreaming beside the giant thing that had brought me safely through the earth's crust, my traveling companion, the hideous Mahar, emerged from the interior of the prospector and stood beside me. For a long time she remained motionless.

What thoughts were passing through the convolutions of her reptilian brain?

I do not know.

She was a member of the dominant race of Pellucidar. By a strange freak of evolution her kind had first developed the power of reason in that world of anomalies.

To her, creatures such as I were of a lower order. As Perry had discovered among the writings of her kind in the buried city of Phutra, it was still an open question among the Mahars as to whether man possessed means of intelligent communication or the power of reason.

Her kind believed that in the center of all-pervading solidity there was a single, vast, spherical cavity, which was Pellucidar. This cavity had been left there for the sole purpose of providing a place for the creation and propagation of the Mahar race. Everything within it had been put there for the uses of the Mahar.

I wondered what this particular Mahar might think now. I found pleasure in speculating upon just what the effect had been upon her of passing through the earth's crust, and coming out into a world that one of even less intelligence than the great Mahars could easily see was a different world from her own Pellucidar.

What had she thought of the outer world's tiny sun?

What had been the effect upon her of the moon and myriad stars of the clear African nights?

How had she explained them?

With what sensations of awe must she first have watched the sun moving slowly across the heavens to disappear at last beneath the western horizon, leaving in his wake that which the Mahar had never before witnessed – the darkness of night? For upon Pellucidar there is no night. The stationary sun hangs forever in the center of the Pellucidarian sky – directly overhead.

Then, too, she must have been impressed by the wondrous mechanism of the prospector which had bored its way from world to world and back again. And that it had been driven by a rational being must also have occurred to her.

Too, she had seen me conversing with other men upon the earth's surface. She had seen the arrival of the caravan of books and arms, and ammunition, and the balance of the heterogeneous collection which I had crammed into the cabin of the iron mole for transportation to Pellucidar.

She had seen all these evidences of a civilization and brain-power transcending in scientific achievement anything that her race had produced; nor once had she seen a creature of her own kind.

There could have been but a single deduction in the mind of the Mahar – there were other worlds than Pellucidar, and the *gilak* was a rational being.

Now the creature at my side was creeping slowly toward the near-by sea. At my hip hung a long-barreled six-shooter – somehow I had been unable to find the same sensation of security in the new-fangled automatics that had been perfected since my first departure from the outer world – and in my hand was a heavy express rifle.

I could have shot the Mahar with ease, for I knew intuitively that she was escaping – but I did not.

I felt that if she could return to her own kind with the story of her adventures, the position of the human race within Pellucidar would be advanced immensely at a single stride, for at once man would take his proper place in the considerations of the reptilia.

At the edge of the sea the creature paused and looked back at me. Then she slid sinuously into the surf.

For several minutes I saw no more of her as she luxuriated in the cool depths.

Then a hundred yards from shore she rose and there for another short while she floated upon the surface.

Finally she spread her giant wings, flapped them vigorously a score of times and rose above the blue sea. A single time she circled far aloft – and then straight as an arrow she sped away.

I watched her until the distant haze enveloped her and she had disappeared. I was alone.

My first concern was to discover where within Pellucidar I might be – and in what direction lay the land of the Sarians where Ghak the Hairy One ruled.

But how was I to guess in which direction lay Sari?

And if I set out to search – what then?

Could I find my way back to the prospector with its priceless freight of books, firearms, ammunition, scientific instruments, and still more books – its great library of reference works upon every conceivable branch of applied sciences?

And if I could not, of what value was all this vast storehouse of potential civilization and progress to be to the world of my adoption?

Upon the other hand, if I remained here alone with it, what could I accomplish single-handed?

Nothing.

But where there was no east, no west, no north, no south, no stars, no moon, and only a stationary midday sun, how was I to find my way back to this spot should ever I get out of sight of it?

I didn't know.

For a long time I stood buried in deep thought, when it occurred to me to try out one of the compasses I had brought and ascertain if it remained steadily fixed upon an unvarying pole. I reentered the prospector and fetched a compass without.

Moving a considerable distance from the prospector that the needle might not be influenced by its great bulk of iron and steel, I turned the delicate instrument about in every direction.

Always and steadily the needle remained rigidly fixed upon a point straight out to sea, apparently pointing toward a large island some ten or twenty miles distant. This then should be north.

I drew my note-book from my pocket and made a careful topographical sketch of the locality within the range of my vision. Due north lay the island, far out upon the shimmering sea.

The spot I had chosen for my observations was the top of a large, flat boulder which rose six or eight feet above the turf. This spot I called Greenwich. The boulder was the 'Royal Observatory.'

I had made a start! I cannot tell you what a sense of relief was imparted to me by the simple fact that there was at least one spot within Pellucidar with a familiar name and a place upon a map.

It was with almost childish joy that I made a little circle in my note-book and traced the word Greenwich beside it.

Now I felt I might start out upon my search with some assurance of finding my way back again to the prospector.

I decided that at first I would travel directly south in the hope that I might in that direction find some familiar landmark. It was as good a direction as any. This much at least might be said of it.

Among the many other things I had brought from the outer world were a number of pedometers. I slipped three of these into my pockets with the idea that I might arrive at a more or less accurate mean from the registrations of them all.

On my map I would register so many paces south, so many east, so many west, and so on. When I was ready to return I would then do so by any route that I might choose.

I also strapped a considerable quantity of ammunition across my shoulders, pocketed some matches, and hooked an aluminum fry-pan and a small stew-kettle of the same metal to my belt.

I was ready – ready to go forth and explore a world!

Ready to search a land area of 124,110,000 square miles for my friends, my incomparable mate, and good old Perry!

And so, after locking the door in the outer shell of the prospector, I set out upon my quest. Due south I traveled, across lovely valleys thick-dotted with grazing herds.

Through dense primeval forests I forced my way and up the slopes of mighty mountains searching for a pass to their farther sides.

Ibex and musk-sheep fell before my good old revolver, so that I lacked not for food in the higher altitudes. The forests and the plains gave plentifully of fruits and wild birds, antelope, aurochsen, and elk.

Occasionally, for the larger game animals and the gigantic beasts of prey, I used my express rifle, but for the most part the revolver filled all my needs.

There were times, too, when faced by a mighty cave bear, a saber-toothed tiger, or huge *felis spelaea*, black-maned and terrible, even my powerful rifle seemed pitifully inadequate – but fortune favored me so that I passed unscathed through adventures that even the recollection of causes the short hairs to bristle at the nape of my neck.

How long I wandered toward the south I do not know, for shortly after I left the prospector something went wrong with my watch, and I was again at the mercy of the baffling timelessness of Pellucidar, forging steadily ahead beneath the great, motionless sun which hangs eternally at noon.

I ate many times, however, so that days must have elapsed, possibly months with no familiar landscape rewarding my eager eyes.

I saw no men nor signs of men. Nor is this strange, for Pellucidar, in its land area, is immense, while the human race there is very young and consequently far from numerous.

Doubtless upon that long search mine was the first human foot to touch the soil in many places – mine the first human eye to rest upon the gorgeous wonders of the landscape.

It was a staggering thought. I could not but dwell upon it often as I made my lonely way through this virgin world. Then, quite suddenly, one day I stepped out of the peace of manless primality into the presence of man – and peace was gone.

It happened thus:

I had been following a ravine downward out of a chain of lofty hills and had paused at its mouth to view the lovely little valley that lay before me. At one side was tangled wood, while straight ahead a river wound peacefully along parallel to the cliffs in which the hills terminated at the valley's edge.

Presently, as I stood enjoying the lovely scene, as insatiate for Nature's wonders as if I had not looked upon similar landscapes countless times, a sound of shouting broke from the direction of the woods. That the harsh, discordant notes rose from the throats of men I could not doubt.

I slipped behind a large boulder near the mouth of the ravine and waited. I could hear the crashing of underbrush in the forest, and I guessed that whoever came, came quickly – pursued and pursuers, doubtless.

In a short time some hunted animal would break into view, and a moment later a score of half-naked savages would come leaping after with spears or clubs or great stone-knives.

I had seen the thing so many times during my life within Pellucidar that I felt that I could anticipate to a nicety precisely what I was about to witness. I hoped that the hunters would prove friendly and be able to direct me toward Sari.

Even as I was thinking these thoughts the quarry emerged from the forest. But it was no terrified four-footed beast. Instead, what I saw was an old man – a terrified old man!

Staggering feebly and hopelessly from what must have been some very terrible fate, if one could judge from the horrified expressions he continually cast behind him toward the wood, he came stumbling on in my direction.

He had covered but a short distance from the forest when I beheld the first of his pursuers – a Sagoth, one of those grim and terrible gorilla-men who guard the mighty Mahars in their buried cities, faring forth from time to time upon slave-raiding or punitive expeditions against the human race of Pellucidar, of whom the dominant race of the inner world think as we think of the bison or the wild sheep of our own world.

Close behind the foremost Sagoth came others until a full dozen raced, shouting after the terror-stricken old man. They would be upon him shortly, that was plain.

One of them was rapidly overhauling him, his back-thrown spear-arm testifying to his purpose.

And then, quite with the suddenness of an unexpected blow, I realized a past familiarity with the gait and carriage of the fugitive.

Simultaneously there swept over me the staggering fact that the old man was – Perry! That he was about to die before my very eyes with no hope that I could reach him in time to avert the awful catastrophe – for to me it meant a real catastrophe!

Perry was my best friend.

Dian, of course, I looked upon as more than friend. She was my mate – a part of me.

I had entirely forgotten the rifle in my hand and the revolvers at my belt; one does not readily synchronize his thoughts with the stone age and the twentieth century simultaneously.

Now from past habit I still thought in the stone age, and in my thoughts of the stone age there were no thoughts of firearms.

The fellow was almost upon Perry when the feel of the gun in my hand awoke me from the lethargy of terror that had gripped me. From behind my boulder I threw up the heavy express rifle – a mighty engine of destruction that might bring down a cave bear or a mammoth at a single shot – and let drive at the Sagoth's broad, hairy breast.

At the sound of the shot he stopped stock-still. His spear dropped from his hand.

Then he lunged forward upon his face.

The effect upon the others was little less remarkable. Perry alone could have possibly guessed the meaning of the loud report or explained its connection with the sudden collapse of the Sagoth. The other gorilla-men halted for but an instant. Then with renewed shrieks of rage they sprang forward to finish Perry.

At the same time I stepped from behind my boulder, drawing one of my revolvers that I might conserve the more precious ammunition of the express rifle. Quickly I fired again with the lesser weapon.

Then it was that all eyes were directed toward me. Another Sagoth fell to the bullet from the revolver; but it did not stop his companions. They were out for revenge as well as blood now, and they meant to have both.

As I ran forward toward Perry I fired four more shots, dropping three of our antagonists. Then at last the remaining seven wavered. It was too much for them, this roaring, death that leaped, invisible, upon them from a great distance.

As they hesitated I reached Perry's side. I have never seen such an expression upon any man's face as that upon Perry's when he recognized me. I have no words where-with to describe it. There was not time to talk then – scarce for a greeting. I thrust the full, loaded revolver into his hand, fired the last shot in my own, and reloaded. There were but six Sagoths left then.

They started toward us once more, though I could see that they were terrified probably as much by the noise of the guns as by their effects. They never reached us. Half-way the three that remained turned and fled, and we let them go.

The last we saw of them they were disappearing into the tangled undergrowth of the forest. And then Perry turned and threw his arms about my neck and, burying his old face upon my shoulder, wept like a child.

2

Traveling with Terror

We made camp there beside the peaceful river. There Perry told me all that had befallen him since I had departed for the outer crust.

It seemed that Hooja had made it appear that I had intentionally left Dian behind, and that I did not purpose ever returning to Pellucidar. He told them that I was of another world and that I had tired of this and of its inhabitants.

To Dian he had explained that I had a mate in the world to which I was returning; that I had never intended taking Dian the Beautiful back with me; and that she had seen the last of me.

Shortly afterward Dian had disappeared from the camp, nor had Perry seen or heard aught of her since.

He had no conception of the time that had elapsed since I had departed, but guessed that many years had dragged their slow way into the past.

Hooja, too, had disappeared very soon after Dian had left. The Sarians, under Ghak the Hairy One, and the Amozites under Dacor the Strong One, Dian's brother, had fallen out over my supposed defection, for Ghak would not believe that I had thus treacherously deceived and deserted them.

The result had been that these two powerful tribes had fallen upon one another with the new weapons that Perry and I had taught them to make and to use. Other tribes of the new federation took sides with the original disputants or set up petty revolutions of their own.

The result was the total demolition of the work we had so well started.

Taking advantage of the tribal war, the Mahars had gathered their Sagoths in force and fallen upon one tribe after another in rapid succession, wreaking awful havoc among them and reducing them for the most part to as pitiable a state of terror as that from which we had raised them.

Alone of all the once-mighty federation the Sarians and the Amozites with a few other tribes continued to maintain their defiance of the Mahars; but these tribes were still divided among themselves, nor had it seemed at all probable to Perry when he had last been among them that any attempt at re-amalgamation would be made.

'And thus, your majesty,' he concluded, 'has faded back into the oblivion of the Stone Age our wondrous dream and with it has gone the First Empire of Pellucidar.'

We both had to smile at the use of my royal title, yet I was indeed still 'Emperor of Pellucidar,' and some day I meant to rebuild what the vile act of the treacherous Hooja had torn down.

But first I would find my empress. To me she was worth forty empires.

'Have you no clues as to the whereabouts of Dian?' I asked.

'None whatever,' replied Perry. 'It was in search of her that I came to the pretty pass in which you discovered me, and from which, David, you saved me.

'I knew perfectly well that you had not intentionally deserted either Dian or Pellucidar. I guessed that in some way Hooja the Sly One was at the bottom of the matter, and I determined to go to Amoz, where I guessed that Dian might come to the protection of her brother, and do my utmost to convince her, and through her Dacor the Strong One, that we had all been victims of a treacherous plot to which you were no party.

'I came to Amoz after a most trying and terrible journey, only to find that Dian was not among her brother's people and that they knew naught of her whereabouts.

'Dacor, I am sure, wanted to be fair and just, but so great were his grief and anger over the disappearance of his sister that he could not listen to reason, but kept repeating time and again that only your return to Pellucidar could prove the honesty of your intentions.

'Then came a stranger from another tribe, sent I am sure at the instigation of Hooja. He so turned the Amozites against me that I was forced to flee their country to escape assassination.

'In attempting to return to Sari I became lost, and then the Sagoths discovered me. For a long time I eluded them, hiding in caves and wading in rivers to throw them off my trail.

'I lived on nuts and fruits and the edible roots that chance threw in my way.

'I traveled on and on, in what direction I could not even guess; and at last I could elude them no longer and the end came as I had long foreseen that it would come, except that I had not foreseen that you would be there to save me.'

We rested in our camp until Perry had regained sufficient strength to travel again. We planned much, rebuilding all our shattered air-castles; but above all we planned most to find Dian.

I could not believe that she was dead, yet where she might be in this savage world, and under what frightful conditions she might be living, I could not guess.

When Perry was rested we returned to the prospector, where he fitted himself out fully like a civilized human being – under-clothing, socks, shoes, khaki jacket and breeches and good, substantial puttees.

When I had come upon him he was clothed in rough *sadak* sandals, a gee-string and a tunic fashioned from the shaggy hide of a *thag*. Now he wore real clothing again for the first time since the ape-folk had stripped us of our apparel that long-gone day that had witnessed our advent within Pellucidar.

With a bandolier of cartridges across his shoulder, two six-shooters at his hips, and a rifle in his hand he was a much rejuvenated Perry.

Indeed he was quite a different person altogether from the rather shaky old man who had entered the prospector with me ten or eleven years before, for the trial trip that had plunged us into such wondrous adventures and into such a strange and hitherto undreamed-of-world.

Now he was straight and active. His muscles, almost atrophied from disuse in his former life, had filled out.

He was still an old man of course, but instead of appearing ten years older than he really was, as he had when we left the outer world, he now appeared about ten years younger. The wild, free life of Pellucidar had worked wonders for him.

Well, it must need have done so or killed him, for a man of Perry's former physical condition could not long have survived the dangers and rigors of the primitive life of the inner world.

Perry had been greatly interested in my map and in the 'Royal Observatory' at Greenwich. By use of the pedometers we had retraced our way to the prospector with ease and accuracy.

Now that we were ready to set out again we decided to follow a different route on the chance that it might lead us into more familiar territory.

I shall not weary you with a repetition of the countless adventures of our long search. Encounters with wild beasts of gigantic size were of almost daily occurrence; but with our deadly express rifles we ran comparatively little risk when one recalls that previously we had both traversed this world of frightful dangers inadequately armed with crude, primitive weapons and all but naked.

We ate and slept many times – so many that we lost count – and so I do not know how long we roamed, though our map shows the distances and directions quite accurately. We must have covered a great many thousand square miles of territory, and yet we had seen nothing in the way of a familiar landmark, when from the heights of a mountain-range we were crossing I descried far in the distance great masses of billowing clouds.

Now clouds are practically unknown in the skies of Pellucidar. The moment that my eyes rested upon them my heart leaped. I seized Perry's arm and, pointing toward the horizonless distance, shouted:

'The Mountains of the Clouds!"

'They lie close to Phutra, and the country of our worst enemies, the Mahars,' Perry remonstrated.

'I know it,' I replied, 'but they give us a starting-point from which to prosecute our search intelligently. They are at least a familiar landmark.

'They tell us that we are upon the right trail and not wandering far in the wrong direction.

'Furthermore, close to the Mountains of the Clouds dwells a good friend, Ja the Mezop. You did not know him, but you know all that he did for me and all that he will gladly do to aid me.

'At least he can direct us upon the right direction toward Sari.'

'The Mountains of the Clouds constitute a mighty range,' replied Perry. 'They must cover an enormous territory. How are you to find your friend in all the great country that is visible from their rugged flanks?'

'Easily,' I answered him, 'for Ja gave me minute directions. I recall almost his exact words:

'"You need merely come to the foot of the highest peak of the Mountains of the Clouds. There you will find a river that flows into the Lural Az.

'"Directly opposite the mouth of the river you will see three large islands far out – so far that they are barely discernible. The one to the extreme left as you face them from the mouth of the river is Anoroc, where I rule the tribe of Anoroc."'

And so we hastened onward toward the great cloudmass that was to be our guide for several weary marches. At last we came close to the towering crags, Alp-like in their grandeur.

Rising nobly among its noble fellows, one stupendous peak reared its giant head thousands of feet above the others. It was he whom we sought; but at its foot no river wound down toward any sea.

'It must rise from the opposite side,' suggested Perry, casting a rueful glance at the forbidding heights that barred our further progress. 'We cannot endure the arctic cold of those high flung passes, and to traverse the endless miles about this interminable range might require a year or more. The land we seek must lie upon the opposite side of the mountains.'

'Then we must cross them,' I insisted.

Perry shrugged.

'We can't do it, David,' he repeated. 'We are dressed for the tropics. We should freeze to death among the snows and glaciers long before we had discovered a pass to the opposite side.'

'We must cross them,' I reiterated. 'We will cross them.'

I had a plan, and that plan we carried out. It took some time.

First we made a permanent camp part way up the slopes where there was good water. Then we set out in search of the great, shaggy cave bear of the higher altitudes.

He is a mighty animal – a terrible animal. He is but little larger than his cousin of the lesser, lower hills; but he makes up for it in the awfulness of his ferocity and in the length and thickness of his shaggy coat. It was his coat that we were after.

We came upon him quite unexpectedly. I was trudging in advance along a rocky trail worn smooth by the padded feet of countless ages of wild beasts. At a shoulder of the mountain around which the path ran I came face to face with the Titan.

I was going up for a fur coat. He was coming down for breakfast. Each realized that here was the very thing he sought.

With a horrid roar the beast charged me.

At my right the cliff rose straight upward for thousands of feet.

At my left it dropped into a dim, abysmal cañon.

In front of me was the bear.

Behind me was Perry.

I shouted to him in warning, and then I raised my rifle and fired into the broad breast of the creature. There was no time to take aim; the thing was too close upon me.

But that my bullet took effect was evident from the howl of rage and pain that broke from the frothing jowls. It didn't stop him, though.

I fired again, and then he was upon me. Down I went beneath his ton of maddened, clawing flesh and bone and sinew.

I thought my time had come. I remember feeling sorry for poor old Perry, left all alone in this inhospitable, savage world.

And then of a sudden I realized that the bear was gone and that I was quite unharmed. I leaped to my feet, my rifle still clutched in my hand, and looked about for my antagonist.

I thought that I should find him farther down the trail, probably finishing Perry, and so I leaped in the direction I supposed him to be, to find Perry perched upon a projecting rock several feet above the trail. My cry of warning had given him time to reach this point of safety.

There he squatted, his eyes wide and his mouth ajar, the picture of abject terror and consternation.

'Where is he?' he cried when he saw me. 'Where is he?'

'Didn't he come this way?' I asked.

'Nothing came this way,' replied the old man. 'But I heard his roars – he must have been as large as an elephant.'

'He was,' I admitted; 'but where in the world do you suppose he disappeared to?'

Then came a possible explanation to my mind. I returned to the point at which the bear had hurled me down and peered over the edge of the cliff into the abyss below.

Far, far down I saw a small brown blotch near the bottom of the cañon. It was the bear.

My second shot must have killed him, and so his dead body, after hurling me to the path, had toppled over into the abyss. I shivered at the thought of how close I, too, must have been to going over with him.

It took us a long time to reach the carcass, and arduous labor to remove the great pelt. But at last the thing was accomplished, and we returned to camp dragging the heavy trophy behind us.

Here we devoted another considerable period to scraping and curing it. When this was done to our satisfaction we made heavy boots, trousers, and coats of the shaggy skin, turning the fur in.

From the scraps we fashioned caps that came down around our ears, with flaps that fell about our shoulders and breasts. We were now fairly well equipped for our search for a pass to the opposite side of the Mountains of the Clouds.

Our first step now was to move our camp upward to the very edge of the perpetual snows which cap this lofty range. Here we built a snug, secure little hut, which we provisioned and stored with fuel for its diminutive fireplace.

With our hut as a base we sallied forth in search of a pass across the range.

Our every move was carefully noted upon our maps which we now kept in duplicate. By this means we were saved tedious and unnecessary retracing of ways already explored.

Systematically we worked upward in both directions from our base, and when we had at last discovered what seemed might prove a feasible pass we moved our belongings to a new hut farther up.

It was hard work – cold, bitter, cruel work. Not a step did we take in advance but the grim reaper strode silently in our tracks.

There were the great cave bears in the timber, and gaunt, lean wolves – huge creatures twice the size of our Canadian timber-wolves. Farther up we were assailed by enormous white bears – hungry, devilish fellows, who came roaring across the rough glacier tops at the first glimpse of us, or stalked us stealthily by scent when they had not yet seen us.

It is one of the peculiarities of life within Pellucidar that man is more often the hunted than the hunter. Myriad are the huge-bellied carnivora of this primitive world. Never, from birth to death, are those great bellies sufficiently filled, so always are their mighty owners prowling about in search of meat.

Terribly armed for battle as they are, man presents to them in his primal state an easy prey, slow of foot, puny of strength, ill-equipped by nature with natural weapons of defense.

The bears looked upon us as easy meat. Only our heavy rifles saved us from prompt extinction. Poor Perry never was a raging lion at heart, and I am convinced that the terrors of that awful period must have caused him poignant mental anguish.

When we were abroad pushing our trail farther and farther toward the distant break which, we assumed, marked a feasible way across the range, we never knew at what second some great engine of clawed and fanged destruction might rush upon us from behind, or lie in wait for us beyond an ice-hummock or a jutting shoulder of the craggy steeps.

The roar of our rifles was constantly shattering the world-old silence of stupendous cañons upon which the eye of man had never before gazed. And when in the comparative safety of our hut we lay down to sleep the great beasts roared and fought without the walls, clawed and battered at the door, or rushed their colossal frames headlong against the hut's sides until it rocked and trembled to the impact.

Yes, it was a gay life.

Perry had got to taking stock of our ammunition each time we returned to the hut. It became something of an obsession with him.

He'd count our cartridges one by one then try to figure how long it would be before the last was expended and we must either remain in the hut until we starved to death or venture forth, empty, to fill the belly of some hungry bear.

I must admit that I, too, felt worried, for our progress was indeed snail-like, and our ammunition could not last forever. In discussing the problem, finally we came to the decision to burn our bridges behind us and make one last supreme effort to cross the divide.

It would mean that we must go without sleep for a long period, and with the further chance that when the time came that sleep could no longer be denied we might still be high in the frozen regions of perpetual snow and ice, where sleep would mean certain death, exposed as we would be to the attacks of wild beasts and without shelter from the hideous cold.

But we decided that we must take these chances, and so at last we set forth from our hut for the last time, carrying such necessities as we felt we could least afford to do without. The bears seemed unusually troublesome and determined that time, and as we clambered slowly upward beyond the highest point to which we had previously attained, the cold became infinitely more intense.

Presently, with two great bears dogging our footsteps we entered a dense fog.

We had reached the heights that are so often cloud-wrapped for long periods. We could see nothing a few paces beyond our noses.

We dared not turn back into the teeth of the bears which we could hear grunting behind us. To meet them in this bewildering fog would have been to court instant death.

Perry was almost overcome by the hopelessness of our situation. He flopped down on his knees and began to pray.

It was the first time I had heard him at his old habit since my return to Pellucidar, and I had thought that he had given up his little idiosyncrasy; but he hadn't. Far from it.

I let him pray for a short time undisturbed, and then as I was about to suggest that we had better be pushing along one of the bears in our rear let out a roar that made the earth faintly tremble beneath our feet.

It brought Perry to his feet as if he had been stung by a wasp, and sent him racing ahead through the blinding fog at a gait that I knew must soon end in disaster were it not checked.

Crevasses in the glacier-ice were far too frequent to permit of reckless speed even in a clear atmosphere, and then there were hideous precipices along the edges of which our way often led us. I shivered as I thought of the poor old fellow's peril.

At the top of my lungs I called to him to stop, but he did not answer me. And then I hurried on in the direction he had gone, faster by far than safety dictated.

For a while I thought I heard him ahead of me, but at last, though I paused often to listen and to call to him, I heard nothing more, not even the grunting of the bears that had been behind us. All was deathly silence – the silence of the tomb. About me lay the thick, impenetrable fog.

I was alone. Perry was gone – gone forever, I had not the slightest doubt.

Somewhere near by lay the mouth of a treacherous fissure, and far down at its icy bottom lay all that was mortal of my old friend, Abner Perry. There would his body lie preserved in its icy sepulcher for countless ages, until on some far distant day the slow-moving river of ice had wound its snail-like way down to the warmer level, there to disgorge its grisly evidence of grim tragedy, and what in that far future age, might mean baffling mystery.

3

Shooting the Chutes – and After

Through the fog I felt my way along by means of my compass. I no longer heard the bears, nor did I encounter one within the fog.

Experience has since taught me that these great beasts are as terror-stricken by this phenomenon as a landsman by a fog at sea, and that no sooner does a fog envelop them than they make the best of their way to lower levels and a clear atmosphere. It was well for me that this was true.

I felt very sad and lonely as I crawled along the difficult footing. My own predicament weighed less heavily upon me than the loss of Perry, for I loved the old fellow.

That I should ever win the opposite slopes of the range I began to doubt, for though I am naturally sanguine, I imagine that the bereavement which had befallen me had cast such a gloom over my spirits that I could see no slightest ray of hope for the future.

Then, too, the blighting, gray oblivion of the cold, damp clouds through which I wandered was dispersing. Hope thrives best in sunlight, and I am sure that it does not thrive at all in a fog.

But the instinct of self-preservation is stronger than hope. It thrives, fortunately, upon nothing. It takes root upon the brink of the grave, and blossoms in the jaws of death. Now it flourished bravely upon the breast of dead hope, and urged me onward and upward in a stern endeavor to justify its existence.

As I advanced the fog became denser. I could see nothing beyond my nose. Even the snow and ice I trod were invisible.

I could not see below the breast of my bearskin coat. I seemed to be floating in a sea of vapor.

To go forward over a dangerous glacier under such conditions was little short of madness; but I could not have stopped going had I known positively that death lay two paces before my nose. In the first place, it was too cold to stop, and in the second, I should have gone mad but for the excitement of the perils that beset each forward step.

For some time the ground had been rougher and steeper, until I had been forced to scale a considerable height that had carried me from the glacier entirely. I was sure from my compass that I was following the right general direction, and so I kept on.

Once more the ground was level. From the wind that blew about me I guessed that I must be upon some exposed peak of ridge.

And then quite suddenly I stepped out into space. Wildly I turned and clutched at the ground that had slipped from beneath my feet.

Only a smooth, icy surface was there. I found nothing to clutch or stay my fall, and a moment later so great was my speed that nothing could have stayed me.

As suddenly as I had pitched into space, with equal suddenness did I emerge from the fog, out of which I shot like a projectile from a cannon into clear daylight. My speed was so great that I could see nothing about me but a blurred and indistinct sheet of smooth and frozen snow, that rushed past me with express-train velocity.

I must have slid downward thousands of feet before the steep incline curved gently on to a broad, smooth, snow-covered plateau. Across this I hurtled with slowly diminishing velocity, until at last objects about me began to take definite shape.

Far ahead, miles and miles away, I saw a great valley and mighty woods, and beyond these a broad expanse of waters. In the nearer foreground I discerned a small, dark blob of color upon the shimmering whiteness of the snow.

'A bear,' thought I, and thanked the instinct that had impelled me to cling tenaciously to my rifle during the moments of my awful tumble.

At the rate I was going it would be but a moment before I should be quite abreast the thing; nor was it long before I came to a sudden stop in soft snow, upon which the sun was shining, not twenty paces from the object of my most immediate apprehension.

It was standing upon its hind legs waiting for me. As I scrambled to my feet to meet it, I dropped my gun in the snow and doubled up with laughter.

It was Perry.

The expression upon his face, combined with the relief I felt at seeing him again safe and sound, was too much for my overwrought nerves.

'David!' he cried. 'David, my boy! God has been good to an old man. He has answered my prayer.'

It seems that Perry in his mad flight had plunged over the brink at about the same point as that at which I had stepped over it a short time later.

Chance had done for us what long periods of rational labor had failed to accomplish.

We had crossed the divide. We were upon the side of the Mountains of the Clouds that we had for so long been attempting to reach.

We looked about. Below us were green trees and warm jungles. In the distance was a great sea.

'The Lural Az,' I said, pointing toward its blue-green surface.

Somehow – the gods alone can explain it – Perry, too, had clung to his rifle during his mad descent of the icy slope. For that there was cause for great rejoicing.

Neither of us was worse for his experience, so after shaking the snow from our clothing, we set off at a great rate down toward the warmth and comfort of the forest and the jungle.

The going was easy by comparison with the awful obstacles we had had to encounter upon the opposite side of the divide. There were beasts, of course, but we came through safely.

Before we halted to eat or rest, we stood beside a little mountain brook beneath the wondrous trees of the primeval forest in an atmosphere of warmth and comfort. It reminded me of an early June day in the Maine woods.

We fell to work with our short axes and cut enough small trees to build a rude protection from the fiercer beasts. Then we lay down to sleep.

How long we slept I do not know. Perry says that inasmuch as there is no means of measuring time within Pellucidar, there can be no such thing as time here, and that we may have slept an outer earthly year, or we may have slept but a second.

But this I know. We had stuck the ends of some of the saplings into the ground in the building of our shelter, first stripping the leaves and branches from them, and when we awoke we found that many of them had thrust forth sprouts.

Personally, I think that we slept at least a month; but who may say? The sun marked midday when we closed our eyes; it was still in the same position when we opened them; nor had it varied a hair's breadth in the interim.

It is most baffling, this question of elapsed time within Pellucidar.

Anyhow, I was famished when we awoke. I think that it was the pangs of hunger that awoke me. Ptarmigan and wild boar fell before my revolver within a dozen moments of my awakening. Perry soon had a roaring fire blazing by the brink of the little stream.

It was a good and delicious meal we made. Though we did not eat the entire boar, we made a very large hole in him, while the ptarmigan was but a mouthful.

Having satisfied our hunger, we determined to set forth at once in search of Anoroc and my old friend, Ja the Mezop. We each thought that by follow-ing the little stream downward, we should come upon the large river which Ja had told me emptied into the Lural Az opposite his island.

We did so; nor were we disappointed, for at last after a pleasant journey – and what journey would not be pleasant after the hardships we had endured among the peaks of the Mountains of the Clouds – we came upon a broad flood that rushed majestically onward in the direction of the great sea we had seen from the snowy slopes of the mountains.

For three long marches we followed the left bank of the growing river, until at last we saw it roll its mighty volume into the vast waters of the sea. Far out across the rippling ocean we described three islands. The one to the left must be Anoroc.

At last we had come close to a solution of our problem – the road to Sari.

But how to reach the islands was now the foremost question in our minds. We must build a canoe.

Perry is a most resourceful man. He has an axiom which carries the thought-kernel that what man has done, man can do, and it doesn't cut any figure with Perry whether a fellow knows how to do it or not.

He set out to make gunpowder once, shortly after our escape from Phutra and at the beginning of the confederation of the wild tribes of Pellucidar. He said that some one, without any knowledge of the fact that such a thing might be concocted, had once stumbled upon it by accident, and so he couldn't see why a fellow who knew all about powder except how to make it couldn't do as well.

He worked mighty hard mixing all sorts of things together, until finally he evolved a substance that looked like powder. He had been very proud of the stuff, and had gone about the village of the Sarians exhibiting it to every one who would listen to him, and explaining what its purpose was and what terrific havoc it would work, until finally the natives became so terrified at the stuff that they wouldn't come within a rod of Perry and his invention.

Finally, I suggested that we experiment with it and see what it would do, so Perry built a fire, after placing the powder at a safe distance, and then touched a glowing ember to a minute particle of the deadly explosive. It extinguished the ember.

Repeated experiments with it determined me that in searching for a high explosive, Perry had stumbled upon a fire-extinguisher that would have made his fortune for him back in our own world.

So now he set himself to work to build a scientific canoe. I had suggested that we construct a dugout, but Perry convinced me that we must build something more in keeping with our positions of supermen in this world of the Stone Age.

'We must impress these natives with our superiority,' he explained. 'You must not forget, David, that you are emperor of Pellucidar. As such you may not with dignity approach the shores of a foreign power in so crude a vessel as a dugout.'

I pointed out to Perry that it wasn't much more incongruous for the emperor to cruise in a canoe, than it was for the prime minister to attempt to build one with his own hands.

He had to smile at that; but in extenuation of his act he assured me that it was quite customary for prime ministers to give their personal attention to the building of imperial navies; 'and this,' he said, 'is the imperial navy of his Serene Highness, David I, Emperor of the Federated Kingdoms of Pellucidar.'

I grinned; but Perry was quite serious about it. It had always seemed rather more or less of a joke to me that I should be addressed as majesty and all the rest of it. Yet my imperial power and dignity had been a very real thing during my brief reign.

Twenty tribes had joined the federation, and their chiefs had sworn eternal fealty to one another and to me. Among them were many powerful though savage nations. Their chiefs we had made kings; their tribal lands kingdoms.

We had armed them with bows and arrows and swords, in addition to their own more primitive weapons. I had trained them in military discipline and in so much of the art of war as I had gleaned from extensive reading of the campaigns of Napoleon, Von Moltke, Grant, and the ancients.

We had marked out as best we could natural boundaries dividing the various kingdoms. We had warned tribes beyond these boundaries that they must not trespass, and we had marched against and severely punished those who had.

We had met and defeated the Mahars and the Sagoths. In short, we had demonstrated our rights to empire, and very rapidly were we being recognized and heralded abroad when my departure for the outer world and Hooja's treachery had set us back.

But now I had returned. The work that fate had undone must be done again, and though I must need smile at my imperial honors, I none the less felt the weight of duty and obligation that rested upon my shoulders.

Slowly the imperial navy progressed toward completion. She was a wondrous craft, but I had my doubts about her. When I voiced them to Perry, he reminded me gently that my people for many generations had been mine-owners, not ship-builders, and consequently I couldn't be expected to know much about the matter.

I was minded to inquire into his hereditary fitness to design battleships; but inasmuch as I already knew that his father had been a minister in a backwoods village far from the coast, I hesitated lest I offend the dear old fellow.

He was immensely serious about his work, and I must admit that in so far as appearance went he did extremely well with the meager tools and assistance at his command. We had only two short axes and our hunting knives; yet with these we hewed trees, split them into planks, surfaced and fitted them.

The 'navy' was some forty feet in length by ten feet beam. Her sides were quite straight and fully ten feet high – 'for the purpose,' explained Perry, 'of adding dignity to her appearance and rendering it less easy for an enemy to board her.'

As a matter of fact, I knew that he had had in mind the safety of her crew under javelin-fire – the lofty sides made an admirable shelter. Inside she reminded me of nothing so much as a floating trench. There was also some slight analogy to a huge coffin.

Her prow sloped sharply backward from the water-line – quite like a line of battleship. Perry had designed her more for moral effect upon an enemy, I think, than for any real harm she might inflict, and so those parts which were to show were the most imposing.

Below the water-line she was practically non-existent. She should have had considerable draft; but, as the enemy couldn't have seen it, Perry decided to do away with it, and so made her flat-bottomed. It was this that caused my doubts about her.

There was another little idiosyncrasy of design that escaped us both until she was about ready to launch – there was no method of propulsion. Her sides were far too high to permit the use of sweeps, and when Perry suggested that we pole her, I remonstrated on the grounds that it would be a most undignified and awkward manner of sweeping down upon the foe, even if we could find or wield poles that would reach to the bottom of the ocean.

Finally I suggested that we convert her into a sailing vessel. When once the idea took hold Perry was most enthusiastic about it, and nothing would do but a four-masted, full-rigged ship.

Again I tried to dissuade him, but he was simply crazy over the psychological effect which the appearance of this strange and mighty craft would have upon the natives of Pellucidar. So we rigged her with thin hides for sails and dried gut for rope.

Neither of us know much about sailing a full-rigged ship; but that didn't worry me a great deal, for I was confident that we should never be called upon to do so, and as the day of launching approached I was positive of it.

We had built her upon a low bank of the river close to where it empties into the sea, and just above high tide. Her keel we had laid upon several rollers cut from small trees, the ends of the rollers in turn resting upon parallel tracks of long saplings. Her stern was toward the water.

A few hours before we were ready to launch her she made quite an imposing picture, for Perry had insisted upon setting every shred of 'canvas.' I told him that I didn't know much about it, but I was sure that at launching the hull only should have been completed, everything else being completed after she had floated safely.

At the last minute there was some delay while we sought a name for her. I wanted her christened the Perry in honor both of her designer and that other great naval genius of another world, Captain Oliver Hazard Perry, of the United States Navy. But Perry was too modest; he wouldn't hear of it.

We finally decided to establish a system in the naming of the fleet. Battle-ships of the first-class should bear the names of kingdoms of the federation; armored cruisers the names of kings; cruisers the names of cities, and so on down the line. Therefore, we decided to name the first battle-ship *Sari*, after the first of the federated kingdoms.

The launching of the *Sari* proved easier than I contemplated. Perry wanted me to get in and break something over the bow as she floated out upon the bosom of the river, but I told him that I should feel safer on dry land until I saw which side up the *Sari* would float.

I could see by the expression of the old man's face that my words had hurt him; but I noticed that he didn't offer to get in himself, and so I felt less contrition than I might otherwise.

When we cut the ropes and removed the blocks that held the *Sari* in place she started for the water with a lunge. Before she hit it she was going at a reckless speed, for we had laid our tracks quite down to the water, greased them, and at intervals placed rollers all ready to receive the ship as she moved forward with stately dignity. But there was no dignity in the *Sari*.

When she touched the surface of the river she must have been going twenty or thirty miles an hour. Her momentum carried her well out into the stream, until she came to a sudden halt at the end of the long line which we had had the foresight to attach to her bow and fasten to a large tree upon the bank.

The moment her progress was checked she promptly capsized. Perry was overwhelmed. I didn't upbraid him, nor remind him that I had 'told him so.'

His grief was so genuine and so apparent that I didn't have the heart to reproach him, even were I inclined to that particular sort of meanness.

'Come, come, old man!' I cried. 'It's not as bad as it looks. Give me a hand with this rope, and we'll drag her up as far as we can; and then when the tide goes out we'll try another scheme. I think we can make a go of her yet.'

Well, we managed to get her up into shallow water. When the tide receded she lay there on her side in the mud, quite a pitiable object for the premier battle-ship of a world – 'the terror of the seas' was the way Perry had occasionally described her.

We had to work fast; but before the tide came in again we had stripped her of her sails and masts, righted her, and filler her about a quarter full of rock ballast. If she didn't stick too fast in the mud I was sure that she would float this time right side up.

I can tell you that it was with palpitating hearts that we sat upon the riverbank and watched that tide come slowly in. The tides of Pellucidar don't amount to much by comparison with our higher tides of the outer world, but I knew that it ought to prove ample to float the *Sari*.

Nor was I mistaken. Finally we had the satisfaction of seeing the vessel rise out of the mud and float slowly upstream with the tide. As the water rose we pulled her in quite close to the bank and clambered aboard.

She rested safely now upon an even keel; nor did she leak, for she was well calked with fiber and tarry pitch. We rigged up a single short mast and light sail, fastened planking down over the ballast to form a deck, worked her out into midstream with a couple of sweeps, and dropped our primitive stone anchor to await the turn of the tide that would bear us out to sea.

While we waited we devoted the time to the construction of an upper deck, since the one immediately above the ballast was some seven feet from the gunwale. The second deck was four feet above this. In it was a large, commodious hatch, leading to the lower deck. The sides of the ship rose three feet above the upper deck, forming an excellent breastwork, which we loopholed at intervals that we might lie prone and fire upon an enemy.

Though we were sailing out upon a peaceful mission in search of my friend Ja, we knew that we might meet with people of some other island who would prove unfriendly.

At last the tide turned. We weighed anchor. Slowly we drifted down the great river toward the sea.

About us swarmed the mighty denizens of the primeval deep – plesiosauri and ichthyosauria with all their horrid, slimy cousins whose names were as the names of aunts and uncles to Perry, but which I have never been able to recall an hour after having heard them.

At last we were safely launched upon the journey to which we had looked forward for so long, and the results of which meant so much to me.

4

Friendship and Treachery

The *Sari* proved a most erratic craft. She might have done well enough upon a park lagoon if safely anchored, but upon the bosom of a mighty ocean she left much to be desired.

Sailing with the wind she did her best; but in quartering or when close-hauled she drifted terribly, as a nautical man might have guessed she would. We couldn't keep within miles of our course, and our progress was pitifully slow.

Instead of making for the island of Anoroc, we bore far to the right, until it became evident that we should have to pass between the two right-hand islands and attempt to return toward Anoroc from the opposite side.

As we neared the islands Perry was quite overcome by their beauty. When we were directly between two of them he fairly went into raptures; nor could I blame him.

The tropical luxuriance of the foliage that dripped almost to the water's edge and the vivid colors of the blooms that shot the green made a most gorgeous spectacle.

Perry was right in the midst of a flowery panegyric on the wonders of the peaceful beauty of the scene when a canoe shot out from the nearest island. There were a dozen warriors in it; it was quickly followed by a second and third.

Of course we couldn't know the intentions of the strangers, but we could pretty well guess them.

Perry wanted to man the sweeps and try to get away from them, but I soon convinced him that any speed of which the *Sari* was capable would be far too slow to outdistance the swift, though awkward, dugouts of the Mezops.

I waited until they were quite close enough to hear me, and then I hailed them. I told them we were friends of the Mezops, and that we were upon a visit to Ja of Anoroc, to which they replied that they were at war with Ja, and that if we would wait a minute they'd board us and throw our corpses to the azdyryths.

I warned them that they would get the worst of it if they didn't leave us alone, but they only shouted in derision and paddled swiftly toward us. It was evident that they were considerably impressed by the appearance and dimensions of our craft, but as these fellows know no fear they were not at all awed.

Seeing that they were determined to give battle, I leaned over the rail of the *Sari* and brought the imperial battle-squadron of the Emperor of Pellucidar into action for the first time in the history of a world. In other and simpler words, I fired my revolver at the nearest canoe.

The effect was magical. A warrior rose from his knees, threw his paddle aloft, stiffened into rigidity for an instant, and then toppled overboard.

The others ceased paddling, and, with wide eyes, looked first at me and then at the battling sea-things which fought for the corpse of their comrade. To them it must have seemed a miracle that I should be able to stand at thrice the range of the most powerful javelin-thrower and with a loud noise and a smudge of smoke slay one of their number with an invisible missile.

But only for an instant were they paralyzed with wonder. Then, with savage shouts, they fell once more to their paddles and forged rapidly toward us.

Again and again I fired. At each shot a warrior sank to the bottom of the canoe or tumbled overboard.

When the prow of the first craft touched the side of the *Sari* it contained only dead and dying men. The other two dugouts were approaching rapidly, so I turned my attention toward them.

I think that they must have been commencing to have some doubts – those wild, naked, red warriors – for when the first man fell in the second boat the others stopped paddling and commenced to jabber among themselves.

The third boat pulled up alongside the second and its crews joined in the conference. Taking advantage of the lull in the battle, I called out to the survivors to return to their shore.

'I have no fight with you,' I cried, and then I told them who I was and added that if they would live in peace they must sooner or later join forces with me.

'Go back now to your people,' I counseled them, 'and tell them that you have seen David I, Emperor of the Federated Kingdom of Pellucidar, and that singlehanded he has overcome you, just as he intends overcoming the Mahars and the Sagoths and any other peoples of Pellucidar who threaten the peace and welfare of his empire.'

Slowly they turned the noses of their canoes toward land. It was evident that they were impressed; yet that they were loath to give up without further contesting my claim to naval supremacy was also apparent, for some of their number seemed to be exhorting the others to a renewal of the conflict.

However, at last they drew slowly away, and the *Sari*, which had not decreased her snail-like speed during this, her first engagement, continued upon her slow, uneven way.

Presently Perry stuck his head up through the hatch and hailed me. 'Have the scoundrels departed?' he asked. 'Have you killed them all?'

'Those whom I failed to kill have departed, Perry,' I replied.

He came out on deck and, peering over the side, descried the lone canoe floating a short distance astern with its grim and grisly freight. Farther his eyes wandered to the retreating boats.

'David,' said he at last, 'this is a notable occasion. It is a great day in the annals of Pellucidar. We have won a glorious victory.

'Your majesty's navy has routed a fleet of the enemy thrice its own size, manned by ten times as many men. Let us give thanks.'

I could scarce restrain a smile at Perry's use of the pronoun 'we,' yet I was glad to share the rejoicing with him as I shall always be glad to share everything with the dear old fellow.

Perry is the only male coward I have ever known whom I could respect and love. He was not created for fighting; but I think that if the occasion should ever arise where it became necessary he would give his life cheerfully for me – yes, I *know* it.

It took us a long time to work around the islands and draw in close to Anoroc. In the leisure afforded we took turns working on our map, and by means of the compass and a little guesswork we set down the shoreline we had left and the three islands with fair accuracy.

Crossed sabers marked the spot where the first great naval engagement of a world had taken place. In a notebook we jotted down, as had been our custom, details that would be of historical value later.

Opposite Anoroc we came to anchor quite close to shore. I knew from my previous experience with the tortuous trails of the island that I could never find my way inland to the hidden tree-village of the Mezop chieftain, Ja; so we remained aboard the *Sari*, firing our express rifles at intervals to attract the attention of the natives.

After some ten shots had been fired at considerable intervals a body of copper-colored warriors appeared upon the shore. They watched us for a moment and then I hailed them, asking the whereabouts of my old friend Ja.

They did not reply at once, but stood with their heads together in serious and animated discussion. Continually they turned their eyes toward our strange craft. It was evident that they were greatly puzzled by our appearance as well as unable to explain the source of the loud noises that had attracted their attention to us. At last one of the warriors addressed us.

'Who are you who seek Ja?' he asked. 'What would you of our chief?'

'We are friends,' I replied. 'I am David. Tell Ja that David, whose life he once saved from a *sithic*, has come again to visit him.

'If you will send out a canoe we will come ashore. We cannot bring our great warship closer in.'

Again they talked for a considerable time. Then two of them entered a canoe that several dragged from its hiding-place in the jungle and paddled swiftly toward us.

They were magnificent specimens of manhood. Perry had never seen a member of this red race close to before. In fact, the dead men in the canoe we had left astern after the battle and the survivors who were paddling rapidly toward their shore were the first he ever had seen. He had been greatly impressed by their physical beauty and the promise of superior intelligence which their well-shaped skulls gave.

The two who now paddled out received us into their canoe with dignified courtesy. To my inquiries relative to Ja they explained that he had not been in the village when our signals were heard, but that runners had been sent out after him and that doubtless he was already upon his way to the coast.

One of the men remembered me from the occasion of my former visit to the island; he was extremely agreeable the moment that he came close enough to recognize me. He said that Ja would be delighted to welcome me, and that all the tribe of Anoroc knew of me by repute, and had received explicit instructions from their chieftain that if any of them should ever come upon me to show me every kindness and attention.

Upon shore we were received with equal honor. While we stood conversing with our bronze friends a tall warrior leaped suddenly from the jungle.

It was Ja. As his eyes fell upon me his face lighted with pleasure. He came quickly forward to greet me after the manner of his tribe.

Toward Perry he was equally hospitable. The old man fell in love with the savage giant as completely as had I. Ja conducted us along the maze-like trail to his strange village, where he gave over one of the tree-houses for our exclusive use.

Perry was much interested in the unique habitation, which resembled nothing so much as a huge wasp's nest built around the bole of a tree well above the ground.

After we had eaten and rested Ja came to see us with a number of his head men. They listened attentively to my story, which included a narrative of the events leading to the formation of the federated kingdoms, the battle with the Mahars, my journey to the outer world, and my return to Pellucidar and search for Sari and my mate.

Ja told me that the Mezops had heard something of the federation and had been much interested in it. He had even gone so far as to send a party of warriors toward Sari to investigate the reports, and to arrange for the entrance of Anoroc into the empire in case it appeared that there was any truth in the rumors that one of the aims of the federation was the overthrow of the Mahars.

The delegation had met with a party of Sagoths. As there had been a truce between the Mahars and the Mezops for many generations, they camped with these warriors of the reptiles, from whom they learned that the federation had gone to pieces. So the party returned to Anoroc.

When I showed Ja our map and explained its purpose to him, he was much interested. The location of Anoroc, the Mountains of the Clouds, the river, and the strip of seacoast were all familiar to him.

He quickly indicated the position of the inland sea and close beside it, the city of Phutra, where one of the powerful Mahar nations had its seat. He likewise showed us where Sari should be and carried his own coast-line as far north and south as it was known to him.

His additions to the map convinced us that Greenwich lay upon the verge of this same sea, and that it might be reached by water more easily than by the arduous crossing of the mountains or the dangerous approach through Phutra, which lay almost directly in line between Anoroc and Greenwich to the northwest.

If Sari lay upon the same water then the shore-line must bend far back toward the southwest of Greenwich – an assumption which, by the way, we found later to be true. Also, Sari was upon a lofty plateau at the southern end of a mighty gulf of the Great Ocean.

The location which Ja gave to distant Amoz puzzled us, for it placed it due north of Greenwich, apparently in mid-ocean. As Ja had never been so far and knew only of Amoz through hearsay, we thought that he must be mistaken; but he was not. Amoz lies directly north of Greenwich across the mouth of the same gulf as that upon which Sari is.

The sense of direction and location of these primitive Pellucidarians is little short of uncanny, as I have had occasion to remark in the past. You may take one of them to the uttermost ends of his world, to places of which he has never even heard, yet without sun or moon or stars to guide him, without map or compass, he will travel straight for home in the shortest direction.

Mountains, rivers, and seas may have to be gone around, but never once does his sense of direction fail him – the homing instinct is supreme.

In the same remarkable way they never forget the location of any place to which they have ever been, and know that of many of which they have only heard from others who have visited them.

In short, each Pellucidarian is a walking geography of his own district and of much of the country contiguous thereto. It always proved of the greatest aid to Perry and me; nevertheless we were anxious to enlarge our map, for we at least were not endowed with the homing instinct.

After several long councils it was decided that, in order to expedite matters, Perry should return to the prospector with a strong party of Mezops and fetch the freight I had brought from the outer world. Ja and his warriors were much impressed by our firearms, and were also anxious to build boats with sails.

As we had arms at the prospector and also books on boat-building we thought that it might prove an excellent idea to start these naturally maritime people upon the construction of a well built navy of staunch sailing-vessels. I was sure that with definite plans to go by Perry could oversee the construction of an adequate flotilla.

I warned him, however, not to be too ambitious, and to forget about dreadnoughts and armored cruisers for a while and build instead a few small sailing-boats that could be manned by four or five men.

I was to proceed to Sari, and while prosecuting my search for Dian attempt at the same time the rehabilitation of the federation. Perry was going as far as possible by water, with the chances that the entire trip might be made in that manner, which proved to be the fact.

With a couple of Mezops as companions I started for Sari. In order to avoid crossing the principal range of the Mountains of the Clouds we took a route that passed a little way south of Phutra. We had eaten four times and slept once, and were, as my companions told me, not far from the great Mahar city, when we were suddenly confronted by a considerable band of Sagoths.

They did not attack us, owing to the peace which exists between the Mahars and the Mezops, but I could see that they looked upon me with considerable suspicion. My friends told them that I was a stranger from a remote country, and as we had previously planned against such a contingency I pretended ignorance of the language which the human beings of Pellucidar employ in conversing with the gorilla-like soldiery of the Mahars.

I noticed, and not without misgivings, that the leader of the Sagoths eyed me with an expression that betokened partial recognition. I was sure that he had seen me before during the period of my incarceration in Phutra and that he was trying to recall my identity.

It worried me not a little. I was extremely thankful when we bade them adieu and continued upon our journey.

Several times during the next few marches I became acutely conscious of the sensation of being watched by unseen eyes, but I did not speak of my suspicions to my companions. Later I had reason to regret my reticence, for—

Well, this is how it happened:

We had killed an antelope and after eating our fill I had lain down to sleep. The Pellucidarians, who seem seldom if ever to require sleep, joined me in this instance, for we had had a very trying march along the northern foothills of the Mountains of the Clouds, and now with their bellies filled with meat they seemed ready for slumber.

When I awoke it was with a start to find a couple of huge Sagoths astride me. They pinioned my arms and legs, and later chained my wrists behind my back. Then they let me up.

I saw my companions; the brave fellows lay dead where they had slept, javelined to death without a chance at self-defense.

I was furious. I threatened the Sagoth leader with all sorts of dire reprisals; but when he heard me speak the hybrid language that is the medium of communication between his kind and the human race of the inner world he only grinned, as much as to say, 'I thought so!'

They had not taken my revolvers or ammunition away from me because they did not know what they were; but my heavy rifle I had lost. They simply left it where it had lain beside me.

So low in the scale of intelligence are they, that they had not sufficient interest in this strange object even to fetch it along with them.

I knew from the direction of our march that they were taking me to Phutra. Once there I did not need much of an imagination to picture what my fate would be. It was the arena and a wild thag or fierce tarag for me – unless the Mahars elected to take me to the pits.

In that case my end would be no more certain, though infinitely more horrible and painful, for in the pits I should be subjected to cruel vivisection. From what I had once seen of their methods in the pits of Phutra I knew them to be the opposite of merciful, whereas in the arena I should be quickly despatched by some savage beast.

Arrived at the underground city, I was taken immediately before a slimy Mahar. When the creature had received the report of the Sagoth its cold eyes glistened with malice and hatred as they were turned balefully upon me.

I knew then that my identity had been guessed. With a show of excitement that I had never before seen evinced by a member of the dominant race of Pellucidar, the Mahar hustled me away, heavily guarded, through the main avenue of the city to one of the principal buildings.

Here we were ushered into a great hall where presently many Mahars gathered.

In utter silence they conversed, for they have no oral speech since they are without auditory nerves. Their method of communication Perry has likened to the projection of a sixth sense into a fourth dimension, where it becomes cognizable to the sixth sense of their audience.

Be that as it may, however, it was evident that I was the subject of discussion, and from the hateful looks bestowed upon me not a particularly pleasant subject.

How long I waited for their decision I do not know, but it must have been a very long time. Finally one of the Sagoths addressed me. He was acting as interpreter for his masters.

'The Mahars will spare your life,' he said, 'and release you on one condition.'

'And what is that condition?' I asked, though I could guess its terms.

'That you return to them that which you stole from the pits of Phutra when you killed the four Mahars and escaped,' he replied.

I had thought that that would be it. The great secret upon which depended the continuance of the Mahar race was safely hid where only Dian and I knew.

I ventured to imagine that they would have given me much more than my liberty to have it safely in their keeping again; but after that – what?

Would they keep their promise?

I doubted it. With the secret of artificial propagation, once more in their hands their numbers would soon be made so to overrun the world of Pellucidar that there could be no hope for the eventual supremacy of the human race, the cause for which I so devoutly hoped, for which I had consecrated my life, and for which I was willing to give my life.

Yes! In that moment as I stood before the heartless tribunal I felt that my life would be a very little thing to give could it save to the human race of Pellucidar the chance to come into its own by insuring the eventual extinction of the hated, powerful Mahars.

'Come!' exclaimed the Sagoths. 'The mighty Mahars await your reply.'

'You may say to them,' I answered, 'that I shall not tell them where the great secret is hid.'

When this had been translated to them there was a great beating of reptilian wings, gaping of sharp-fanged jaws, and hideous hissing. I thought that they were about to fell upon me on the spot, and so I laid my hands upon my revolvers; but at length they became more quiet and presently transmitted some command to my Sagoth guard, the chief of which laid a heavy hand upon my arm and pushed me roughly before him from the audience-chamber.

They took me to the pits, where I lay carefully guarded. I was sure that I was to be taken to the vivisection laboratory, and it required all my courage to fortify myself against the terrors of so fearful a death. In Pellucidar, where there is no time, death-agonies may endure for eternities.

Accordingly, I had to steel myself against an endless doom, which now stared me in the face!

5

Surprises

But at last the allotted moment arrived – the moment for which I had been trying to prepare myself, for how long I could not even guess. A great Sagoth came and spoke some words of command to those who watched over me. I was jerked roughly to my feet and with little consideration hustled upward toward the higher levels.

Out into the broad avenue they conducted me, where, amid huge throngs of Mahars, Sagoths, and heavily guarded slaves, I was led, or, rather, pushed and shoved roughly, along in the same direction that the mob moved. I had seen such a concourse of people once before in the buried city of Phutra; I guessed, and rightly, that we were bound for the great arena where slaves who are condemned to death meet their end.

Into the vast amphitheater they took me, stationing me at the extreme end of the arena. The queen came, with her slimy, sickening retinue. The seats were filled. The show was about to commence.

Then, from a little doorway in the opposite end of the structure, a girl was led into the arena. She was at a considerable distance from me. I could not see her features.

I wondered what fate awaited this other poor victim and myself, and why they had chosen to have us die together. My own fate, or rather, my thought of it, was submerged in the natural pity I felt for this lone girl, doomed to die horribly beneath the cold, cruel eyes of her awful captors. Of what crime could she be guilty that she must expiate it in the dreaded arena?

As I stood thus thinking, another door, this time at one of the long sides of the arena, was thrown open, and into the theater of death slunk a mighty tarag, the huge cave tiger of the Stone Age. At my sides were my revolvers. My captors had not taken them from me, because they did not yet realize their nature. Doubtless they thought them some strange manner of war-club, and as those who are condemned to the arena are permitted weapons of defense, they let me keep them.

The girl they had armed with a javelin. A brass pin would have been almost as effective against the ferocious monster they had loosed upon her.

The tarag stood for a moment looking about him – first up at the vast audience and then about the arena. He did not seem to see me at all, but his eyes fell presently upon the girl. A hideous roar broke from his titanic lungs

– a roar which ended in a long-drawn scream that is more human than the death-cry of a tortured woman – more human but more awesome. I could scarce restrain a shudder.

Slowly the beast turned and moved toward the girl. Then it was that I came to myself and to a realization of my duty. Quickly and as noiselessly as possible I ran down the arena in pursuit of the grim creature. As I ran I drew one of my pitifully futile weapons. Ah! Could I but have had my lost express-gun in my hands at that moment! A single well-placed shot would have crumbled even this great monster. The best I could hope to accomplish was to divert the thing from the girl to myself and then to place as many bullets as possible in it before it reached and mauled me into insensibility and death.

There is a certain unwritten law of the arena that vouchsafes freedom and immunity to the victor, be he beast or human being – both of whom, by the way, are all the same to the Mahar. That is, they were accustomed to look upon man as a lower animal before Perry and I broke through the Pellucidarian crust, but I imagine that they were beginning to alter their views a trifle and to realize that in the *gilak* – their word for human being – they had a highly organized, reasoning being to contend with.

Be that as it may, the chances were that the tarag alone would profit by the law of the arena. A few more of his long strides, a prodigious leap, and he would be upon the girl. I raised a revolver and fired. The bullet struck him in the left hind leg. It couldn't have damaged him much; but the report of the shot brought him around, facing me.

I think the snarling visage of a huge, enraged, saber-toothed tiger is one of the most terrible sights in the world. Especially if he be snarling at you and there be nothing between the two of you but bare sand.

Even as he faced me a little cry from the girl carried my eyes beyond the brute to her face. Hers was fastened upon me with an expression of incredulity that baffles description. There was both hope and horror in them, too.

'Dian!' I cried. 'My Heavens, Dian!'

I saw her lips form the name David, as with raised javelin she rushed forward upon the tarag. She was a tigress then – a primitive savage female defending her loved one. Before she could reach the beast with her puny weapon, I fired again at the point where the tarag's neck met his left shoulder. If I could get a bullet through there it might reach his heart. The bullet didn't reach his heart, but it stopped him for an instant.

It was then that a strange thing happened. I heard a great hissing from the stands occupied by the Mahars, and as I glance toward them I saw three mighty *thipdars* – the winged dragons that guard the queen, or, as Perry calls them, pterodactyls – rise swiftly from their rocks and dart lightning-like, toward the center of the arena. They are huge, powerful reptiles.

One of them, with the advantage which his wings might give him, would easily be a match for a cave bear or a tarag.

These three, to my consternation, swooped down upon the tarag as he was gathering himself for a final charge upon me. They buried their talons in his back and lifted him bodily from the arena as if he had been a chicken in the clutches of a hawk.

What could it mean?

I was baffled for an explanation; but with the tarag gone I lost no time in hastening to Dian's side. With a little cry of delight she threw herself into my arms. So lost were we in the ecstasy of reunion that neither of us – to this day – can tell what became of the tarag.

The first thing we were aware of was the presence of a body of Sagoths about us. Gruffly they commanded us to follow them. They led us from the arena and back through the streets of Phutra to the audience chamber in which I had been tried and sentenced. Here we found ourselves facing the same cold, cruel tribunal.

Again a Sagoth acted an interpreter. He explained that our lives had been spared because at the last moment Tu-al-sa had returned to Phutra, and seeing me in the arena had prevailed upon the queen to spare my life.

'Who is Tu-al-sa?' I asked.

'A Mahar whose last male ancestor was – ages ago – the last of the male rulers among the Mahars,' he replied.

'Why should she wish to have my life spared?'

He shrugged his shoulders and then repeated my question to the Mahar spokesman. When the latter had explained in the strange sign-language that passes for speech between the Mahars and their fighting men the Sagoth turned again to me:

'For a long time you had Tu-al-sa in your power,' he explained. 'You might easily have killed her or abandoned her in a strange world – but you did neither. You did not harm her, and you brought her back with you to Pellucidar and set her free to return to Phutra. This is your reward.'

Now I understood. The Mahar who had been my involuntary companion upon my return to the outer world was Tu-al-sa. This was the first time that I had learned the lady's name. I thanked fate that I had not left her upon the sands of the Sahara – or put a bullet in her, as I had been tempted to do. I was surprised to discover that gratitude was a characteristic of the dominant race of Pellucidar. I could never think of them as, aught but cold-blooded, brainless reptiles, though Perry had devoted much time in explaining to me that owing to a strange freak of evolution among all the genera of the inner world, this species of the reptilia had advanced to a position quite analogous to that which man holds upon the outer crust.

He had often told me that there was every reason to believe from their writings, which he had learned to read while we were incarcerated in Phutra, that they were a just race, and that in certain branches of science and arts they were quite well advanced, especially in genetics and metaphysics, engineering and architecture.

While it had always been difficult for me to look upon these things as other than slimy, winged crocodiles – which, by the way, they do not at all resemble – I was now forced to a realization of the fact that I was in the hands of enlightened creatures – for justice and gratitude are certain hallmarks of rationality and culture.

But what they purposed for us further was of most imminent interest to me. They might save us from the tarag and yet not free us. They looked upon us yet, to some extent, I knew, as creatures of a lower order, and so as we are unable to place ourselves in the position of the brutes we enslave – thinking that they are happier in bondage than in the free fulfillment of the purposes for which nature intended them – the Mahars, too, might consider our welfare better conserved in captivity than among the dangers of the savage freedom we craved. Naturally, I was next impelled to inquire their further intent.

To my question, put through the Sagoth interpreter, I received the reply that having spared my life they considered that Tu-al-sa's debt of gratitude was canceled. They still had against me, however, the crime of which I had been guilty – the unforgivable crime of stealing the great secret. They, therefore, intended holding Dian and me prisoners until the manuscript was returned to them.

They would, they said, send an escort of Sagoths with me to fetch the precious document from its hiding-place, keeping Dian at Phutra as a hostage and releasing us both the moment that the document was safely restored to their queen.

There was no doubt but that they had the upper hand. However, there was so much more at stake than the liberty or even the lives of Dian and myself, that I did not deem it expedient to accept their offer without giving the matter careful thought.

Without the great secret this maleless race must eventually become extinct. For ages they had fertilized their eggs by an artificial process, the secret of which lay hidden in the little cave of a far-off valley where Dian and I had spent our honeymoon. I was none too sure that I could find the valley again, nor that I cared to. So long as the powerful reptilian race of Pellucidar continued to propagate, just so long would the position of man within the inner world be jeopardized. There could not be two dominant races.

I said as much to Dian.

'You used to tell me,' she replied, 'of the wonderful things you could accomplish with the inventions of your own world. Now you have returned with all that is necessary to place this great power in the hands of the men of Pellucidar.

'You told me of great engines of destruction which would cast a bursting ball of metal among our enemies, killing hundreds of them at one time.

'You told me of mighty fortresses of stone which a thousand men armed with big and little engines such as these could hold forever against a million Sagoths.

'You told me of great canoes which moved across the water without paddles, and which spat death from holes in their sides.

'All these may now belong to the men of Pellucidar. Why should we fear the Mahars?

'Let them breed! Let their numbers increase by thousands. They will be helpless before the power of the Emperor of Pellucidar.

'But if you remain a prisoner in Phutra, what may we accomplish?

'What could the men of Pellucidar do without you to lead them?

'They would fight among themselves, and while they fought the Mahars would fall upon them, and even though the Mahars race should die out, of what value would the emancipation of the human race be to them without the knowledge, which you alone may wield, to guide them toward the wonderful civilization of which you have told me so much that I long for its comforts and luxuries as I never before longed for anything.

'No, David; the Mahars cannot harm us if you are at liberty. Let them have their secret that you and I may return to our people, and lead them to the conquest of all Pellucidar.'

It was plain that Dian was ambitious, and that her ambition had not dulled her reasoning faculties. She was right. Nothing could be gained by remaining bottled up in Phutra for the rest of our lives.

It was true that Perry might do much with the contents of the prospector, or iron mole, in which I had brought down the implements of outer-world civilization; but Perry was a man of peace. He could never weld the warring factions of the disrupted federation. He could never win new tribes to the empire. He would fiddle around manufacturing gun-powder and trying to improve upon it until some one blew him up with his own invention. He wasn't practical. He never would get anywhere without a balance-wheel – without some one to direct his energies.

Perry needed me and I needed him. If we were going to do anything for Pellucidar we must be free to do it together.

The outcome of it all was that I agreed to the Mahars' proposition. They promised that Dian would be well treated and protected from every indignity during my absence. So I set out with a hundred Sagoths in search of the little valley which I had stumbled upon by accident, and which I might and might not find again.

We traveled directly toward Sari. Stopping at the camp where I had been captured I recovered my express rifle, for which I was very thankful. I found it lying where I had left it when I had been overpowered in my sleep by the Sagoths who had captured me and slain my Mezop companions.

On the way I added materially to my map, an occupation which did not elicit from the Sagoths even a shadow of interest. I felt that the human race of Pellucidar had little to fear from these gorilla-men. They were fighters – that was all. We might even use them later ourselves in this same capacity. They had not sufficient brain power to constitute a menace to the advancement of the human race.

As we neared the spot where I hoped to find the little valley I became more and more confident of success. Every landmark was familiar to me, and I was sure now that I knew the exact location of the cave.

It was at about this time that I sighted a number of the half-naked warriors of the human race of Pellucidar. They were marching across our front. At sight of us they halted; that there would be a fight I could not doubt. These Sagoths would never permit an opportunity for the capture of slaves for their Mahar masters to escape them.

I saw that the men were armed with bows and arrows, long lances and swords, so I guessed that they must have been members of the federation, for only my people had been thus equipped. Before Perry and I came the men of Pellucidar had only the crudest weapons wherewith to slay one another.

The Sagoths, too, were evidently expecting battle. With savage shouts they rushed forward toward the human warriors.

Then a strange thing happened. The leader of the human beings stepped forward with upraised hands. The Sagoths ceased their war-cries and advanced slowly to meet him. There was a long parley during which I could see that I was often the subject of their discourse. The Sagoths' leader pointed in the direction in which I had told him the valley lay. Evidently he was explaining the nature of our expedition to the leader of the warriors. It was all a puzzle to me.

What human being could be upon such excellent terms with the gorilla-men?

I couldn't imagine. I tried to get a good look at the fellow, but the Sagoths had left me in the rear with a guard when they had advanced to battle, and the distance was too great for me to recognize the features of any of the human beings.

Finally the parley was concluded and the men continued on their way while the Sagoths returned to where I stood with my guard. It was time for eating, so we stopped where we were and made our meal. The Sagoths didn't tell me who it was they had met, and I did not ask, though I must confess that I was quite curious.

They permitted me to sleep at this halt. Afterward we took up the last leg of our journey. I found the valley without difficulty and led my guard directly to the cave. At its mouth the Sagoths halted and I entered alone.

I noticed as I felt about the floor in the dim light that there was a pile of fresh-turned rubble there. Presently my hands came to the spot where the great secret had been buried. There was a cavity where I had carefully smoothed the earth over the hiding-place of the document – the manuscript was gone!

Frantically I searched the whole interior of the cave several times over, but without other result than a complete confirmation of my worst fears. Someone had been here ahead of me and stolen the great secret.

The one thing within Pellucidar which might free Dian and me was gone, nor was it likely that I should ever learn its whereabouts. If a Mahar had found it, which was quite improbable, the chances were that the dominant race would never divulge the fact that they had recovered the precious document. If a cave man had happened upon it he would have no conception of its meaning or value, and as a consequence it would be lost or destroyed in short order.

With bowed head and broken hopes I came out of the cave and told the Sagoth chieftain what I had discovered. It didn't mean much to the fellow, who doubtless had but little better idea of the contents of the document I had been sent to fetch to his masters than would the cave man who in all probability had discovered it.

The Sagoth knew only that I had failed in my mission, so he took advantage of the fact to make the return journey to Phutra as disagreeable as possible. I did not rebel, thought I had with me the means to destroy them all. I did not dare rebel because of the consequences to Dian. I intended demanding her release on the grounds that she was in no way guilty of the theft, and that my failure to recover the document had not lessened the value of the good faith I had had in offering to do so. The Mahars might keep me in slavery if they chose, but Dian should be returned safely to her people.

I was full of my scheme when we entered Phutra and I was conducted directly to the great audience-chamber. The Mahars listened to the report of the Sagoth chieftain, and so difficult is it to judge their emotions from their almost expressionless countenance, that I was at a loss to know how terrible might be their wrath as they learned that their great secret, upon which rested the fate of their race, might now be irretrievably lost.

Presently I could see that she who presided was communicating something to the Sagoth interpreter – doubtless something to be transmitted to me which might give me a forewarning of the fate which lay in store for me. One thing I had decided definitely: If they would not free Dian I should turn loose upon Phutra with my little arsenal. Alone I might even win to freedom, and if I could learn where Dian was imprisoned it would be worth the attempt to free her. My thoughts were interrupted by the interpreter.

'The mighty Mahars,' he said, 'are unable to reconcile your statement that the document is lost with your action in sending it to them by special messenger. They wish to know if you have so soon forgotten the truth or if you are merely ignoring it.'

'I sent them no document,' I cried. 'Ask them what they mean.'

'They say,' he went on after conversing with the Mahar for a moment, 'that just before your return to Phutra, Hooja the Sly One came, bringing the great secret with him. He said that you had sent him ahead with it, asking him to deliver it and return to Sari where you would await him, bringing the girl with him.'

'Dian?' I gasped. 'The Mahars have given over Dian into the keeping of Hooja?'

'Surely,' he replied. 'What of it? She is only a gilak,' as you or I would say, 'She is only a cow.'

6

A Pendent World

The Mahars set me free as they had promised, but with strict injunctions never to approach Phutra or any other Mahar city. They also made it perfectly plain that they considered me a dangerous creature, and that having wiped the slate clean in so far as they were under obligations to me, they now considered me fair prey. Should I again fall into their hands, they intimated it would go ill with me.

They would not tell me in which direction Hooja had set forth with Dian, so I departed from Phutra, filled with bitterness against the Mahars, and rage toward the Sly One who had once again robbed me of my greatest treasure.

At first I was minded to go directly back to Anoroc; but upon second thought turned my face toward Sari, as I felt that somewhere in that direction Hooja would travel, his own country lying in that general direction.

Of my journey to Sari it is only necessary to say that it was fraught with the usual excitement and adventure incident to all travel across the face of savage Pellucidar. The dangers, however, were greatly reduced through the medium of my armament. I often wondered how it had happened that I had ever survived the first ten years of my life within the inner world, when, naked and primitively armed, I had traversed great areas of her beast-ridden surface.

With the aid of my map, which I had kept with great care during my march with the Sagoths in search of the great secret, I arrived at Sari at last. As I topped the lofty plateau in whose rocky cliffs the principal tribe of Sarians find their cave-homes, a great hue and cry arose from those who first discovered me.

Like wasps from their nests the hairy warriors poured from their caves. The bows with their poison-tipped arrows, which I had taught them to fashion and to use, were raised against me. Swords of hammered iron – another of my innovations – menaced me, as with lusty shouts the horde charged down.

It was a critical moment. Before I should be recognized I might be dead. It was evident that all semblance of intertribal relationship had ceased with my going, and that my people had reverted to their former savage, suspicious hatred of all strangers. My garb must have puzzled them, too, for never before of course had they seen a man clothed in khaki and puttees.

Leaning my express rifle against my body I raised both hands aloft. It was the peace-sign that is recognized everywhere upon the surface of Pellucidar. The charging warriors paused and surveyed me. I looked for my friend Ghak, the Hairy One, king of Sari, and presently I saw him coming from a distance. Ah, but it was good to see his mighty, hairy form once more! A friend was Ghak – a friend well worth the having; and it had been some time since I had seen a friend.

Shouldering his way through the throng of warriors, the mighty chieftain advanced toward me. There was an expression of puzzlement upon his fine features. He crossed the space between the warriors and myself, halting before me.

I did not speak. I did not even smile. I wanted to see if Ghak, my principal lieutenant, would recognize me. For some time he stood there looking me over carefully. His eyes took in my large pith helmet, my khaki jacket, and bandoleers of cartridges, the two revolvers swinging at my hips, the large rifle resting against my body. Still I stood with my hands above my head. He examined my puttees and my strong tan shoes – a little the worse for wear now. Then he glanced up once more to my face. As his gaze rested there quite steadily for some moments I saw recognition tinged with awe creep across his countenance.

Presently without a word he took one of my hands in his and dropping to one knee raised my fingers to his lips. Perry had taught them this trick, nor ever did the most polished courtier of all the grand courts of Europe perform the little act of homage with greater grace and dignity.

Quickly I raised Ghak to his feet, clasping both his hands in mine. I think there must have been tears in my eyes then – I know I felt too full for words. The king of Sari turned toward his warriors.

'Our emperor has come back,' he announced. 'Come hither and—'

But he got no further, for the shouts that broke from those savage throats would have drowned the voice of heaven itself. I had never guessed how much they thought of me. As they clustered around, almost fighting for the chance to kiss my hand, I saw again the vision of empire which I had thought faded forever.

With such as these I could conquer a world. With such as these I *would* conquer one! If the Sarians had remained loyal, so too would the Amozites be loyal still, and the Kalians, and the Suvians, and all the great tribes who had formed the federation that was to emancipate the human race of Pellucidar.

Perry was safe with the Mezops; I was safe with the Sarians; now if Dian were but safe with me the future would look bright indeed.

It did not take long to outline to Ghak all that had befallen me since I had departed from Pellucidar, and to get down to the business of finding Dian, which to me at that moment was of even greater importance than the very empire itself.

When I told him that Hooja had stolen her, he stamped his foot in rage.

'It is always the Sly One!' he cried. 'It was Hooja who caused the first trouble between you and the Beautiful One.

'It was Hooja who betrayed our trust, and all but caused our recapture by the Sagoths that time we escaped from Phutra.

'It was Hooja who tricked you and substituted a Mahar for Dian when you started upon your return journey to your own world.

'It was Hooja who schemed and lied until he had turned the kingdoms one against another and destroyed the federation.

'When we had him in our power we were foolish to let him live. Next time—'

Ghak did not need to finish his sentence.

'He has become a very powerful enemy now,' I replied. 'That he is allied in some way with the Mahars is evidenced by the familiarity of his relations with the Sagoths who were accompanying me in search of the great secret, for it must have been Hooja whom I saw conversing with them just before we reached the valley. Doubtless they told him of our quest and he hastened on ahead of us, discovered the cave and stole the document. Well does he deserve his appellation of the Sly One.'

With Ghak and his head men I held a number of consultations. The upshot of them was a decision to combine our search for Dian with an attempt to rebuild the crumbled federation. To this end twenty warriors were despatched in pairs of ten to the leading kingdoms, with instructions to make every effort to discover the whereabouts of Hooja and Dian, while prosecuting their missions to the chieftains to whom they were sent.

Ghak was to remain at home to receive the various delegations which we invited to come to Sari on the business of the federation. Four hundred warriors were started for Anoroc to fetch Perry and the contents of the prospector to the capitol of the empire, which was also the principal settlement of the Sarians.

At first it was intended that I remain at Sari, that I might be in readiness to hasten forth at the first report of the discovery of Dian; but I found the inaction in the face of my deep solicitude for the welfare of my mate so galling that scarce had the several units departed upon their missions before I, too, chafed to be actively engaged upon the search.

It was after my second sleep, subsequent to the departure of the warriors, as I recall, that I at last went to Ghak with the admission that I could no longer support the intolerable longing to be personally upon the trail of my lost love.

Ghak tried to dissuade me, though I could tell that his heart was with me in my wish to be away and really doing something. It was while we were arguing upon the subject that a stranger, with hands above his head, entered the village. He was immediately surrounded by warriors and conducted to Ghak's presence.

The fellow was a typical cave man – squat, muscular, and hairy, and of a type I had not seen before. His features, like those of all the primeval men of Pellucidar, were regular and fine. His weapons consisted of a stone ax and knife and a heavy knobbed bludgeon of wood. His skin was very white.

'Who are you?' asked Ghak. 'And whence come you?'

'I am Kolk, son of Goork, who is chief of the Thurians,' replied the stranger. 'From Thuria I have come in search of the land of Amoz, where dwells Dacor, the Strong One, who stole my sister, Canda, the Graceful One, to be his mate.

'We of Thuria had heard of a great chieftain who has bound together many tribes, and my father has sent me to Dacor to learn if there be truth in these stories, and if so to offer the services of Thuria to him whom we have heard called emperor.'

'The stories are true,' replied Ghak, 'and here is the emperor of whom you have heard. You need travel no farther.'

Kolk was delighted. He told us much of the wonderful resources of Thuria, the Land of Awful Shadow, and of his long journey in search of Amoz.

'And why,' I asked, 'does Goork, your father, desire to join his kingdom to the empire?'

'There are two reasons,' replied the young man. 'Forever have the Mahars, who dwell beyond the Sidi Plains which lie at the farther rim of the Land of Awful Shadow, taken heavy toll of our people, whom they either force into lifelong slavery or fatten for their feasts. We have heard that the great emperor makes successful war upon the Mahars, against whom we should be glad to fight.

'Recently has another reason come. Upon a great island which lies in the Sojar Az, but a short distance from our shores, a wicked man has collected a great band of outcast warriors of all tribes. Even are there many Sagoths among them, sent by the Mahars to aid the Wicked One.

'This band makes raids upon our villages, and it is constantly growing in size and strength, for the Mahars give liberty to any of their male prisoners who will promise to fight with this band against the enemies of the Mahars. It is the purpose of the Mahars thus to raise a force of our own kind to combat the growth and menace of the new empire of which I have come to seek information. All this we learned from one of our own warriors who had pretended to sympathize with this band and had then escaped at the first opportunity.'

'Who could this man be,' I asked Ghak, 'who leads so vile a movement against his own kind?'

'His name is Hooja,' spoke up Kolk, answering my question.

Ghak and I looked at each other. Relief was written upon his countenance and I know that it was beating strongly in my heart. At last we had discovered a tangible clue to the whereabouts of Hooja – and with the clue a guide!

But when I broached the subject to Kolk he demurred. He had come a long way, he explained, to see his sister and to confer with Dacor. Moreover, he had instructions from his father which he could not ignore lightly. But even so he would return with me and show me the way to the island of the Thurian shore if by doing so we might accomplish anything.

'But we cannot,' he urged. 'Hooja is powerful. He has thousands of warriors. He has only to call upon his Mahar allies to receive a countless horde of Sagoths to do his bidding against his human enemies.

'Let us wait until you may gather an equal horde from the kingdoms of your empire. Then we may march against Hooja with some show of success.

'But first must you lure him to the mainland, for who among you knows how to construct the strange things that carry Hooja and his band back and forth across the water?

'We are not island people. We do not go upon the water. We know nothing of such things.'

I couldn't persuade him to do more than direct me upon the way. I showed him my map, which now included a great area of country extending from Anoroc upon the east to Sari upon the west, and from the river south of the Mountains of the Clouds north to Amoz. As soon as I had explained it to him he drew a line with his finger, showing a sea-coast far to the west and south of Sari, and a great circle which he said marked the extent of the Land of Awful Shadow in which lay Thuria.

The shadow extended southeast of the coast out into the sea half-way to a large island, which he said was the seat of Hooja's traitorous government. The island itself lay in the light of the noonday sun. Northwest of the coast and embracing a part of Thuria lay the Lidi Plains, upon the northwestern verge of which was situated the Mahar city which took such heavy toll of the Thurians.

Thus were the unhappy people now between two fires, with Hooja upon one side and the Mahars on the other. I did not wonder that they sent out an appeal for succor.

Though Ghak and Kolk both attempted to dissuade me, I was determined to set out at once, nor did I delay longer than to make a copy of my map to be given to Perry that he might add to his that which I had set down since we parted. I left a letter for him as well, in which among other things, I advanced the theory that the Sojar Az, or Great Sea, which Kolk mentioned as stretching eastward from Thuria, might indeed be the same mighty ocean as that which, swinging around the southern end of a continent ran northward along the shore opposite Phutra, mingling its waters with the huge gulf upon which lay Sari, Amoz, and Greenwich.

Against this possibility I urged him to hasten the building of a fleet of small sailing-vessels, which we might utilize should I find it impossible to entice Hooja's horde to the mainland.

I told Ghak what I had written, and suggested that as soon as he could he should make new treaties with the various kingdoms of the empire, collect an army and march toward Thuria – this of course against the possibility of my detention through some cause or other.

Kolk gave me a sign to his father – a *lidi*, or beast of burden, crudely scratched upon a bit of bone, and beneath the lidi a man and a flower; all very rudely done perhaps, but none the less effective as I well knew from my long years among the primitive men of Pellucidar.

The lidi is the tribal beast of the Thurians; the man and the flower in the combination in which they appeared bore a double significance, as they constituted not only a message to the effect that the bearer came in peace, but were also Kolk's signature.

And so, armed with my credentials and my small arsenal, I set out alone upon my quest for the dearest girl in this world or yours.

Kolk gave me explicit directions, though with my map I do not believe that I could have gone wrong. As a matter of fact I did not need the map at all, since the principal landmark of the first half of my journey, a gigantic mountainpeak, was plainly visible from Sari, though a good hundred miles away.

At the southern base of this mountain a river rose and ran in a westerly direction, finally turning south and emptying into the Sojar Az some forty miles northeast of Thuria. All that I had to do was follow this river to the sea and then follow the coast to Thuria.

Two hundred and forty miles of wild mountain and primeval jungle, of untracked plain, of nameless rivers, of deadly swamps and savage forests lay ahead of me, yet never had I been more eager for an adventure than now, for never had more depended upon haste and success.

I do not know how long a time that journey required, and only half did I appreciate the varied wonders that each new march unfolded before me, for my mind and heart were filled with but a single image – that of a perfect girl whose great, dark eyes looked bravely forth from a frame of raven hair.

It was not until I had passed the high peak and found the river that my eyes first discovered the pendent world, the tiny satellite which hangs low over the surface of Pellucidar casting its perpetual shadow always upon the same spot – the area that is known here as the Land of Awful Shadow, in which dwells the tribe of Thuria.

From the distance and the elevation of the highlands where I stood the Pellucidarian noonday moon showed half in sunshine and half in shadow, while directly beneath it was plainly visible the round dark spot upon the surface of Pellucidar where the sun has never shone. From where I stood the moon appeared to hang so low above the ground as almost to touch it; but later I was to learn that it floats a mile above the surface – which seems indeed quite close for a moon.

Following the river downward I soon lost sight of the tiny planet as I entered the mazes of a lofty forest. Nor did I catch another glimpse of it for some time – several marches at least. However, when the river led me to the sea, or rather just before it reached the sea, of a sudden the sky became overcast and the size and luxuriance of the vegetation diminished as by magic – as if an omnipotent hand had drawn a line upon the earth, and said:

'Upon this side shall the trees and the shrubs, the grasses and the flowers, riot in profusion of rich colors, gigantic size and bewildering abundance; and upon that side shall they be dwarfed and pale and scant.'

Instantly I looked above, for clouds are so uncommon in the skies of Pellucidar – they are practically unknown except above the mightiest mountain ranges – that it had given me something of a start to discover the sun obliterated. But I was not long in coming to a realization of the cause of the shadow.

Above me hung another world. I could see its mountains and valleys, ocean, lakes, and rivers, its broad, grassy plains and dense forests. But too great was the distance and too deep the shadow of its under side for me to distinguish any movement as of animal life.

Instantly a great curiosity was awakened within me. The questions which the sight of this planet, so tantalizingly close, raised in my mind were numerous and unanswerable.

Was it inhabited?

If so, by what manner and form of creature?

Were its people as relatively diminutive as their little world, or were they as disproportionately huge as the lesser attraction of gravity upon the surface of their globe would permit of their being?

As I watched it, I saw that it was revolving upon an axis that lay parallel to the surface of Pellucidar, so that during each revolution its entire surface was once exposed to the world below and once bathed in the heat of the great sun above. The little world had that which Pellucidar could not have – a day and night, and – greatest of boons to one outer-earthly born – time.

Here I saw a chance to give time to Pellucidar, using this mighty clock, revolving perpetually in the heavens, to record the passage of the hours for the earth below. Here should be located an observatory, from which might be flashed by wireless to every corner of the empire the correct time once each day. That this time would be easily measured I had no doubt, since so plain were the landmarks upon the under surface of the satellite that it would be but necessary to erect a simple instrument and mark the instant of passage of a given landmark across the instrument.

But then was not the time for dreaming; I must devote my mind to the purpose of my journey. So I hastened onward beneath the great shadow. As I advanced I could not but note the changing nature of the vegetation and the paling of its hues.

The river led me a short distance within the shadow before it emptied into the Sojar Az. Then I continued in a southerly direction along the coast toward the village of Thuria, where I hoped to find Goork and deliver to him my credentials.

I had progressed no great distance from the mouth of the river when I discerned, lying some distance at sea, a great island. This I assumed to be the stronghold of Hooja, nor did I doubt that upon it even now was Dian.

The way was most difficult, since shortly after leaving the river I encountered lofty cliffs split by numerous long, narrow fiords, each of which necessitated a considerable detour. As the crow flies it is about twenty miles from the mouth of the river to Thuria, but before I had covered half of it I was fagged. There was no familiar fruit or vegetable growing upon the rocky soil of the cliff-tops, and I would have fared ill for food had not a hare broken cover almost beneath my nose.

I carried bow and arrows to conserve my ammunition-supply, but so quick was the little animal that I had no time to draw and fit a shaft. In fact my dinner was a hundred yards away and going like the proverbial bat when I dropped my six-shooter on it. It was a pretty shot and when coupled with a good dinner made me quite contented with myself.

After eating I lay down and slept. When I awoke I was scarcely so self-satisfied, for I had not more than opened my eyes before I became aware of the presence, barely a hundred yards from me, of a pack of some twenty huge wolf-dogs – the things which Perry insisted upon called hyaenodons – and almost simultaneously I discovered that while I slept my revolvers, rifle, bow, arrows, and knife had been stolen from me.

And the wolf-dog pack was preparing to rush me.

7

From Plight to Plight

I have never been much of a runner; I hate running. But if ever a sprinter broke into smithereens all world's records it was that day when I fled before those hideous beasts along the narrow spit of rocky cliff between two narrow fiords toward the Sojar Az. Just as I reached the verge of the cliff the foremost of the brutes was upon me. He leaped and closed his massive jaws upon my shoulder.

The momentum of his flying body, added to that of my own, carried the two of us over the cliff. It was a hideous fall. The cliff was almost perpendicular. At its foot broke the sea against a solid wall of rock.

We struck the cliff-face once in our descent and then plunged into the salt sea. With the impact with the water the hyaenodon released his hold upon my shoulder.

As I came sputtering to the surface I looked about for some tiny foot- or hand-hold where I might cling for a moment of rest and recuperation. The cliff itself offered me nothing, so I swam toward the mouth of the fiord.

At the far end I could see that erosion from above had washed down sufficient rubble to form a narrow ribbon of beach. Toward this I swam with all my strength. Not once did I look behind me, since every unnecessary movement in swimming detracts so much from one's endurance speed. Not until I had drawn myself safely out upon the beach did I turn my eyes back toward the sea for the hyaenodon. He was swimming slowly and apparently painfully towards the beach upon where I stood.

I watched him for a long time, wondering why it was that such a doglike animal was not a better swimmer. As he neared me I realized that he was weakening rapidly. I had gathered a handful of stones to be ready for his assault when he landed, but in a moment I let them fall from my hands. It was evident that the brute either was no swimmer or else was severely injured, for by now he was making practically no headway. Indeed, it was with quite apparent difficulty that he kept his nose above the surface of the sea.

He was not more than fifty yards from shore when he went under. I watched the spot where he had disappeared, and in a moment I saw his head reappear. The look of dumb misery in his eyes struck a chord in my breast, for I loved dogs. I forgot that he was a vicious, primordial wolf-thing – a man-eater, a scourge, and a terror. I saw only the sad eyes that looked like the eyes of Raja, my dead collie of the outer world.

I did not stop to weigh and consider. In other words, I did not stop to think, which I believe must be the way of men who do things – in contra- distinction to those who think much and do nothing. Instead, I leaped back into the water and swam out toward the drowning beast. At first he showed his teeth at my approach, but just before I reached him he went under for the second time, so that I had to dive to get him.

I grabbed him by the scruff of the neck, and though he weighed as much as a Shetland pony, I managed to drag him to shore and well up upon the beach. Here I found that one of his forelegs was broken – the crash against the cliff-face must have done it.

By this time all the fight was out of him, so that when I had gathered a few tiny branches from some of the stunted trees that grew in the crevices of the cliff, and returned to him he permitted me to set his broken leg and bind it in splints. I had to tear part of my shirt into bits to obtain a bandage, but at last the job was done. Then I sat stroking the savage head and talking to the beast in the man-dog talk with which you are familiar, if you ever owned and loved a dog.

When he is well, I thought, he probably will turn upon me and attempt to devour me, and against that eventuality I gathered together a pile of rocks and set to work to fashion a stone-knife. We were bottled up at the head of the fiord as completely as if we had been behind prison bars. Before us spread the Sojar Az, and elsewhere about us rose unscalable cliffs.

Fortunately a little rivulet trickled down the side of the rocky wall, giving us ample supply of fresh water – some of which I kept constantly beside the hyaenodon in a huge, bowl-shaped shell, of which there were countless numbers among the rubble of the beach.

For food we subsisted upon shellfish and an occasional bird that I succeeded in knocking over with a rock, for long practice as a pitcher on prep-school and varsity nines had made me an excellent shot with a hand-thrown missile.

It was not long before the hyaenodon's leg was sufficiently mended to permit him to rise and hobble about on three legs. I shall never forget with what intent interest I watched his first attempt. Close at my hand lay my pile of rocks. Slowly the beast came to his three good feet. He stretched himself, lowered his head, and lapped water from the drinking-shell at his side, turned and looked at me, and then hobbled off toward the cliffs.

Thrice he traversed the entire extent of our prison, seeking, I imagine, a loop-hole for escape, but finding none he returned in my direction. Slowly he came quite close to me, sniffed at my shoes, my puttees, my hands, and then limped off a few feet and lay down again.

Now that he was able to get around, I was a little uncertain as to the wisdom of my impulsive mercy.

How could I sleep with that ferocious thing prowling about the narrow confines of our prison?

Should I close my eyes it might be to open them again to the feel of those mighty jaws at my throat. To say the least, I was uncomfortable.

I have had too much experience with dumb animals to bank very strongly on any sense of gratitude which may be attributed to them by inexperienced sentimentalists. I believe that some animals love their masters, but I doubt very much if their affection is the outcome of gratitude – a characteristic that is so rare as to be only occasionally traceable in the seemingly unselfish acts of man himself.

But finally I was forced to sleep. Tired nature would be put off no longer. I simply fell asleep, willy nilly, as I sat looking out to sea. I had been very uncomfortable since my ducking in the ocean, for though I could see the sunlight on the water half-way toward the island and upon the island itself, no ray of it fell upon us. We were well within the Land of Awful Shadow. A perpetual half-warmth pervaded the atmosphere, but clothing was slow in drying, and so from loss of sleep and great physical discomfort, I at last gave way to nature's demands and sank into profound slumber.

When I awoke it was with a start, for a heavy body was upon me. My first thought was that the hyaenodon had at last attacked me, but as my eyes opened and I struggled to rise, I saw that a man was astride me and three others bending close above him.

I am no weakling – and never have been. My experience in the hard life of the inner world has turned my thews to steel. Even such giants as Ghak the Hairy One have praised my strength; but to it is added another quality which they lack – science.

The man upon me held me down awkwardly, leaving me many openings – one of which I was not slow in taking advantage of, so that almost before the fellow knew that I was awake I was upon my feet with my arms over his shoulders and about his waist and had hurled him heavily over my head to the hard rubble of the beach, where he lay quite still.

In the instant that I arose I had seen the hyaenodon lying asleep beside a boulder a few yards away. So nearly was he the color of the rock that he was scarcely discernible. Evidently the newcomers had not seen him.

I had not more than freed myself from one of my antagonists before the other three were upon me. They did not work silently now, but charged me with savage cries – a mistake upon their part. The fact that they did not draw their weapons against me convinced me that they desired to take me alive; but I fought as desperately as if death loomed immediate and sure.

The battle was short, for scarce had their first wild whoop reverberated through the rocky fiord, and they had closed upon me, than a hairy mass of demoniacal rage hurtled among us.

It was the hyaenodon!

In an instant he had pulled down one of the men, and with a single shake, terrier-like, had broken his neck. Then he was upon another. In their efforts to vanquish the wolfdog the savages forgot all about me, thus giving me an instant in which to snatch a knife from the loin-string of him who had first fallen and account for another of them. Almost simultaneously the hyaenodon pulled down the remaining enemy, crushing his skull with a single bite of those fearsome jaws.

The battle was over – unless the beast considered me fair prey, too. I waited, ready for him with knife and bludgeon – also filched from a dead foeman; but he paid no attention to me, falling to work instead to devour one of the corpses.

The beast had been handicapped but little by his splinted leg; but having eaten he lay down and commenced to gnaw at the bandage. I was sitting some little distance away devouring shellfish, of which, by the way, I was becoming exceedingly tired.

Presently, the hyaenodon arose and came toward me. I did not move. He stopped in front of me and deliberately raised his bandaged leg and pawed my knee. His act was as intelligible as words – he wished the bandage removed.

I took the great paw in one hand and with the other hand untied and unwound the bandage, removed the splints and felt of the injured member. As far as I could judge the bone was completely knit. The joint was stiff; when I bent it a little the brute winced – but he neither growled nor tried to pull away. Very slowly and gently I rubbed the joint and applied pressure to it for a few moments.

Then I set it down upon the ground. The hyaenodon walked around me a few times, and then lay down at my side, his body touching mine. I laid my hand upon his head. He did not move. Slowly, I scratched about his ears and neck and down beneath the fierce jaws. The only sign he gave was to raise his chin a trifle that I might better caress him.

That was enough! From that moment I have never again felt suspicion of Raja, as I immediately named him. Somehow all sense of loneliness vanished, too – I had a dog! I had never guessed precisely what it was that was lacking to life in Pellucidar, but now I knew it was the total absence of domestic animals.

Man here had not yet reached the point where he might take the time from slaughter and escaping slaughter to make friends with any of the brute creation. I must qualify this statement a trifle and say that this was true of those tribes with which I was most familiar. The Thurians do domesticate the colossal lidi, traversing the great Lidi Plains upon the backs of these grotesque and stupendous monsters, and possibly there may also be other, far-distant peoples within the great world, who have tamed others of the wild things of jungle, plain or mountain.

The Thurians practice agriculture in a crude sort of way. It is my opinion that this is one of the earliest steps from savagery to civilization. The taming of wild beasts and their domestication follows.

Perry argues that wild dogs were first domesticated for hunting purposes; but I do not agree with him. I believe that if their domestication were not purely the result of an accident, as, for example, my taming of the hyaenodon, it came about through the desire of tribes who had previously domesticated flocks and herds to have some strong, ferocious beast to guard their roaming property. However, I lean rather more strongly to the theory of accident.

As I sat there upon the beach of the little fiord eating my unpalatable shell-fish, I commenced to wonder how it had been that the four savages had been able to reach me, though I had been unable to escape from my natural prison. I glanced about in all directions, searching for an explanation. At last my eyes fell upon the bow of a small dugout protruding scarce a foot from behind a large boulder lying half in the water at the edge of the beach.

At my discovery I leaped to my feet so suddenly that it brought Raja, growling and bristling, upon all fours in an instant. For the moment I had forgotten him. But his savage rumbling did not cause me any uneasiness.

He glanced quickly about in all directions as if searching for the cause of my excitement. Then, as I walked rapidly down toward the dugout, he slunk silently after me.

The dugout was similar in many respects to those which I had seen in use by the Mezops. In it were four paddles. I was much delighted, as it promptly offered me the escape I had been craving.

I pushed it out into the water that would float it, stepped in and called to Raja to enter. At first he did not seem to understand what I wished of him, but after I had paddled out a few yards he plunged through the surf and swam after me. When he had come alongside I grasped the scruff of his neck, and after a considerable struggle, in which I several times came near to overturning the canoe, I managed to drag him aboard, where he shook himself vigorously and squatted down before me.

After emerging from the fiord, I paddled southward along the coast, where presently the lofty cliffs gave way to lower and more level country. It was here somewhere that I should come upon the principal village of the Thurians. When, after a time, I saw in the distance what I took to be huts in a clearing near the shore, I drew quickly into land, for though I had been furnished credentials by Kolk, I was not sufficiently familiar with the tribal characteristics of these people to know whether I should receive a friendly welcome or not; and in case I should not, I wanted to be sure of having a canoe hidden safely away so that I might undertake the trip to the island, in any event – provided, of course, that I escaped the Thurians should they prove belligerent.

At the point where I landed the shore was quite low. A forest of pale, scrubby ferns ran down almost to the beach. Here I dragged up the dugout, hiding it well within the vegetation, and with some loose rocks built a cairn upon the beach to mark my cache. Then I turned my steps toward the Thurian village.

As I proceeded I began to speculate upon the possible actions of Raja when we should enter the presence of other men than myself. The brute was padding softly at my side, his sensitive nose constantly atwitch and his fierce eyes moving restlessly from side to side – nothing would ever take Raja unawares!

The more I thought upon the matter the greater became my perturbation. I did not want Raja to attack any of the people upon whose friendship I so greatly depended, nor did I want him injured or slain by them.

I wondered if Raja would stand for a leash. His head as he paced beside me was level with my hip. I laid my hand upon it caressingly. As I did so he turned and looked up into my face, his jaws parting and his red tongue lolling as you have seen your own dog's beneath a love pat.

'Just been waiting all your life to be tamed and loved, haven't you, old man?' I asked. 'You're nothing but a good pup, and the man who put the hyaeno in your name ought to be sued for libel.'

Raja bared his mighty fangs with upcurled, snarling lips and licked my hand.

'You're grinning, you old fraud, you!' I cried. 'If you're not, I'll eat you. I'll be a doughnut you're nothing but some kid's poor old Fido, masquerading around as a real, live man-eater.'

Raja whined. And so we walked on together toward Thuria – I talking to the beast at my side, and he seeming to enjoy my company no less than I enjoyed his. If you don't think it's lonesome wandering all by yourself through savage, unknown Pellucidar, why, just try it, and you will not wonder that I was glad of the company of this first dog – this living replica of the fierce and now extinct hyaenodon of the outer crust that hunted in savage packs the great elk across the snows of southern France, in the days when the mastodon roamed at will over the broad continent of which the British Isles were then a part, and perchance left his footprints and his bones in the sands of Atlantis as well.

Thus I dreamed as we moved on toward Thuria. My dreaming was rudely shattered by a savage growl from Raja. I looked down at him. He had stopped in his tracks as one turned to stone. A thin ridge of stiff hair bristled along the entire length of his spine. His yellow green eyes were fastened upon the scrubby jungle at our right.

I fastened my fingers in the bristles at his neck and turned my eyes in the direction that his pointed. At first I saw nothing. Then a slight movement of the bushes riveted my attention. I thought it must be some wild beast, and was glad of the primitive weapons I had taken from the bodies of the warriors who had attacked me.

Presently I distinguished two eyes peering at us from the vegetation. I took a step in their direction, and as I did so a youth arose and fled precipitately in the direction we had been going. Raja struggled to be after him, but I held tightly to his neck, an act which he did not seem to relish, for he turned on me with bared fangs.

I determined that now was as good a time as any to discover just how deep was Raja's affection for me. One of us could be master, and logically I was the one. He growled at me. I cuffed him sharply across the nose. He looked at me for a moment in surprised bewilderment, and then he growled again. I made another feint at him, expecting that it would bring him at my throat; but instead he winced and crouched down.

Raja was subdued!

I stooped and patted him. Then I took a piece of the rope that constituted a part of my equipment and made a leash for him.

Thus we resumed our journey toward Thuria. The youth who had seen us was evidently of the Thurians. That he had lost no time in racing homeward and spreading the word of my coming was evidenced when we had come within sight of the clearing, and the village – the first real village, by the way, that I had ever seen constructed by human Pellucidarians. There was a rude rectangle walled with logs and boulders, in which were a hundred or more thatched huts of similar construction. There was no gate. Ladders that could be removed by night led over the palisade.

Before the village were assembled a great concourse of warriors. Inside I could see the heads of women and children peering over the top of the wall; and also, farther back, the long necks of lidi, topped by their tiny heads. Lidi, by the way, is both the singular and plural form of the noun that describes the huge beasts of burden of the Thurians. They are enormous quadrupeds, eighty or a hundred feet long, with very small heads perched at the top of very long, slender necks. Their heads are quite forty feet from the ground. Their gait is slow and deliberate, but so enormous are their strides that, as a matter of fact, they cover the ground quite rapidly.

Perry has told me that they are almost identical with the fossilized remains of the diplodocus of the outer crust's Jurassic age. I have to take his word for it – and I guess you will, unless you know more of such matters than I.

As we came in sight of the warriors the men set up a great jabbering. Their eyes were wide in astonishment – only, I presume, because of my strange garmenture, but as well from the fact that I came in company with a jalok, which is the Pellucidarian name of the hyaenodon.

Raja tugged at his leash, growling and showing his long white fangs. He would have liked nothing better than to be at the throats of the whole aggregation; but I held him in with the leash, though it took all my strength to do it. My free hand I held above my head, palm out, in token of peacefulness of my mission.

In the foreground I saw the youth who had discovered us, and I could tell from the way he carried himself that he was quite overcome by his own importance. The warriors about him were all fine looking fellows, though shorter and squatter than the Sarians or the Amozites. Their color, too, was a bit lighter, owing, no doubt, to the fact that much of their lives is spent within the shadow of the world that hangs forever above their country.

A little in advance of the others was a bearded fellow tricked out in many ornaments. I didn't need to ask to know that he was the chieftain – doubtless Goork, father of Kolk. Now to him I addressed myself.

'I am David,' I said, 'Emperor of the Federated Kingdoms of Pellucidar. Doubtless you have heard of me?'

He nodded his head affirmatively.

'I come from Sari,' I continued, 'where I just met Kolk, the son of Goork.

I bear a token from Kolk to his father, which will prove that I am a friend.'

Again the warrior nodded. 'I am Goork,' he said. 'Where is the token?'

'Here,' I replied, and fished into the game-bag where I had placed it.

Goork and his people waited in silence. My hand searched the inside of the bag.

It was empty!

The token had been stolen with my arms!

8

Captive

When Goork and his people saw that I had no token they commenced to taunt me.

'You do not come from Kolk, but from the Sly One!' they cried. 'He has sent you from the island to spy upon us. Go away, or we will set upon you and kill you.'

I explained that all my belongings had been stolen from me, and that the robber must have taken the token too; but they didn't believe me. As proof that I was one of Hooja's people, they pointed to my weapons, which they said were ornamented like those of the island clan. Further, they said that no good man went in company with a jalok – and that by this line of reasoning I certainly was a bad man.

I saw that they were not naturally a war-like tribe, for they preferred that I leave in peace rather than force them to attack me, whereas the Sarians would have killed a suspicious stranger first and inquired into his purposes later.

I think Raja sensed their antagonism, for he kept tugging at his leash and growling ominously. They were a bit in awe of him, and kept at a safe distance. It was evident that they could not comprehend why it was that this savage brute did not turn upon me and rend me.

I wasted a long time there trying to persuade Goork to accept me at my own valuation, but he was too canny. The best he would do was to give us food, which he did, and direct me as to the safest portion of the island upon which to attempt a landing, though even as he told me I am sure that he thought my request for information but a blind to deceive him as to my true knowledge of the insular stronghold.

At last I turned away from them – rather disheartened, for I had hoped to be able to enlist a considerable force of them in an attempt to rush Hooja's horde and rescue Dian. Back along the beach toward the hidden canoe we made our way.

By the time we came to the cairn I was dog-tired. Throwing myself upon the sand I soon slept, and with Raja stretched out beside me I felt a far greater security than I had enjoyed for a long time.

I awoke much refreshed to find Raja's eyes glued upon me. The moment I opened mine he rose, stretched himself, and without a backward glance plunged into the jungle. For several minutes I could hear him crashing through the brush. Then all was silent.

I wondered if he had left me to return to his fierce pack. A feeling of loneliness overwhelmed me. With a sigh I turned to the work of dragging the canoe down to the sea. As I entered the jungle where the dugout lay a hare darted from beneath the boat's side, and a well-aimed cast of my javelin brought it down. I was hungry – I had not realized it before – so I sat upon the edge of the canoe and devoured my repast. The last remnants gone, I again busied myself with preparations for my expedition to the island.

I did not know for certain that Dian was there; but I surmised as much. Nor could I guess what obstacles might confront me in an effort to rescue her. For a time I loitered about after I had the canoe at the water's edge, hoping against hope that Raja would return; but he did not, so I shoved the awkward craft through the surf and leaped into it.

I was still a little downcast by the desertion of my newfound friend, though I tried to assure myself that it was nothing but what I might have expected.

The savage brute had served me well in the short time that we had been together, and had repaid his debt of gratitude to me, since he had saved my life, or at least my liberty, no less certainly than I had saved his life when he was injured and drowning.

The trip across the water to the island was uneventful. I was mighty glad to be in the sunshine again when I passed out of the shadow of the dead world about halfway between the mainland and the island. The hot rays of the noonday sun did a great deal toward raising my spirits, and dispelling the mental gloom in which I had been shrouded almost continually since entering the Land of Awful Shadow. There is nothing more dispiriting to me than absence of sunshine.

I had paddled to the southwestern point, which Goork said he believed to be the least frequented portion of the island, as he had never seen boats put off from there. I found a shallow reef running far out into the sea and rather precipitous cliffs running almost to the surf. It was a nasty place to land, and I realized now why it was not used by the natives; but at last I managed, after a good wetting, to beach my canoe and scale the cliffs.

The country beyond them appeared more open and park-like than I had anticipated, since from the mainland the entire coast that is visible seems densely clothed with tropical jungle. This jungle, as I could see from the vantage-point of the cliff-top, formed but a relatively narrow strip between the sea and the more open forest and meadow of the interior. Farther back there was a range of low but apparently very rocky hills, and here and there all about were visible flat-topped masses of rock – small mountains, in fact – which reminded me of pictures I had seen of landscapes in New Mexico. Altogether, the country was very much broken and very beautiful. From where I stood I counted no less than a dozen streams winding down from among the table-buttes and emptying into a pretty river which flowed away in a northeasterly direction toward the opposite end of the island.

As I let my eyes roam over the scene I suddenly became aware of figures moving upon the flat top of a far-distant butte. Whether they were beast or human, though, I could not make out; but at least they were alive, so I determined to prosecute my search for Hooja's stronghold in the general direction of this butte.

To descend to the valley required no great effort. As I swung along through the lush grass and the fragrant flowers, my cudgel swinging in my hand and my javelin looped across my shoulders with its auroch's-hide strap, I felt equal to any emergency, ready for any danger.

I had covered quite a little distance, and I was passing through a strip of wood which lay at the foot of one of the flat-topped hills, when I became conscious of the sensation of being watched. My life within Pellucidar has rather quickened my senses of sight, hearing, and smell, and, too, certain primitive intuitive or instinctive qualities that seem blunted in civilized man. But, though I was positive that eyes were upon me, I could see no sign of any living thing within the wood other than the many, gay-plumaged birds and little monkeys which filled the trees with life, color, and action.

To you it may seem that my conviction was the result of an overwrought imagination, or to the actual reality of the prying eyes of the little monkeys or the curious ones of the birds; but there is a difference which I cannot explain between the sensation of casual observation and studied espionage. A sheep might gaze at you without transmitting a warning through your subjective mind, because you are in no danger from a sheep. But let a tiger gaze fixedly at you from ambush, and unless your primitive instincts are completely calloused you will presently commence to glance furtively about and be filled with vague, unreasoning terror.

Thus was it with me then. I grasped my cudgel more firmly and unslung my javelin, carrying it in my left hand. I peered to left and right, but I saw nothing. Then, all quite suddenly, there fell about my neck and shoulders, around my arms and body, a number of pliant fiber ropes.

In a jiffy I was trussed up as neatly as you might wish. One of the nooses dropped to my ankles and was jerked up with a suddenness that brought me to my face upon the ground. Then something heavy and hairy sprang upon my back. I fought to draw my knife, but hairy hands grasped my wrists and, dragging them behind my back, bound them securely.

Next my feet were bound. Then I was turned over upon my back to look up into the faces of my captors.

And what faces! Imagine if you can a cross between a sheep and a gorilla, and you will have some conception of the physiognomy of the creature that bent close above me, and of those of the half-dozen others that clustered about. There was the facial length and great eyes of the sheep, and the bull-neck and hideous fangs of the gorilla. The bodies and limbs were both man and gorilla-like.

As they bent over me they conversed in a monosyllabic tongue that was perfectly intelligible to me. It was something of a simplified language that had no need for aught but nouns and verbs, but such words as it included were the same as those of the human beings of Pellucidar. It was amplified by many gestures which filled in the speech-gaps.

I asked them what they intended doing with me; but, like our own North American Indians when questioned by a white man, they pretend not to understand me. One of them swung me to his shoulder as lightly as if I had been a shoat. He was a huge creature, as were his fellows, standing fully seven feet upon his short legs and weighing considerably more than a quarter of a ton.

Two went ahead of my bearer and three behind. In this order we cut to the right through the forest to the foot of the hill where precipitous cliffs appeared to bar our farther progress in this direction. But my escort never paused. Like ants upon a wall, they scaled that seemingly unscalable barrier, clinging, Heaven knows how, to its ragged perpendicular face. During most of the short journey to the summit I must admit that my hair stood on end. Presently, however, we topped the thing and stood upon the level mesa which crowned it.

Immediately from all about, out of burrows and rough, rocky lairs, poured a perfect torrent of beasts similar to my captors. They clustered about, jabbering at my guards and attempting to get their hands upon me, whether from curiosity or a desire to do me bodily harm I did not know, since my escort with bared fangs and heavy blows kept them off.

Across the mesa we went, to stop at last before a large pile of rocks in which an opening appeared. Here my guards set me upon my feet and called out a word which sounded like 'Gr-gr-gr!' and which I later learned was the name of their king.

Presently there emerged from the cavernous depths of the lair a monstrous creature, scarred from a hundred battles, almost hairless and with an empty socket where one eye had been. The other eye, sheeplike in its mildness, gave the most startling appearance to the beast, which but for that single timid orb was the most fearsome thing that one could imagine.

I had encountered the black, hairless, long-tailed ape-things of the mainland – the creatures which Perry thought might constitute the link between the higher orders of apes and man – but these brute-men of Gr-gr-gr seemed to set that theory back to zero, for there was less similarity between the black ape-men and these creatures than there was between the latter and man, while both had many human attributes; some of which were better developed in one species and some in the other.

The black apes were hairless and built thatched huts in their arboreal retreats; they kept domesticated dogs and ruminants, in which respect they were farther advanced than the human beings of Pellucidar; but they appeared to have only a meager language, and sported long, apelike tails.

On the other hand, Gr-gr-gr's people were, for the most part, quite hairy, but they were tailless and had a language similar to that of the human race of Pellucidar; nor were they arboreal. Their skins, where skin showed, were white.

From the foregoing facts and others that I have noted during my long life within Pellucidar, which is now passing through an age analogous to some pre-glacial age of the outer crust, I am constrained to the belief that evolution is not so much a gradual transition from one form to another as it is an accident of breeding, either by crossing or the hazards of birth. In other words, it is my belief that the first man was a freak of nature – nor would one have to draw over-strongly upon his credulity to be convinced that Gr-gr-gr and his tribe were also freaks.

The great man-brute seated himself upon a flat rock – his throne, I imagine – just before the entrance to his lair. With elbows on knees and chin in palms he regarded me intently through his lone sheep-eye while one of my captors told of my taking.

When all had been related Gr-gr-gr questioned me. I shall not attempt to quote these people in their own abbreviated tongue – you would have even greater difficulty in interpreting them than did I. Instead, I shall put the words into their mouths which will carry to you the ideas which they intended to convey.

'You are an enemy,' was Gr-gr-gr's initial declaration. 'You belong to the tribe of Hooja.'

Ah! So they knew Hooja and he was their enemy! Good!

'I am an enemy of Hooja,' I replied. 'He has stolen my mate and I have come here to take her away from him and punish Hooja.'

'How could you do that alone?'

'I do not know,' I answered, 'but I should have tried had you not captured me. What do you intend to do with me?'

'You shall work for us.'

'You will not kill me?' I asked.

'We do not kill except in self-defense,' he replied; 'self-defense and punishment. Those who would kill us and those who do wrong we kill. If we knew you were one of Hooja's people we might kill you, for all Hoojas' people are bad people; but you say you are an enemy of Hooja. You may not speak the truth, but until we learn that you have lied we shall not kill you. You shall work.'

'If you hate Hooja,' I suggested, 'why not let me, who hate him, too, go and punish him?'

For some time Gr-gr-gr sat in thought. Then he raised his head and addressed my guard.

'Take him to his work,' he ordered.

His tone was final. As if to emphasize it he turned and entered his burrow. My guard conducted me farther into the mesa, where we came presently to a tiny depression or valley, at one end of which gushed a warm spring.

The view that opened before me was the most surprising that I have ever seen. In the hollow, which must have covered several hundred acres, were numerous fields of growing things, and working all about with crude implements or with no implements at all other than their bare hands were many of the brute-men engaged in the first agriculture that I had seen within Pellucidar.

They put me to work cultivating in a patch of melons. I never was a farmer nor particularly keen for this sort of work, and I am free to confess that time never had dragged so heavily as it did during the hour or the year I spent there at that work. How long it really was I do not know, of course; but it was all too long.

The creatures that worked about me were quite simple and friendly. One of them proved to be a son of Gr-gr-gr. He had broken some minor tribal law, and was working out his sentence in the fields. He told me that his tribe had lived upon this hilltop always, and that there were other tribes like them dwelling upon other hilltops. They had no wars and had always lived in peace and harmony, menaced only by the larger carnivora of the island, until my kind had come under a creature called Hooja, and attacked and killed them when they chanced to descend from their natural fortresses to visit their fellows upon other lofty mesas.

Now they were afraid; but some day they would go in a body and fall upon Hooja and his people and slay them all. I explained to him that I was Hooja's enemy, and asked, when they were ready to go, that I be allowed to go with them, or, better still, that they let me go ahead and learn all that I could about the village where Hooja dwelt so that they might attack it with the best chance of success.

Gr-gr-gr's son seemed much impressed by my suggestion. He said that when he was through in the fields he would speak to his father about the matter.

Some time after this Gr-gr-gr came through the fields where we were, and his son spoke to him upon the subject, but the old gentleman was evidently in anything but a good humor, for he cuffed the youngster and, turning upon me, informed me that he was convinced that I had lied to him, and that I was one of Hooja's people.

'Wherefore,' he concluded, 'we shall slay you as soon as the melons are cultivated. Hasten, therefore.'

And hasten I did. I hastened to cultivate the weeds which grew among the melon-vines. Where there had been one sickly weed before, I nourished two healthy ones. When I found a particularly promising variety of weed growing elsewhere than among my melons, I forthwith dug it up and transplanted it among my charges.

My masters did not seem to realize my perfidy. They saw me always laboring diligently in the melon-patch, and as time enters not into the reckoning of Pellucidarians – even of human beings and much less of brutes and half brutes – I might have lived on indefinitely through this subterfuge had not that occurred which took me out of the melon-patch for good and all.

9

Hooja's Cutthroats Appear

I had built a little shelter of rocks and brush where I might crawl in and sleep out of the perpetual light and heat of the noonday sun. When I was tired or hungry I retired to my humble cot.

My masters never interposed the slightest objection. As a matter of fact, they were very good to me, nor did I see aught while I was among them to indicate that they are ever else than a simple, kindly folk when left to themselves. Their awe-inspiring size, terrific strength, mighty fighting-fangs, and hideous appearance are but the attributes necessary to the successful waging of their constant battle for survival, and well do they employ them when the need arises. The only flesh they eat is that of herbivorous animals and birds. When they hunt the mighty thag, the prehistoric bos of the outer crust, a single male, with his fiber rope, will catch and kill the greatest of the bulls.

Well, as I was about to say, I had this little shelter at the edge of my mel-on-patch. Here I was resting from my labors on a certain occasion when I heard a great hub-bub in the village, which lay about a quarter of a mile away.

Presently a male came racing toward the field, shouting excitedly. As he approached I came from my shelter to learn what all the commotion might be about, for the monotony of my existence in the melon-patch must have fostered that trait of my curiosity from which it had always been my secret boast I am peculiarly free.

The other workers also ran forward to meet the messenger, who quickly unburdened himself of his information, and as quickly turned and scamp-ered back toward the village. When running these beast-men often go upon all fours. Thus they leap over obstacles that would slow up a human being, and upon the level attain a speed that would make a thoroughbred look to his laurels. The result in this instance was that before I had more than assimilated the gist of the word which had been brought to the fields, I was alone, watching my co-workers speeding villageward.

I was alone! It was the first time since my capture that no beast-man had been within sight of me. I was alone! And all my captors were in the village at the opposite edge of the mesa repelling an attack of Hooja's horde!

It seemed from the messenger's tale that two of Gr-gr-gr's great males had been set upon by a half-dozen of Hooja's cutthroats while the former were peaceably returning from the thag hunt. The two had returned to the village un-scratched, while but a single one of Hooja's half-dozen had escaped to report the outcome of the battle to their leader. Now Hooja was coming to punish Gr-gr-gr's people. With his large force, armed with the bows and arrows that Hooja had learned from me to make, with long lances and sharp knives, I feared that even the mighty strength of the beastmen could avail them but little.

At last had come the opportunity for which I waited! I was free to make for the far end of the mesa, find my way to the valley below, and while the two forces were engaged in their struggle, continue my search for Hooja's village, which I had learned from the beast-men lay farther on down the river that I had been following when taken prisoner.

As I turned to make for the mesa's rim the sounds of battle came plainly to my ears – the hoarse shouts of men mingled with the half-beastly roars and growls of the brute-folk.

Did I take advantage of my opportunity?

I did not. Instead, lured by the din of strife and by the desire to deliver a stroke, however feeble, against hated Hooja, I wheeled and ran directly toward the village.

When I reached the edge of the plateau such a scene met my astonished gaze as never before had startled it, for the unique battle-methods of the half-brutes were rather the most remarkable I had ever witnessed. Along the very edge of the cliff-top stood a thin line of mighty males – the best rope-throwers of the tribe. A few feet behind these the rest of the males, with the exception of about twenty, formed a second line. Still farther in the rear all the women and young children were clustered into a single group under the protection of the remaining twenty fighting males and all the old males.

But it was the work of the first two lines that interested me. The forces of Hooja – a great horde of savage Sagoths and primeval cave men – were working their way up the steep cliff-face, their agility but slightly less than that of my captors who had clambered so nimbly aloft – even he who was burdened by my weight.

As the attackers came on they paused occasionally wherever a projection gave them sufficient foothold and launched arrows and spears at the defenders above them. During the entire battle both sides hurled taunts and insults at one another – the human beings naturally excelling the brutes in the coarseness and vileness of their vilification and invective.

The 'firing-line' of the brute-men wielded no weapon other than their long fiber nooses. When a foeman came within range of them a noose would settle unerringly about him and he would be dragged, fighting and yelling, to the cliff-top, unless, as occasionally occurred, he was quick enough to draw his knife and cut the rope above him, in which event he usually plunged downward to a no less certain death than that which awaited him above.

Those who were hauled up within reach of the powerful clutches of the defenders had the nooses snatched from them and were catapulted back through the first line to the second, where they were seized and killed by the simple expedient of a single powerful closing of mighty fangs upon the backs of their necks.

But the arrows of the invaders were taking a much heavier toll than the nooses of the defenders and I foresaw that it was but a matter of time before Hooja's forces must conquer unless the brute-men changed their tactics, or the cave men tired of the battle.

Gr-gr-gr was standing in the center of the first line. All about him were boulders and large fragments of broken rock. I approached him and without a word toppled a large mass of rock over the edge of the cliff. It fell directly upon the head of an archer, crushing him to instant death and carrying his mangled corpse with it to the bottom of the declivity, and on its way brushing three more of the attackers into the hereafter.

Gr-gr-gr turned toward me in surprise. For an instant he appeared to doubt the sincerity of my motives. I felt that perhaps my time had come when he reached for me with one of his giant paws; but I dodged him, and running a few paces to the right hurled down another missile. It, too, did its allotted work of destruction. Then I picked up smaller fragments and with all the control and accuracy for which I had earned justly deserved fame in my collegiate days I rained down a hail of death upon those beneath me.

Gr-gr-gr was coming toward me again. I pointed to the litter of rubble upon the cliff-top.

'Hurl these down upon the enemy!' I cried to him. 'Tell your warriors to throw rocks down upon them!'

At my words the others of the first line, who had been interested spectators of my tactics, seized upon great boulders or bits of rock, whichever came first to their hands, and, without waiting for a command from Gr-gr-gr, deluged the terrified cave men with a perfect avalanche of stone. In less than no time the cliff-face was stripped of enemies and the village of Gr-gr-gr was saved.

Gr-gr-gr was standing beside me when the last of the cave men disappeared in rapid flight down the valley. He was looking at me intently.

'Those were your people,' he said. 'Why did you kill them?'

'They were not my people,' I returned. 'I have told you that before, but you would not believe me. Will you believe me now when I tell you that I hate Hooja and his tribe as much as you do? Will you believe me when I tell you that I wish to be the friend of Gr-gr-gr?'

For some time he stood there beside me, scratching his head. Evidently it was no less difficult for him to readjust his preconceived conclusions than it is for most human beings; but finally the idea percolated – which it might never have done had he been a man, or I might qualify that statement by saying had he been some men. Finally he spoke.

'Gilak,' he said, 'you have made Gr-gr-gr ashamed. He would have killed you. How can he reward you?'

'Set me free,' I replied quickly.

'You are free,' he said. 'You may go down when you wish, or you may stay with us. If you go you may always return. We are your friends.'

Naturally, I elected to go. I explained all over again to Gr-gr-gr the nature of my mission. He listened attentively; after I had done he offered to send some of his people with me to guide me to Hooja's village. I was not slow in accepting his offer.

First, however, we must eat. The hunters upon whom Hooja's men had fallen had brought back the meat of a great thag. There would be a feast to commemorate the victory – a feast and dancing.

I had never witnessed a tribal function of the brutefolk, though I had often heard strange sounds coming from the village, where I had not been allowed since my capture. Now I took part in one of their orgies.

It will live forever in my memory. The combination of bestiality and humanity was oftentimes pathetic, and again grotesque or horrible. Beneath the glaring noonday sun, in the sweltering heat of the mesa-top, the huge, hairy creatures leaped in a great circle. They coiled and threw their fiber-ropes; they hurled taunts and insults at an imaginary foe; they fell upon the carcass of the thag and literally tore it to pieces; and they ceased only when, gorged, they could no longer move.

I had to wait until the processes of digestion had released my escort from its torpor. Some had eaten until their abdomens were so distended that I thought they must burst, for beside the thag there had been fully a hundred antelopes of various sizes and varied degrees of decomposition, which they had unearthed from burial beneath the floors of their lairs to grace the banquet-board.

But at last we were started – six great males and myself. Gr-gr-gr had returned my weapons to me, and at last I was once more upon my oft-interrupted way toward my goal. Whether I should find Dian at the end of my journey or no I could not even surmise; but I was none the less impatient to be off, for if only the worst lay in store for me I wished to know even the worst at once.

I could scarce believe that my proud mate would still be alive in the power of Hooja; but time upon Pellucidar is so strange a thing that I realized that to her or to him only a few minutes might have elapsed since his subtle trickery had enabled him to steal her away from Phutra. Or she might have found the means either to repel his advances or escape him.

As we descended the cliff we disturbed a great pack of large hyena-like beasts – *hyaena spelaeus*, Perry calls them – who were busy among the corpses of the cave men fallen in battle. The ugly creatures were far from the cowardly things that our own hyenas are reputed to be; they stood their ground with bared fangs as we approached them. But, as I was later to learn, so formidable are the brute-folk that there are few even of the larger carnivora that will not make way for them when they go abroad. So the hyenas moved a little from our line of march, closing in again upon their feasts when we had passed.

We made our way steadily down the rim of the beautiful river which flows the length of the island, coming at last to a wood rather denser than any that I had before encountered in this country. Well within this forest my escort halted.

'There!' they said, and pointed ahead. 'We are to go no farther.'

Thus having guided me to my destination they left me. Ahead of me, through the trees, I could see what appeared to be the foot of a steep hill. Toward this I made my way. The forest ran to the very base of a cliff, in the face of which were the mouths of many caves. They appeared untenanted;

but I decided to watch for a while before venturing farther. A large tree, densely foliaged, offered a splendid vantage-point from which to spy upon the cliff, so I clambered among its branches where, securely hidden, I could watch what transpired about the caves.

It seemed that I had scarcely settled myself in a comfortable position before a party of cave men emerged from one of the smaller apertures in the cliff-face, about fifty feet from the base. They descended into the forest and disappeared. Soon after came several others from the same cave, and after them, at a short interval, a score of women and children, who came into the wood to gather fruit. There were several warriors with them – a guard, I presume.

After this came other parties, and two or three groups who passed out of the forest and up the cliff-face to enter the same cave. I could not understand it. All who came out had emerged from the same cave. All who returned reentered it. No other cave gave evidence of habitation, and no cave but one of extraordinary size could have accommodated all the people whom I had seen pass in and out of its mouth.

For a long time I sat and watched the coming and going of great numbers of the cave-folk. Not once did one leave the cliff by any other opening save that from which I had seen the first party come, nor did any re-enter the cliff through another aperture.

What a cave it must be, I thought, that houses an entire tribe! But dissatisfied of the truth of my surmise, I climbed higher among the branches of the tree that I might get a better view of other portions of the cliff. High above the ground I reached a point whence I could see the summit of the hill. Evidently it was a flat-topped butte similar to that on which dwelt the tribe of Gr-gr-gr.

As I sat gazing at it a figure appeared at the very edge. It was that of a young girl in whose hair was a gorgeous bloom plucked from some flowering tree of the forest. I had seen her pass beneath me but a short while before and enter the small cave that had swallowed all of the returning tribesmen.

The mystery was solved. The cave was but the mouth of a passage that led upward through the cliff to the summit of the hill. It served merely as an avenue from their lofty citadel to the valley below.

No sooner had the truth flashed upon me than the realization came that I must seek some other means of reaching the village, for to pass unobserved through this well-traveled thoroughfare would be impossible. At the moment there was no one in sight below me, so I slid quickly from my arboreal watch-tower to the ground and moved rapidly away to the right with the intention of circling the hill if necessary until I had found an unwatched spot where I might have some slight chance of scaling the heights and reaching the top unseen.

I kept close to the edge of the forest, in the very midst of which the hill seemed to rise. Though I carefully scanned the cliff as I traversed its base, I saw no sign of any other entrance than that to which my guides had led me.

After some little time the roar of the sea broke upon my ears. Shortly after I came upon the broad ocean which breaks at this point at the very foot of the great hill where Hooja had found safe refuge for himself and his villains.

I was just about to clamber along the jagged rocks which lie at the base of the cliff next to the sea, in search of some foothold to the top, when I chanced to see a canoe rounding the end of the island. I threw myself down behind a large boulder where I could watch the dugout and its occupants without myself being seen.

They paddled toward me for a while and then, about a hundred yards from me, they turned straight in toward the foot of the frowning cliffs. From where I was it seemed that they were bent upon self-destruction, since the roar of the breakers beating upon the perpendicular rock-face appeared to offer only death to any one who might venture within their relentless clutch.

A mass of rock would soon hide them from my view; but so keen was the excitement of the instant that I could not refrain from crawling forward to a point whence I could watch the dashing of the small craft to pieces on the jagged rocks that loomed before her, although I risked discovery from above to accomplish my design.

When I had reached a point where I could again see the dugout, I was just in time to see it glide unharmed between two needle-pointed sentinels of granite and float quietly upon the unruffled bosom of a tiny cove.

Again I crouched behind a boulder to observe what would next transpire; nor did I have long to wait. The dugout, which contained but two men, was drawn close to the rocky wall. A fiber rope, one end of which was tied to the boat, was made fast about a projection of the cliff face.

Then the two men commenced the ascent of the almost perpendicular wall toward the summit several hundred feet above. I looked on in amazement, for, splendid climbers though the cave men of Pellucidar are, I never before had seen so remarkably a feat performed. Upwardly they moved without a pause, to disappear at last over the summit.

When I felt reasonably sure that they had gone for a while at least I crawled from my hiding-place and at the risk of a broken neck leaped and scrambled to the spot where their canoe was moored.

If they had scaled that cliff I could, and if I couldn't I should die in the attempt.

But when I turned to the accomplishment of the task I found it easier than

I had imagined it would be, since I immediately discovered that shallow hand and footholds had been scooped in the cliff's rocky face, forming a crude ladder from the base to the summit.

At last I reached the top, and very glad I was, too. Cautiously I raised my head until my eyes were above the cliff-crest. Before me spread a rough mesa, liberally sprinkled with large boulders. There was no village in sight nor any living creature.

I drew myself to level ground and stood erect. A few trees grew among the boulders. Very carefully I advanced from tree to tree and boulder to boulder toward the inland end of the mesa. I stopped often to listen and look cautiously about me in every direction.

How I wished that I had my revolvers and rifle! I would not have to worm my way like a scared cat toward Hooja's village, nor did I relish doing so now; but Dian's life might hinge upon the success of my venture, and so I could not afford to take chances. To have met suddenly with discovery and had a score or more of armed warriors upon me might have been very grand and heroic; but it would have immediately put an end to all my earthly activities, nor have accomplished aught in the service of Dian.

Well, I must have traveled nearly a mile across that mesa without seeing a sign of anyone, when all of a sudden, as I crept around the edge of a boulder, I ran plump into a man, down on all fours like myself, crawling toward me.

10

The Raid on the Cave-Prison

His head was turned over his shoulder as I first saw him – he was looking back toward the village. As I leaped for him his eyes fell upon me. Never in my life have I seen a more surprised mortal than this poor cave man. Before he could utter a single scream of warning or alarm I had my fingers on his throat and had dragged him behind the boulder, where I proceeded to sit upon him, while I figured out what I had best do with him.

He struggled a little at first, but finally lay still, and so I released the pressure of my fingers at his windpipe, for which I imagine he was quite thankful – I know that I should have been.

I hated to kill him in cold blood; but what else I was to do with him I could not see, for to turn him loose would have been merely to have the entire village aroused and down upon me in a moment. The fellow lay looking up at me with the surprise still deeply written on his countenance. At last, all of a sudden, a look of recognition entered his eyes.

'I have seen you before,' he said. 'I saw you in the arena at the Mahars' city of Phutra when the thipdars dragged the tarag from you and your mate. I never understood that. Afterward they put me in the arena with two warriors from Gombul.'

He smiled in recollection.

'It would have been the same had there been ten warriors from Gombul. I slew them, winning my freedom. Look!'

He half turned his left shoulder toward me, exhibiting the newly healed scar of the Mahars' branded mark.

'Then,' he continued, 'as I was returning to my people I met some of them fleeing. They told me that one called Hooja the Sly One had come and seized our village, putting our people into slavery. So I hurried hither to learn the truth, and, sure enough, here I found Hooja and his wicked men living in my village, and my father's people but slaves among them.

'I was discovered and captured, but Hooja did not kill me. I am the chief's son, and through me he hoped to win my father's warriors back to the village to help him in a great war he says that he will soon commence.

'Among his prisoners is Dian the Beautiful One, whose brother, Dacor the Strong One, chief of Amoz, once saved my life when he came to Thuria to steal a mate. I helped him capture her, and we are good friends. So when I learned that Dian the Beautiful One was Hooja's prisoner, I told him that I would not aid him if he harmed her.

'Recently one of Hooja's warriors overheard me talking with another prisoner. We were planning to combine all the prisoners, seize weapons, and when most of Hooja's warriors were away, slay the rest and retake our hilltop. Had we done so we could have held it, for there are only two entrances – the narrow tunnel at one end and the steep path up the cliffs at the other.

'But when Hooja heard what we had planned he was very angry, and ordered that I die. They bound me hand and foot and placed me in a cave until all the warriors should return to witness my death; but while they were away I heard someone calling me in a muffled voice which seemed to come from the wall of the cave. When I replied the voice, which was a woman's, told me that she had overheard all that had passed between me and those who had brought me thither, and that she was Dacor's sister and would find a way to help me.

'Presently a little hole appeared in the wall at the point from which the voice had come. After a time I saw a woman's hand digging with a bit of stone. Dacor's sister made a hole in the wall between the cave where I lay bound and that in which she had been confined, and soon she was by my side and had cut my bonds.

'We talked then, and I offered to make the attempt to take her away and back to the land of Sari, where she told me she would be able to learn the whereabouts of her mate. Just now I was going to the other end of the island to see if a boat lay there, and if the way was clear for our escape. Most of the boats are always away now, for a great many of Hooja's men and nearly all the slaves are upon the Island of Trees, where Hooja is having many boats built to carry his warriors across the water to the mouth of a great river which he discovered while he was returning from Phutra – a vast river that empties into the sea there.'

The speaker pointed toward the northeast.

'It is wide and smooth and slow-running almost to the land of Sari,' he added.

'And where is Dian the Beautiful One now?' I asked.

I had released my prisoner as soon as I found that he was Hooja's enemy, and now the pair of us were squatting beside the boulder while he told his story.

'She returned to the cave where she had been imprisoned,' he replied, 'and is awaiting me there.'

'There is no danger that Hooja will come while you are away?'

'Hooja is upon the Island of Trees,' he replied.

'Can you direct me to the cave so that I can find it alone?' I asked.

He said he could, and in the strange yet explicit fashion of the Pellucidarians he explained minutely how I might reach the cave where he had been imprisoned, and through the hole in its wall reach Dian.

I thought it best for but one of us to return, since two could accomplish but little more than one and would double the risk of discovery. In the meantime he could make his way to the sea and guard the boat, which I told him lay there at the foot of the cliff.

I told him to await us at the cliff-top, and if Dian came alone to do his best to get away with her and take her to Sari, as I thought it quite possible that, in case of detection and pursuit, it might be necessary for me to hold off Hooja's people while Dian made her way alone to where my new friend was to await her. I impressed upon him the fact that he might have to resort to trickery or even to force to get Dian to leave me; but I made him promise that he would sacrifice everything, even his life, in an attempt to rescue Dacor's sister.

Then we parted – he to take up his position where he could watch the boat and await Dian, I to crawl cautiously on toward the caves. I had no difficulty in following the directions given me by Juag, the name by which Dacor's friend said he was called. There was the leaning tree, my first point he told

182

me to look for after rounding the boulder where we had met. After that I crawled to the balanced rock, a huge boulder resting upon a tiny base no longer than the palm of your hand.

From here I had my first view of the village of caves. A low bluff ran diagonally across one end of the mesa, and in the face of this bluff were the mouths of many caves. Zig-zag trails led up to them, and narrow ledges scooped from the face of the soft rock connected those upon the same level.

The cave in which Juag had been confined was at the extreme end of the cliff nearest me. By taking advantage of the bluff itself, I could approach within a few feet of the aperture without being visible from any other cave. There were few people about at the time; most of these were congregated at the foot of the far end of the bluff, where they were so engrossed in excited conversation that I felt but little fear of detection. However, I exercised the greatest care in approaching the cliff. After watching for a while until I caught an instant when every head was turned away from me, I darted, rabbitlike, into the cave.

Like many of the man-made caves of Pellucidar, this one consisted of three chambers, one behind another, and all unlit except for what sunlight filtered in through the external opening. The result was gradually increasing darkness as one passed into each succeeding chamber.

In the last of the three I could just distinguish objects, and that was all. As I was groping around the walls for the hole that should lead into the cave where Dian was imprisoned, I heard a man's voice quite close to me.

The speaker had evidently but just entered, for he spoke in a loud tone, demanding the whereabouts of one whom he had come in search of.

'Where are you, woman?' he cried. 'Hooja has sent for you.'

And then a woman's voice answered him:

'And what does Hooja want of me?'

The voice was Dian's. I groped in the direction of the sounds, feeling for the hole.

'He wishes you brought to the Island of Trees,' replied the man; 'for he is ready to take you as his mate.'

'I will not go,' said Dian. 'I will die first.'

'I am sent to bring you, and bring you I shall.'

I could hear him crossing the cave toward her.

Frantically I clawed the wall of the cave in which I was in an effort to find the elusive aperture that would lead me to Dian's side.

I heard the sound of a scuffle in the next cave. Then my fingers sank into loose rock and earth in the side of the cave. In an instant I realized why I had been unable to find the opening while I had been lightly feeling the surface of the walls – Dian had blocked up the hole she had made lest it arouse suspicion and lead to an early discovery of Juag's escape.

Plunging my weight against the crumbling mass, I sent it crashing into the adjoining cavern. With it came I, David, Emperor of Pellucidar. I doubt if any other potentate in a world's history ever made a more undignified entrance. I landed head first on all fours, but I came quickly and was on my feet before the man in the dark guessed what had happened.

He saw me, though, when I arose and, sensing that no friend came thus precipitately, turned to meet me even as I charged him. I had my stone knife in my hand, and he had his. In the darkness of the cave there was little opportunity for a display of science, though even at that I venture to say that we fought a very pretty duel.

Before I came to Pellucidar I do not recall that I ever had seen a stone knife, and I am sure that I never fought with a knife of any description; but now I do not have to take my hat off to any of them when it comes to wielding that primitive yet wicked weapon.

I could just see Dian in the darkness, but I knew that she could not see my features or recognize me; and I enjoyed in anticipation, even while I was fighting for her life and mine, her dear joy when she should discover that it was I who was her deliverer.

My opponent was large, but he also was active and no mean knife-man. He caught me once fairly in the shoulder – I carry the scar yet, and shall carry it to the grave. And then he did a foolish thing, for as I leaped back to gain a second in which to calm the shock of the wound he rushed after me and tried to clinch. He rather neglected his knife for the moment in his greater desire to get his hands on me. Seeing the opening, I swung my left fist fairly to the point of his jaw.

Down he went. Before ever he could scramble up again I was on him and had buried my knife in his heart. Then I stood up – and there was Dian facing me and peering at me through the dense gloom.

'You are not Juag!' she exclaimed. 'Who are you?'

I took a step toward her, my arms outstretched.

'It is I, Dian,' I said. 'It is David.'

At the sound of my voice she gave a little cry in which tears were mingled – a pathetic little cry that told me all without words how far hope had gone from her – and then she ran forward and threw herself in my arms. I covered her perfect lips and her beautiful face with kisses, and stroked her thick black hair, and told her again and again what she already knew – what she had known for years – that I loved her better than all else which two worlds had to offer. We couldn't devote much time, though, to the happiness of lovemaking, for we were in the midst of enemies who might discover us at any moment.

I drew her into the adjoining cave. Thence we made our way to the mouth of the cave that had given me entrance to the cliff. Here I reconnoitered for a moment, and seeing the coast clear, ran swiftly forth with Dian at my side. We dodged around the cliff-end, then paused for an instant, listening. No sound reached our ears to indicate that any had seen us, and we moved cautiously onward along the way by which I had come.

As we went Dian told me that her captors had informed her how close I had come in search of her – even to the Land of Awful Shadow – and how one of Hooja's men who knew me had discovered me asleep and robbed me of all my possessions. And then how Hooja had sent four others to find me and take me prisoner. But these men, she said, had not yet returned, or at least she had not heard of their return.

'Nor will you ever,' I responded, 'for they have gone to that place whence none ever returns.' I then related my adventure with these four.

We had come almost to the cliff-edge where Juag should be awaiting us when we saw two men walking rapidly toward the same spot from another direction. They did not see us, nor did they see Juag, whom I now discovered hiding behind a low bush close to the verge of the precipice which drops into the sea at this point. As quickly as possible, without exposing ourselves too much to the enemy, we hastened forward that we might reach Juag as quickly as they.

But they noticed him first and immediately charged him, for one of them had been his guard, and they had both been sent to search for him, his escape having been discovered between the time he left the cave and the time when I reached it. Evidently they had wasted precious moments looking for him in other portions of the mesa.

When I saw that the two of them were rushing him, I called out to attract their attention to the fact that they had more than a single man to cope with. They paused at the sound of my voice and looked about.

When they discovered Dian and me they exchanged a few words, and one of them continued toward Juag while the other turned upon us. As he came nearer I saw that he carried in his hand one of my six-shooters, but he was holding it by the barrel, evidently mistaking it for some sort of warclub or tomahawk.

I could scarce refrain a grin when I thought of the wasted possibilities of that deadly revolver in the hands of an untutored warrior of the stone age. Had he but reversed it and pulled the trigger he might still be alive; maybe he is for all I know, since I did not kill him then. When he was about twenty feet from me I flung my javelin with a quick movement that I had learned from Ghak. He ducked to avoid it, and instead of receiving it in his heart, for which it was intended, he got it on the side of the head.

Down he went all in a heap. Then I glanced toward Juag. He was having a most exciting time. The fellow pitted against Juag was a veritable giant; he was hacking and hewing away at the poor slave with a villainous-looking knife that might have been designed for butchering mastodons. Step by step, he was forcing Juag back toward the edge of the cliff with a fiendish cunning that permitted his adversary no chance to side-step the terrible consequences of retreat in this direction. I saw quickly that in another moment Juag must deliberately hurl himself to death over the precipice or be pushed over by his foeman.

And as I saw Juag's predicament I saw, too, in the same instant, a way to relieve him. Leaping quickly to the side of the fellow I had just felled. I snatched up my fallen revolver. It was a desperate chance to take, and I realized it in the instant that I threw the gun up from my hip and pulled the trigger. There was no time to aim. Juag was upon the very brink of the chasm. His relentless foe was pushing him hard, beating at him furiously with the heavy knife.

And then the revolver spoke – loud and sharp. The giant threw his hands above his head, whirled about like a huge top, and lunged forward over the precipice.

And Juag?

He cast a single affrighted glance in my direction – never before, of course, had he heard the report of a firearm – and with a howl of dismay he, too, turned and plunged headforemost from sight. Horror-struck, I hastened to the brink of the abyss just in time to see two splashes upon the surface of the little cove below.

For an instant I stood there watching with Dian at my side. Then, to my utter amazement, I saw Juag rise to the surface and swim strongly toward the boat.

The fellow had dived that incredible distance and come up unharmed!

I called to him to await us below, assuring him that he need have no fear of my weapon, since it would harm only my enemies. He shook his head and muttered something which I could not hear at so great a distance; but when I pushed him he promised to wait for us. At the same instant Dian caught my arm and pointed toward the village. My shot had brought a crowd of natives on the run toward us.

The fellow whom I had stunned with my javelin had regained consciousness and scrambled to his feet. He was now racing as fast as he could go back toward his people. It looked mighty dark for Dian and me with that ghastly descent between us and even the beginnings of liberty, and a horde of savage enemies advancing at a rapid run.

There was but one hope. That was to get Dian started for the bottom without delay. I took her in my arms just for an instant – I felt, somehow, that it might be for the last time. For the life of me I couldn't see how both of us could escape.

I asked her if she could make the descent alone – if she were not afraid. She smiled up at me bravely and shrugged her shoulders. She afraid! So beautiful is she that I am always having difficulty in remembering that she is a primitive, half-savage cave girl of the stone age, and often find myself mentally limiting her capacities to those of the effete and overcivilized beauties of the outer crust.

'And you?' she asked as she swung over the edge of the cliff.

'I shall follow you after I take a shot or two at our Mends,' I replied. 'I just want to give them a taste of this new medicine which is going to cure Pellucidar of all its ills. That will stop them long enough for me to join you. Now hurry, and tell Juag to be ready to shove off the moment I reach the boat, or the instant that it becomes apparent that I cannot reach it.

'You, Dian, must return to Sari if anything happens to me, that you may devote your life to carrying out with Perry the hopes and plans for Pellucidar that are so dear to my heart. Promise me, dear.'

She hated to promise to desert me, nor would she; only shaking her head and making no move to descend. The tribesmen were nearing us. Juag was shouting up to us from below. It was evident that he realized from my actions that I was attempting to persuade Dian to descend, and that grave danger threatened us from above.

'Dive!' he cried. 'Dive!'

I looked at Dian and then down at the abyss below us. The cove appeared no larger than a saucer. How Juag ever had hit it I could not guess.

'Dive!' cried Juag. 'It is the only way – there is no time to climb down.'

11

Escape

Dian glanced downward and shuddered. Her tribe were hill people – they were not accustomed to swimming other than in quiet rivers and placid lakelets. It was not the steep that appalled her. It was the ocean – vast, mysterious, terrible.

To dive into it from this great height was beyond her. I couldn't wonder, either. To have attempted it myself seemed too preposterous even for thought. Only one consideration could have prompted me to leap headforemost from that giddy height – suicide; or at least so I thought at the moment.

'Quick!' I urged Dian. 'You cannot dive; but I can hold them until you reach safety.'

'And you?' she asked once more. 'Can you dive when they come too close? Otherwise you could not escape if you waited here until I reached the bottom.'

I saw that she would not leave me unless she thought that I could make that frightful dive as we had seen Juag make it. I glanced once downward; then with a mental shrug I assured her that I would dive the moment that she reached the boat. Satisfied, she began the descent carefully, yet swiftly. I watched her for a moment, my heart in my mouth lest some slight misstep or the slipping of a finger-hold should pitch her to a frightful death upon the rocks below.

Then I turned toward the advancing Hoojans – 'Hoosiers,' Perry dubbed them – even going so far as to christen this island where Hooja held sway Indiana; it is so marked now upon our maps. They were coming on at a great rate. I raised my revolver, took deliberate aim at the foremost warrior, and pulled the trigger. With the bark of the gun the fellow lunged forward. His head doubled beneath him. He rolled over and over two or three times before he came to a stop, to lie very quietly in the thick grass among the brilliant wild flowers.

Those behind him halted. One of them hurled a javelin toward me, but it fell short – they were just beyond javelin-range. There were two armed with bows and arrows; these I kept my eyes on. All of them appeared awe-struck and frightened by the sound and effect of the firearm. They kept looking from the corpse to me and jabbering among themselves.

I took advantage of the lull in hostilities to throw a quick glance over the edge toward Dian. She was half-way down the cliff and progressing finely. Then I turned back toward the enemy. One of the bowmen was fitting an arrow to his bow. I raised my hand.

'Stop!' I cried. 'Whoever shoots at me or advances toward me I shall kill as I killed him!'

I pointed at the dead man. The fellow lowered his bow. Again there was animated discussion. I could see that those who were not armed with bows were urging something upon the two who were.

At last the majority appeared to prevail, for simultaneously the two archers raised their weapons. At the same instant I fired at one of them, dropping him in his tracks. The other, however, launched his missile, but the report of my gun had given him such a start that the arrow flew wild above my head. A second after and he, too, was sprawled upon the sward with a round hole between his eyes. It had been a rather good shot.

I glanced over the edge again. Dian was almost at the bottom. I could see Juag standing just beneath her with his hands upstretched to assist her.

A sullen roar from the warriors recalled my attention toward them. They stood shaking their fists at me and yelling insults. From the direction of the village I saw a single warrior coming to join them. He was a huge fellow, and when he strode among them I could tell by his bearing and their deference toward him that he was a chieftain. He listened to all they had to tell of the happenings of the last few minutes; then with a command and a roar he started for me with the whole pack at his heels. All they had needed had arrived – namely, a brave leader.

I had two unfired cartridges in the chambers of my gun. I let the big warrior have one of them, thinking that his death would stop them all. But I guess they were worked up to such a frenzy of rage by this time that nothing would have stopped them. At any rate, they only yelled the louder as he fell and increased their speed toward me. I dropped another with my remaining cartridge.

Then they were upon me – or almost. I thought of my promise to Dian – the awful abyss was behind me – a big devil with a huge bludgeon in front of me. I grasped my six-shooter by the barrel and hurled it squarely in his face with all my strength.

Then, without waiting to learn the effect of my throw, I wheeled, ran the few steps to the edge, and leaped as far out over that frightful chasm as I could. I know something of diving, and all that I know I put into that dive, which I was positive would be my last.

For a couple of hundred feet I fell in horizontal position. The momentum I gained was terrific. I could feel the air almost as a solid body, so swiftly I hurtled through it. Then my position gradually changed to the vertical, and with hands outstretched I slipped through the air, cleaving it like a flying arrow. Just before I struck the water a perfect shower of javelins fell all about. My enemies had rushed to the brink and hurled their weapons after me. By a miracle I was untouched.

In the final instant I saw that I had cleared the rocks and was going to strike the water fairly. Then I was in and plumbing the depths. I suppose I didn't really go very far down, but it seemed to me that I should never stop. When at last I dared curve my hands upward and divert my progress toward the surface, I thought that I should explode for air before I ever saw the sun again except through a swirl of water. But at last my head popped above the waves, and I filled my lungs with air.

Before me was the boat, from which Juag and Dian were clambering. I couldn't understand why they were deserting it now, when we were about to set out for the mainland in it; but when I reached its side I understood. Two heavy javelins, missing Dian and Juag by but a hair's breadth, had sunk deep into the bottom of the dugout in a straight line with the grain of the wood, and split her almost in two from stem to stern. She was useless.

Juag was leaning over a near-by rock, his hand outstretched to aid me in clambering to his side; nor did I lose any time in availing myself of his proffered assistance. An occasional javelin was still dropping perilously close to us, so we hastened to draw as close as possible to the cliff side, where we were comparatively safe from the missiles.

Here we held a brief conference, in which it was decided that our only hope now lay in making for the opposite end of the island as quickly as we could, and utilizing the boat that I had hidden there to continue our journey to the mainland.

Gathering up three of the least damaged javelins that had fallen about us, we set out upon our journey, keeping well toward the south side of the island, which Juag said was less frequented by the Hoojans than the central portion where the river ran. I think that this ruse must have thrown our pursuers off our track, since we saw nothing of them nor heard any sound of pursuit during the greater portion of our march the length of the island.

But the way Juag had chosen was rough and roundabout, so that we consumed one or two more marches in covering the distance than if we had followed the river. This it was which proved our undoing.

Those who sought us must have sent a party up the river immediately after we escaped; for when we came at last onto the river-trail not far from our destination, there can be no doubt but that we were seen by Hoojans who were just ahead of us on the stream. The result was that as we were passing through a clump of bush a score of warriors leaped out upon us, and before we could scarce strike a blow in defense, had disarmed and bound us.

For a time thereafter I seemed to be entirely bereft of hope. I could see no ray of promise in the future – only immediate death for Juag and me, which didn't concern me much in the face of what lay in store for Dian.

Poor child! What an awful life she had led! From the moment that I had first seen her chained in the slave caravan of the Mahars until now, a prisoner of a no less cruel creature, I could recall but a few brief intervals of peace and quiet in her tempestuous existence. Before I had known her, Jubal the Ugly One had pursued her across a savage world to make her his mate. She had eluded him, and finally I had slain him; but terror and privations, and exposure to fierce beasts had haunted her footsteps during all her lonely flight from him. And when I had returned to the outer world the old trials had recommenced with Hooja in Jubal's role. I could almost have wished for death to vouchsafe her that peace which fate seemed to deny her in this life.

I spoke to her on the subject, suggesting that we expire together.

'Do not fear, David,' she replied. 'I shall end my life before ever Hooja can harm me; but first I shall see that Hooja dies.'

She drew from her breast a little leathern thong, to the end of which was fastened a tiny pouch.

'What have you there?' I asked.

'Do you recall that time you stepped upon the thing you call viper in your world?' she asked.

I nodded.

'The accident gave you the idea for the poisoned arrows with which we fitted the warriors of the empire,' she continued. 'And, too, it gave me an idea. For a long time I have carried a viper's fang in my bosom. It has given me strength to endure many dangers, for it has always assured me immunity from the ultimate insult. I am not ready to die yet. First let Hooja embrace the viper's fang.'

So we did not die together, and I am glad now that we did not. It is always a foolish thing to contemplate suicide; for no matter how dark the future may appear today, tomorrow may hold for us that which will alter our whole life in an instant, revealing to us nothing but sunshine and happiness. So, for my part, I shall always wait for tomorrow.

In Pellucidar, where it is always today, the wait may not be so long, and so it proved for us. As we were passing a lofty, flat-topped hill through a parklike wood a perfect network of fiber ropes fell suddenly about our guard, enmeshing them. A moment later a horde of our friends, the hairy gorilla-men, with the mild eyes and long faces of sheep, leaped among them.

It was a very interesting fight. I was sorry that my bonds prevented me from taking part in it, but I urged on the brutemen with my voice, and cheered old Gr-gr-gr, their chief, each time that his mighty jaws crunched out the life of a Hoojan. When the battle was over we found that a few of our captors had escaped, but the majority of them lay dead about us. The gorilla-men paid no further attention to them. Gr-gr-gr turned to me.

'Gr-gr-gr and all his people are your friends,' he said. 'One saw the warriors of the Sly One and followed them. He saw them capture you, and then he flew to the village as fast as he could go and told me all that he had seen. The rest you know. You did much for Gr-gr-gr and Gr-gr-gr's people. We shall always do much for you.'

I thanked him; and when I had told him of our escape and our destination, he insisted on accompanying us to the sea with a great number of his fierce males. Nor were we at all loath to accept his escort. We found the canoe where I had hidden it, and bidding Gr-gr-gr and his warriors farewell, the three of us embarked for the mainland.

I questioned Juag upon the feasibility of attempting to cross to the mouth of the great river of which he had told me, and up which he said we might paddle almost to Sari; but he urged me not to attempt it, since we had but a single paddle and no water or food. I had to admit the wisdom of his advice, but the desire to explore this great waterway was strong upon me, arousing in me at last a determination to make the attempt after first gaining the mainland and rectifying our deficiencies.

We landed several miles north of Thuria in a little cove that seemed to offer protection from the heavier seas which sometimes run, even upon these usually pacific oceans of Pellucidar. Here I outlined to Dian and Juag the plans I had in mind. They were to fit the canoe with a small sail, the purposes of which I had to explain to them both – since neither had ever seen or heard of such a contrivance before. Then they were to hunt for food which we could transport with us, and prepare a receptacle for water.

These two latter items were more in Juag's line, but he kept muttering about the sail and the wind for a long time. I could see that he was not even half convinced that any such ridiculous contraption could make a canoe move through the water.

We hunted near the coast for a while, but were not rewarded with any particular luck. Finally we decided to hide the canoe and strike inland in search of game. At Juag's suggestion we dug a hole in the sand at the upper edge of the beach and buried the craft, smoothing the surface over nicely and throwing aside the excess material we had excavated. Then we set out away from the sea. Traveling in Thuria is less arduous than under the midday sun which perpetually glares down on the rest of Pellucidar's surface; but it has its drawbacks, one of which is the depressing influence exerted by the everlasting shade of the Land of Awful Shadow.

The farther inland we went the darker it became, until we were moving at last through an endless twilight. The vegetation here was sparse and of a weird, colorless nature, though what did grow was wondrous in shape and form. Often we saw huge lidi, or beasts of burden, striding across the dim landscape, browsing upon the grotesque vegetation or drinking from the slow and sullen rivers that run down from the Lidi Plains to empty into the sea in Thuria.

What we sought was either a thag – a sort of gigantic elk – or one of the larger species of antelope, the flesh of either of which dries nicely in the sun. The bladder of the thag would make a fine water-bottle, and its skin, I figured, would be a good sail. We traveled a considerable distance inland, entirely crossing the Land of Awful Shadow and emerging at last upon that portion of the Lidi Plains which lies in the pleasant sunlight. Above us the pendent world revolved upon its axis, filling me especially – and Dian to an almost equal state – with wonder and insatiable curiosity as to what strange forms of life existed among the hills and valleys and along the seas and rivers, which we could plainly see.

Before us stretched the horizonless expanses of vast Pellucidar, the Lidi Plains rolling up about us, while hanging high in the heavens to the northwest of us I thought I discerned the many towers which marked the entrances to the distant Mahar city, whose inhabitants preyed upon the Thurians.

Juag suggested that we travel to the northeast, where, he said, upon the verge of the plain we would find a wooded country in which game should be plentiful. Acting upon his advice, we came at last to a forest-jungle, through which wound innumerable game-paths. In the depths of this forbidding wood we came upon the fresh spoor of thag.

Shortly after, by careful stalking, we came within javelin-range of a small herd. Selecting a great bull, Juag and I hurled our weapons simultaneously, Dian reserving hers for an emergency. The beast staggered to his feet, bellowing. The rest of the herd was up and away in an instant, only the wounded bull remaining, with lowered head and roving eyes searching for the foe.

Then Juag exposed himself to the view of the bull – it is a part of the tactics of the hunt – while I stepped to one side behind a bush. The moment that the savage beast saw Juag he charged him. Juag ran straight away, that the bull might be lured past my hiding-place. On he came – tons of mighty bestial strength and rage.

Dian had slipped behind me. She, too, could fight a thag should emergency require. Ah, such a girl! A rightful empress of a stone age by every standard which two worlds might bring to measure her!

Crashing down toward us came the bull thag, bellowing and snorting, with the power of a hundred outer-earthly bulls. When he was opposite me I sprang for the heavy mane that covered his huge neck. To tangle my fingers in it was the work of but an instant. Then I was running along at the beast's shoulder.

Now, the theory upon which this hunting custom is based is one long ago discovered by experience, and that is that a thag cannot be turned from his charge once he has started toward the object of his wrath, so long as he can still see the thing he charges. He evidently believes that the man clinging to his mane is attempting to restrain him from overtaking his prey, and so he pays no attention to this enemy, who, of course, does not retard the mighty charge in the least.

Once in the gait of the plunging bull, it was but a slight matter to vault to his back, as cavalrymen mount their chargers upon the run. Juag was still running in plain sight ahead of the bull. His speed was but a trifle less than that of the monster that pursued him. These Pellucidarians are almost as fleet as deer; because I am not is one reason that I am always chosen for the close-in work of the thag-hunt. I could not keep in front of a charging thag long enough to give the killer time to do his work. I learned that the first – and last – time I tried it.

Once astride the bull's neck, I drew my long stone knife and, setting the point carefully over the brute's spine, drove it home with both hands. At the same instant I leaped clear of the stumbling animal. Now, no vertebrate can progress far with a knife through his spine, and the thag is no exception to the rule.

The fellow was down instantly. As he wallowed Juag returned, and the two of us leaped in when an opening afforded the opportunity and snatched our javelins from his side. Then we danced about him, more like two savages than anything else, until we got the opening we were looking for, when simultaneously, our javelins pierced his wild heart, stilling it forever.

The thag had covered considerable ground from the point at which I had leaped upon him. When, after despatching him, I looked back for Dian, I could see nothing of her. I called aloud, but receiving no reply, set out at a brisk trot to where I had left her. I had no difficulty in finding the self-same bush behind which we had hidden, but Dian was not there. Again and again I called, to be rewarded only by silence. Where could she be? What could have become of her in the brief interval since I had seen her standing just behind me?

12

KIDNAPPED!

I searched about the spot carefully. At last I was rewarded by the discovery of her javelin, a few yards from the bush that had concealed us from the charging thag – her javelin and the indications of a struggle revealed by the trampled vegetation and the overlapping footprints of a woman and a man. Filled with consternation and dismay, I followed these latter to where they suddenly disappeared a hundred yards from where the struggle had occurred. There I saw the huge imprints of a lidi's feet.

The story of the tragedy was all too plain. A Thurian had either been following us, or had accidentally espied Dian and taken a fancy to her. While Juag and I had been engaged with the thag, he had abducted her. I ran swiftly back to where Juag was working over the kill. As I approached him I saw that something was wrong in this quarter as well, for the islander was standing upon the carcass of the thag, his javelin poised for a throw.

When I had come nearer I saw the cause of his belligerent attitude. Just beyond him stood two large jaloks, or wolf-dogs, regarding him intently – a male and a female. Their behavior was rather peculiar, for they did not seem preparing to charge him. Rather, they were contemplating him in an attitude of questioning.

Juag heard me coming and turned toward me with a grin. These fellows

PELLUCIDAR

love excitement. I could see by his expression that he was enjoying in anticipation the battle that seemed imminent. But he never hurled his javelin. A shout of warning from me stopped him, for I had seen the remnants of a rope dangling from the neck of the male jalok.

Juag again turned toward me, but this time in surprise. I was abreast him in a moment and, passing him, walked straight toward the two beasts. As I did so the female crouched with bared fangs. The male, however, leaped forward to meet me, not in deadly charge, but with every expression of delight and joy which the poor animal could exhibit.

It was Raja – the jalok whose life I had saved, and whom I then had tamed! There was no doubt that he was glad to see me. I now think that his seeming desertion of me had been but due to a desire to search out his ferocious mate and bring her, too, to live with me.

When Juag saw me fondling the great beast he was filled with consternation, but I did not have much time to spare to Raja while my mind was filled with the grief of my new loss. I was glad to see the brute, and I lost no time in taking him to Juag and making him understand that Juag, too, was to be Raja's friend. With the female the matter was more difficult, but Raja helped us out by growling savagely at her whenever she bared her fangs against us.

I told Juag of the disappearance of Dian, and of my suspicions as to the explanation of the catastrophe. He wanted to start right out after her, but I suggested that with Raja to help me it might be as well were he to remain and skin the thag, remove its bladder, and then return to where we had hidden the canoe on the beach. And so it was arranged that he was to do this and await me there for a reasonable time. I pointed to a great lake upon the surface of the pendent world above us, telling him that if after this lake had appeared four times I had not returned to go either by water or land to Sari and fetch Ghak with an army. Then, calling Raja after me, I set out after Dian and her abductor. First I took the wolf dog to the spot where the man had fought with Dian. A few paces behind us followed Raja's fierce mate. I pointed to the ground where the evidences of the struggle were plainest and where the scent must have been strong to Raja's nostrils.

Then I grasped the remnant of leash that hung about his neck and urged him forward upon the trail. He seemed to understand. With nose to ground he set out upon his task. Dragging me after him, he trotted straight out upon the Lidi Plains, turning his steps in the direction of the Thurian village. I could have guessed as much!

Behind us trailed the female. After a while she closed upon us, until she ran quite close to me and at Raja's side. It was not long before she seemed as easy in my company as did her lord and master.

We must have covered considerable distance at a very rapid pace, for we had re-entered the great shadow, when we saw a huge lidi ahead of us, moving leisurely across the level plain. Upon its back were two human figures. If I could have known that the jaloks would not harm Dian I might have turned them loose upon the lidi and its master; but I could not know, and so dared take no chances.

However, the matter was taken out of my hands presently when Raja raised his head and caught sight of his quarry. With a lunge that hurled me flat and jerked the leash from my hand, he was gone with the speed of the wind after the giant lidi and its riders. At his side raced his shaggy mate, only a trifle smaller than he and no whit less savage.

They did not give tongue until the lidi itself discovered them and broke into a lumbering, awkward, but none the less rapid gallop. Then the two hound-beasts commenced to bay, starting with a low, plaintive note that rose, weird and hideous, to terminate in a series of short, sharp yelps. I feared that it might be the hunting-call of the pack; and if this were true, there would be slight chance for either Dian or her abductor – or myself, either, as far as that was concerned. So I redoubled my efforts to keep pace with the hunt; but I might as well have attempted to distance the bird upon the wing; as I have often reminded you, I am no runner. In that instance it was just as well that I am not, for my very slowness of foot played into my hands; while had I been fleeter, I might have lost Dian that time forever.

The lidi, with the hounds running close on either side, had almost disappeared in the darkness that enveloped the surrounding landscape, when I noted that it was bearing toward the right. This was accounted for by the fact that Raja ran upon his left side, and unlike his mate, kept leaping for the great beast's shoulder. The man on the lidi's back was prodding at the hyaenodon with his long spear, but still Raja kept springing up and snapping.

The effect of this was to turn the lidi toward the right, and the longer I watched the procedure the more convinced I became that Raja and his mate were working together with some end in view, for the she-dog merely galloped steadily at the lidi's right about opposite his rump.

I had seen jaloks hunting in packs, and I recalled now what for the time I had not thought of – the several that ran ahead and turned the quarry back toward the main body. This was precisely what Raja and his mate were doing – they were turning the lidi back toward me, or at least Raja was. Just why the female was keeping out of it I did not understand, unless it was that she was not entirely clear in her own mind as to precisely what her mate was attempting.

At any rate, I was sufficiently convinced to stop where I was and await developments, for I could readily realize two things. One was that I could never overhaul them before the damage was done if they should pull the lidi down now. The other thing was that if they did not pull it down for a few minutes it would have completed its circle and returned close to where I stood.

And this is just what happened. The lot of them were almost swallowed up in the twilight for a moment. Then they reappeared again, but this time far to the right and circling back in my general direction. I waited until I could get some clear idea of the right spot to gain that I might intercept the lidi; but even as I waited I saw the beast attempt to turn still more to the right – a move that would have carried him far to my left in a much more circumscribed circle than the hyaenodons had mapped out for him. Then I saw the female leap forward and head him; and when he would have gone too far to the left, Raja sprang, snapping at his shoulder and held him straight.

Straight for me the two savage beasts were driving their quarry! It was wonderful.

It was something else, too, as I realized while the monstrous beast neared me. It was like standing in the middle of the tracks in front of an approaching express-train. But I didn't dare waver; too much depended upon my meeting that hurtling mass of terrified flesh with a well-placed javelin. So I stood there, waiting to be run down and crushed by those gigantic feet, but determined to drive home my weapon in the broad breast before I fell.

The lidi was only about a hundred yards from me when Raja gave a few barks in a tone that differed materially from his hunting-cry. Instantly both he and his mate leaped for the long neck of the ruminant.

Neither missed. Swinging in mid-air, they hung tenaciously, their weight dragging down the creature's head and so retarding its speed that before it had reached me it was almost stopped and devoting all its energies to attempting to scrape off its attackers with its forefeet.

Dian had seen and recognized me, and was trying to extricate herself from the grasp of her captor, who, handicapped by his strong and agile prisoner, was unable to wield his lance effectively upon the two jaloks. At the same time I was running swiftly toward them.

When the man discovered me he released his hold upon Dian and sprang to the ground, ready with his lance to meet me. My javelin was no match for his longer weapon, which was used more for stabbing than as a missile. Should I miss him at my first cast, as was quite probable, since he was prepared for me, I would have to face his formidable lance with nothing more than a stone knife. The outlook was scarcely entrancing. Evidently I was soon to be absolutely at his mercy.

Seeing my predicament, he ran toward me to get rid of one antagonist before he had to deal with the other two. He could not guess, of course, that the two jaloks were hunting with me; but he doubtless thought that after they had finished the lidi they would make after the human prey – the beasts are notorious killers, often slaying wantonly.

But as the Thurian came Raja loosened his hold upon the lidi and dashed for him, with the female close after. When the man saw them he yelled to me to help him, protesting that we should both be killed if we did not fight together. But I only laughed at him and ran toward Dian.

Both the fierce beasts were upon the Thurian simultaneously – he must have died almost before his body tumbled to the ground. Then the female wheeled toward Dian. I was standing by her side as the thing charged her, my javelin ready to receive her.

But again Raja was too quick for me. I imagined he thought she was making for me, for he couldn't have known anything of my relations toward Dian. At any rate he leaped full upon her back and dragged her down. There ensued forthwith as terrible a battle as one would wish to see if battles were gaged by volume of noise and riotous-ness of action. I thought that both the beasts would be torn to shreds.

When finally the female ceased to struggle and rolled over on her back, her forepaws limply folded, I was sure that she was dead. Raja stood over her, growling, his jaws close to her throat. Then I saw that neither of them bore a scratch. The male had simply administered a severe drubbing to his mate. It was his way of teaching her that I was sacred.

After a moment he moved away and let her rise, when she set about smoothing down her rumpled coat, while he came stalking toward Dian and me. I had an arm about Dian now. As Raja came close I caught him by the neck and pulled him up to me. There I stroked him and talked to him, bidding Dian do the same, until I think he pretty well understood that if I was his friend, so was Dian.

For a long time he was inclined to be shy of her, often baring his teeth at her approach, and it was a much longer time before the female made friends with us. But by careful kindness, by never eating without sharing our meat with them, and by feeding them from our hands, we finally won the confidence of both animals. However, that was a long time after.

With the two beasts trotting after us, we returned to where we had left Juag. Here I had the dickens' own time keeping the female from Juag's throat. Of all the venomous, wicked, cruel-hearted beasts on two worlds, I think a female hyaenodon takes the palm.

But eventually she tolerated Juag as she had Dian and me, and the five of us set out toward the coast, for Juag had just completed his labors on the thag when we arrived. We ate some of the meat before starting, and gave the hounds some. All that we could we carried upon our backs.

On the way to the canoe we met with no mishaps. Dian told me that the fellow who had stolen her had come upon her from behind while the roaring of the thag had drowned all other noises, and that the first she had known he had disarmed her and thrown her to the back of his lidi, which had been lying down close by waiting for him. By the time the thag had ceased bellowing the fellow had got well away upon his swift mount. By holding one palm over her mouth he had prevented her calling for help.

'I thought,' she concluded, 'that I should have to use the viper's tooth, after all.'

We reached the beach at last and unearthed the canoe. Then we busied ourselves stepping a mast and rigging a small sail – Juag and I, that is – while Dian cut the thag meat into long strips for drying when we should be out in the sunlight once more.

At last all was done. We were ready to embark. I had no difficulty in getting Raja aboard the dugout; but Ranee – as we christened her after I had explained to Dian the meaning of Raja and its feminine equivalent – positively refused for a time to follow her mate aboard. In fact, we had to shove off without her. After a moment, however, she plunged into the water and swam after us.

I let her come alongside, and then Juag and I pulled her in, she snapping and snarling at us as we did so; but, strange to relate, she didn't offer to attack us after we had ensconced her safely in the bottom alongside Raja.

The canoe behaved much better under sail than I had hoped – infinitely better than the battle-ship *Sari* had – and we made good progress almost due west across the gulf, upon the opposite side of which I hoped to find the mouth of the river of which Juag had told me.

The islander was much interested and impressed by the sail and its results. He had not been able to understand exactly what I hoped to accomplish with it while we were fitting up the boat; but when he saw the clumsy dugout move steadily through the water without paddles, he was as delighted as a child. We made splendid headway on the trip, coming into sight of land at last.

Juang had been terror-stricken when he had learned that I intended crossing the ocean, and when we passed out of sight of land he was in a blue funk. He said that he had never heard of such a thing before in his life, and that always he had understood that those who ventured far from land never returned; for how could they find their way when they could see no land to steer for?

I tried to explain the compass to him; and though he never really grasped the scientific explanation of it, yet he did learn to steer by it quite as well as I. We passed several islands on the journey – islands which Juag told me were entirely unknown to his own island folk. Indeed, our eyes may have been the first ever to rest upon them. I should have liked to stop off and explore them, but the business of empire would brook no unnecessary delays.

I asked Juag how Hooja expected to reach the mouth of the river which we were in search of if he didn't cross the gulf, and the islander explained that Hooja would undoubtedly follow the coast around. For some time we sailed up the coast searching for the river, and at last we found it. So great was it that I thought it must be a mighty gulf until the mass of driftwood that came out upon the first ebb tide convinced me that it was the mouth of a river. There were the trunks of trees uprooted by the undermining of the river banks, giant creepers, flowers, grasses, and now and then the body of some land animal or bird.

I was all excitement to commence our upward journey when there occurred that which I had never before seen within Pellucidar – a really terrific wind-storm. It blew down the river upon us with a ferocity and suddenness that took our breaths away, and before we could get a chance to make the shore it became too late. The best that we could do was to hold the scudding craft before the wind and race along in a smother of white spume. Juag was terrified. If Dian was, she hid it; for was she not the daughter of a once great chief, the sister of a king, and the mate of an emperor?

Raja and Ranee were frightened. The former crawled close to my side and buried his nose against me. Finally even fierce Ranee was moved to seek sympathy from a human being. She slunk to Dian, pressing close against her and whimpering, while Dian stroked her shaggy neck and talked to her as I talked to Raja.

There was nothing for us to do but try to keep the canoe right side up and straight before the wind. For what seemed an eternity the tempest neither increased nor abated. I judged that we must have blown a hundred miles before the wind and straight out into an unknown sea!

As suddenly as the wind rose it died again, and when it died it veered to blow at right angles to its former course in a gentle breeze. I asked Juag then what our course was, for he had had the compass last. It had been on a leather thong about his neck. When he felt for it, the expression that came into his eyes told me as plainly as words what had happened – the compass was lost! The compass was lost!

And we were out of sight of land without a single celestial body to guide us! Even the pendent world was not visible from our position!

Our plight seemed hopeless to me, but I dared not let Dian and Juag guess how utterly dismayed I was; though, as I soon discovered, there was nothing to be gained by trying to keep the worst from Juag – he knew it quite as well as I. He had always known, from the legends of his people, the dangers of the open sea beyond the sight of land. The compass, since he had learned its uses from me, had been all that he had to buoy his hope of eventual salvation from the watery deep. He had seen how it had guided me across the water to the very coast that I desired to reach, and so he had implicit confidence in it. Now that it was gone, his confidence had departed, also.

There seemed but one thing to do; that was to keep on sailing straight before the wind – since he could travel most rapidly along that course – until we sighted land of some description. If it chanced to be the mainland, well and good; if an island – well, we might live upon an island. We certainly could not live long in this little boat, with only a few strips of dried thag and a few quarts of water left.

Quite suddenly a thought occurred to me. I was surprised that it had not come before as a solution to our problem. I turned toward Juag.

'You Pellucidarians are endowed with a wonderful instinct,' I reminded him, 'an instinct that points the way straight to your homes, no matter in what strange land you may find yourself. Now all we have to do is let Dian guide us toward Amoz, and we shall come in a short time to the same coast whence we just were blown.'

As I spoke I looked at them with a smile of renewed hope; but there was no answering smile in their eyes. It was Dian who enlightened me.

'We could do all this upon land,' she said. 'But upon the water that power is denied us. I do not know why; but I have always heard that this is true – that only upon the water may a Pellucidarian be lost. This is, I think, why we all fear the great ocean so – even those who go upon its surface in canoes. Juag has told us that they never go beyond the sight of land.'

We had lowered the sail after the blow while we were discussing the best course to pursue. Our little craft had been drifting idly, rising and falling with the great waves that were now diminishing. Sometimes we were upon the crest – again in the hollow. As Dian ceased speaking she let her eyes range across the limitless expanse of billowing waters. We rose to a great height upon the crest of a mighty wave. As we topped it Dian gave an exclamation and pointed astern.

'Boats!' she cried. 'Boats! Many, many boats!'

Juag and I leaped to our feet; but our little craft had now dropped to the trough, and we could see nothing but walls of water close upon either hand. We waited for the next wave to lift us, and when it did we strained our eyes in the direction that Dian had indicated. Sure enough, scarce half a mile away were several boats, and scattered far and wide behind us as far as we could see were many others! We could not make them out in the distance or in the brief glimpse that we caught of them before we were plunged again into the next wave cañon; but they were boats.

And in them must be human beings like ourselves.

13

Racing For Life

At last the sea subsided, and we were able to get a better view of the armada of small boats in our wake. There must have been two hundred of them. Juag said that he had never seen so many boats before in all his life. Where had they come from? Juag was first to hazard a guess.

'Hooja,' he said, 'was building many boats to carry his warriors to the great river and up it toward Sari. He was building them with almost all his warriors and many slaves upon the Island of Trees. No one else in all the history of Pellucidar has ever built so many boats as they told me Hooja was building. These must be Hooja's boats.'

'And they were blown out to sea by the great storm just as we were,' suggested Dian.

'There can be no better explanation of them,' I agreed.

'What shall we do?' asked Juag.

'Suppose we make sure that they are really Hooja's people,' suggested Dian. 'It may be that they are not, and that if we run away from them before we learn definitely who they are, we shall be running away from a chance to live and find the mainland. They may be a people of whom we have never even heard, and if so we can ask them to help us – if they know the way to the mainland.'

'Which they will not,' interposed Juag.

'Well,' I said, 'it can't make our predicament any more trying to wait until we find out who they are. They are heading for us now. Evidently they have spied our sail, and guess that we do not belong to their fleet.'

'They probably want to ask the way to the mainland themselves,' said Juag, who was nothing if not a pessimist.

'If they want to catch us, they can do it if they can paddle faster than we can sail,' I said. 'If we let them come close enough to discover their identity, and can then sail faster than they can paddle, we can get away from them anyway, so we might as well wait.'

And wait we did.

The sea calmed rapidly, so that by the time the foremost canoe had come within five hundred yards of us we could see them all plainly. Every one was headed for us. The dugouts, which were of unusual length, were manned by twenty paddlers, ten to a side. Besides the paddlers there were twenty-five or more warriors in each boat.

When the leader was a hundred yards from us Dian called our attention to the fact that several of her crew were Sagoths. That convinced us that the flotilla was indeed Hooja's. I told Juag to hail them and get what information he could, while I remained in the bottom of our canoe as much out of sight as possible. Dian lay down at full length in the bottom; I did not want them to see and recognize her if they were in truth Hooja's people.

'Who are you?' shouted Juag, standing up in the boat and making a megaphone of his palms.

A figure arose in the bow of the leading canoe – a figure that I was sure I recognized even before he spoke.

'I am Hooja!' cried the man, in answer to Juag.

For some reason he did not recognize his former prisoner and slave – possibly because he had so many of them.

'I come from the Island of Trees,' he continued. 'A hundred of my boats were lost in the great storm and all their crews drowned. Where is the land? What are you, and what strange thing is that which flutters from the little tree in the front of your canoe?'

He referred to our sail, flapping idly in the wind.

'We, too, are lost,' replied Juag. 'We know not where the land is. We are going back to look for it now.'

So saying he commenced to scull the canoe's nose before the wind, while I made fast the primitive sheets that held our crude sail. We thought it time to be going.

There wasn't much wind at the time, and the heavy, lumbering dugout was slow in getting under way. I thought it never would gain any momentum. And all the while Hooja's canoe was drawing rapidly nearer, propelled by the strong arms of his twenty paddlers. Of course, their dugout was much larger than ours, and, consequently, infinitely heavier and more cumbersome; nevertheless, it was coming along at quite a clip, and ours was yet but barely moving. Dian and I remained out of sight as much as possible, for the two craft were now well within bow-shot of one another, and I knew that Hooja had archers.

Hooja called to Juag to stop when he saw that our craft was moving. He was much interested in the sail, and not a little awed, as I could tell by his shouted remarks and questions. Raising my head, I saw him plainly. He would have made an excellent target for one of my guns, and I had never been sorrier that I had lost them.

We were now picking up speed a trifle, and he was not gaining upon us so fast as at first. In consequence, his requests that we stop suddenly changed to commands as he became aware that we were trying to escape him.

'Come back!' he shouted. 'Come back, or I'll fire!'

I use the word fire because it more nearly translates into English the Pellucidarian word *trag*, which covers the launching of any deadly missile.

But Juag only seized his paddle more tightly – the paddle that answered the purpose of rudder, and commenced to assist the wind by vig-
orous strokes. Then Hooja gave the command to some of his archers to
fire upon us. I couldn't lie hidden in the bottom of the boat, leaving Juag
alone exposed to the deadly shafts, so I arose and, seizing another paddle,
set to work to help him. Dian joined me, though I did my best to persuade her to remain sheltered; but being a woman, she must have her own
way.

The instant that Hooja saw us he recognized us. The whoop of triumph
he raised indicated how certain he was that we were about to fall into his
hands. A shower of arrows fell about us. Then Hooja caused his men to cease
firing – he wanted us alive. None of the missiles struck us, for Hooja's archers were not nearly the marksmen that are my Sarians and Amozites.

We had now gained sufficient headway to hold our own on about even
terms with Hooja's paddlers. We did not seem to be gaining, though; and
neither did they. How long this nerve-racking experience lasted I cannot
guess, though we had pretty nearly finished our meager supply of provisions
when the wind picked up a bit and we commenced to draw away.

Not once yet had we sighted land, nor could I understand it, since so
many of the seas I had seen before were thickly dotted with islands. Our
plight was anything but pleasant, yet I think that Hooja and his forces were
even worse off than we, for they had no food nor water at all.

Far out behind us in a long line that curved upward in the distance, to
be lost in the haze, strung Hooja's two hundred boats. But one would have
been enough to have taken us could it have come alongside. We had drawn
some fifty yards ahead of Hooja – there had been times when we were scarce
ten yards in advance – and were feeling considerably safer from capture.
Hooja's men, working in relays, were commencing to show the effects of the
strain under which they had been forced to work without food or water, and
I think their weakening aided us almost as much as the slight freshening of
the wind.

Hooja must have commenced to realize that he was going to lose us, for he
again gave orders that we be fired upon. Volley after volley of arrows struck
about us. The distance was so great by this time that most of the arrows fell
short, while those that reached us were sufficiently spent to allow us to ward
them off with our paddles. However, it was a most exciting ordeal.

Hooja stood in the bow of his boat, alternately urging his men to greater
speed and shouting epithets at me. But we continued to draw away from
him. At last the wind rose to a fair gale, and we simply raced away from our
pursuers as if they were standing still. Juag was so tickled that he forgot all
about his hunger and thirst. I think that he had never been entirely reconciled to the heathenish invention which I called a sail, and that down in the

bottom of his heart he believed that the paddlers would eventually overhaul us; but now he couldn't praise it enough.

We had a strong gale for a considerable time, and eventually dropped Hooja's fleet so far astern that we could no longer discern them. And then – ah, I shall never forget that moment – Dian sprang to her feet with a cry of 'Land!'

Sure enough, dead ahead, a long, low coast stretched across our bow. It was still a long way off, and we couldn't make out whether it was island or mainland; but at least it was land. If ever shipwrecked mariners were grateful, we were then. Raja and Ranee were commencing to suffer for lack of food, and I could swear that the latter often cast hungry glances upon us, though I am equally sure that no such hideous thoughts ever entered the head of her mate. We watched them both most closely, however. Once while stroking Ranee I managed to get a rope around her neck and make her fast to the side of the boat. Then I felt a bit safer for Dian. It was pretty close quarters in that little dugout for three human beings and two practically wild, man-eating dogs; but we had to make the best of it, since I would not listen to Juag's suggestion that we kill and eat Raja and Ranee.

We made good time to within a few miles of the shore. Then the wind died suddenly out. We were all of us keyed up to such a pitch of anticipation that the blow was doubly hard to bear. And it was a blow, too, since we could not tell in what quarter the wind might rise again; but Juag and I set to work to paddle the remaining distance.

Almost immediately the wind rose again from precisely the opposite direction from which it had formerly blow, so that it was mighty hard work making progress against it. Next it veered again so that we had to turn and run with it parallel to the coast to keep from being swamped in the trough of the seas.

And while we were suffering all these disappointments Hooja's fleet appeared in the distance!

They evidently had gone far to the left of our course, for they were now almost behind us as we ran parallel to the coast; but we were not much afraid of being overtaken in the wind that was blowing. The gale kept on increasing, but it was fitful, swooping down upon us in great gusts and then going almost calm for an instant. It was after one of these momentary calms that the catastrophe occurred. Our sail hung limp and our momentum decreased when of a sudden a particularly vicious squall caught us. Before I could cut the sheets the mast had snapped at the thwart in which it was stepped.

The worst had happened; Juag and I seized paddles and kept the canoe with the wind; but that squall was the parting shot of the gale, which died out immediately after, leaving us free to make for the shore, which we lost no time in attempting. But Hooja had drawn closer in toward shore than we, so it looked as if he might head us off before we could land. However, we did our best to distance him, Dian taking a paddle with us.

We were in a fair way to succeed when there appeared, pouring from among the trees beyond the beach, a horde of yelling, painted savages, brandishing all sorts of devilish-looking primitive weapons. So menacing was their attitude that we realized at once the folly of attempting to land among them.

Hooja was drawing closer to us. There was no wind. We could not hope to outpaddle him. And with our sail gone, no wind would help us, though, as if in derision at our plight, a steady breeze was now blowing. But we had no intention of sitting idle while our fate overtook us, so we bent to our paddles and, keeping parallel with the coast, did our best to pull away from our pursuers.

It was a grueling experience. We were weakened by lack of food. We were suffering the pangs of thirst. Capture and death were close at hand. Yet I think that we gave a good account of ourselves in our final effort to escape. Our boat was so much smaller and lighter than any of Hooja's that the three of us forced it ahead almost as rapidly as his larger craft could go under their twenty paddles.

As we raced along the coast for one of those seemingly interminable periods that may draw hours into eternities where the labor is soul-searing and there is no way to measure time, I saw what I took for the opening to a bay or the mouth of a great river a short distance ahead of us. I wished that we might make for it; but with the menace of Hooja close behind and the screaming natives who raced along the shore parallel to us, I dared not attempt it.

We were not far from shore in that mad flight from death. Even as I paddled I found opportunity to glance occasionally toward the natives. They were white, but hideously painted. From their gestures and weapons I took them to be a most ferocious race. I was rather glad that we had not succeeded in landing among them.

Hooja's fleet had been in much more compact formation when we sighted them this time than on the occasion following the tempest. Now they were moving rapidly in pursuit of us, all well within the radius of a mile. Five of them were leading, all abreast, and were scarce two hundred yards from us. When I glanced over my shoulder I could see that the archers had already fitted arrows to their bows in readiness to fire upon us the moment that they should draw within range.

Hope was low in my breast. I could not see the slightest chance of escaping them, for they were overhauling us rapidly now, since they were able to work their paddles in relays, while we three were rapidly wearying beneath the constant strain that had been put upon us.

It was then that Juag called my attention to the rift in the shore-line which I had thought either a bay or the mouth of a great river. There I saw moving slowly out into the sea that which filled my soul with wonder.

14

Gore and Dreams

It was a two-masted Felucca with lateen sails! the craft was long and low. In it were more than fifty men, twenty or thirty of whom were at oars with which the craft was being propelled from the lee of the land. I was dumbfounded.

Could it be that the savage, painted natives I had seen on shore had so perfected the art of navigation that they were masters of such advanced building and rigging as this craft proclaimed? It seemed impossible! And as I looked I saw another of the same type swing into view and follow its sister through the narrow strait out into the ocean.

Nor were these all. One after another, following closely upon one another's heels, came fifty of the trim, graceful vessels. They were cutting in between Hooja's fleet and our little dugout.

When they came a bit closer my eyes fairly popped from my head at what I saw, for in the eye of the leading felucca stood a man with a sea-glass leveled upon us. Who could they be? Was there a civilization within Pellucidar of such wondrous advancement as this? Were there far-distant lands of which none of my people had ever heard, where a race had so greatly outstripped all other races of this inner world?

The man with the glass had lowered it and was shouting to us. I could not make out his words, but presently I saw that he was pointing aloft. When I looked I saw a pennant fluttering from the peak of the forward lateen yard – a red, white, and blue pennant, with a single great white star in a field of blue.

Then I knew. My eyes went even wider than they had before. It was the navy! It was the navy of the empire of Pellucidar which I had instructed Perry to build in my absence. It was *my* navy!

I dropped my paddle and stood up and shouted and waved my hand. Juag and Dian looked at me as if I had gone suddenly mad. When I could stop shouting I told them, and they shared my joy and shouted with me.

But still Hooja was coming nearer, nor could the leading felucca overhaul him before he would be alongside or at least within bow-shot.

Hooja must have been as much mystified as we were as to the identity of the strange fleet; but when he saw me waving to them he evidently guessed that they were friendly to us, so he urged his men to redouble their efforts to reach us before the felucca cut him off.

He shouted word back to others of his fleet – word that was passed back until it had reached them all – directing them to run alongside the strangers and board them, for with his two hundred craft and his eight or ten thousand warriors he evidently felt equal to overcoming the fifty vessels of the enemy, which did not seem to carry over three thousand men all told.

His own personal energies he bent to reaching Dian and me first, leaving the rest of the work to his other boats. I thought that there could be little doubt that he would be successful in so far as we were concerned, and I feared for the revenge that he might take upon us should the battle go against his force, as I was sure it would; for I knew that Perry and his Mezops must have brought with them all the arms and ammunition that had been contained in the prospector. But I was not prepared for what happened next.

As Hooja's canoe reached a point some twenty yards from us a great puff of smoke broke from the bow of the leading felucca, followed almost simultaneously by a terrific explosion, and a solid shot screamed close over the heads of the men in Hooja's craft, raising a great splash where it clove the water just beyond them.

Perry had perfected gunpowder and built cannon! It was marvelous! Dian and Juag, as much surprised as Hooja, turned wondering eyes toward me. Again the cannon spoke. I suppose that by comparison with the great guns of modern naval vessels of the outer world it was a pitifully small and inadequate thing; but here in Pellucidar, where it was the first of its kind, it was about as awe-inspiring as anything you might imagine.

With the report an iron cannon-ball about five inches in diameter struck Hooja's dugout just above the waterline, tore a great splintering hole in its side, turned it over, and dumped its occupants into the sea.

The four dugouts that had been abreast of Hooja had turned to intercept the leading felucca. Even now, in the face of what must have been a withering catastrophe to them, they kept bravely on toward the strange and terrible craft.

In them were fully two hundred men, while but fifty lined the gunwale of the felucca to repel them. The commander of the felucca, who proved to be Ja, let them come quite close and then turned loose upon them a volley of shots from small-arms.

The cave men and Sagoths in the dugouts seemed to wither before that blast of death like dry grass before a prairie fire. Those who were not hit dropped their bows and javelins and, seizing upon paddles, attempted to escape. But the felucca pursued them relentlessly, her crew firing at will.

At last I heard Ja shouting to the survivors in the dugouts – they were all quite close to us now – offering them their lives if they would surrender. Perry was standing close behind Ja, and I knew that this merciful action was prompted, perhaps commanded, by the old man; for no Pellucidarian would have thought of showing leniency to a defeated foe.

As there was no alternative save death, the survivors surrendered and a moment later were taken aboard the *Amoz*, the name that I could now see printed in large letters upon the felucca's bow, and which no one in that whole world could read except Perry and I.

When the prisoners were aboard, Ja brought the felucca alongside our dugout. Many were the willing hands that reached down to lift us to her decks. The bronze faces of the Mezops were broad with smiles, and Perry was fairly beside himself with joy.

Dian went aboard first and then Juag, as I wished to help Raja and Ranee aboard myself, well knowing that it would fare ill with any Mezop who touched them. We got them aboard at last, and a great commotion they caused among the crew, who had never seen a wild beast thus handled by man before.

Perry and Dian and I were so full of questions that we fairly burst, but we had to contain ourselves for a while, since the battle with the rest of Hooja's fleet had scarce commenced. From the small forward decks of the feluccas Perry's crude cannon were belching smoke, flame, thunder, and death. The air trembled to the roar of them. Hooja's horde, intrepid, savage fighters that they were, were closing in to grapple in a last death-struggle with the Mezops who manned our vessels.

The handling of our fleet by the red island warriors of Ja's clan was far from perfect. I could see that Perry had lost no time after the completion of the boats in setting out upon this cruise. What little the captains and crews had learned of handling feluccas they must have learned principally since they embarked upon this voyage, and while experience is an excellent teacher and had done much for them, they still had a great deal to learn. In maneuvering for position they were continually fouling one another, and on two occasions shots from our batteries came near to striking our own ships.

No sooner, however, was I aboard the flagship than I attempted to rectify this trouble to some extent. By passing commands by word of mouth from one ship to another I managed to get the fifty feluccas into some sort of line, with the flag-ship in the lead. In this formation we commenced slowly to circle the position of the enemy. The dugouts came for us right along in an attempt to board us, but by keeping on the move in one direction and circling, we managed to avoid getting in each other's way, and were enabled to fire our cannon and our small arms with less danger to our own comrades.

When I had a moment to look about me, I took in the felucca on which I was. I am free to confess that I marveled at the excellent construction and stanch yet speedy lines of the little craft. That Perry had chosen this type of vessel seemed rather remarkable, for though I had warned him against turreted battleships, armor, and like useless show, I had fully expected that when I beheld his navy I should find considerable attempt at grim and terrible magnificence, for it was always Perry's idea to overawe these ignorant cave men when we had to contend with them in battle. But I had soon learned that while one might easily astonish them with some new engine of war, it was an utter impossibility to frighten them into surrender.

I learned later that Ja had gone carefully over the plans of various craft with Perry. The old man had explained in detail all that the text told him of them. The two had measured out dimensions upon the ground, that Ja might see the sizes of different boats. Perry had built models, and Ja had had him read carefully and explain all that they could find relative to the handling of sailing vessels. The result of this was that Ja was the one who had chosen the felucca. It was well that Perry had had so excellent a balance wheel, for he had been wild to build a huge frigate of the Nelsonian era – he told me so himself.

One thing that had inclined Ja particularly to the felucca was the fact that it included oars in its equipment. He realized the limitations of his people in the matter of sails, and while they had never used oars, the implement was so similar to a paddle that he was sure they quickly could master the art – and they did. As soon as one hull was completed Ja kept it on the water constantly, first with one crew and then with another, until two thousand red warriors had learned to row. Then they stepped their masts and a crew was told off for the first ship.

While the others were building they learned to handle theirs. As each succeeding boat was launched its crew took it out and practiced with it under the tutorage of those who had graduated from the first ship, and so on until a full complement of men had been trained for every boat.

Well, to get back to the battle: The Hoojans kept on coming at us, and as fast as they came we mowed them down. It was little else than slaughter. Time and time again I cried to them to surrender, promising them their lives if they would do so. At last there were but ten boatloads left. These turned in flight. They thought they could paddle away from us – it was pitiful! I passed the word from boat to boat to cease firing – not to kill another Hoojan unless they fired on us. Then we set out after them. There was a

nice little breeze blowing and we bowled along after our quarry as gracefully and as lightly as swans upon a park lagoon. As we approached them I
could see not only wonder but admiration in their eyes. I hailed the nearest
dugout.

'Throw down your arms and come aboard us,' I cried, 'and you shall not
be harmed. We will feed you and return you to the mainland. Then you
shall go free upon your promise never to bear arms against the Emperor of
Pellucidar again!'

I think it was the promise of food that interested them most. They could
scarce believe that we would not kill them. But when I exhibited the prisoners we already had taken, and showed them that they were alive and unharmed, a great Sagoth in one of the boats asked me what guarantee I could
give that I would keep my word.

'None other than my word,' I replied. 'That I do not break.'

The Pellucidarians themselves are rather punctilious about this same
matter, so the Sagoth could understand that I might possibly be speaking
the truth. But he could not understand why we should not kill them unless
we meant to enslave them, which I had as much as denied already when I
had promised to set them free. Ja couldn't exactly see the wisdom of my
plan, either. He thought that we ought to follow up the ten remaining dugouts and sink them all; but I insisted that we must free as many as possible
of our enemies upon the mainland.

'You see,' I explained, 'these men will return at once to Hooja's Island,
to the Mahar cities from which they come, or to the countries from which
they were stolen by the Mahars. They are men of two races and of many
countries. They will spread the story of our victory far and wide, and while
they are with us, we will let them see and hear many other wonderful things
which they may carry back to their friends and their chiefs. It's the finest
chance for free publicity, Perry,' I added to the old man, 'that you or I have
seen in many a day.'

Perry agreed with me. As a matter of fact, he would have agreed to anything that would have restrained us from killing the poor devils who fell
into our hands. He was a great fellow to invent gunpowder and firearms
and cannon; but when it came to using these things to kill people, he was as
tender-hearted as a chicken.

The Sagoth who had spoken was talking to other Sagoths in his boat.
Evidently they were holding a council over the question of the wisdom of
surrendering.

'What will become of you if you don't surrender to us?' I asked. 'If we
do not open up our batteries on you again and kill you all, you will simply
drift about the sea helplessly until you die of thirst and starvation. You
cannot return to the islands, for you have seen as well as we that the natives

there are very numerous and warlike. They would kill you the moment you landed.'

The upshot of it was that the boat of which the Sagoth speaker was in charge surrendered. The Sagoths threw down their weapons, and we took them aboard the ship next in line behind the *Amoz*. First Ja had to impress upon the captain and crew of the ship that the prisoners were not to be abused or killed. After that the remaining dugouts paddled up and surrendered. We distributed them among the entire fleet lest there be too many upon any one vessel. Thus ended the first real naval engagement that the Pellucidarian seas had ever witnessed – though Perry still insists that the action in which the *Sari* took part was a battle of the first magnitude.

The battle over and the prisoners disposed of and fed – and do not imagine that Dian, Juag, and I, as well as the two hounds were not fed also – I turned my attention to the fleet. We had the feluccas close in about the flag-ship, and with all the ceremony of a medieval potentate on parade I received the commanders of the forty-nine feluccas that accompanied the flag-ship – Dian and I together – the empress and the emperor of Pellucidar.

It was a great occasion. The savage, bronze warriors entered into the spirit of it, for as I learned later dear old Perry had left no opportunity neglected for impressing upon them that David was emperor of Pellucidar, and that all that they were accomplishing and all that he was accomplishing was due to the power, and redounded to the glory of David. The old man must have rubbed it in pretty strong, for those fierce warriors nearly came to blows in their efforts to be among the first of those to kneel before me and kiss my hand. When it came to kissing Dian's I think they enjoyed it more; I know I should have.

A happy thought occurred to me as I stood upon the little deck of the *Amoz* with the first of Perry's primitive cannon behind me. When Ja kneeled at my feet, the first to do me homage, I drew from its scabbard at his side the sword of hammered iron that Perry had taught him to fashion. Striking him lightly on the shoulder I created him king of Anoroc. Each captain of the forty-nine other feluccas I made a duke. I left it to Perry to enlighten them as to the value of the honors I had bestowed upon them.

During these ceremonies Raja and Ranee had stood beside Dian and me. Their bellies had been well filled, but still they had difficulty in permitting so much edible humanity to pass unchallenged. It was a good education for them though, and never after did they find it difficult to associate with the human race without arousing their appetites.

After the ceremonies were over we had a chance to talk with Perry and Ja. The former told me that Ghak, king of Sari, had sent my letter and map to him by a runner, and that he and Ja had at once decided to set out on the completion of the fleet to ascertain the correctness of my theory that the Lural Az, in which the Anoroc Islands lay, was in reality the same ocean as that which lapped the shores of Thuria under the name of Sojar Az, or Great Sea.

Their destination had been the island retreat of Hooja, and they had sent word to Ghak of their plans that we might work in harmony with them. The tempest that had blown us off the coast of the continent had blown them far to the south also. Shortly before discovering us they had come into a great group of islands, from between the largest two of which they were sailing when they saw Hooja's fleet pursuing our dugout.

I asked Perry if he had any idea as to where we were, or in what direction lay Hooja's island or the continent. He replied by producing his map, on which he had carefully marked the newly discovered islands – there described as the Unfriendly Isles – which showed Hooja's island northwest of us about two points west.

He then explained that with compass, chronometer, log and reel, they had kept a fairly accurate record of their course from the time they had set out. Four of the feluccas were equipped with these instruments, and all of the captains had been instructed in their use.

I was very greatly surprised at the ease with which these savages had mastered the rather intricate detail of this unusual work, but Perry assured me that they were a wonderfully intelligent race, and had been quick to grasp all that he had tried to teach them.

Another thing that surprised me was the fact that so much had been accomplished in so short a time, for I could not believe that I had been gone from Anoroc for a sufficient period to permit of building a fleet of fifty feluccas and mining iron ore for the cannon and balls, to say nothing of manufacturing these guns and the crude muzzle-loading rifles with which every Mezop was armed, as well as the gunpowder and ammunition they had in such ample quantities.

'Time!' exclaimed Perry. 'Well, how long *were* you gone from Anoroc before we picked you up in the Sojar Az?'

That was a puzzler, and I had to admit it. I didn't know how much time had elapsed and neither did Perry, for time is nonexistent in Pellucidar.

'Then, you see, David,' he continued, 'I had almost unbelievable resources at my disposal. The Mezops inhabiting the Anoroc Islands, which stretch far out to sea beyond the three principal isles with which you are familiar, number well into the millions, and by far the greater part of them are friendly to Ja. Men, women, and children turned to and worked the moment Ja explained the nature of our enterprise.

'And not only were they anxious to do all in their power to hasten the day when the Mahars should be overthrown, but – and this counted for most of all – they are simply ravenous for greater knowledge and for better ways of doing things.

'The contents of the prospector set their imaginations to working over-time, so that they craved to own, themselves, the knowledge which had made it possible for other men to create and build the things which you brought back from the outer world.

'And then,' continued the old man, 'the element of time, or, rather, lack of time, operated to my advantage. There being no nights, there was no laying off from work – they labored incessantly stopping only to eat and, on rare occasions, to sleep. Once we had discovered iron ore we had enough mined in an incredibly short time to build a thousand cannon. I had only to show them once how a thing should be done, and they would fall to work by thousands to do it.

'Why, no sooner had we fashioned the first muzzle-loader and they had seen it work successfully, than fully three thousand Mezops fell to work to make rifles. Of course there was much confusion and lost motion at first, but eventually Ja got them in hand, detailing squads of them under competent chiefs to certain work.

'We now have a hundred expert gun-makers. On a little isolated isle we have a great powder-factory. Near the iron-mine, which is on the main-land, is a smelter, and on the eastern shore of Anoroc, a well equipped ship-yard. All these industries are guarded by forts in which several cannon are mounted and where warriors are always on guard.

'You would be surprised now, David, at the aspect of Anoroc. I am sur-prised myself; it seems always to me as I compare it with the day that I first set foot upon it from the deck of the *Sari* that only a miracle could have worked the change that has taken place.'

'It is a miracle,' I said; 'it is nothing short of a miracle to transplant all the wondrous possibilities of the twentieth century back to the Stone Age. It is a miracle to think that only five hundred miles of earth separate two epochs that are really ages and ages apart.

'It is stupendous, Perry! But still more stupendous is the power that you and I wield in this great world. These people look upon us as little less than supermen. We must show them that we are all of that.

'We must give them the best that we have, Perry.'

'Yes,' he agreed; 'we must. I have been thinking a great deal lately that some kind of shrapnel shell or explosive bomb would be a most splendid innovation in their warfare. Then there are breech-loading rifles and those with magazines that I must hasten to study out and learn to reproduce as soon as we get settled down again; and—'

'Hold on, Perry!' I cried. 'I didn't mean these sorts of things at all. I said that we must give them the best we have. What we have given them so far has been the worst. We have given them war and the munitions of war. In a single day we have made their wars infinitely more terrible and bloody than in all their past ages they have been able to make them with their crude, primitive weapons.

'In a period that could scarcely have exceeded two outer earthly hours, our fleet practically annihilated the largest armada of native canoes that the Pellucidarians ever before had gathered together. We butchered some eight thousand warriors with the twentieth-century gifts we brought. Why, they wouldn't have killed that many warriors in the entire duration of a dozen of their wars with their own weapons! No, Perry; we've got to give them something better than scientific methods of killing one another.'

The old man looked at me in amazement. There was reproach in his eyes, too.

'Why, David!' he said sorrowfully. 'I thought that you would be pleased with what I had done. We planned these things together, and I am sure that it was you who suggested practically all of it. I have done only what I thought you wished done and I have done it the best that I know how.'

I laid my hand on the old man's shoulder.

'Bless your heart, Perry!' I cried. 'You've accomplished miracles. You have done precisely what I should have done, only you've done it better. I'm not finding fault; but I don't wish to lose sight myself, or let you lose sight, of the greater work which must grow out of this preliminary and necessary carnage. First we must place the empire upon a secure footing, and we can do so only by putting the fear of us in the hearts of our enemies; but after that—

'Ah, Perry! That is the day I look forward to! When you and I can build sewing-machines instead of battleships, harvesters of crops instead of harvesters of men, plow-shares and telephones, schools and colleges, printing-presses and paper! When our merchant marine shall ply the great Pellucidarian seas, and cargoes of silks and typewriters and books shall forge their ways where only hideous saurians have held sway since time began!'

'Amen!' said Perry.

And Dian, who was standing at my side, pressed my hand.

15

Conquest and Peace

The fleet sailed directly for Hooja's island, coming to anchor at its north-eastern extremity before the flat-topped hill that had been Hooja's stronghold.

I sent one of the prisoners ashore to demand an immediate surrender; but as he told me afterward they wouldn't believe all that he told them, so they congregated on the cliff-top and shot futile arrows at us.

In reply I had five of the feluccas cannonade them. When they scampered away at the sound of the terrific explosions, and at sight of the smoke and the iron balls, I landed a couple of hundred red warriors and led them to the opposite end of the hill into the tunnel that ran to its summit. Here we met a little resistance; but a volley from the muzzle-loaders turned back those who disputed our right of way, and presently we gained the mesa. Here again we met resistance, but at last the remnant of Hooja's horde surrendered.

Juag was with me, and I lost no time in returning to him and his tribe the hilltop that had been their ancestral home for ages until they were robbed of it by Hooja. I created a kingdom of the island, making Juag king there. Before we sailed I went to Gr-gr-gr, chief of the beast-men, taking Juag with me. There the three of us arranged a code of laws that would permit the brute-folk and the human beings of the island to live in peace and harmony. Gr-gr-gr sent his son with me back to Sari, capital of my empire, that he might learn the ways of the human beings. I have hopes of turning this race into the greatest agriculturists of Pellucidar.

When I returned to the fleet I found that one of the islanders of Juag's tribe, who had been absent when we arrived, had just returned from the mainland with the news that a great army was encamped in the Land of Awful Shadow, and that they were threatening Thuria. I lost no time in weighing anchors and setting out for the continent, which we reached after a short and easy voyage.

From the deck of the *Amoz* I scanned the shore through the glasses that Perry had brought with him. When we were close enough for the glasses to be of value I saw that there was indeed a vast concourse of warriors entirely encircling the walled village of Goork, chief of the Thurians. As we approached smaller objects became distinguishable. It was then that I discovered numerous flags and pennants floating above the army of the besiegers.

I called Perry and passed the glasses to him.

'Ghak of Sari,' I said.

Perry looked through the lenses of a moment, and then turned to me with a smile.

'The red, white, and blue of the empire,' he said. 'It is indeed your majesty's army.'

It soon became apparent that we had been sighted by those on shore, for a great multitude of warriors had congregated along the beach watching us. We came to anchor as close in as we dared, which with our light feluccas was within easy speaking-distance of the shore. Ghak was there and his eyes were mighty wide, too; for, as he told us later, though he knew this must be Perry's fleet it was so wonderful to him that he could not believe the testimony of his own eyes even while he was watching it approach.

To give the proper effect to our meeting I commanded that each felucca fire twenty-one guns as a salute to His Majesty Ghak, King of Sari. Some of the gunners, in the exuberance of their enthusiasm, fired solid shot; but fortunately they had sufficient good judgment to train their pieces on the open sea, so no harm was done. After this we landed – an arduous task since each felucca carried but a single light dugout.

I learned from Ghak that the Thurian chieftain, Goork, had been inclined to haughtiness, and had told Ghak, the Hairy One, that he knew nothing of me and cared less; but I imagine that the sight of the fleet and the sound of the guns brought him to his senses, for it was not long before he sent a deputation to me, inviting me to visit him in his village. Here he apologized for the treatment he had accorded me, very gladly swore allegiance to the empire, and received in return the title of king.

We remained in Thuria only long enough to arrange the treaty with Goork, among the other details of which was his promise to furnish the imperial army with a thousand lidi, or Thurian beasts of burden, and drivers for them. These were to accompany Ghak's army back to Sari by land, while the fleet sailed to the mouth of the great river from which Dian, Juag, and I had been blown.

The voyage was uneventful. We found the river easily, and sailed up it for many miles through as rich and wonderful a plain as I have ever seen. At the head of navigation we disembarked, leaving a sufficient guard for the feluccas, and marched the remaining distance to Sari.

Ghak's army, which was composed of warriors of all the original tribes of the federation, showing how successful had been his efforts to rehabilitate the empire, marched into Sari some time after we arrived. With them were the thousand lidi from Thuria.

At a council of the kings it was decided that we should at once commence the great war against the Mahars, for these haughty reptiles presented the greatest obstacle to human progress within Pellucidar. I laid out a plan of campaign which met with the enthusiastic endorsement of the kings. Pursuant to it, I at once despatched fifty lidi to the fleet with orders to fetch fifty cannon to Sari. I also ordered the fleet to proceed at once to Anoroc, where they were to take aboard all the rifles and ammunition that had been completed since their departure, and with a full complement of men to sail along the coast in an attempt to find a passage to the inland sea near which lay the Mahars' buried city of Phutra.

Ja was sure that a large and navigable river connected the sea of Phutra with the Lural Az, and that, barring accident, the fleet would be before Phutra as soon as the land forces were.

At last the great army started upon its march. There were warriors from every one of the federated kingdoms. All were armed either with bow and arrows or muzzle-loaders, for nearly the entire Mezop contingent had been enlisted for this march, only sufficient having been left aboard the feluccas to man them properly. I divided the forces into divisions, regiments, battalions, companies, and even to platoons and sections, appointing the full complement of officers and noncommissioned officers. On the long march I schooled them in their duties, and as fast as one learned I sent him among the others as a teacher.

Each regiment was made up of about a thousand bowmen, and to each was temporarily attached a company of Mezop musketeers and a battery of artillery – the latter, our naval guns, mounted upon the broad backs of the mighty lidi. There was also one full regiment of Mezop musketeers and a regiment of primitive spearmen. The rest of the lidi that we brought with us were used for baggage animals and to transport our women and children, for we had brought them with us, as it was our intention to march from one Mahar city to another until we had subdued every Mahar nation that menaced the safety of any kingdom of the empire.

Before we reached the plain of Phutra we were discovered by a company of Sagoths, who at first stood to give battle; but upon seeing the vast numbers of our army they turned and fled toward Phutra. The result of this was that when we came in sight of the hundred towers which mark the entrances to the buried city we found a great army of Sagoths and Mahars lined up to give us battle.

At a thousand yards we halted, and, placing our artillery upon a slight eminence at either flank, we commenced to drop solid shot among them. Ja, who was chief artillery officer, was in command of this branch of the service, and he did some excellent work, for his Mezop gunners had become rather proficient by this time. The Sagoths couldn't stand much of this sort of warfare, so they charged us, yelling like fiends. We let them come quite close, and then the musketeers who formed the first line opened up on them.

The slaughter was something frightful, but still the remnants of them kept on coming until it was a matter of hand-to-hand fighting. Here our spearmen were of value, as were also the crude iron swords with which most of the imperial warriors were armed.

We lost heavily in the encounter after the Sagoths reached us; but they were absolutely exterminated – not one remained even as a prisoner. The Mahars, seeing how the battle was going, had hastened to the safety of their buried city. When we had overcome their gorilla-men we followed after them.

But here we were doomed to defeat, at least temporarily; for no sooner had the first of our troops descended into the subterranean avenues than many of them came stumbling and fighting their way back to the surface, half-choked by the fumes of some deadly gas that the reptiles had liberated upon them. We lost a number of men here. Then I sent for Perry, who had remained discreetly in the rear, and had him construct a little affair that I had had in my mind against the possibility of our meeting with a check at the entrances to the underground city.

Under my direction he stuffed one of his cannon full of powder, small bullets, and pieces of stone, almost to the muzzle. Then he plugged the muzzle tight with a cone-shaped block of wood, hammered and jammed in as tight as it could be. Next he inserted a long fuse. A dozen men rolled the cannon to the top of the stairs leading down into the city, first removing it from its carriage. One of them then lit the fuse and the whole thing was given a shove down the stairway, while the detachment turned and scampered to a safe distance.

For what seemed a very long time nothing happened. We had commenced to think that the fuse had been put out while the piece was rolling down the stairway, or that the Mahars had guessed its purpose and extinguished it themselves, when the ground about the entrance rose suddenly into the air, to be followed by a terrific explosion and a burst of smoke and flame that shot high in company with dirt, stone, and fragments of cannon.

Perry had been working on two more of these giant bombs as soon as the first was completed. Presently we launched these into two of the other entrances. They were all that were required, for almost immediately after the third explosion a stream of Mahars broke from the exits furthest from us, rose upon their wings, and soared northward. A hundred men on lidi were despatched in pursuit, each lidi carrying two riflemen in addition to its driver. Guessing that the inland sea, which lay not far north of Phutra, was their destination, I took a couple of regiments and followed.

A low ridge intervenes between the Phutra plain where the city lies, and the inland sea where the Mahars were wont to disport themselves in the cool waters. Not until we had topped this ridge did we get a view of the sea.

Then we beheld a scene that I shall never forget so long as I may live.

Along the beach were lined up the troop of lidi, while a hundred yards from shore the surface of the water was black with the long snouts and cold, reptilian eyes of the Mahars. Our savage Mezop riflemen, and the shorter, squatter, white-skinned Thurian drivers, shading their eyes with their hands, were gazing seaward beyond the Mahars, whose eyes were fastened upon the same spot. My heart leaped when I discovered that which was chaining the attention of them all. Twenty graceful feluccas were moving smoothly across the waters of the sea toward the reptilian horde!

The sight must have filled the Mahars with awe and consternation, for never had they seen the like of these craft before. For a time they seemed unable to do aught but gaze at the approaching fleet; but when the Mezops opened on them with their muskets the reptiles swam rapidly in the direction of the feluccas, evidently thinking that these would prove the easier to overcome. The commander of the fleet permitted them to approach within a hundred yards. Then he opened on them with all the cannon that could be brought to bear, as well as with the small arms of the sailors.

A great many of the reptiles were killed at the first volley. They wavered for a moment, then dived; nor did we see them again for a long time.

But finally they rose far out beyond the fleet, and when the feluccas came about and pursued them they left the water and flew away toward the north.

Following the fall of Phutra I visited Anoroc, where I found the people busy in the shipyards and the factories that Perry had established. I discovered something, too, that he had not told me of – something that seemed infinitely more promising than the powder-factory or the arsenal. It was a young man poring over one of the books I had brought back from the outer world! He was sitting in the log cabin that Perry had had built to serve as his sleeping quarters and office. So absorbed was he that he did not notice our entrance. Perry saw the look of astonishment in my eyes and smiled.

'I started teaching him the alphabet when we first reached the prospector, and were taking out its contents,' he explained. 'He was much mystified by the books and anxious to know of what use they were. When I explained he asked me to teach him to read, and so I worked with him whenever I could. He is very intelligent and learns quickly. Before I left he had made great progress, and as soon as he is qualified he is going to teach others to read. It was mighty hard work getting started, though, for everything had to be translated into Pellucidarian.

'It will take a long time to solve this problem, but I think that by teaching a number of them to read and write English we shall then be able more quickly to give them a written language of their own.'

And this was the nucleus about which we were to build our great system of schools and colleges – this almost naked red warrior, sitting in Perry's little cabin upon the island of Anoroc, picking out words letter by letter from a work on intensive farming. Now we have—

But I'll get to all that before I finish.

While we were at Anoroc I accompanied Ja in an expedition to South Island, the southernmost of the three largest which form the Anoroc group – Perry had given it its name – where we made peace with the tribe there that had for long been hostile toward Ja. They were now glad enough to make friends with him and come into the federation. From there we sailed with sixty-five feluccas for distant Luana, the main island of the group where dwell the hereditary enemies of Anoroc.

Twenty-five of the feluccas were of a new and larger type than those with which Ja and Perry had sailed on the occasion when they chanced to find and rescue Dian and me. They were longer, carried much larger sails, and were considerably swifter. Each carried four guns instead of two, and these were so arranged that one or more of them could be brought into action no matter where the enemy lay.

The Luana group lies just beyond the range of vision from the mainland. The largest island of it alone is visible from Anoroc; but when we neared it we found that it comprised many beautiful islands, and that they were thickly populated. The Luanians had not, of course, been ignorant of all that had been going on in the domains of their nearest and dearest enemies. They knew of our feluccas and our guns, for several of their riding-parties had had a taste of both. But their principal chief, an old man, had never seen either. So, when he sighted us, he put out to overwhelm us, bringing with him a fleet of about a hundred large war-canoes, loaded to capacity with javelin-armed warriors. It was pitiful, and I told Ja as much. It seemed a shame to massacre these poor fellows if there was any way out of it.

To my surprise Ja felt much as I did. He said he had always hated to war with other Mezops when there were so many alien races to fight against. I suggested that we hail the chief and request a parley; but when Ja did so the old fool thought that we were afraid, and with loud cries of exultation urged his warriors upon us.

So we opened up on them, but at my suggestion centered our fire upon the chief's canoe. The result was that in about thirty seconds there was nothing left of that war dugout but a handful of splinters, while its crew – those who were not killed – were struggling in the water, battling with the myriad terrible creatures that had risen to devour them.

We saved some of them, but the majority died just as had Hooja and the crew of his canoe that time our second shot capsized them.

Again we called to the remaining warriors to enter into a parley with us; but the chief's son was there and he would not, now that he had seen his father killed. He was all for revenge. So we had to open up on the brave fellows with all our guns; but it didn't last long at that, for there chanced to be wiser heads among the Luanians than their chief or his son had possessed. Presently, an old warrior who commanded one of the dugouts surrendered. After that they came in one by one until all had laid their weapons upon our decks.

Then we called together upon the flag-ship all our captains, to give the affair greater weight and dignity, and all the principal men of Luana. We had conquered them, and they expected either death or slavery; but they deserved neither, and I told them so. It is always my habit here in Pellucidar to impress upon these savage people that mercy is as noble a quality as physical bravery, and that next to the men who fight shoulder to shoulder with one, we should honor the brave men who fight against us, and if we are victorious, award them both the mercy and honor that are their due.

By adhering to this policy I have won to the federation many great and noble peoples, who under the ancient traditions of the inner world would have been massacred or enslaved after we had conquered them; and thus I won the Luanians. I gave them their freedom, and returned their weapons to them after they had sworn loyalty to me and friendship and peace with Ja, and I made the old fellow, who had had the good sense to surrender, king of Luana, for both the old chief and his only son had died in the battle.

When I sailed away from Luana she was included among the kingdoms of the empire, whose boundaries were thus pushed eastward several hundred miles.

We now returned to Anoroc and thence to the mainland, where I again took up the campaign against the Mahars, marching from one great buried city to another until we had passed far north of Amoz into a country where I had never been. At each city we were victorious, killing or capturing the Sagoths and driving the Mahars further away.

I noticed that they always fled toward the north. The Sagoth prisoners we usually found quite ready to transfer their allegiance to us, for they are little more than brutes, and when they found that we could fill their stomachs and give them plenty of fighting, they were nothing loath to march with us against the next Mahar city and battle with men of their own race.

Thus we proceeded, swinging in a great half-circle north and west and south again until we had come back to the edge of the Lidi Plains north of Thuria. Here we overcame the Mahar city that had ravaged the Land of Awful Shadow for so many ages. When we marched on to Thuria, Goork and his people went mad with joy at the tidings we brought them.

During this long march of conquest we had passed through seven countries, peopled by primitive human tribes who had not yet heard of the federation, and succeeded in joining them all to the empire. It was noticeable that each of these peoples had a Mahar city situated near by, which had drawn upon them for slaves and human food for so many ages that not even in legend had the population any folk-tale which did not in some degree reflect an inherent terror of the reptilians.

In each of these countries I left an officer and warriors to train them in military discipline, and prepare them to receive the arms that I intended furnishing them as rapidly as Perry's arsenal could turn them out, for we felt that it would be a long, long time before we should see the last of the Mahars.

That they had flown north but temporarily until we should be gone with our great army and terrifying guns I was positive, and equally sure was I that they would presently return.

The task of ridding Pellucidar of these hideous creatures is one which in all probability will never be entirely completed, for their great cities must abound by the hundreds and thousands of the far-distant lands that no subject of the empire has ever laid eyes upon.

But within the present boundaries of my domain there are now none left that I know of, for I am sure we should have heard indirectly of any great Mahar city that had escaped us, although of course the imperial army has by no means covered the vast area which I now rule.

After leaving Thuria we returned to Sari, where the seat of government is located. Here, upon a vast, fertile plateau, overlooking the great gulf that runs into the continent from the Lural Az, we are building the great city of Sari. Here we are erecting mills and factories. Here we are teaching men and women the rudiments of agriculture. Here Perry has built the first printing-press, and a dozen young Sarians are teaching their fellows to read and write the language of Pellucidar.

We have just laws and only a few of them. Our people are happy because they are always working at something which they enjoy. There is no money, nor is any money value placed upon any commodity. Perry and I were as one in resolving that the root of all evil should not be introduced into Pellucidar while we lived.

A man may exchange that which he produces for something which he desires that another has produced; but he cannot dispose of the thing he thus acquires. In other words, a commodity ceases to have pecuniary value the instant that it passes out of the hands of its producer. All excess reverts to government; and, as this represents the production of the people as a government, government may dispose of it to other peoples in exchange for that which they produce. Thus we are establishing a trade between kingdoms, the profits from which go to the betterment of the people – to building factories for the manufacture of agricultural implements, and machinery for the various trades we are gradually teaching the people.

Already Anoroc and Luana are vying with one another in the excellence of the ships they build. Each has several large ship-yards. Anoroc makes gunpowder and mines iron ore, and by means of their ships they carry on a very lucrative trade with Thuria, Sari, and Amoz. The Thurians breed lidi, which, having the strength and intelligence of an elephant, make excellent draft animals.

Around Sari and Amoz the men are domesticating the great striped antelope, the meat of which is most delicious. I am sure that it will not be long before they will have them broken to harness and saddle. The horses of

Pellucidar are far too diminutive for such uses, some species of them being little larger than fox-terriers.

Dian and I live in a great palace overlooking the gulf. There is no glass in our windows, for we have no windows, the walls rising but a few feet above the floor-line, the rest of the space being open to the ceilings; but we have a roof to shade us from the perpetual noon-day sun. Perry and I decided to set a style in architecture that would not curse future generations with the white plague, so we have plenty of ventilation. Those of the people who prefer, still inhabit their caves, but many are building houses similar to ours.

At Greenwich we have located a town and an observatory – though there is nothing to observe but the stationary sun directly overhead. Upon the edge of the Land of Awful Shadow is another observatory, from which the time is flashed by wireless to every corner of the empire twenty-four times a day. In addition to the wireless, we have a small telephone system in Sari. Everything is yet in the early stages of development; but with the science of the outer-world twentieth century to draw upon we are making rapid progress, and with all the faults and errors of the outer world to guide us clear of dangers, I think that it will not be long before Pellucidar will become as nearly a Utopia as one may expect to find this side of heaven.

Perry is away just now, laying out a railway-line from Sari to Amoz. There are immense anthracite coal-fields at the head of the gulf not far from Sari, and the railway will tap these. Some of his students are working on a locomotive now. It will be a strange sight to see an iron horse puffing through the primeval jungles of the stone age, while cave bears, saber-toothed tigers, mastodons and the countless other terrible creatures of the past look on from their tangled lairs in wide-eyed astonishment.

We are very happy, Dian and I, and I would not return to the outer world for all the riches of all its princes. I am content here. Even without my imperial powers and honors I should be content, for have I not that greatest of all treasures, the love of a good woman – my wondrous empress, Dian the Beautiful?

TANAR OF PELLUCIDAR

PROLOGUE

Jason Gridley is a radio bug. Had he not been, this story never would have been written. Jason is twenty-three and scandalously good looking – too good looking to be a bug of any sort. As a matter of fact, he does not seem buggish at all – just a normal, sane, young American, who knows a great deal about many things in addition to radio; aeronautics, for example, and golf, and tennis, and polo.

But this is not Jason's story – he is only an incident – an important incident in my life that made this story possible, and so, with a few more words of explanation, we shall leave Jason to his tubes and waves and amplifiers, concerning which he knows everything and I nothing.

Jason is an orphan with an income, and after he graduated from Stanford, he came down and bought a couple of acres at Tarzana, and that is how and when I met him.

While he was building he made my office his headquarters and was often in my study and afterward I returned the compliment by visiting him in his new 'lab,' as he calls it – a quite large room at the rear of his home, a quiet, restful room in a quiet, restful house of the Spanish-American farm type – or we rode together in the Santa Monica Mountains in the cool air of early morning.

Jason is experimenting with some new principle of radio concerning which the less I say the better it will be for my reputation, since I know nothing whatsoever about it and am likely never to.

Perhaps I am too old, perhaps I am too dumb, perhaps I am just not interested – I prefer to ascribe my abysmal and persistent ignorance of all things pertaining to radio to the last state; that of disinterestedness; it salves my pride.

I do know this, however, because Jason has told me, that the idea he is playing with suggests an entirely new and unsuspected – well, let us call it wave.

He says the idea was suggested to him by the vagaries of static and in groping around in search of some device to eliminate this he discovered in the ether an undercurrent that operated according to no previously known scientific laws.

At his Tarzana home he has erected a station and a few miles away, at the back of my ranch, another. Between these stations we talk to one another through some strange, ethereal medium that seems to pass through all other waves and all other stations, unsuspected and entirely harmless – so harmless is it that it has not the slightest effect upon Jason's regular set, standing in the same room and receiving over the same aerial.

But this, which is not very interesting to any one except Jason, is all by the way of getting to the beginning of the amazing narrative of the adventures of Tanar of Pellucidar.

Jason and I were sitting in his 'lab' one evening discussing, as we often did, innumerable subjects, from 'cabbages to kings,' and coming back, as Jason usually did, to the Gridley wave, which is what we have named it.

Much of the time Jason kept on his ear phones, than which there is no greater discourager of conversation. But this does not irk me as much as most of the conversations one has to listen to through life. I like long silences and my own thoughts.

Presently, Jason removed the headpiece. 'It is enough to drive a fellow to drink!' he exclaimed.

'What?' I asked.

'I am getting that same stuff again,' he said. 'I can hear voices, very faintly, but, unmistakably, human voices. They are speaking a language unknown to man. It is maddening.'

'Mars, perhaps,' I suggested, 'or Venus.'

He knitted his brows and then suddenly smiled one of his quick smiles. 'Or Pellucidar.'

I shrugged.

'Do you know, Admiral,' he said (he calls me Admiral because of a yachting cap I wear at the beach), 'that when I was a kid I used to believe every word of those crazy stories of yours about Mars and Pellucidar. The inner world at the earth's core was as real to me as the High Sierras, the San Joaquin Valley, or the Golden Gate, and I felt that I knew the twin cities of Helium better than I did Los Angeles.

'I saw nothing improbable at all in that trip of David Innes and old man Perry through the earth's crust to Pellucidar. Yes, sir, that was all gospel to me when I was a kid.'

'And now you are twenty-three and know that it can't be true,' I said, with a smile.

'You are trying to tell me it is true, are you?' he demanded, laughing.

'I never have told any one that it is true,' I replied; 'I let people think what they think, but I reserve the right to do likewise.'

'Why, you know perfectly well that it would be impossible for that iron mole of Perry's to have penetrated five hundred miles of the earth's crust, you know there is no inner world peopled by strange reptiles and men of the stone age, you know there is no Emperor of Pellucidar.' Jason was becoming excited, but his sense of humor came to our rescue and he laughed.

'I like to believe that there is a Dian the Beautiful,' I said.

'Yes,' he agreed, 'but I am sorry you killed off Hooja the Sly One. He was a corking villain.'

'There are always plenty of villains,' I reminded him.

'They help the girls to keep their "figgers" and their school girl complexions,' he said.

'How?' I asked.

'The exercise they get from being pursued.'

'You are making fun of me,' I reproached him, 'but remember, please, that I am but a simple historian. If damsels flee and villains pursue I must truthfully record the fact.'

'Baloney!' he exclaimed in the pure university English of America.

Jason replaced his headpiece and I returned to the perusal of the narrative of an ancient liar, who should have made a fortune out of the credulity of book readers, but seems not to have. Thus we sat for some time.

Presently Jason removed his ear phones and turned toward me. 'I was getting music,' he said; 'strange, weird music, and then suddenly there came loud shouts and it seemed that I could hear blows struck and there were screams and the sound of shots.'

'Perry, you know, was experimenting with gunpowder down there below, in Pellucidar,' I reminded Jason, with a grin; but he was inclined to be serious and did not respond in kind.

'You know, of course,' he said, 'that there really has been a theory of an inner world for many years.'

'Yes,' I replied, 'I have read works expounding and defending such a theory.'

'It supposes polar openings leading into the interior of the earth,' said Jason.

'And it is substantiated by many seemingly irrefutable scientific facts,' I reminded him – 'open polar sea, warmer water farthest north, tropical vegetation floating southward from the polar regions, the northern lights, the magnetic pole, the persistent stories of the Eskimos that they are descended from a race that came from a warm country far to the north.'

'I'd like to make a try for one of the polar openings,' mused Jason as he replaced the ear phones.

Again there was a long silence, broken at last by a sharp exclamation from Jason. He pushed an extra headpiece toward me.

'Listen!' he exclaimed.

As I adjusted the ear phones I heard that which we had never before received on the Gridley wave – code! No wonder that Jason Gridley was excited, since there was no station on earth, other than his own, attuned to the Gridley wave.

Code! What could it mean? I was torn by conflicting emotions – to tear off the ear phones and discuss this amazing thing with Jason, and to keep them on and listen.

I am not what one might call an expert in the intricacies of code, but I had no difficulty in understanding the simple signal of two letters, repeated in groups of three, with a pause after each group: 'D.I., D.I., D.I.,' pause; 'D.I., D.I., D.I.,' pause.

I glanced up at Jason. His eyes, filled with puzzled questioning, met mine, as though to ask, what does it mean?

The signals ceased and Jason touched his own key, sending his initials, 'J.G., J.G., J.G.' in the same grouping that we had received the D.I. signal. Almost instantly he was interrupted – you could feel the excitement of the sender.

'D.I., D.I., D.I., Pellucidar,' rattled against our ear-drums like machine gun fire. Jason and I sat in dumb amazement, staring at one another.

'It is a hoax!' I exclaimed, and Jason, reading my lips, shook his head.

'How can it be a hoax?' he asked. 'There is no other station on earth equipped to send or to receive over the Gridley wave, so there can be no means of perpetrating such a hoax.'

Our mysterious station was on the air again: 'If you get this, repeat my signal,' and he signed off with 'D.I., D.I., D.I.'

'That would be David Innes,' mused Jason.

'Emperor of Pellucidar,' I added.

Jason sent the message, 'D.I., D.I., D.I.,' followed by, 'what station is this,' and 'who is sending?'

'This is the Imperial Observatory at Greenwich, Pellucidar; Abner Perry sending. Who are you?'

'This is the private experimental laboratory of Jason Gridley, Tarzana, California; Gridley sending,' replied Jason.

'I want to get into communication with Edgar Rice Burroughs; do you know him?'

'He is sitting here, listening in with me,' replied Jason.

'Thank God, if that is true, but how am I to know that it is true?' demanded Perry.

I hastily scribbled a note to Jason: 'Ask him if he recalls the fire in his first gunpowder factory and that the building would have been destroyed had they not extinguished the fire by shoveling his gunpowder onto it?'

Jason grinned as he read the note, and sent it.

'It was unkind of David to tell of that,' came back the reply, 'but now I know that Burroughs is indeed there, as only he could have known of that incident. I have a long message for him. Are you ready?'

'Yes,' replied Jason.

'Then stand by.'

And this is the message that Abner Perry sent from the bowels of the earth; from The Empire of Pellucidar.

INTRODUCTION

It must be some fifteen years since David Innes and I broke through the inner surface of the earth's crust and emerged into savage Pellucidar, but when a stationary sun hangs eternally at high noon and there is no restless moon and there are no stars, time is measureless and so it may have been a hundred years ago or one. Who knows?

Of course, since David returned to earth and brought back many of the blessings of civilization we have had the means to measure time, but the people did not like it. They found that it put restrictions and limitations upon them that they never had felt before and they came to hate it and ignore it until David, in the goodness of his heart, issued an edict abolishing time in Pellucidar.

It seemed a backward step to me, but I am resigned now, and, perhaps, happier, for when all is said and done, time is a hard master, as you of the outer world, who are slaves of the sun, would be forced to admit were you to give the matter thought.

Here, in Pellucidar, we eat when we are hungry, we sleep when we are tired, we set out upon journeys when we leave and we arrive at our destinations when we get there; nor are we old because the earth has circled the sun seventy times since our birth, for we do not know that this has occurred.

Perhaps I have been here fifteen years, but what matter. When I came I knew nothing of radio – my researches and studies were along other lines – but when David came back from the outer world he brought many scientific works and from these I learned all that I know of radio, which has been enough to permit me to erect two successful stations; one here at Greenwich and one at the capital of The Empire of Pellucidar.

But, try as I would, I never could get anything from the outer world, and after a while I gave up trying, convinced that the earth's crust was impervious to radio.

In fact we used our stations but seldom, for, after all, Pellucidar is only commencing to emerge from the stone age, and in the economy of the stone age there seems to be no crying need for radio.

But sometimes I played with it and upon several occasions I thought that I heard voices and other sounds that were not of Pellucidar. They were too faint to be more than vague suggestions of intriguing possibilities, but yet they did suggest something most alluring, and so I set myself to making changes and adjustments until this wonderful thing that has happened but now was made possible.

And my delight in being able to talk with you is second only to my relief in being able to appeal to you for help. David is in trouble. He is a captive in the north, or what he and I call north, for there are no points of compass known to Pellucidarians.

I have heard from him, however. He has sent me a message and in it he suggests a startling theory that would make aid from the outer crust possible if – but first let me tell you the whole story; the story of the disaster that befell David Innes and what led up to it and then you will be in a better position to judge as to the practicability of sending succor to David from the outer crust.

The whole thing dates from our victories over the Mahars, the once dominant race of Pellucidar. When, with our well organized armies, equipped with firearms and other weapons unknown to the Mahars or their gorilla-like mercenaries, the Sagoths, we defeated the reptilian monsters and drove their slimy hordes from the confines of The Empire, the human race of the inner world for the first time in its history took its rightful place among the orders of creation.

But our victories laid the foundation for the disaster that has overwhelmed us.

For a while there was no Mahar within the boundaries of any of the kingdoms that constitute The Empire of Pellucidar; but presently we had word of them here and there – small parties living upon the shores of sea or lake far from the haunts of man.

They gave us no trouble – their old power had crumbled beyond recall; their Sagoths were now numbered among the regiments of The Empire; the Mahars had no longer the means to harm us; yet we did not want them among us. They are eaters of human flesh and we had no assurance that lone hunters would be safe from their voracious appetites.

We wanted them to be gone and so David sent a force against them, but with orders to treat with them first and attempt to persuade them to leave The Empire peacefully rather than embroil themselves in another war that might mean total extermination.

Sagoths accompanied the expedition, for they alone of all the creatures of Pellucidar can converse in the sixth sense, fourth dimension language of the Mahars.

The story that the expedition brought back was rather pitiful and aroused David's sympathies, as stories of persecution and unhappiness always do.

After the Mahars had been driven from The Empire they had sought a haven where they might live in peace. They assured us that they had accepted the inevitable in a spirit of philosophy and entertained no thoughts

234

of renewing their warfare against the human race or in any way attempting to win back their lost ascendancy.

Far away upon the shores of a mighty ocean, where there were no signs of man, they settled in peace, but their peace was not for long.

A great ship came, reminding the Mahars of the first ships they had seen – the ships that David and I had built – the first ships, as far as we knew, that ever had sailed the silent seas of Pellucidar.

Naturally it was a surprise to us to learn that there was a race within the inner world sufficiently far advanced to be able to build ships, but there was another surprise in store for us. The Mahars assured us that these people possessed firearms and that because of their ships and their firearms they were fully as formidable as we and they were much more ferocious; killing for the pure sport of slaughter.

After the first ship had sailed away the Mahars thought they might be allowed to live in peace, but this dream was short lived, as presently the first ship returned and with it were many others manned by thousands of bloodthirsty enemies against whose weapons the great reptiles had little or no defense.

Seeking only escape from man, the Mahars left their new home and moved back a short distance toward The Empire, but now their enemies seemed bent only upon persecution; they hunted them, and when they found them the Mahars were again forced to fall back before the ferocity of their continued attacks.

Eventually they took refuge within the boundaries of The Empire, and scarcely had David's expedition to them returned with its report when we had definite proof of the veracity of their tale through messages from our northernmost frontier bearing stories of invasion by a strange, savage race of white men.

Frantic was the message from Goork, King of Thuria, whose far-flung frontier stretches beyond the Land of Awful Shadow.

Some of his hunters had been surprised and all but a few killed or captured by the invaders.

He had sent warriors, then, against them, but these, too, had met a like fate, being greatly outnumbered, and so he sent a runner to David begging the Emperor to rush troops to his aid.

Scarcely had the first runner arrived when another came, bearing tidings of the capture and sack of the principal town of the Kingdom of Thuria; and then a third arrived from the commander of the invaders demanding that David come with tribute or they would destroy his country and slay the prisoners they held as hostages.

In reply David dispatched Tanar, son of Ghak, to demand the release of all prisoners and the departure of the invaders.

Immediately runners were sent to the nearest kingdoms of The Empire and ere Tanar had reached the Land of Awful Shadow, ten thousand warriors were marching along the same trail to enforce the demands of the Emperor and drive the savage foe from Pellucidar.

As David approached the Land of Awful Shadow that lies beneath Pellucidar's mysterious satellite, a great column of smoke was observable in the horizonless distance ahead.

It was not necessary to urge the tireless warriors to greater speed, for all who saw guessed that the invaders had taken another village and put it to the torch.

And then came the refugees – women and children only – and behind them a thin line of warriors striving to hold back swarthy, bearded strangers, armed with strange weapons that resembled ancient harquebuses with bell-shaped muzzles – huge, unwieldy things that belched smoke and flame and stones and bits of metal.

That the Pellucidarians, outnumbered ten to one, were able to hold back their savage foes at all was due to the more modern firearms that David and I had taught them to make and use.

Perhaps half the warriors of Thuria were armed with these and they were all that saved them from absolute rout, and, perhaps, total annihilation.

Loud were the shouts of joy when the first of the refugees discovered and recognized the force that had come to their delivery.

Goork and his people had been wavering in allegiance to The Empire, as were several other distant kingdoms, but I believe that this practical demonstration of the value of the Federation ended their doubts forever and left the people of the Land of Awful Shadow and their king the most loyal subjects that David possessed.

The effect upon the enemy of the appearance of ten thousand well-armed warriors was quickly apparent. They halted, and, as we advanced, they withdrew, but though they retreated they gave us a good fight.

David learned from Goork that Tanar had been retained as a hostage, but though he made several attempts to open negotiations with the enemy for the purpose of exchanging some prisoners that had fallen into our hands, for Tanar and other Pellucidarians, he never was able to do so.

Our forces drove the invaders far beyond the limits of The Empire to the shores of a distant sea, where, with difficulty and the loss of many men, they at last succeeded in embarking their depleted forces on ships that were as archaic in design as were their ancient harquebuses.

These ships rose to exaggerated heights at stern and bow, the sterns being built up in several stories, or housed decks, one atop another. There was much carving in seemingly intricate designs everywhere above the water line and each ship carried at her prow a figurehead painted, like the balance of the ship, in gaudy colors – usually a life size or a heroic figure of a naked woman or a mermaid.

The men themselves were equally bizarre and colorful, wearing gay cloths about their heads, wide sashes of bright colors and huge boots with flapping tops – those that were not half naked and barefoot.

Besides their harquebuses they carried huge pistols and knives stuck in their belts and at their hips were cutlasses. Altogether, with their bushy whiskers and fierce faces, they were at once a bad looking and a picturesque lot.

From some of the last prisoners he took during the fighting at the seashore, David learned that Tanar was still alive and that the chief of the invaders had determined to take him home with him in the hope that he could learn from Tanar the secrets of our superior weapons and gunpowder, for, notwithstanding my first failures, I had, and not without some pride, finally achieved a gunpowder that would not only burn, but that would ignite with such force as to be quite satisfactory. I am now perfecting a noiseless, smokeless powder, though honesty compels me to confess that my first experiments have not been entirely what I had hoped they might be, the first batch detonated having nearly broken my ear-drums and so filled my eyes with smoke that I thought I had been blinded.

When David saw the enemy ships sailing away with Tanar he was sick with grief, for Tanar always has been an especial favorite of the Emperor and his gracious Empress, Dian the Beautiful. He was like a son to them.

We had no ships upon this sea and David could not follow with his army; neither, being David, could he abandon the son of his best friend to a savage enemy before he had exhausted every resource at his command in an effort toward rescue.

In addition to the prisoners that had fallen into his hands David had captured one of the small boats that the enemy had used in embarking his forces, and this it was that suggested to David the mad scheme upon which he embarked.

The boat was about sixteen feet long and was equipped with both oars and a sail. It was broad of beam and had every appearance of being staunch and seaworthy, though pitifully small in which to face the dangers of an unknown sea, peopled, as are all the waters of Pellucidar, with huge monsters possessing short tempers and long appetites.

Standing upon the shore, gazing after the diminishing outlines of the departing ships, David reached his decision. Surrounding him were, the captains and the kings of the Federated Kingdoms of Pellucidar and behind these ten thousand warriors, leaning upon their arms. To one side the sullen prisoners, heavily guarded, gazed after their departing comrades, with what sensations of hopelessness and envy one may guess.

David turned toward his people. 'Those departing ships have borne away Tanar, the son of Ghak, and perhaps a score more of the young men of Pellucidar. It is beyond reason to expect that the enemy ever will bring our comrades back to us, but it is easy to imagine the treatment they will receive at the hands of this savage, bloodthirsty race.

'We may not abandon them while a single avenue of pursuit remains open to us. Here is that avenue.' He waved his hand across the broad ocean. 'And here the means of traversing it.' He pointed to the small boat.

'It would carry scarce twenty men,' cried one, who stood near the Emperor.

'It need carry but three,' replied David, 'for it will sail to rescue, not by force, but by strategy; or perhaps only to locate the stronghold of the enemy, that we may return and lead a sufficient force upon it to overwhelm it.'

'I shall go,' concluded the Emperor. 'Who will accompany me?'

Instantly every man within hearing of his voice, saving the prisoners only, flashed a weapon above his head and pressed forward to offer his services. David smiled.

'I knew as much,' he said, 'but I cannot take you all. I shall need only one and that shall be Ja of Anoroc, the greatest sailor of Pellucidar.'

A great shout arose, for Ja, the King of Anoroc, who is also the chief officer of the navy of Pellucidar, is vastly popular throughout The Empire, and, though all were disappointed in not being chosen, yet they appreciated the wisdom of David's selection.

'But two is too small a number to hope for success,' argued Ghak, 'and I, the father of Tanar, should be permitted to accompany you.'

'Numbers, such as we might crowd in that little boat, would avail us nothing,' replied David, 'so why risk a single additional life? If twenty could pass through the unknown dangers that lie ahead of us, two may do the same, while with fewer men we can carry a far greater supply of food and water against the unguessed extent of the great sea that we face and the periods of calm and the long search.'

'But two are too few to man the boat,' expostulated another, 'and Ghak is right – the father of Tanar should be among his rescuers.'

'Ghak is needed by The Empire,' replied David. 'He must remain to command the armies for the Empress until I return, but there shall be a third who will embark with us.'

'Who?' demanded Ghak.

'One of the prisoners,' replied David. 'For his freedom we should readily find one willing to guide us to the country of the enemy.'

Nor was this difficult since every prisoner volunteered when the proposal was submitted to them.

David chose a young fellow who said his name was Fitt and who seemed to possess a more open and honest countenance than any of his companions.

And then came the provisioning of the boat. Bladders were filled with fresh water, and quantities of corn and dried fish and jerked meat, as well as vegetables and fruits, were packed into other bladders, and all were stored in the boat until it seemed that she might carry no more. For three men the supplies might have been adequate for a year's voyage upon the outer crust, where time enters into all calculations.

The prisoner, Fitt, who was to accompany David and Ja, assured David that one fourth the quantity of supplies would be ample and that there were points along the route they might take where their water supply could be replenished and where game abounded, as well as native fruits, nuts and vegetables, but David would not cut down by a single ounce the supplies that he had decided upon.

As the three were about to embark David had a last word with Ghak.

'You have seen the size and the armament of the enemy ships, Ghak,' he said. 'My last injunction to you is to build at once a fleet that can cope successfully with these great ships of the enemy and while the fleet is building – and it must be built upon the shores of this sea – send expeditions forth to search for a waterway from this ocean to our own. Can you find it, all of our ships can be utilized and the building of the greater navy accelerated by utilizing the shipyards of Anoroc.

'When you have completed and manned fifty ships set forth to our rescue if we have not returned by then. Do not destroy these prisoners, but preserve them well for they alone can guide you to their country.'

And then David I, Emperor of Pellucidar, and Ja, King of Anoroc, with the prisoner, Fitt, boarded the tiny boat; friendly hands pushed them out upon the long, oily swells of a Pellucidarian sea; ten thousand throats cheered them upon their way and ten thousand pairs of eyes watched them until they had melted into the mist of the upcurving, horizonless distance of a Pellucidarian seascape.

David had departed upon a vain but glorious adventure, and, in the distant capital of The Empire, Dian the Beautiful would be weeping.

1

Stellara

The great ship trembled to the recoil of the cannon; the rattle of musketry. The roar of the guns aboard her sister ships and the roar of her own were deafening. Below decks the air was acrid with the fumes of burnt powder.

Tanar of Pellucidar, chained below with other prisoners, heard these sounds and smelled the smoke. He heard the rattle of the anchor chain; he felt the straining of the mast to which his shackles were bent and the altered motion of the hull told him that the ship was under way.

Presently the firing ceased and the regular rising and falling of the ship betokened that it was on its course. In the darkness of the hold Tanar could see nothing. Sometimes the prisoners spoke to one another, but their thoughts were not happy ones, and so, for the most part, they remained silent – waiting. For what?

They grew very hungry and very thirsty. By this they knew that the ship was far at sea. They knew nothing of time. They only knew that they were hungry and thirsty and that the ship should be far at sea – far out upon an unknown sea, setting its course for an unknown port.

Presently a hatch was raised and men came with food and water – poor, rough food and water that smelled badly and tasted worse; but it was water and they were thirsty.

One of the men said: 'Where is he who is called Tanar?'

'I am Tanar,' replied the son of Ghak.

'You are wanted on deck,' said the man, and with a huge key he unlocked the massive, hand-wrought lock that held Tanar chained to the mast. 'Follow me!'

The bright light of Pellucidar's perpetual day blinded the Sarian as he clambered to the deck from the dark hole in which he had been confined and it was a full minute before his eyes could endure the light, but his guard hustled him roughly along and Tanar was already stumbling up the long stairs leading to the high deck at the ship's stern before he regained the use of his eyes.

As he mounted the highest deck he saw the chiefs of the Korsar horde assembled and with them were two women. One appeared elderly and ill favored, but the other was young and beautiful, but for neither did Tanar have any eyes – he was interested only in the enemy men, for these he could fight, these he might kill, which was the sole interest that an enemy could hold for Tanar, the Sarian, and being what he was Tanar could not fight women, not even enemy women; but he could ignore them, and did.

He was led before a huge fellow whose bushy whiskers almost hid his face – a great, blustering fellow with a scarlet scarf bound about his head. But for an embroidered, sleeveless jacket, open at the front, the man was naked above the waist, about which was wound another gaudy sash into which were stuck two pistols and as many long knives, while at his side dangled a cutlass, the hilt of which was richly ornamented with inlays of pearl and semi-precious stones.

A mighty man was The Cid, chief of the Korsars – a burly, blustering, bully of a man, whose position among the rough and quarrelsome Korsars might be maintained only by such as he.

Surrounding him upon the high poop of his ship was a company of beefy ruffians of similar mold, while far below, in the waist of the vessel, a throng of lesser cutthroats, the common sailors, escaped from the dangers and demands of an arduous campaign, relaxed according to their various whims.

Stark brutes were most of these, naked but for shorts and the inevitable gaudy sashes and head cloths – an unlovely company, yet picturesque.

At The Cid's side stood a younger man who well could boast as hideous a countenance as any sun ever shone upon, for across a face that might have taxed even a mother's love, ran a repulsive scar from above the left eye to below the right hand corner of the mouth, cleaving the nose with a deep, red gash. The left eye was lidless and gazed perpetually upward and outward, as a dead eye might, while the upper lip was permanently drawn upward at the right side in a sardonic sneer that exposed a single fang-like tooth. No, Bohar the Bloody was not beautiful.

Before these two, The Cid and The Bloody One, Tanar was roughly dragged.

'They call you Tanar?' bellowed The Cid.

Tanar nodded.

'And you are the son of a king!' and he laughed loudly. 'With a ship's company I could destroy your father's entire kingdom and make a slave of him, as I have of his son.'

'You had many ships' companies,' replied Tanar; 'but I did not see any of them destroying the kingdom of Sari. The army that chased them into the ocean was commanded by my father, under the Emperor.'

The Cid scowled. 'I have made men walk the plank for less than that,' he growled.

'I do not know what you mean,' said Tanar.

'You shall,' barked The Cid; 'and then, by the beard of the sea god, you'll keep a civil tongue in your head. Hey!' he shouted to one of his officers, 'have a prisoner fetched and the plank run out. We'll show this son of a king who The Cid is and that he is among real men now.'

'Why fetch another?' demanded Bohar the Bloody. 'This fellow can walk and learn his lesson at the same time.'

'But he could not profit by it,' replied The Cid.

'Since when did The Cid become a dry nurse to an enemy?' demanded Bohar, with a sneer.

Without a word The Cid wheeled and swung an ugly blow to Bohar's chin, and as the man went down the chief whipped a great pistol from his sash and stood over him, the muzzle pointed at Bohar's head.

'Perhaps that will knock your crooked face straight or bump some brains into your thick head,' roared The Cid.

Bohar lay on his back glaring up at his chief.

'Who is your master?' demanded The Cid.

'You are,' growled Bohar.

'Then get up and keep a civil tongue in your head,' ordered The Cid.

As Bohar arose he turned a scowling face upon Tanar. It was as though his one good eye had gathered all the hate and rage and venom in the wicked heart of the man and was concentrating them upon the Sarian, the indirect cause of his humiliation, and from that instant Tanar knew that Bohar the Bloody hated him with a personal hatred distinct from any natural antipathy that he might have felt for an alien and an enemy.

On the lower deck men were eagerly running a long plank out over the starboard rail and making the inboard end fast to cleats with stout lines.

From an opened hatch others were dragging a strapping prisoner from the kingdom of Thuria, who had been captured in the early fighting in the Land of Awful Shadow.

The primitive warrior held his head high and showed no terror in the presence of his rough captors. Tanar, looking down upon him from the upper deck, was proud of this fellow man of the Empire. The Cid was watching, too.

'That tribe needs taming,' he said.

The younger of the two women, both of whom had stepped to the edge of the deck and were looking down upon the scene in the waist, turned to The Cid.

'They seem brave men; all of them,' she said. 'It is a pity to kill one needlessly.'

'Poof! girl,' exclaimed The Cid. 'What do you know of such things? It is the blood of your mother that speaks. By the beards of the gods, I would that you had more of your father's blood in your veins.'

'It is brave blood, the blood of my mother,' replied the girl, 'for it does not fear to be itself before all men. The blood of my father dares not reveal its good to the eyes of men because it fears ridicule. It boasts of its courage to hide its cowardice.'

The Cid swore a mighty oath. 'You take advantage of our relationship, Stellara,' he said, 'but do not forget that there is a limit beyond which even you may not go with The Cid, who brooks no insults.'

The girl laughed. 'Reserve that talk for those who fear you,' she said.

During this conversation, Tanar, who was standing near, had an opportunity to observe the girl more closely and was prompted to do so by the nature of her remarks and the quiet courage of her demeanor. For the first time he noticed her hair, which was like gold in warm sunlight, and because the women of his own country were nearly all dark haired the color of her hair impressed him. He thought it very lovely and when he looked more closely at her features he realized that they, too, were lovely, with a sunny, golden loveliness that seemed to reflect like qualities of heart and character. There was a certain feminine softness about her that was sometimes lacking in the sturdy, self-reliant, primitive women of his own race. It was not in any sense a weakness, however, as was evidenced by her fearless attitude toward The Cid and by the light of courage that shone from her brave eyes. Intelligent eyes they were, too – brave, intelligent and beautiful.

But there Tanar's interest ceased and he was repulsed by the thought that this woman belonged to the uncouth bully, who ruled with an iron hand the whiskered brutes of the great fleet, for The Cid's reference to their relationship left no doubt in the mind of the Sarian that the woman was his mate.

And now the attention of all was focused on the actors in the tragedy below. Men had bound the wrists of the prisoner together behind his back and placed a blindfold across his eyes.

'Watch below, son of a king,' said The Cid to Tanar, 'and you will know what it means to walk the plank.'

'I am watching,' said Tanar, 'and I see that it takes many of your people to make one of mine do this thing, whatever it may be.'

The girl laughed, but The Cid scowled more deeply, while Bohar cast a venomous glance at Tanar.

Now men with drawn knives and sharp pikes lined the plank on either side of the ship's rail and others lifted the prisoner to the inboard end so that he faced the opposite end of the plank that protruded far out over the sea, where great monsters of the deep cut the waves with giant backs as they paralleled the ship's course – giant saurians, long extinct upon the outer crust.

Prodding the defenseless man with knife and pike they goaded him forward along the narrow plank to the accompaniment of loud oaths and vulgar jests and hoarse laughter.

Erect and proud, the Thurian marched fearlessly to his doom. He made no complaint and when he reached the outer end of the plank and his foot found no new place beyond he made no outcry. Just for an instant he drew back his foot and hesitated and then, silently, he leaped far out, and, turning, dove head foremost into the sea.

Tanar turned his eyes away and it chanced that he turned them in the direction of the girl. To his surprise he saw that she, too, had refused to look at the last moment and in her face, turned toward his; he saw an expression of suffering.

Could it be that this woman of The Cid's brutal race felt sympathy and sorrow for a suffering enemy?

Tanar doubted it. More likely that something she had eaten that day had disagreed with her.

'Now,' cried The Cid, 'you have seen a man walk the plank and know what I may do with you, if I choose.'

Tanar shrugged. 'I hope I may be as indifferent to my fate as was my comrade,' he said, 'for you certainly got little enough sport out of him.'

'If I turn you over to Bohar we shall have sport,' replied The Cid. 'He has other means of enlivening a dull day that far surpass the tame exercise on the plank.'

The girl turned angrily upon The Cid. 'You shall not do that!' she cried. 'You promised me that you would not torture any prisoners while I was with the fleet.'

'If he behaves I shall not,' said The Cid, 'but if he does not I shall turn him over to Bohar the Bloody. Do not forget that I am Chief of Korsar and that even you may be punished if you interfere.'

Again the girl laughed. 'You can frighten the others, Chief of Korsar,' she said, 'but not me.'

'If she were mine,' muttered Bohar threateningly, but the girl interrupted him.

'I am not, nor ever shall be,' she said.

'Do not be too sure of that,' growled The Cid. 'I can give you to whom I please; let the matter drop.' He turned to the Sarian prisoner. 'What is your name, son of a king?' he asked.

'Tanar.'

'Listen well, Tanar,' said The Cid impressively. 'Our prisoners do not live beyond the time that they be of service to us. Some of you will be kept to exhibit to the people of Korsar, after which they will be of little use to me, but you can purchase life and, perhaps, freedom.'

'How?' demanded Tanar.

'Your people were armed with weapons far better than ours,' explained The Cid; 'your powder was more powerful and more dependable. Half the time ours fails to ignite at the first attempt.'

'That must be embarrassing,' remarked Tanar.

'It is fatal,' said The Cid.

'But what has it to do with me?' asked the prisoner.

'If you will teach us how to make better weapons and such powder as your people have you shall be spared and shall have your freedom.'

Tanar made no reply – he was thinking – thinking of the supremacy that their superior weapons gave his people – thinking of the fate that lay in store for him and for those poor devils in the dark, foul hole below deck.

'Well?' demanded The Cid.

'Will you spare the others, too?' he asked.

'Why should I?'

'I shall need their help,' said Tanar. 'I do not know all that is necessary to make the weapons and the powder.'

As a matter of fact he knew nothing about the manufacture of either, but he saw here a chance to save his fellow prisoners, or at least to delay their destruction and gain time in which they might find means to escape, nor did he hesitate to deceive The Cid, for is not all fair in war?

'Very well,' said the Korsar chief; 'if you and they give me no trouble you shall all live – provided you teach us how to make weapons and powder like your own.'

'We cannot live in the filthy hole in which we are penned,' retorted the Sarian; 'neither can we live without food. Soon we shall all sicken and die. We are people of the open air – we cannot be smothered in dark holes filled with vermin and be starved, and live.'

'You shall not be returned to the hole,' said The Cid. 'There is no danger that you will escape.'

'And the others?' demanded Tanar.

'They remain where they are!'

'They will all die, and without them I cannot make powder,' Tanar reminded him.

The Cid scowled. 'You would have my ship overrun with enemies,' he growled.

'They are unarmed.'

'Then they certainly would be killed,' said The Cid. 'No one would survive long among that pack an' he were not armed;' he waved a hand contemptuously toward the half naked throng below.

'Then leave the hatches off and give them decent air and more and better food.'

'I'll do it,' said The Cid. 'Bohar, have the forward hatches removed, place a guard there with orders to kill any prisoner who attempts to come on deck and any of our men who attempts to go below; see, too, that the prisoners get the same rations as our own men.'

It was with a feeling of relief that amounted almost to happiness that Tanar saw Bohar depart to carry out the orders of The Cid, for he knew well that his people could not long survive the hideous and unaccustomed confinement and the vile food that had been his lot and theirs since they had been brought aboard the Korsar ship.

Presently The Cid went to his cabin and Tanar, left to his own devices, walked to the stern and leaning on the rail gazed into the hazy up-curving distance where lay the land of the Sarians, his land, beyond the haze.

Far astern a small boat rose and fell with the great, long billows. Fierce denizens of the deep constantly threatened it, storms menaced it, but on it forged in the wake of the great fleet – a frail and tiny thing made strong and powerful by the wills of three men.

But this Tanar did not see, for the mist hid it. He would have been heartened to know that his Emperor was risking his life to save him.

As he gazed and dreamed he became conscious of a presence near him, but he did not turn, for who was there upon that ship who might have access to this upper deck, whom he might care to see or speak with?

Presently he heard a voice at his elbow, a low, golden voice that brought him around facing its owner. It was the girl.

'You are looking back toward your own country?' she said.

'Yes.'

'You will never see it again,' she said, a note of sadness in her voice, as though she understood his feelings and sympathized.

'Perhaps not, but why should you care? I am an enemy.'

'I do not know why I should care,' replied the girl. 'What is your name?'

'Tanar.'

'Is that all?'

'I am called Tanar the Fleet One.'

'Why?'

'Because in all Sari none can outdistance me.'

'Sari – is that the name of your country?'

'Yes.'

'What is it like?'

'It is a high plateau among the mountains. It is a very lovely country, with leaping rivers and great trees. It is filled with game. We hunt the great ryth there and the tarag for meat and for sport and there are countless lesser animals that give us food and clothing.'

'Have you no enemies? You are not a warlike people as are the Korsars.'

'We defeated the warlike Korsars,' he reminded her.

'I would not speak of that too often,' she said. 'The tempers of the Korsars are short and they love to kill.'

'Why do you not kill me then?' he demanded. 'You have a knife and a pistol in your sash, like the others.'

The girl only smiled.

'Perhaps you are not a Korsar,' he exclaimed. 'You were captured as I was and are a prisoner.'

'I am no prisoner,' she replied.

'But you are not a Korsar,' he insisted.

'Ask The Cid – he will doubtless cutlass you for your impertinence; but why do you think I am not a Korsar?'

'You are too beautiful and too fine,' he replied. 'You have shown sympathy and that is a finer sentiment far beyond their mental capability. They are—'

'Be careful, enemy; perhaps I am a Korsar!'

'I do not believe it,' said Tanar.

'Then keep your beliefs to yourself, prisoner,' retorted the girl in a haughty tone.

'What is this?' demanded a rough voice behind Tanar. 'What has this thing said to you, Stellara?'

Tanar wheeled to face Bohar the Bloody.

'I questioned that she was of the same race as you,' snapped Tanar before the girl could reply. 'It is inconceivable that one so beautiful could be tainted by the blood of Korsar.'

His face flaming with rage, Bohar laid a hand upon one of his knives and stepped truculently toward the Sarian. 'It is death to insult the daughter of The Cid,' he cried, whipping the knife from his sash and striking a wicked blow at Tanar.

The Sarian, light of foot, trained from childhood in the defensive as well as offensive use of edged weapons, stepped quickly to one side and then as quickly in again and once more Bohar the Bloody sprawled upon the deck to a well delivered blow.

Bohar was fairly foaming at the mouth with rage as he jerked his heavy pistol from his gaudy sash and aiming it at Tanar's chest from where he lay upon the deck, pulled the trigger. At the same instant the girl sprang forward as though to prevent the slaying of the prisoner.

It all happened so quickly that Tanar scarcely knew the sequence of events, but what he did know was that the powder failed to ignite, and then he laughed.

'You had better wait until I have taught you how to make powder that will burn before you try to murder me, Bohar,' he said.

The Bloody One scrambled to his feet and Tanar stood ready to receive the expected charge, but the girl stepped between them with an imperious gesture.

'Enough of this!' she cried. 'It is The Cid's wish that this man live. Would you like to have The Cid know that you tried to pistol him, Bohar?'

The Bloody One stood glaring at Tanar for several seconds, then he wheeled and strode away without a word.

'It would seem that Bohar does not like me,' said Tanar, smiling.

'He dislikes nearly every one,' said Stellara, 'but he hates you – now.'

'Because I knocked him down, I suppose. I cannot blame him.'

'That is not the real reason,' said the girl.

'What is, then?'

She hesitated and then she laughed. 'He is jealous. Bohar wants me for his mate.'

'But why should he be jealous of me?'

Stellara looked Tanar up and down and then she laughed again. 'I do not know,' she said. 'You are not much of a man beside our huge Korsars – with your beardless face and your small waist. It would take two of you to make one of them.'

To Tanar her tone implied thinly veiled contempt and it piqued him, but why it should he did not know and that annoyed him, too. What was she but the savage daughter of a savage, boorish Korsar?

When he had first learned from Bohar's lips that she was the daughter and not the mate of The Cid he had felt an unaccountable relief, half unconsciously and without at all attempting to analyze his reaction.

Perhaps it was the girl's beauty that had made such a relationship with The Cid seem repulsive, perhaps it was her lesser ruthlessness, which seemed superlative gentleness by contrast with the brutality of Bohar and The Cid, but now she seemed capable of a refined cruelty, which was, after all, what he might have expected to find in one form or another in the daughter of the Chief of the Korsars.

As one will, when piqued, and just at random, Tanar loosed a bolt in the hope that it might annoy her. 'Bohar knows you better than I,' he said; 'perhaps he knew that he had cause for jealousy.'

'Perhaps,' she replied, enigmatically, 'but no one will ever know, for Bohar will kill you – I know *him* well enough to know that.'

2

Disaster

Upon the timeless seas of Pellucidar a voyage may last for an hour or a year – that depends not upon its duration, but upon the important occurrences which mark its course.

Curving upward along the inside of the arc of a great circle the Korsar fleet ploughed the restless sea. Favorable winds carried the ships onward. The noonday sun hung perpetually at zenith. Men ate when they were hungry, slept when they were tired, or slept against the time when sleep might be denied them, for the people of Pellucidar seem endowed with a faculty that permits them to store sleep, as it were, in times of ease, against the time when sleep might be denied them, against the more strenuous periods of hunting and warfare when there is no opportunity for sleep. Similarly, they eat with unbelievable irregularity.

Tanar had slept and eaten several times since his encounter with Bohar, whom he had seen upon various occasions since without an actual meeting. The Bloody One seemed to be biding his time.

Stellara had kept to her cabin with the old woman, who Tanar surmised was her mother. He wondered if Stellara would look like the mother or. The Cid when she was older, and he shuddered when he considered either eventuality.

As he stood thus musing, Tanar's attention was attracted by the actions of the men on the lower deck. He saw them looking across the port bow and upward and, following the direction of their eyes with his, he saw the rare phenomenon of a cloud in the brilliant sky.

Some one must have notified The Cid at about the same time, for he came from his cabin and looked long and searchingly at the heavens.

In his loud voice The Cid bellowed commands and his wild crew scrambled to their stations like monkeys, swarming aloft or standing by on deck ready to do his bidding.

Down came the great sails and reefed were the lesser ones, and throughout the fleet, scattered over the surface of the shining sea, the example of the Commander was followed.

The cloud was increasing in size and coming rapidly nearer. No longer was it the small white cloud that had first attracted their attention, but a great, bulging, ominous, black mass that frowned down upon the ocean, turning it a sullen gray where the shadow lay.

The wind that had been blowing gently ceased suddenly. The ship fell off and rolled in the trough of the sea. The silence that followed cast a spell of terror over the ship's company.

Tanar, watching, saw the change. If these rough seafaring men blenched before the threat of the great cloud the danger must be great indeed.

The Sarians were mountain people. Tanar knew little of the sea, but if Tanar feared anything on Pellucidar it was the sea. The sight, therefore, of these savage Korsar sailors cringing in terror was far from reassuring.

Someone had come to the rail and was standing at his side.

'When that has passed,' said a voice, 'there will be fewer ships in the fleet of Korsar and fewer men to go home to their women.'

He turned and saw Stellara looking upward at the cloud.

'You do not seem afraid,' he said.

'Nor you,' replied the girl. 'We seem the only people aboard who are not afraid.'

'Look down at the prisoners,' he told her. 'They show no fear.'

'Why?' she asked.

'They are Pellucidarians,' he replied, proudly.

'We are all of Pellucidar,' she reminded him.

'I refer to The Empire,' he said.

'Why are you not afraid?' she asked. 'Are you so much braver than the Korsars?' There was no sarcasm in her tone.

'I am very much afraid,' replied Tanar. 'Mine are mountain people – we know little of the sea or its ways.'

'But you show no fear,' insisted Stellara.

'That is the result of heredity and training,' he replied.

'The Korsars show their fear,' she mused. She spoke as one who was of different blood. 'They boast much of their bravery,' she continued as though speaking to herself, 'but when the sky frowns they show fear.' There seemed a little note of contempt in her voice. 'See!' she cried. 'It is coming!'

The cloud was tearing toward them now and beneath it the sea was lashed to fury. Shreds of cloud whirled and twisted at the edges of the great cloud mass. Shreds of spume whirled and twisted-above the angry waves. And then the storm struck the ship, laying it over on its side.

What ensued was appalling to a mountaineer, unaccustomed to the sea – the chaos of watery mountains, tumbling, rolling, lashing at the wallowing ship; the shrieking wind; the driving, blinding spume; the terror-stricken crew, cowed, no longer swaggering bullies.

Reeling, staggering, clutching at the rail Bohar the Bloody passed Tanar where he clung with one arm about a stanchion and the other holding Stellara, who would have been hurled to the deck but for the quick action of the Sarian.

The face of Bohar was an ashen mask against which the red gash of his ugly scar stood out in startling contrast. He looked at Tanar and Stellara, but he passed them by, mumbling to himself.

Beyond them was The Cid, screaming orders that no one could hear. Toward him Bohar made his way. Above the storm Tanar heard The Bloody One screaming at his chief.

'Save me! Save me!' he cried. 'The boats – lower the boats! The ship is lost.'

It was apparent, even to a landsman, that no small boat could live in such a sea even if one could have been lowered.

The Cid paid no attention to his lieutenant, but clung where he was, bawling commands.

A mighty sea rose suddenly above the bow; it hung there for an instant and then rolled in upon the lower deck – tons of crushing, pitiless, insensate sea – rolled in upon the huddled, screaming seamen. Naught but the high prow and the lofty poop showed above the angry waves – just for an instant the great ship strained and shuddered, battling for life.

'It is the end!' cried Stellara.

Bohar screamed like a dumb brute in the agony of death. The Cid knelt on the deck, his face buried in his arms. Tanar stood watching, fascinated by the terrifying might of the elements. He saw man shrink to puny insignificance before a gust of wind, and a slow smile crossed his face.

The wave receded and the ship, floundering, staggered upward, groaning. The smile left Tanar's lips as his eyes gazed down upon the lower deck. It was almost empty now. A few broken forms lay huddled in the scuppers; a dozen men, clinging here and there, showed signs of life. The others, all but those who had reached safety below deck, were gone.

The girl clung tightly to the man. 'I did not think she could live through that,' she said.

'Nor I,' said Tanar.

'But you were not afraid,' she said. 'You seemed the only one who was not afraid.'

'Of what use was Bohar's screaming?' he asked. 'Did it save him?'

'Then you were afraid, but you hid it?'

He shrugged. 'Perhaps,' he said. 'I do not know what you mean by fear. I did not want to die, if that is what you mean.'

'Here comes another!' cried Stellara, shuddering, and pressing closer to him.

Tanar's arm tightened about the slim figure of the girl. It was an unconscious gesture of the protective instinct of the male.

'Do not be afraid,' he said.

'I am not – now,' she replied.

At the instant that the mighty comber engulfed the ship the angry hurricane struck suddenly with renewed fury – struck at a new angle – and the masts, already straining even to the minimum of canvas that had been necessary to give the ship headway and keep its nose into the storm, snapped like dry bones and crashed by the board in a tangle of cordage. The ship's head fell away and she rolled in the trough of the great seas, a hopeless derelict.

Above the screaming of the wind rose Bohar's screams. 'The boats! The boats!' he repeated like a trained parrot gone mad from terror.

As though sated for the moment and worn out by its own exertions the storm abated, the wind died, but the great seas rose and fell and the great ship rolled, helpless. At the bottom of each watery gorge it seemed that it must be engulfed by the gray green cliff toppling above it and at the crest of each liquid mountain certain destruction loomed inescapable.

Bohar, still screaming, scrambled to the lower deck. He found men, by some miracle still alive in the open, and others cringing in terror below deck. By dint of curses and blows and the threat of his pistol he gathered them together and though they whimpered in fright he forced them to make a boat ready.

There were twenty of them and their gods or their devils must have been with them, for they lowered a boat and got clear of the floundering hulk in safety and without the loss of a man.

The Cid, seeing what Bohar contemplated, had tried to prevent the seemingly suicidal act by bellowing orders at him from above, but they had no effect and at the last moment The Cid had descended to the lower deck to enforce his commands, but he had arrived too late.

Now he stood staring unbelievingly at the small boat riding the great seas in seeming security while the dismasted ship, pounded by the stumps of its masts, seemed doomed to destruction.

From corners where they had been hiding came the balance of the ship's company and when they saw Bohar's boat and the seemingly relative safety of the crew they clamored for escape by the other boats. With the idea once implanted in their minds there followed a mad panic as the half-brutes fought for places in the remaining boats.

'Come!' cried Stellara. 'We must hurry or they will go without us.' She started to move toward the companionway, but Tanar restrained her.

'Look at them,' he said. 'We are safer at the mercy of the sea and the storm.'

Stellara shrank back close to him. She saw men knifing one another – those behind knifing those ahead. Men dragging others from the boats and killing them on deck or being killed. She saw The Cid pistol a seaman in the back and leap to his place in the first boat to be lowered. She saw men leaping from the rail in a mad effort to reach this boat and falling into the sea, or being thrown in if they succeeded in boarding the tossing shell.

She saw the other boats being lowered and men crushed between them and the ship's side – she saw the depths to which fear can plunge the braggart and the bully as the last of the ship's company, failing to win places in the last boat, deliberately leaped into the sea and were drowned.

Standing there upon the high poop of the rolling derelict, Tanar and Stellara watched the frantic efforts of the oarsmen in the overcrowded small boats. They saw one boat foul another and both founder. They watched the drowning men battling for survival. They heard their hoarse oaths and their screams above the roaring of the sea and the shriek of the wind as the storm returned as though fearing that some might escape its fury.

'We are alone,' said Stellara. 'They have all gone.'

'Let them go,' replied Tanar. 'I would not exchange places with them.'

'But there can be no hope for us,' said the girl.

'There is no more for them,' replied the Sarian, 'and at least we are not crowded into a small boat filled with cutthroats.'

'You are more afraid of the men than you are of the sea,' she said.

'For you, yes,' he replied.

'Why should you fear for me?' she demanded. 'Am I not also your enemy?'

He turned his eyes quickly upon her and they were filled with surprise. 'That is so,' he said; 'but, somehow, I had forgotten it – you do not seem like an enemy, as the others do. You do not seem like one of them, even.'

Clinging to the rail and supporting the girl upon the lurching deck, Tanar's lips were close to Stellara's ear as he sought to make himself heard above the storm. He sensed the faint aroma of a delicate sachet that was ever after to be a part of his memory of Stellara.

A sea struck the staggering ship throwing Tanar forward so that his cheek touched the cheek of the girl and as she turned her head his lips brushed hers. Each realized that it was an accident, but the effect was none the less surprising. Tanar, for the first time, felt the girl's body against his and consciousness of contact must have been reflected in his eyes for Stellara shrank back and there was an expression of fear in hers.

Tanar saw the fear in the eyes of an enemy, but it gave him no pleasure. He tried to think only of the treatment that would have been accorded a woman of his tribe had one been at the mercy of the Korsars, but that, too, failed to satisfy him as it only could if he were to admit that he was of the same ignoble clay as the men of Korsar.

But whatever thoughts were troubling the minds of Stellara and Tanar were temporarily submerged by the grim tragedy of the succeeding few moments as another tremendous sea, the most gigantic that had yet assailed the broken ship, hurled its countless tons upon her shivering deck.

To Tanar it seemed, indeed, that this must mark the end since it was inconceivable that the unmanageable hulk could rise again from the smother of water that surged completely over her almost to the very highest deck of the towering poop, where the two clung against the tearing wind and the frightful pitching of the derelict.

But, as the sea rolled on, the ship slowly, sluggishly struggled to the surface like an exhausted swimmer who, drowning, struggles weakly against the inevitability of fate and battles upward for one last gasp of air that will, at best, but prolong the agony of death.

As the main deck slowly emerged from the receding waters, Tanar was horrified by the discovery that the forward hatch had been stove in. That the ship must have taken in considerable water, and that each succeeding wave that broke over it would add to the quantity, affected the Sarian less than knowledge of the fact that it was beneath this hatch that his fellow prisoners were confined.

Through the black menace of his almost hopeless situation had shone a single bright ray of hope that, should the ship weather the storm, there would be aboard her a score of his fellow Pellucidarians and that together they might find the means to rig a makeshift sail and work their way back to the mainland from which they had embarked; but with the gaping hatch and the almost certain conclusion to be drawn from it he realized that it would, indeed, be a miracle if there remained alive aboard the derelict any other than Stellara and himself.

The girl was looking down at the havoc wrought below and now she turned her face toward his.

'They must all be drowned,' she said, 'and they were your people. I am sorry.'

'Perhaps they would have chosen it in preference to what might have awaited them in Korsar,' he said.

'And they have been released only a little sooner than we shall be,' she continued. 'Do you notice how low the ship rides now and how sluggish she is? The hold must be half filled with water – another such sea as the last one will founder her.'

For some time they stood in silence, each occupied with his own thoughts. The hulk rolled in the trough and momentarily it seemed that she might not roll back in time to avert the disaster of the next menacing comber, yet each time she staggered drunkenly to oppose a high side to the hungry waters.

'I believe the storm has spent itself,' said Tanar.

'The wind has died and there has been no sea like the great one that stove in the forward hatch,' said Stellara, hopefully.

The noonday sun broke from behind the black cloud that had shrouded it and the sea burst into a blaze of blue and silver beauty. The storm had passed. The seas diminished. The derelict rolled heavily upon the great swells, low in the water, but temporarily relieved of the menace of immediate disaster.

Tanar descended the companionway to the lower deck and approached the forward hatch. A single glance below revealed only what he could have anticipated – floating corpses rolling with the roll of the derelict. All below were dead. With a sigh he turned away and returned to the upper deck.

The girl did not even question him for she could read in his demeanor the story of what his eyes had beheld.

'You and I are the only living creatures that remain aboard,' he said.

She waved a hand in a broad gesture that took in the sea about them. 'Doubtless we alone of the entire ship's company have survived,' she said. 'I see no other ship nor any of the small boats.'

Tanar strained his eyes in all directions. 'Nor I,' said he; 'but perhaps some of them have escaped.'

She shook her head. 'I doubt it.'

'Yours has been a heavy loss,' sympathized the Sarian. 'Besides so many of your people, you have lost your father and your mother.'

Stellara looked up quickly into his eyes. 'They were not my people,' she said.

'What?' exclaimed Tanar. 'They were not your people? But your father, The Cid, was Chief of the Korsars.'

'He was not my father,' replied the girl.

'And the woman was not your mother?'

'May the gods forbid!' she exclaimed.

'But The Cid! He treated you like a daughter.'

'He thought I was his daughter, but I am not.'

'I do not understand,' said Tanar; 'yet I am glad that you are not. I could not understand how you, who are so different from them, could be a Korsar.'

'My mother was a native of the island of Amiocap and there The Cid, raiding for women, seized her. She told me about it many times before she died.

'Her mate was absent upon a great tandor hunt and she never saw him again. When I was born The Cid thought that I was his daughter, but my mother knew better for I bore upon my left shoulder a small, red birthmark identical with one upon the left shoulder of the mate from whom she had been stolen – my father.

'My mother never told The Cid the truth, for fear that he would kill me in accordance with the custom the Korsars follow of destroying the children of their captives if a Korsar is not the father.'

'And the woman who was with you on board was not your mother?'

'No, she was The Cid's mate, but not my mother, who is dead.'

Tanar felt a distinct sense of relief that Stellara was not a Korsar, but why this should be so he did not know, nor, perhaps, did he attempt to analyze his feelings.

'I am glad,' he said again.

'But why?' she asked.

'Now we do not have to be enemies,' he replied.

'Were we before?'

He hesitated and then he laughed. 'I was not your enemy,' he said, 'but you reminded me that you were mine.'

'It has been the habit of a lifetime to think of myself as a Korsar,' exclaimed Stellara, 'although I knew that I was not. I felt no enmity toward you.'

'Whatever we may have been we must of necessity be friends now,' he told her.

'That will depend upon you,' she replied.

3

Amiocap

The blue waters of the great sea known as Korsar Az wash the shores of a green island far from the mainland – a long, narrow island with verdure clad hills and plateaus, its coast line indented by coves and tiny bays – Amiocap, an island of mystery and romance.

At a distance, and when there is a haze upon the waters, it looks like two islands, rather than one, so low and narrow it is at one point, where coves run in on either side and the sea almost meets.

Thus it appeared to the two survivors from the deck of the Korsar derelict drifting helplessly with the sluggish run of an ocean current and at the whim of vagrant winds.

Time is not even a word to the people of Pellucidar, so Tanar had given no thought to that. They had eaten many times, but as there was still an ample supply of provisions, even for a large ship's company, he felt no concern upon that score, but he had been worried by the depletion of their supply of good water, for the contents of many casks that he had broached had been undrinkable.

They had slept much, which is the way of Pellucidarians when there is naught else to do, storing energy for possible future periods of long drawn exertion.

They had been sleeping thus, for how long who may say in the measureless present of Pellucidar. Stellara was the first to come on deck from the cabin she had occupied next to that of The Cid. She looked about for Tanar, but not seeing him she let her eyes wander out over the upcurving expanse of water that merged in every direction with the blue domed vault of the brilliant sky, in the exact center of which hung the great noonday sun.

But suddenly her gaze was caught and held by something beside the illimitable waters and the ceaseless sun. She voiced a surprised and joyous cry and, turning, ran across the deck toward the cabin in which Tanar slept.

'Tanar! Tanar!' she cried, pounding upon the paneled door. 'Land, Tanar, land!'

The door swung open and the Sarian stepped out upon the deck where Stellara stood pointing across the starboard rail of the drifting derelict.

Close by rose the green hills of a long shore line that stretched away in both directions for many miles, but whether was the mainland or an island they could not tell.

'Land!' breathed Tanar. 'How good it looks!'

'The pleasant green of the soft foliage often hides terrible beasts and savage men,' Stellara reminded him.

'But they are the dangers that I know – it is the unknown dangers of the sea that I do not like. I am not of the sea.'

'You hate the sea?'

'No,' he replied, 'I do not hate it; I do not understand it – that is all. But there is something that I do understand,' and he pointed toward the land.

There was that in Tanar's tone that caused Stellara to look quickly in the direction that he indicated.

'Men!' she exclaimed.

'Warriors,' said Tanar.

'There must be twenty of them in that canoe,' she said.

'And here comes another canoeful behind them.'

From the mouth of a narrow cove the canoes were paddling out into the open sea.

'Look!' cried Stellara. 'There are many more coming.'

One after another twenty canoes moved in a long column out upon the quiet waters and as they drew steadily toward the ship the survivors saw that each was filled with almost naked warriors. Short, heavy spears, bone-tipped, bristled menacingly; stone knives protruded from every G-string and stone hatchets swung at every hip.

As the flotilla approached, Tanar went to a cabin and returned with two of the heavy pistols left behind by a fleeing Korsar when the ship had been abandoned.

'Do you expect to repulse four hundred warriors with those?' asked the girl.

Tanar shrugged. 'If they have never heard the report of a firearm a few shots may suffice to frighten them away, for a time at least,' he explained, 'and if we do not go on the shore the current will carry us away from them in time.'

'But suppose they do not frighten so easily?' she demanded.

'Then I can do no more than my best with the crude weapons and the inferior powder of the Korsars,' he said with the conscious superiority of one who had, with his people, so recently emerged from the stone age that he often instinctively grasped a pistol by the muzzle and used it as a war club in sudden emergencies when at close quarters.

'Perhaps they will not be unfriendly,' suggested Stellara.

Tanar laughed. 'Then they are not of Pellucidar,' he said, 'but of some wondrous country inhabited by what Perry calls angels.'

'Who is Perry?' she demanded. 'I never heard of him.'

'He is a madman who says that Pellucidar is the inside of a hollow stone that is as round as the strange world that hangs forever above the Land of Awful Shadow, and that upon the outside are seas and mountains and plains and countless people and a great country from which he comes.'

'He must be quite mad,' said the girl.

'Yet he and David, our Emperor, have brought us many advantages that were before unknown in Pellucidar, so that now we can kill more warriors in a single battle than was possible before during the course of a whole war. Perry calls this civilization and it is indeed a very wonderful thing.'

'Perhaps he came from the frozen world from which the ancestors of the Korsars came,' suggested the girl. 'They say that that country lies outside of Pellucidar.'

'Here is the enemy,' said Tanar. 'Shall I fire at that big fellow standing in the bow of the first canoe?' Tanar raised one of the heavy pistols and took aim, but the girl laid a hand upon his arm.

'Wait,' she begged. 'They may be friendly. Do not fire unless you must – I hate killing.'

'I can well believe that you are no Korsar,' he said, lowering the muzzle of his weapon.

There came a hail from the leading canoe. 'We are prepared for you, Korsars,' shouted the tall warrior standing in the bow. 'You are few in numbers. We are many. Your great canoe is a useless wreck; ours are manned by twenty warriors each. You are helpless. We are strong. It is not always thus and this time it is not we who shall be taken prisoners, but you, if you attempt to land.

'But we are not like you, Korsars. We do not want to kill or capture. Go away and we shall not harm you.'

'We cannot go away,' replied Tanar. 'Our ship is helpless. We are only two and our food and water are nearly exhausted. Let us land and remain until we can prepare to return to our own countries.'

The warrior turned and conversed with the others in his canoe. Presently he faced Tanar again.

'No,' he said; 'my people will not permit Korsars to come among us. They do not trust you. Neither do I. If you do not go away we shall take you as prisoners and your fate will be in the hands of the Council of the Chiefs.'

'But we are not Korsars,' explained Tanar.

The warrior laughed. 'You speak a lie,' he said. 'Do you think that we do not know the ships of Korsar?'

'This is a Korsar ship,' replied Tanar; 'but we are not Korsars. We were prisoners and when they abandoned their ship in a great storm they left us aboard.'

Again the warriors conferred and those in other canoes that had drawn alongside the first joined in the discussion.

'Who are you then?' demanded the spokesman.

'I am Tanar of Pellucidar. My father is King of Sari.'

'We are all of Pellucidar,' replied the warrior; 'but we never heard of a country called Sari. And the woman – she is your mate?'

'No!' cried Stellara, haughtily. 'I am not his mate.'

'Who are you? Are you a Sarian, also?'

'I am no Sarian. My father and mother were of Amiocap.'

Again the warriors talked among themselves, some seeming to favor one idea, some another.

'Do you know the name of this country?' finally demanded the leading warrior, addressing Stellara.

'No,' she replied.

'We were about to ask you that very question,' said Tanar.

'And the woman is from Amiocap?' demanded the warrior.

'No other blood flows in my veins,' said Stellara, proudly.

'Then it is strange that you do not recognize your own land and your own people,' cried the warrior. 'This is the island of Amiocap!'

Stellara voiced a low cry of pleased astonishment. 'Amiocap!' she breathed softly, as to herself. The tone was a caress, but the warriors in the canoes were too far away to hear her. They thought she was silent and embarrassed because they had discovered her deception.

'Go away!' they cried again.

'You will not send me away from the land of my parents!' cried Stellara, in astonishment.

'You have lied to us,' replied the tall warrior. 'You are not of Amiocap. You do not know us, nor do we know you.'

'Listen!' cried Tanar. 'I was a prisoner aboard this ship and, being no Korsar, the girl told me her story long before we sighted this land. She could not have known that we were near your island. I do not know that she even knew its location, but nevertheless I believe that her story is true.

'She has never said that she was from Amiocap, but that her parents were. She has never seen the island before now. Her mother was stolen by the Korsars before she was born.'

Again the warriors spoke together in low tones for a moment and then, once more, the spokesman addressed Stellara. 'What was your mother's name?' he demanded. 'Who was your father?'

'My mother was called Allara,' replied the girl. 'I never saw my father, but my mother said that he was a chief and a great tandor hunter, called Fedol.'

At a word from the tall warrior in the bow of the leading canoe from the warriors paddled slowly nearer the drifting hulk, and as they approached the ship's waist Tanar and Stellara descended to the main deck, which was now almost awash, so deep the ship rode because of the water in her hold, and as the canoe drifted alongside, the warriors, with the exception of a couple, laid down their paddles and stood ready with their bone-tipped spears.

Now the two upon the ship's deck and the tall warrior in the canoe stood almost upon the same level and face to face. The latter was a smooth-faced man with finely molded features and clear, gray eyes that bespoke intelligence and courage. He was gazing intently at Stellara, as though he would search her very soul for proof of the veracity or falsity of her statements. Presently he spoke.

'You might well be her daughter,' he said; 'the resemblance is apparent.'

'You knew my mother?' exclaimed Stellara.

'I am Vulhan. You have heard her speak of me?'

'My mother's brother!' exclaimed Stellara, with deep emotion, but there was no answering emotion in the manner of the Amiocap warrior. 'My father, where is he? Is he alive?'

'That is the question,' said Vulhan, seriously. 'Who is your father! Your mother was stolen by a Korsar. If the Korsar is your father, you are a Korsar.'

'But he is not my father. Take me to my own father – although he has never seen me he will know me and I shall know him.'

'It will do no harm,' said a warrior who stood close to Vulhan. 'If the girl is a Korsar we shall know what to do with her.'

'If she is the spawn of the Korsar who stole Allara, Vulhan and Fedol will know how to treat her,' said Vulhan savagely.

'I am not afraid,' said Stellara.

'And this other,' said Vulhan, nodding toward Tanar. 'What of him?'

'He was a prisoner of war that the Korsars were taking back to Korsar. Let him come with you. His people are not sea people. He could not survive by the sea alone.'

'You are sure that he is no Korsar?' demanded Vulhan.

'Look at him!' exclaimed the girl. 'The men of Amiocap must know the people of Korsar well by sight. Does this one look like a Korsar?'

Vulhan was forced to admit that he did not. 'Very well,' he said, 'he may come with us, but whatever your fate, he must share it.'

'Gladly,' agreed Tanar.

The two quit the deck of the derelict as places were made for them in the canoe and as the little craft was paddled rapidly toward shore neither felt any sorrow at parting from the drifting hulk that had been their home for so long. The last they saw of her, just as they were entering the cove, from which they had first seen the canoes emerge, she was drifting slowly with the ocean current parallel with the green shore of Amiocap.

At the upper end of the cove the canoes were beached and dragged beneath the concealing foliage of the luxuriant vegetation. Here they were turned bottom side up and left until occasion should again demand their use.

The warriors of Amiocap conducted their two prisoners into the jungle that grew almost to the water's edge. At first there was no sign of trail and the leading warriors forced their way through the lush vegetation, which fortunately was free from thorns and briers, but presently they came upon a little path which opened into a broad, well beaten trail along which the party moved in silence.

During the march Tanar had an opportunity to study the men of Amiocap more closely and he saw that almost without exception they were symmetrically built, with rounded, flowing muscles that suggested a combination of agility and strength. Their features were regular, and there was not among them one who might be termed ugly. On the whole their expressions were open rather than cunning and kindly rather than ferocious; yet the scars upon the bodies of many of them and their well worn and efficient looking, though crude, weapons suggested that they might be bold hunters and fierce warriors. There was a marked dignity in their carriage and demeanor which appealed to Tanar as did their taciturnity, for the Sarians themselves are not given to useless talk.

Stellara, walking at his side, appeared unusually happy and there was an expression of contentment upon her face that the Sarian had never seen there before. She had been watching him as well as the Amiocapians, and now she addressed him in a whisper.

'What do you think of my people?' she asked, proudly. 'Are they not wonderful?'

'They are a fine race,' he replied, 'and I hope for your sake that they will believe that you are one of them.'

'It is all just as I have dreamed it so many times,' said the girl, with a happy sigh. 'I have always known that some day I should come to Amiocap and that it would be just as my mother told me that it was – the great trees, the giant ferns, the gorgeous, flowering vines and bushes. There are fewer savage beasts here than in other parts of Pellucidar and the people seldom war among themselves, so that for the most part they live in peace and contentment, broken only by the raids of the Korsars or an occasional raid upon their fields and villages by the great tandors. Do you know what tandors are, Tanar? Do you have them in your country?'

Tanar nodded. 'I have heard of them in Amoz,' he said, 'though they are rare in Sari.'

'There are thousands of them upon the island of Amiocap,' said the girl, 'and my people are the greatest tandor hunters in Pellucidar.'

Again they walked on in silence, Tanar wondering what the attitude of the Amiocapians would be towards them, and if friendly whether they would be able to assist him in making his way back to the distant mainland, where Sari lay. To this primitive mountaineer it seemed little short of hopeless even to dream of returning to his native land, for the sea appalled him, nor did he have any conception as to how he might set a course across its savage bosom, or navigate any craft that he might later find at his disposal; yet so powerful is the homing instinct in the Pellucidarians that there was no doubt in his mind that so long as he lived he would always be searching for a way back to Sari.

He was glad that he did not have to worry about Stellara, for if it was true that she was among her own people she could remain upon Amiocap and there would rest upon him no sense of responsibility for her return to Korsar; but if they did not accept her – that was another matter; then Tanar would have to seek for means of escape from an island peopled by enemies and he would have to take Stellara with him.

But this train of thought was interrupted by a sudden exclamation from Stellara. 'Look!' she cried. 'Here is a village; perhaps it is the very village of my mother.'

'What did you say?' inquired a warrior, walking near them.

'I said that perhaps this is the village where my mother lived before she was stolen by the Korsars.'

'And you say that your mother was Allara?' inquired the warrior.

'Yes.'

'This was indeed the village in which Allara lived,' said the warrior; 'but do not hope, girl, that you will received as one of them; for unless your father also was of Amiocap, you are not an Amiocapian. It will be hard to convince any one that you are not the daughter of a Korsar father, and as such you are a Korsar and no Amiocapian.'

'But how can you know that my father was a Korsar?' demanded Stellara.

'We do not have to know,' replied the warrior; 'it is merely a matter of what we believe, but that is a question that will have to be settled by Zural, the chief of the village of Lar.'

'Lar,' repeated Stellara. 'That is the village of my mother? I have heard her speak of it many times. This, then, must be Lar.'

'It is,' replied the warrior, 'and presently you shall see Zural.'

The village of Lar consisted of perhaps a hundred thatched huts, each of which was divided into two or more rooms, one of which was invariably an open sitting room without walls, in the center of which was a stone fireplace. The other rooms were ordinarily tightly walled and windowless, affording the necessary darkness for the Amiocapians when they wished to sleep.

The entire clearing was encircled by the most remarkable fence that Tanar had ever seen. The posts, instead of being set in the ground, were suspended from a heavy fiber rope that ran from tree to tree, the lower ends of the posts hanging at least four feet above the ground. Holes had been bored through the posts at intervals of twelve or eighteen inches and into these were inserted hardwood stakes, four or five feet in length and sharpened at either end. These stakes protruded from the posts in all directions, parallel with the ground, and the posts were hung at such a distance from one another that the points of the stakes, protruding from contiguous posts, left intervals of from two to four feet between. As a safeguard against an attacking enemy they seemed futile to Tanar, for in entering the village the party had passed through the open spaces between the posts without being hindered by the barrier.

But conjecture as to the purpose of this strange barrier was crowded from his thoughts by other more interesting occurrences, for no sooner had they entered the village than they were surrounded by a horde of men, women and children.

'Who are these?' demanded some.

'They say that they are friends,' replied Vulhan, 'but we believe that they are from Korsar.'

'Korsars!' cried the villagers.

'I am no Korsar,' cried Stellara, angrily. 'I am the daughter of Allara, the sister of Vulhan.'

'Let her tell that to Zural. It is his business to listen, not ours,' cried one. 'Zural will know what to do with Korsars. Did they not steal his daughter and kill his son?'

'Yes, take them to Zural,' cried another.

'It is to Zural that I am taking them,' replied Vulhan.

The villagers made way for the warriors and their prisoners and as the latter passed through the aisles thus formed many were the ugly looks cast upon them and many the expressions of hatred that they overheard, but no violence was offered them and presently they were conducted to a large hut near the center of the village.

Like the other dwellings of the village of Lar, the floors of the chief's house were raised a foot or eighteen inches above the ground. The thatched roof of the great, open living room, into which they were conducted, was supported by enormous ivory tusks of the giant tandors. The floor, which appeared to be constructed of unglazed tile, was almost entirely covered by the hides of wild animals. There were a number of low, wooden stools standing about the room, and one higher one that might almost have been said to have attained the dignity of a chair.

Upon this larger stool was seated a stern faced man, who scrutinized them closely and silently as they were halted before him. For several seconds no one spoke, and then the man upon the chair turned to Vulhan.

'Who are these,' he demanded, 'and what do they in the village of Lar?'

'We took them from a Korsar ship that was drifting helplessly with the ocean current,' said Vulhan, 'and we have brought them to Zural, chief of the village of Lar, that he may hear their story and judge whether they be the friends they claim to be, or the Korsar enemies that we believe them to be. This one,' and Vulhan pointed to Stellara, 'says that she is the daughter of Allara.'

'I am the daughter of Allara,' said Stellara.

'And who was your father?' demanded Zural.

'My father's name is Fedol,' replied Stellara.

'How do you know?' asked Zural.

'My mother told me.'

'Where were you born?' demanded Zural.

'In the Korsar city of Allaban,' replied Stellara.

'Then you are a Korsar,' stated Zural with finality. 'And this one, what has he to say for himself?' asked Zural, indicating Tanar with a nod.

'He claims that he was a prisoner of the Korsars and that he comes from a distant kingdom called Sari.'

'I have never heard of such a kingdom,' said Zural. 'Is there any warrior here who has ever heard of it?' he demanded. 'If there is, let him in justice to the prisoner, speak.' But the Amiocapians only shook their heads for there was none who had ever heard of the kingdom of Sari. 'It is quite plain,' continued Zural, 'that they are enemies and that they are seeking by falsehood to gain our confidence. If there is a drop of Amiocapian blood in one of them, we are sorry for that drop. Take them away, Vulhan. Keep them under guard until we decide how they shall be destroyed.'

'My mother told me that the Amiocapians were a just and kindly people,' said Stellara; 'but it is neither just nor kindly to destroy this man who is not an enemy simply because you have never heard of the country from which he comes. I tell you that he is no Korsar. I was on one of the ships of the fleet when the prisoners were brought aboard. I heard The Cid and Bohar the Bloody when they were questioning this man, and I know that he is no Korsar and that he comes from a kingdom known as Sari. They did not doubt his word, so why should you? If you are a just and kindly people how can you destroy me without giving me an opportunity to talk with Fedol, my father. He will believe me; he will know that I am his daughter.'

'The gods frown upon us if we harbor enemies in our village,' replied Zural. 'We should have bad luck, as all Amiocapians know. Wild beasts would kill our hunters and the tandors would trample our fields and destroy our villages. But worst of all the Korsars would come and rescue you from us. As for Fedol, no man knows where he is. He is not of this village and the people of his own village have slept and eaten many times since they saw Fedol. They have slept and eaten many times since Fedol set forth upon his last tandor hunt. Perhaps the tandors have avenged the killing of many of their fellows, or perhaps Fedol fell into the clutches of the Buried People. These things we do not know, but we do know that Fedol went away to hunt tandors and that he never came back and that we do not know where to find him. Take them away, Vulhan, and we shall hold a council of the chiefs and then we shall decide what shall be done with them.'

'You are a cruel and wicked man, Zural,' cried Stellara, 'and no better than the Korsars themselves.'

'It is useless, Stellara,' said Tanar, laying a hand upon the girl's arm. 'Let us go quietly with Vulhan;' and then in a low whisper, 'Do not anger them, for there is yet hope for us in the council of the chiefs if we do not antagonize them.' And so without further word Stellara and Tanar were led from the house of Zural the chief surrounded by a dozen stalwart warriors.

4

Letari

Stellara and Tanar were conducted to a small hut in the outskirts of the village. The building consisted of but two rooms; the open living room with the fireplace and a small dark, sleeping apartment. Into the latter the prisoners were thrust and a single warrior was left on guard in the living room to prevent their escape.

In a world where the sun hangs perpetually at zenith there is no darkness and without darkness there is little opportunity to escape from the clutches of a watchful enemy. Yet never for a moment was the thought of escape absent from the mind of Tanar the Sarian. He studied the sentries and as each one was relieved he tried to enter into conversation with his successor, but all to no avail – the warriors would not talk to him. Sometimes the guards dozed, but the village and the clearing about it were always alive with people so that it appeared unlikely that any opportunity for escape might present itself.

The sentries were changed, food was brought to the prisoners and when they felt so inclined they slept. Thus only might they measure the lapse of time, if such a thing occurred to them, which doubtless it did not. They talked together and sometimes Stellara sang – sang the songs of Amiocap that her mother had taught her, and they were happy and contented, although each knew that the specter of death hovered constantly above them. Presently he would strike, but in the meantime they were happy.

'When I was a youth,' said Tanar, 'I was taken prisoner by the black people with tails. They build their villages among the high branches of lofty trees and at first they put me in a small hut as dark as this and much dirtier and I was very miserable and very unhappy for I have always been free and I love my freedom, but now I am again a prisoner in a dark hut and in addition I know that I am going to die and I do not want to die, yet I am not unhappy. Why is it, Stellara, do you know?'

'I have wondered about the same thing myself,' replied the girl. 'It seems to me that I have never been so happy before in my life, but I do not know the reason.'

They were sitting close together upon a fiber mat that they had placed near the doorway that they might obtain as much light and air as possible. Stellara's soft eyes looked thoughtfully out upon the little world framed by the doorway of their prison cell. One hand rested listlessly on the mat between them. Tanar's eyes rested upon her profile, and slowly his hand went out and covered hers.

'Perhaps,' he said, 'I should not be happy if you were not here.'

The girl turned half frightened eyes upon him and withdrew her hand. 'Don't,' she said.

'Why?' he asked.

'I do not know, only that it makes me afraid.'

The man was about to speak again when a figure darkened the opening in the doorway. A girl had come bringing food. Heretofore it had been a man – a taciturn man who had replied to none of Tanar's questions. But there was no suggestion of taciturnity upon the beautiful, smiling countenance of the girl.

'Here is food,' she said. 'Are you hungry?'

'Where there is nothing else to do but eat I am always hungry,' said Tanar. 'But where is the man who brought our food before?'

'That was my father,' replied the girl. 'He has gone to hunt and I have brought the food in his stead.'

'I hope that he never returns from the hunt,' said Tanar.

'Why?' demanded the girl. 'He is a good father. Why do you wish him harm?'

'I wish him no harm,' replied Tanar, laughing. 'I only wish that his daughter would continue to bring our food. She is far more agreeable and much better looking.'

The girl flushed, but it was evident that she was pleased.

'I wanted to come before,' she said, 'but my father would not let me. I saw you when they brought you into the village and I have wanted to see you again. I never before saw a man who looked like you. You are different from the Amiocapians. Are all the men of Sari as good looking as you?'

Tanar laughed. 'I am afraid I have never given much thought to that subject,' he replied. 'In Sari we judge our men by what they do and not by what they look like.'

'But you must be a great hunter,' said the girl. 'You look like a great hunter.'

'How do great hunters look?' demanded Stellara with some asperity.

'They look like this man,' replied the girl. 'Do you know,' she continued, 'I have dreamed about you many times.'

'What is your name?' asked Tanar.

'Letari,' replied the girl.

'Letari,' repeated Tanar. 'That is a pretty name. I hope, Letari, that you will bring our food to us often.'

'I shall never bring it again,' she said, sadly.

'And why?' demanded Tanar.

'Because no one will bring it again,' she said.

'And why is that? Are they going to starve us to death?'

'No, the council of the chiefs has decided that you are both Korsars and that you must be destroyed.'

'And when will that be?' asked Stellara.

'As soon as the hunters return with food. We are going to have a great feast and dance, but I shall not enjoy it. I shall be very unhappy for I do not wish to see Tanar die.'

'How are they going to destroy us?' asked the man.

'Look,' said the girl, pointing through the open doorway. There, in the distance, the two prisoners saw men setting two stakes into the ground. 'There were many who wanted to give you to the Buried People,' said Letari, 'but Zural said that it has been so long since we have had a feast and a dance that he thought that we should celebrate the killing of two Korsars rather than let the Buried People have all the pleasure, and so they are going to tie you to those two stakes and pile dry wood and brush around you and burn you to death.'

Stellara shuddered. 'And my mother taught me that you were a kindly people,' she said.

'Oh, we do not mean to be unkind,' said Letari, 'but the Korsars have been very cruel to us and Zural believes that the gods will take word to the Korsars that you were burned to death and that perhaps it will frighten them and keep them away from Amiocap.'

Tanar arose to his feet and stood very straight and stiff. The horror of the situation almost overwhelmed him. He looked down at Stellara's golden head and shuddered. 'You cannot mean,' he said, 'that the men of Amiocap intend to burn this girl alive?'

'Why, yes,' said Letari. 'It would do no good to kill her first for then her spirit could not tell the gods that she was burned and they could not tell the Korsars.'

'It is hideous,' cried Tanar; 'and you, a girl yourself, have you no sympathy; have you no heart?'

'I am very sorry that they are going to burn you,' said Letari, 'but as for her, she is a Korsar and I feel nothing but hatred and loathing for her, but you are different. I know that you are not a Korsar and I wish that I could save you.'

'Will you – would you, if you could?' demanded Tanar.

'Yes, but I cannot.'

The conversation relative to escape had been carried on in low whispers, so that the guard would not overhear, but evidently it had aroused his suspicion for now he arose and came to the doorway of the hut. 'What are you talking about?' he demanded. 'Why do you stay in here so long, Letari, talking with these Korsars? I heard what you said and I believe that you are in love with this man.'

'What if I am?' demanded the girl. 'Do not our gods demand that we love? What else do we live for upon Amiocap but love?'

'The gods do not say that we should love our enemies.'

'They do not say that we should not,' retorted Letari. 'If I choose to love Tanar it is my own affair.'

'Clear out!' snapped the warrior. 'There are plenty of men in Lar for you to love.'

'Ah!' sighed the girl as she passed through the doorway, 'but there is none like Tanar.'

'The hateful little wanton,' cried Stellara after the girl had left.

'She does not hesitate to reveal what is in her heart,' said Tanar. 'The girls of Sari are not like that. They would die rather than reveal their love before the man had declared his. But perhaps she is only a child and did not realize what she said.'

'A child nothing,' snapped Stellara. 'She knew perfectly well what she was saying and it is quite apparent that you liked it. Very well, when she comes to save you, go with her.'

'You do not think that I intended to go with her alone even though an opportunity for escape presented itself through her, do you?' demanded Tanar.

'She told you that she would not help me to escape,' Stellara reminded him.

'I know that, but it would be only in the hope of helping you to escape that I would take advantage of her help.'

'I would rather be burned alive a dozen times than to escape with her help.'

There was a venom in the girl's voice that had never been there before and Tanar looked at her in surprise. 'I do not understand you, Stellara,' he said.

'I do not understand myself,' said the girl, and burying her face in her hands she burst into tears.

Tanar knelt quickly beside her and put an arm about her. 'Don't,' he begged, 'please don't.'

She pushed him from her. 'Go away,' she cried. 'Don't touch me. I hate you.'

Tanar was about to speak again when he was interrupted by a great commotion at the far end of the village. There were shouts and yells from men, mingled with a thunderous noise that fairly shook the ground, and then the deep booming of drums.

Instantly the men setting the stakes in the ground, where Tanar and Stellara were to be burned, stopped their work, seized their weapons and rushed in the direction from which the noise was coming.

The prisoners saw men, women and children running from their huts and all directed their steps toward the same point. The guard before their door leaped to his feet and stood for a moment looking at the running villagers. Then, without a word or backward glance, he dashed off after them.

Tanar, realizing that for the moment at least they were unguarded, stepped from the dark cell out into the open living apartment and looked in the direction toward which the villagers were running. There he saw the cause of the disturbance and also an explanation of the purpose for which the strange hanging barrier had been erected.

Just beyond the barrier loomed two gigantic mammoths – huge tandors, towering sixteen feet or more in height – their wicked eyes red with hate and rage; their great tusks gleaming in the sunlight; their long, powerful trunks seeking to drag down the barrier from the sharpened stakes of which their flesh recoiled. Facing the mammoths was a shouting horde of warriors, screaming women and children, and above all rose the thundering din of the drums.

Each time the tandors sought to force their way through the barrier, or brush aside its posts, these swung about so that the sharpened stakes threatened their eyes or pricked the tender flesh of their trunks, while bravely facing them the shouting warriors hurled their stone-tipped spears.

But however interesting or inspiring the sight might be, Tanar had no time to spare to follow the course of this strange encounter, Turning to Stellara, he seized her hand. 'Come,' he cried. 'Now is our chance!' And while the villagers were engrossed with the tandors at the far end of the village, Tanar and Stellara ran swiftly across the clearing and entered the lush vegetation of the forest beyond.

There was no trail and it was with difficulty that they forced their way through the underbrush for a short distance before Tanar finally halted.

'We shall never escape them in this way,' he said. 'Our spoor is as plain as the spoor of a dyryth after a rain.'

'How else then may we escape?' asked Stellara.

Tanar was looking upward into the trees examining them closely. 'When I was a prisoner among the black people with long tails,' he said, 'I had to learn to travel through the trees and this knowledge and the ability have stood me in good stead many times since and I believe that they may prove our salvation now.'

'You go then,' said Stellara, 'and save yourself, for certainly I cannot travel through the trees, and there is no reason why we should both be recaptured when one of us can escape.'

Tanar smiled. 'You know that I would not do that,' he said.

'But what else may you do?' demanded Stellara. 'They will follow the trail we are making and recapture us before we are out of hearing of the village.'

'We shall leave no trail,' said Tanar. 'Come,' and leaping lightly to a lower branch he swung himself into the tree that spread above them. 'Give me your hand,' he said, reaching down to Stellara, and a moment later he had drawn the girl to his side. Then he stood erect and steadied the girl while she arose to her feet. Before them a maze of branches stretched away to be lost in the foliage.

'We shall leave no spoor here,' said Tanar.

'I am afraid,' said Stellara. 'Hold me tightly.'

'You will soon become accustomed to it,' said Tanar, 'and then you will not be afraid. At first I was afraid, but later I could swing through the trees almost as rapidly as the black men themselves.'

'I cannot even take a single step,' said Stellara. 'I know that I shall fall.'

'You do not have to take a step,' said Tanar. 'Put your arms around my neck and hold on tightly,' and then he stooped and lifted her with his left arm while she clung tightly to him, her soft white arms encircling his neck.

'How easily you lifted me!' she said; 'how strong you are; but no man living could carry my weight through these trees and not fall.'

Tanar did not reply, but instead he moved off among the branches seeking sure footing and secure handholds as he went. The girl's soft body was pressed close to his and in his nostrils was the delicate sachet that he had sensed in his first contact with Stellara aboard the Korsar ship and which now seemed a part of her.

As Tanar swung through the forest, the girl marveled at the strength of the man. She had always considered him a weakling by comparison with the beefy Korsars, but now she realized that in those smoothly rolling muscles was concealed the power of a superman.

She found a fascination in watching him. He moved so easily and he did not seem to tire. Once she let her lips fall until they touched his thick, black hair and then, just a little, almost imperceptibly, she tightened her arms about his neck.

Stellara was very happy and then, of a sudden, she recalled Letari and she straightened up and relaxed her hold. 'The vile wanton,' she said.

'Who?' demanded Tanar. 'What are you talking about?'

'That creature, Letari,' said Stellara.

'Why she is not vile,' said Tanar. 'I thought she was very nice and she is certainly beautiful.'

'I believe you are in love with her,' snapped Stellara.

'That would not be difficult,' said Tanar. 'She seemed very lovable.'

'Do you love her?' demanded Stellara.

'Why shouldn't I?' asked Tanar.

'Do you?' insisted the girl.

'Would you care if I did?' asked Tanar, softly.

'Most certainly not,' said Stellara.

'Then why do you ask?'

'I didn't ask,' said Stellara. 'I do not care.'

'Oh,' said Tanar. 'I misunderstood,' and he moved on in silence, for the men of Sari are not talkative, and Stellara did not know what was in his mind for his face did not reflect the fact that he was laughing inwardly, and, anyway, Stellara could not see his face.

Tanar moved always in one direction and his homing instinct assured him that the direction lay toward Sari. As far as the land went he could move unerringly toward the spot in Pellucidar where he was born. Every Pellucidarian can do that, but put them on the water, out of sight of land, and that instinct leaves them and they have no more conception of direction than would you or I if we were transported suddenly to a land where there are no points of compass since the sun hangs perpetually at zenith and there is no moon and no stars. Tanar's only wish at present was to put them as far as possible from the village of Lar. He would travel until they reached the coast for, knowing that Amiocap was an island, he knew that eventually they must come to the ocean. What they should do then was rather vague in his mind. He had visions of building a boat and embarking upon the sea, although he knew perfectly well that this would be madness on the part of a hill dweller such as he.

Presently he felt hungry and he knew that they must have traveled a considerable distance.

Sometimes Tanar kept track of distance by computing the number of steps that he took, for by much practice he had learned to count them almost mechanically, leaving his mind free for other perceptions and thoughts, but here among the branches of the trees, where his steps were not of uniform length, he had thought it not worth the effort to count them and so he could only tell by the recurrence of hunger that they must have covered considerable distance since they left the village of Lar.

During their flight through the forest they had seen birds and monkeys and other animals and, on several occasions, they had paralleled or crossed game trails, but as the Amiocapians had stripped him of his weapons he had no means of obtaining meat until he could stop long enough to fashion a bow and some arrows and a spear.

How he missed his spear! From childhood it had been his constant companion and for a long time he had felt almost helpless without it. He had never become entirely accustomed or reconciled to carrying firearms, feeling in the bottom of his primitive and savage heart that there was nothing more dependable than a sturdy, stone shod spear.

He had rather liked the bow and arrows that Innes and Perry had taught him to make and use, as the arrows had seemed like little spears. At least one could see them, whereas with the strange and noisy weapons, which belched forth smoke and flame, one could not see the projectile at all. It was most unnatural and uncanny.

But Tanar's mind was not occupied with such thoughts at this time. Food was dominant.

Presently they came to a small, natural clearing beside a crystal brook and Tanar swung lightly to the ground.

'We shall stop here,' he said, 'until I can make weapons and get meat for us.'

With the feel of the ground beneath her feet again Stellara felt more independent. 'I am not hungry,' she said.

'I am,' said Tanar.

'There are berries and fruits and nuts in plenty,' she insisted. 'We should not wait here to be overtaken by the warriors from Lar.'

'We shall wait here until I have made weapons,' said Tanar, with finality, 'and then I shall not only be in a position to make a kill for meat, but I shall be able better to defend you against Zural's warriors.'

'I wish to go on,' said Stellara. 'I do not wish to stay here,' and she stamped her little foot.

Tanar looked at her in surprise. 'What is the matter with you, Stellara? You were never like this before.'

'I do not know what is the matter with me,' said the girl. 'I only know that I wish I were back in Korsar, in the house of The Cid. There, at least, I should be among friends. Here I am surrounded only by enemies.'

'Then you would have Bohar the Bloody One as a mate, if he survived the storm, or if not he another like him,' Tanar reminded her.

'At least he loved me,' said Stellara.

'And you loved him?' asked Tanar.

'Perhaps,' said Stellara.

There was a peculiar look on Tanar's face as his eyes rested upon the girl. He did not understand her, but he seemed to be trying to. She was looking past him, a strange expression upon her face when suddenly she voiced an exclamation of dismay and pointed past him.

'Look!' she cried. 'Oh, God, look!'

5

The Tandor Hunter

So filled with fear was Stellara's tone that Tanar felt the hair rise upon his scalp as he wheeled about to face the thing that had so filled the girl with horror, but even had he had time to conjure in his imagination a picture worthy of her fright, he could not have imagined a more fearsome or repulsive thing than that which was advancing upon them.

In conformation it was primarily human, but there the similarity ended. It had arms and legs and it walked erect upon two feet; but such feet! They were huge, flat things with nailless toes – short, stubby toes with webs between them. Its arms were short and in lieu of fingers its hands were armed with three heavy claws. It stood somewhere in the neighborhood of five feet in height and there was not a vestige of hair upon its entire naked body, the skin of which was of the sickly pallor of a corpse.

But these attributes lent to it but a fraction of its repulsiveness – it was its head and face that were appalling. It had no external ears, there being only two small orifices on either side of its head where these organs are ordinarily located. Its mouth was large with loose, flabby lips that were drawn back now into a snarl that exposed two rows of heavy fangs. Two small openings above the center of the mouth marked the spot where a nose should have been and, to add further to the hideousness of its appearance, it was eyeless, unless bulging protuberances forcing out the skin where the eyes should have been might be called eyes. Here the skin upon the face moved as though great, round eyes were rolling beneath. The hideousness of that blank face without eyelids, lashes or eyebrows shocked even the calm and steady nerves of Tanar.

The creature carried no weapons, but what need had it for weapons, armed as it was with those formidable claws and fangs? Beneath its pallid skin surged great muscles that attested its giant strength and upon its otherwise blank face the mouth alone was sufficient to suggest its diabolical ferocity.

'Run, Tanar!' cried Stellara. 'Take to the trees! It is one of the Buried People.' But the thing was too close to him to admit of escape even if Tanar had been minded to desert Stellara, and so he stood there quietly awaiting the encounter and then suddenly, as though to add to the uncanny horror of the situation, the thing spoke. From its flabby, drooling lips issued sounds – mumbled, ghastly sounds that yet took on the semblance of speech until it became intelligible in a distorted way to Tanar and Stellara.

'It is the woman I want,' mumbled the creature. 'Give me the woman, and the man may go.' To Tanar's shocked sensibilities it was as though a mutilated corpse had risen from the grave and spoken, and he fell back a step with a sensation as nearly akin to horror as he had ever experienced.

'You cannot have the woman,' said Tanar. 'Leave us alone, or I will kill you.'

An uncanny scream that was a mixture of laugh and shriek broke from the lips of the thing. 'Then die!' it cried, as it launched itself upon the Sarian.

As it closed it struck upward with its heavy claws in an attempt to disembowel its antagonist, but Tanar eluded its first rush by leaping lightly to one side and then, turning quickly, he hurled himself upon the loathsome body and circling its neck with one powerful arm Tanar turned suddenly and, bending his body forward and downward, hurled the creature over his head and heavily to the ground.

But instantly it was up again and at him. Screaming with rage and frothing at the mouth it struck wildly with its heavy claws, but Tanar had learned certain things from David Innes that men of the stone age ordinarily do not know, for David had taught him, as he had taught many another young Pellucidarian, the art of self-defense, including boxing, wrestling and jiu-jitsu, and now again they came into good stead as they had upon other occasions since he had mastered them and once more he gave thanks for the fortunate circumstance that had brought David Innes from the outer crust to Pellucidar to direct the destinies of its human race as first emperor.

Combined with his knowledge, training and agility was Tanar's great strength, without which these other accomplishments would have been of far lesser value, and so as the creature struck, Tanar parried the blows, fending the wicked talons from his flesh and with a strength that surprised his antagonist since it was fully as great as his own.

But what was still more surprising to the monster was the frequency with which Tanar was able to step in and deliver telling blows to the body and head that, in its awkwardness and lack of skill, it was unable to properly protect.

To one side, watching the battle for which she was the stake, stood Stellara. She might have run away and hidden; she might have made good her escape, but no such thoughts entered her courageous little head. It would have been as impossible for her to desert her champion in the hour of his need as it would have been for him to leave her to her fate and so she stood there, helpless, awaiting the outcome.

To and fro across the clearing the battlers moved, trampling down the lush vegetation that sometimes grew so thickly as to hamper their movements, and now it became apparent to both Stellara and Tanar from the labored breathing of the creature that it was being steadily worn down and that it lacked the endurance of the Sarian. However, probably sensing something of this itself, it now redoubled its efforts and the ferocity of its attack, and, at the same time, Tanar discovered a vulnerable spot at which to aim his blows.

Striking for the face he had accidentally touched one of the bulging protuberances that lay beneath the skin where the eyes should have been. At the impact of the blow, light as it was, the creature screamed and leaped backward, instinctively raising one of its claws to the injured organ and thereafter Tanar directed all his efforts toward placing further and heavier blows upon those two bulging spots.

He struck again and landed cleanly a heavy blow upon one of them. With a shriek of pain the creature stepped back and clamped both paws to its hurt.

They were fighting very close to where Stellara stood. The creature's back was toward her and she could have reached out and touched him, so near was he to her. She saw Tanar spring forward to strike again. The creature dropped back quite abreast of her and then suddenly lowering its head it gave vent to a horrid shriek and charged the Sarian with all the hideous ferocity that it could gather.

It seemed as though it had mustered all its remaining vitality and thrown it into this last, mad charge. Tanar, his mind and muscles coordinating perfectly, quick to see openings and take advantage of them and equally quick to realize the advantages of retreat, leaped backward to avoid the mad charge and the flailing claws, but as he did so one of his heels struck a low bush and he fell heavily to the ground upon his back.

For the moment he was helpless and in that brief moment the creature could be upon him with those horrid fangs and ripping claws.

Tanar knew it. The thing charging him knew it and Stellara, standing so close to them, knew it, and so quickly did she act that Tanar had scarcely struck the ground as she launched herself bodily upon the charging monster from behind.

As a football player hurls himself forward to tackle an opponent so Stellara hurled herself at the creature. Her arms encircled its knees and then slipped down, as he kicked and struggled to free himself, until finally she secured a hold upon one of his skinny ankles just above its huge foot. There she clung and the creature lunged forward just short of Tanar, but instantly, with a howl of rage, it turned to rend the girl. But that brief instant of delay had been sufficient to permit Tanar to regain his feet and ere ever the talons or fangs could sink into the soft flesh of Stellara, Tanar was upon the creature's back. Fingers of steel encircled its throat and though it struggled and struck out with its heavy claws it was at last helpless in the clutches of the Sarian.

Slowly, relentlessly, Tanar choked the life from the monster and then, with an expression of disgust, he cast the corpse aside and stepped quickly to where Stellara was staggering weakly to her feet.

He put his arm about her and for a moment she buried her face in his shoulder and sobbed. 'Do not be afraid,' he said; 'the thing is dead.'

She raised her face toward his. 'Let us go away from here,' she said. 'I am afraid. There may be more of the Buried People about. There must be an entrance to their underworld near here, for they do not wander far from such openings.'

'Yes,' he said, 'until I have weapons I wish to see no more of them.'

'They are horrible creatures,' said Stellara, 'and if there had been two of them we should both have been lost.'

'What are they?' asked Tanar. 'You seem to know about them. Where had you ever seen one before?'

'I have never seen one until just now,' said she, 'but my mother told me about them. They are feared and hated by all Amiocapians. They are Coripies and they inhabit dark caverns and tunnels beneath the surface of the ground. That is why we call them the Buried People. They live on flesh and wandering about the jungle they gather up the remains of our kills and devour the bodies of wild beasts that have died in the forest, but being afraid of our spears they do not venture far from the openings that lead down into their dark world. Occasionally they waylay a lone hunter and less often they come to one of our villages and seize a woman or child. No one has ever entered their world and escaped to tell about it, so that what my mother has told me about them is only what our people have imagined as to the underworld where the Buried People dwell for there has never been any Amiocapian warrior brave enough to venture into the dark recesses of one of their tunnels, or if there has been such he has not returned to tell of it.'

'And if the kindly Amiocapians had not decided to burn us to death, they might have given us to the Buried People?' asked Tanar.

'Yes, they would have taken us and bound us to trees close to one of the entrances to the underworld, but do not blame my mother's people for that as they would have been doing only that which they considered right and proper.'

'Perhaps they are a kindly people,' said Tanar, with a grin, 'for it was certainly far more kindly to accord us death by burning at the stake than to have left us to the horrid attentions of the Coripies. But come, we will take to the trees again, for this spot does not look as beautiful to me now as it did when we first looked upon it.'

Once more they took up their flight among the branches and just as they were commencing to feel the urge to sleep Tanar discovered a small deer in a game trail beneath them, and making his kill the two satisfied their hunger, and then with small branches and great leaves Tanar constructed a platform in a tree – a narrow couch, where Stellara lay down to sleep while he stood guard, and after she had slept he slept, and then once more they resumed their flight.

Strengthened and refreshed by food and sleep they renewed their journey in higher spirits and greater hopefulness. The village of Lar lay far behind and since they had left it they had seen no other village nor any sign of man.

While Stellara had slept Tanar had busied himself in fashioning crude weapons against the time when he might find proper materials for the making of better ones. A slender branch of hard wood, gnawed to a point by his strong, white teeth, must answer him for a spear. His bow was constructed of another branch and strung with tendons taken from the deer he had killed, while his arrows were slender shoots cut from a tough shrub that grew plentifully throughout the forest. He fashioned a second, lighter spear for Stellara, and thus armed each felt a sense of security that had been entirely wanting before.

On and on they went, three times they ate and once again they slept, and still they had not reached the seacoast.

The great sun hung overhead; a gentle, cooling breeze moved through the forest; birds of gorgeous plumage and little monkeys unknown to the outer world flew or scampered, sang or chattered as the man and the woman disturbed them in their passage. It was a peaceful world and to Tanar, accustomed to the savage, carnivorous beasts that overran the great mainland of his birth, it seemed a very safe and colorless world; yet he was content that nothing was interfering with their progress toward escape.

Stellara had said no more about desiring to return to Korsar and the plan that always hovered among his thoughts included taking Stellara back to Sari with him.

The peaceful trend of Tanar's thoughts was suddenly shattered by the sound of shrill trumpeting. So close it sounded that it might almost have been directly beneath him, and an instant later as he parted the foliage ahead of him he saw the cause of the disturbance.

The jungle ended here upon the edge of open meadowland that was dotted with small clumps of trees. In the foreground there were two figures – a warrior fleeing for his life and behind him a huge tandor, which, though going upon three legs, was sure soon to overtake the man.

Tanar took the entire scene in at a glance and was aware that here was a lone tandor hunter who had failed to hamstring his prey in both hind legs.

It is seldom that man hunts the great tandor single-handed and only the bravest or the most rash would essay to do so. Ordinarily there are several hunters, two of whom are armed with heavy, stone axes. While the others make a noise to attract the attention of the tandor and hide the sound of the approach of the axe men, the latter creep cautiously through the underbrush from the rear of the great animal until each is within striking distance of a hind leg. Then simultaneously they hamstring the monster, which, lying helpless, they dispatch with heavy spears and arrows.

He who would alone hamstring a tandor must be endowed not only with great strength and courage, but must be able to strike two unerring blows with his axe in such rapid succession that the beast is crippled almost before it realizes that it has been attacked.

It was evident to Tanar that this hunter had failed to get in his second blow quickly enough and now he was at the mercy of the great beast.

Since they had started upon their flight through the trees Stellara had overcome her fear and was now able to travel alone with only occasional assistance from Tanar. She had been following the Sarian and now she stood at his side, watching the tragedy being enacted below them.

'He will be killed,' she cried. 'Can we not save him?'

This thought had not occurred to Tanar, for was the man not an Amiocapian and an enemy; but there was something in the girl's tone that spurred the Sarian to action. Perhaps it was the instinct in the male to exhibit his prowess before the female. Perhaps it was because at heart Tanar was brave and magnanimous, or perhaps it was because that among all the other women in the world it was Stellara who had spoken. Who may know? Perhaps Tanar did not know himself what prompted his next act.

Shouting a word that is familiar to all tandor hunters and which is most nearly translatable into English as 'Reverse!' he leaped to the ground almost at the side of the charging tandor and simultaneously he carried his spear hand back and drove the heavy shaft deep into the beast's side, just behind its left shoulder. Then he leaped back into the forest expecting that the tandor would do precisely what it did do.

With a squeal of pain it turned upon its new tormentor.

The Amiocapian, who still clung to his heavy axe, had heard, as though it was a miracle from the gods, the familiar signal that had burst so suddenly from Tanar's lips. It had told him what the other would attempt and he was ready, with the result that he turned back toward the beast at the instant that it wheeled to charge after Tanar, and as it crashed into the undergrowth of the jungle in pursuit of the Sarian the Amiocapian overtook it. The great axe moved swiftly as lightning and the huge beast, trumpeting with rage, sank helplessly to the ground and rolled over on its side.

'Down!' shouted the Amiocapian, to advise Tanar that the attack had been successful.

The Sarian returned and together the two warriors dispatched the great beast, while above them Stellara remained among the concealing verdure of the trees, for the women of Pellucidar do not rashly expose themselves to view of enemy warriors. In this instance she knew that it would be safer to wait and discover the attitude of the Amiocapian toward Tanar. Perhaps he would be grateful and friendly, but there was the possibility that he might not.

The beast dispatched, the two men faced one another. 'Who are you,' demanded the Amiocapian, 'who came so bravely to the rescue of a stranger? I do not recognize you. You are not of Amiocap.'

'My name is Tanar and I am from the kingdom of Sari, that lies far away on the distant mainland. I was captured by the Korsars, who invaded the empire of which Sari is a part. They were taking me and other prisoners back to Korsar when the fleet was overtaken by a terrific storm and the ship upon which I was confined was so disabled that it was deserted by its crew. Drifting helplessly with the wind and current it finally bore us to the shores of Amiocap, where we were captured by warriors from the village of Lar. They did not believe our story, but thought that we were Korsars and they were about to destroy us when we succeeded in making our escape.

'If you do not believe me,' continued the Sarian, 'then one of us must die for under no circumstances will we return to Lar to be burned at the stake.'

'Whether I believe you or not,' replied the Amiocapian, 'I should be beneath the contempt of all men were I to permit any harm to befall one who has just saved my life at the risk of his own.'

'Very well,' said Tanar. 'We shall go our way in the knowledge that you will not reveal our whereabouts to the men of the village of Lar.'

'You say "we,"' said the Amiocapian. 'You are not alone then?'

'No, there is another with me,' replied Tanar.

'Perhaps I can help you,' said the Amiocapian. 'It is my duty to do so. In what direction are you going and how do you plan to escape from Amiocap?'

'We are seeking the coast where we hope to be able to build a craft and to cross the ocean to the mainland.'

The Amiocapian shook his head. 'That will be difficult,' he said. 'Nay, impossible.'

'We may only make the attempt,' said Tanar, 'for it is evident that we cannot remain here among the people of Amiocap, who will not believe that we are not Korsars.'

'You do not look at all like the Korsars,' said the warrior. 'Where is your companion? Does he look like one?'

'My companion is a woman,' replied Tanar.

'If she looks no more like a Korsar than you, then it were easy to believe your story and, I, for one, am willing to believe it and willing to help you. There are other villages upon Amiocap than Lar and other chiefs than Zural. We are all bitter against the Korsars, but we are not all blinded by our hate as is Zural. Fetch your companion and if she does not appear to be a Korsar, I will take you to my own village and see that you are well treated. If I am in doubt I will permit you to go your way; nor shall I mention the fact to others that I have seen you.'

'That is fair enough,' said Tanar, and then, turning, he called to the girl. 'Come, Stellara! Here is a warrior who would see if you are a Korsar.'

The girl dropped lightly to the ground from the branches of the tree above the two men.

As the eyes of the Amiocapian fell upon her he stepped back with an exclamation of shock and surprise.

'Gods of Amiocap!' he cried. 'Allara!'

The two looked at him in amazement. 'No, not Allara,' said Tanar, 'but Stellara, her daughter. Who are you that you should so quickly recognize the likeness?'

'I am Fedol,' said the man, 'and Allara was my mate.'

'Then this is your daughter, Fedol,' said Tanar.

The warrior shook his head, sadly. 'No,' he said, 'I can believe that she is the daughter of Allara, but her father must have been a Korsar for Allara was stolen from me by the men of Korsar. She is a Korsar and though my heart urges me to accept her as my daughter, the customs of Amiocap forbid. Go your way in peace. If I can protect you I shall, but I cannot accept you, or take you to my village.'

Stellara came close to Fedol, her eyes searching the tan skin upon his left shoulder. 'You are Fedol,' she said, pointing to the red birthmark upon his skin, 'and here is the proof that my mother gave me, transmitted to me through your blood, that I am the daughter of Fedol,' and she turned her left shoulder to him, and there lay upon the white skin a small, round, red mark identical with that upon the left shoulder of the Amiocapian.

For a moment Fedol stood spellbound, his eyes fixed upon Stellara's shoulder and then he took her into his arms and held her closely.

'My daughter!' he murmured. 'Allara come back to me in the blood of our blood and the flesh of our flesh!'

6

The Island of Love

The noonday sun of Pellucidar shone down upon a happy trio as Fedol guided Stellara and Tanar towards the village of Paraht, where he ruled as chief.

'Will they receive us there as friends,' asked Stellara, 'or will they wish to destroy us as did the men of Lar?'

'I am chief,' said Fedol. 'Even if they questioned you, they will do as I command, but there will be no question for the proof is beyond dispute and they will accept you as the daughter of Fedol and Allara, as I have accepted you.'

'And Tanar?' asked Stellara, 'will you protect him, too?'

'Your word is sufficient that he is not a Korsar,' replied Fedol. 'He may remain with us as long as he wishes.'

'What will Zural think of this?' asked Tanar. 'He has condemned us to die. Will he not insist that the sentence be carried out?'

'Seldom do the villagers of Amiocap war one against the other,' replied Fedol; 'but if Zural wishes war he shall have it ere ever I shall give up you or my daughter to the burning stake of Lar.'

Great was the rejoicing when the people of Paraht saw their chief, whom they had thought lost to them forever, returning. They clustered about him with glad cries of welcome, which were suddenly stilled by loud shouts of 'The Korsars! The Korsars!' as the eyes of some of the people alighted upon Tanar and Stellara.

'Who cried "Korsars"?' demanded Fedol. 'What know you of these people?'

'I know them,' replied a tall warrior. 'I am from Lar. There are six others with me and we have been searching for these Korsars, who escaped just before they were to have been burned at the stake. We will take them back with us and Zural will rejoice that you have captured them.'

'You will take them nowhere,' said Fedol. 'They are not Korsars. This one,' and he placed a hand upon Stellara's shoulder, 'is my daughter, and the man is a warrior from distant Sari. He is the son of the king of that country, which lies far away upon a mainland unknown to us.'

'They told that same story to, Zural,' said the warrior from Lar; 'but we did not believe them. None of us believed them. I was with Vulhan and his party when we took them from the Korsar ship that brought them to Amiocap.'

'At first I did not believe them,' said Fedol, 'but Stellara convinced me that she is my daughter, just as I can convince you of the truth of her statement.'

'How?' demanded the warrior.

'By the birthmark on my left shoulder,' replied Fedol. 'Look at it, and then compare it with the one upon her left shoulder. No one who knew Allara can doubt that Stellara is her daughter, so closely does the girl resemble her mother, and being Allara's daughter how could she inherit the birthmark upon her left shoulder from any other sire than me?'

The warriors from Lar scratched their heads. 'It would seem the best of proof,' replied the warriors' spokesman.

'It is the best of proof,' said Fedol. 'It is all that I need. It is all the people of Paraht need. Take the word to Zural and the people of Lar and I believe that they will accept my daughter and Tanar as we are accepting them, and I believe that they will be willing to protect them as we intend to protect them from all enemies, whether from Amiocap or elsewhere.'

'I shall take your message to Zural,' replied the warrior, and shortly afterward they departed on the trail toward Lar.

Fedol prepared a room in his house for Stellara and assigned Tanar to a large building that was occupied solely by bachelors.

Plans were made for a great feast to celebrate the coming of Stellara and a hundred men were dispatched to fetch the ivory and the meat of the tandor that Fedol and Tanar had slain.

Fedol decked Stellara with ornaments of bone and ivory and gold. She wore the softest furs and the gorgeous plumage of rare birds. The people of Paraht loved her and Stellara was happy.

Tanar was accepted at first by the men of the tribe with some reservations, not untinged with suspicion. He was their guest by the order of their chief and they treated him as such, but presently, when they came to know him and particularly after he had hunted with them, they liked him for himself and made him one of them.

The Amiocapians were, at first, an enigma to Tanar. Their tribal life and all their customs were based primarily upon love and kindness. Harsh words, bickering and scolding were practically unknown among them. These attributes of the softer side of man appeared at first weak and effeminate to the Sarian, but when he found them combined with great strength and rare courage his admiration for the Amiocapians knew no bounds, and he soon recognized in their attitude toward one another and toward life a philosophy that he hoped he might make clear to his own Sarians.

The Amiocapians considered love the most sacred of the gifts of the gods, and the greatest power for good and they practiced liberty of love without license. So that while they were not held in slavery by senseless man-made laws that denied the laws of God and nature, yet they were pure and virtuous to a degree beyond that which he had known in any other people.

With hunting and dancing and feasting, with tests of skill and strength in which the men of Amiocap contended in friendly rivalry, life for Stellara and Tanar was ideally happy.

Less and less often did the Sarian think of Sari. Sometime he would build a boat and return to his native country, but there was no hurry; he would wait, and gradually even that thought faded almost entirely from his mind. He and Stellara were often together. They found a measure of happiness and contentment in one another's society that was lacking at other times or with other people. Tanar had never spoken of love. Perhaps he had not thought of love for it seemed that he was always engaged upon some enterprise of the hunt, or contending in some of the sports and games of the men. His body and his mind were occupied – a condition which sometimes excludes thoughts of love, but wherever he went or whatever he did the face and figure of Stellara hovered ever in the background of his thoughts.

Without realizing it, perhaps, his every thought, his every act was influenced by the sweet loveliness of the chief's daughter. Her friendship he took for granted and it gave him great happiness, but yet he did not speak of love. But Stellara was a woman, and women live on love.

In the village of Paraht she saw the girls openly avowing their love to men, but she was still bound by the customs of Korsar and it would have been impossible for her to bring herself to tell a man that she loved him until he had avowed his love. And so hearing no word of love from Tanar, she was content with his friendship. Perhaps she, too, had given no more thought to the matter of love than he.

But there was another who did harbor thoughts of love. It was Doval, the Adonis of Paraht. In all Amiocap there was no handsomer youth than Doval. Many were the girls who had avowed their love to him, but his heart had been unmoved until he looked upon Stellara.

Doval came often to the house of Fedol the chief. He brought presents of skin and ivory and bone to Stellara and they were much together. Tanar saw and he was troubled, but why he was troubled he did not know.

The people of Paraht had eaten and slept many times since the coming of Tanar and Stellara and as yet no word had come from Zural, or the village of Lar, in answer to the message that Fedol had sent, but now, at last, there entered the village a party of warriors from Lar, and Fedol, sitting upon the chief's chair, received them in the tiled living room of his home.

'Welcome, men of Lar,' said the chief. 'Fedol welcomes you to the village of Paraht and awaits with impatience the message that you bring him from his friend, Zural the chief.'

'We come from Zural and the people of Lar,' said the spokesman, 'with a message of friendship for Fedol and Paraht. Zural, our chief, has commanded us to express to you his deep sorrow for the unintentional wrong that he did your daughter and the warrior from Sari. He is convinced that Stellara is your daughter and that the man is no Korsar if you are convinced of these facts, and he has sent presents to them and to you and with these presents an invitation for you to visit the village of Lar and bring Stellara and Tanar with you that Zural and his people may make amends for the wrong that they unwittingly did them.'

Fedol and Tanar and Stellara accepted the proffered friendship of Zural and his people, and a feast was prepared in honor of the visitors.

While these preparations were in progress a girl entered the village from the jungle. She was a dark-haired girl of extraordinary beauty. Her soft skin was scratched and soiled as from a long journey. Her hair was disheveled, but her eyes were bright with happiness and her teeth gleamed from between lips that were parted in a smile of triumph and expectation.

She made her way directly through the village to the house of Fedol and when the warriors of Lar descried her they exclaimed with astonishment.

'Letari!' cried one of them. 'Where did you come from? What are you doing in the village of Paraht?'

But Letari did not answer. Instead she walked directly to where Tanar stood and halted before him.

'I have come to you,' she said. 'I have died many a death from loneliness and sorrow since you ran away from the village of Lar, and when the warriors returned and said that you were safe in the village of Paraht I determined to come here. And so when Zural sent these warriors to bear his message to Fedol I followed them. The way has been hard and though I kept close behind them there were many times when wild beasts menaced me and I feared that I should never reach you, but at last I am here.'

'But why have you come?' demanded Tanar.

'Because I love you,' replied Letari. 'Before the men of Lar and all the people of Paraht I proclaim my love.'

Tanar flushed. In all his life he had never been in so embarrassing a position. All eyes were turned upon him and among them were the eyes of Stellara.

'Well?' demanded Fedol, looking at Tanar.

'The girl is mad,' said the Sarian. 'She cannot love me for she scarcely knows me. She never spoke to me but once before and that was when she brought food to Stellara and me when we were prisoners in the village of Lar.'

'I am not mad,' said Letari. 'I love you.'

'Will you have her?' asked Fedol.

'I do not love her,' said Tanar.

'We will take her back to the village of Lar with us when we go,' said one of the warriors.

'I shall not go,' cried Letari. 'I love him and I shall stay here forever.'

The girl's declaration of love for Tanar seemed not to surprise any one but the Sarian. It aroused little comment and no ridicule. The Amiocapians, with the possible exception of Stellara, took it as a matter of course. It was the most natural thing in the world for the people of this island of love to declare themselves publicly in matters pertaining to their hearts or to their passions.

That the general effect of such a policy was not nor never had been detrimental to the people as a race was evident by their high intelligence, the perfection of their physique, their great beauty and their unquestioned courage. Perhaps the opposite custom, which has prevailed among most of the people of the outer crust for so many ages, is responsible for the unnumbered millions of unhappy human beings who are warped or twisted mentally, morally or physically.

But with such matters the mind of Letari was not concerned. It was not troubled by any consideration of posterity. All she thought of was that she loved the handsome stranger from Sari and that she wanted to be near him. She came close to him and looked up into his face.

'Why do you not love me?' she asked. 'Am I not beautiful?'

'Yes, you are very beautiful,' he said; 'but no one can explain love, least of all I. Perhaps there are qualities of mind and character – things that we can neither see nor feel nor hear – that draw one heart forever to another.'

'But I am drawn to you,' said the girl. 'Why are not you attracted to me?'

Tanar shook his head for he did not know. He wished that the girl would go away and leave him alone for she made him feel uneasy and restless and entirely uncomfortable, but Letari had no idea of leaving him alone. She was near him and there she intended to stay until they dragged her away and took her back to Lar, if they were successful in so doing, but she had determined in her little head that she should run away from them at the first opportunity and hide in the jungle until she could return to Paraht and Tanar.

'Will you talk to me?' she asked. 'Perhaps if you talk to me you will love me.'

'I will talk to you,' said Tanar, 'but I shall not love you.'

'Let us walk a little way from these people where we may talk,' she said.

'Very well,' said Tanar. He was only too anxious himself to get away where he might hide his embarrassment.

Letari led the way down the village street, her soft arm brushing his. 'I should be a good mate,' she said, 'for I should love only you, and if, after a while, you did not like me you could send me away for that is one of the customs of Amiocap – that when one of two people ceases to love they shall no longer be mates.'

'But they do not become mates unless they both love,' insisted Tanar.

'That is true,' admitted Letari, 'but presently you shall love me. I know that, for all men love me. I could have for my mate any man in Lar that I choose.'

'You do not feel unkindly towards yourself,' said Tanar, with a grin.

'Why should I?' asked Letari. 'Am I not beautiful and young?'

Stellara watched Tanar and Letari walking down the village street. She saw how close together they walked and it seemed that Tanar was very much interested in what Letari had to say to him. Doval was standing at her side. She turned to him.

'It is noisy here,' she said. 'There are too many people. Walk with me to the end of the village.'

It was the first time that Stellara had ever indicated a desire to be alone with him and Doval felt a strange thrill of elation. 'I will walk with you to the end of the village, Stellara, or to the end of Pellucidar, forever, because I love you,' he said.

The girl sighed and shook her head. 'Do not talk about love,' she begged. 'I merely wish to walk and there is no one else here to walk with me.'

'Why will you not love me?' asked Doval, as they left the house of the chief and entered the main street of the village. 'Is it because you love another?'

'No,' cried Stellara, vehemently. 'I love no one. I hate all men.'

Doval shook his head in perplexity. 'I cannot understand you,' he said. 'Many girls have told me that they loved me. I think that I could have almost any girl in Amiocap as my mate if I asked her; but you, the only one that I love, will not have me.'

For a few moments Stellara was silent in thought. Then she turned to the handsome youth at her side. 'You are very sure of yourself, Doval,' she said, 'but I do not believe that you are right. I would be willing to bet that I could name a girl who would not have you; who, no matter how hard you tried to make her, would not love you.'

'If you mean yourself, then there is one,' he said, 'but there is no other.'

'Oh, yes, there is,' insisted Stellara.

'Who is she?' demanded Doval.

'Letari, the girl from Lar,' said Stellara.

Doval laughed. 'She throws her love at the first stranger that comes to Amiocap,' he said. 'She would be too easy.'

'Nevertheless you cannot make her love you,' insisted Stellara.

'I do not intend to try,' said Doval. 'I do not love her. I love only you, and if I made her love me of what good would that be toward making you love me? No, I shall spend my time trying to win you.'

'You are afraid,' said Stellara. 'You know that you would fail.'

'It would do me no good if I succeeded,' insisted Duval. 'It would make me like you very much better than I do now,' said Stellara.

'You mean that?' asked Doval.

'I most certainly do,' said Stellara.

'Then I shall make the girl love me,' said Doval. 'And if I do you promise to be mine?'

'I said nothing of the kind,' said Stellara. 'I only said that I should like you very much better than I do now.'

'Well, that is something,' said Doval. 'If you will like me very much better than you do now that is at least a step in the right direction.'

'However, there is no danger of that,' said Stellara, 'for you cannot make her love you.'

'Wait, and see,' said Doval.

As Tanar and Letari turned to come back along the village street they passed Doval and Stellara, and Tanar saw that they were walking very close together and whispering in low tones. The Sarian scowled; and suddenly he discovered that he did not like Doval and he wondered why because always he had thought Doval a very fine fellow. Presently it occurred to him that the reason was that Doval was not good enough for Stellara, but then if Stellara loved him that was all there was to it and with the thought that perhaps Stellara loved him Tanar became angry with Stellara. What could she see in this Doval, he wondered, and what business had Doval to walk alone with her in the village streets? Had not he, Tanar, always had Stellara to himself? Never before had any one interfered, although all the men liked Stellara. Well, if Stellara liked Doval better than she did him, he would show her that he did not care. He, Tanar the Sarian, son of Ghak, king of Sari, would not let any woman make a fool of him and so he ostentatiously put his arm around the slim shoulders of Letari and walked thus slowly the length of the village street; nor did Stellara fail to see.

At the feast that was given in honor of the messengers sent by Zural, Stellara sat by Doval and Tanar had Letari at his side, and Doval and Letari were happy.

After the feast was over most of the villagers returned to their houses and slept, but Tanar was restless and unhappy and could not sleep so he took his weapons, his heavy spear shod with bone, his bow and his arrows, and his stone knife with the ivory handle, that Fedol the chief had given him, and went alone into the forest to hunt.

If the villagers slept an hour or a day is a matter of no moment, since there was no way of measuring the time. When they awoke – some sooner, some later – they went about the various duties of their life. Letari sought for Tanar, but she could not find him; instead she came upon Doval.

'You are very beautiful,' said the man.

'I know it,' replied Letari.

'You are the most beautiful girl that I have ever seen,' insisted Doval.

Letari looked at him steadily for a few moments. 'I never noticed you before,' she said. 'You are very handsome. You are quite the handsomest man that I ever saw.'

'That is what every one says,' replied Doval. 'Many girls have told me that they loved me, but still I have no mate.'

'A woman wants something beside a handsome face in her mate,' said Letari.

'I am very brave,' said Doval, 'and I am a great hunter. I like you. Come, let us walk together,' and Doval put his arm about the girl's shoulders and together they walked along the village street, while, from the doorway of her sleeping apartment in the home of her father, the chief, Stellara watched, and as she watched, a smile touched her lips.

Over the village of Paraht rested the peace of Amiocap and the calm of eternal noon. The children played at games beneath the shade of the trees that had been left dotting the village here and there when the clearing had been made. The women worked upon skins, strung beads or prepared food. The men looked to their weapons against the next hunt, or lolled idly on furs in their open living rooms – those who were not still sleeping off the effects of the heavy feast. Fedol, the chief, was bidding farewell to Zural's messengers and entrusting to them a gift for the ruler of Lar, when suddenly the peace and quiet was shattered by hoarse cries and a shattering burst of musketry.

Instantly all was pandemonium. Then women and warriors rushed from their homes; shouts, curses and screams filled the air.

'Korsars! Korsars!' rang through the village, as the bearded ruffians, taking advantage of the surprise and confusion of the villagers, rushed rapidly forward to profit by the advantage they had gained.

7

'Korsars!'

Tanar the Sarian hunted through the primeval forest of Amiocap. Already his repute as a hunter stood high among the men of Paraht, but it was not to add further luster to his fame that he hunted now. It was to quiet a restlessness that would not permit him to sleep – restlessness and a strange depression that was almost unhappiness, but his thoughts were not always upon the hunt. Visions of Stellara often walked in front of him, the golden sunlight on her golden hair, and then beside her he saw the handsome Doval with an arm about her shoulder. He closed his eyes and shook his head to dispel the vision, but it persisted and he tried thinking of Letari, the beautiful maiden from Lar. Yes, Letari was beautiful. What eyes she had; and she loved him. Perhaps, after all, it would be as well to mate with her and remain forever upon Amiocap, but presently he found himself comparing Letari with Stellara and he found himself wishing that Letari possessed more of the characteristics of Stellara. She had not the character nor the intelligence of the daughter of Fedol. She offered him none of the restful companionship that had made his association with Stellara so infinitely happy.

He wondered if Stellara loved Doval, and if Doval loved Stellara, and with the thoughts he halted in his tracks and his eyes went wide as a sudden realization burst for the first time upon his consciousness.

'God!' he exclaimed aloud. 'What a fool I have been. I have loved her always and did not know it,' and wheeling about he set off at a brisk trot in the direction of Paraht, all thoughts of his hunt erased from his mind.

Tanar had hunted far, much farther than he had thought, but at last he came to the village of Fedol the chief. As he passed through the hanging barrier of Paraht, the first people that he saw were Letari and Doval. They were walking side by side and very close and the man's arm was about the slim shoulders of the girl.

Letari looked at Tanar in astonishment as she recognized him. 'We all thought the Korsars had taken you with them,' she cried.

'Korsars!' exclaimed Tanar. 'What Korsars?'

'They were here,' said Doval. 'They raided the village, but we drove them off with just a small loss. There were not many of them. Where were you?'

'After the feast I went into the forest to hunt,' said Tanar. 'I did not know that there was a Korsar upon the island of Amiocap.'

'It is just as well that you were not here,' said Letari, 'for while you were away I have learned that I love Doval.'

'Where is Stellara?' demanded Tanar.

'She was taken by the Korsars,' said Doval. 'Thank God that it was not you, Letari,' and, stooping, he kissed the girl upon the lips.

With a cry of grief and rage Tanar ran swiftly to the house of Fedol the chief. 'Where is Stellara?' he demanded, springing unceremoniously into the center of the living room.

An old woman looked up from where she sat with her face buried in her hands. She was the sole occupant of the room. 'The Korsars took her,' she said.

'Where is Fedol then?' demanded Tanar.

'He has gone with warriors to try to rescue her,' said the old woman, 'but it is useless. They, who are taken by the Korsars, never come back.'

'Which way did they go?' asked Tanar.

Sobbing with grief, the old woman pointed in the direction taken by the Korsars, and again she buried her face in her hands, grieving for the misfortune that had overtaken the house of Fedol the chief.

Almost immediately Tanar picked up the trail of the Korsars, which he could identify by the imprints of their heeled boots, and he saw that Fedol and his warriors had not followed the same trail, evidencing the fact that they must have gone in the wrong direction to succor Stellara successfully.

Sick with anguish, maddened by hate, the Sarian plunged on through the forest. Plain to his eyes lay the spoor of his quarry. In his heart was a rage that gave him the strength of many men.

In a little glade, partially surrounded by limestone cliffs, a small company of ragged, bewhiskered men had halted to rest. Where they had halted a tiny spring broke from the base of the cliff and trickled along its winding channel for a short distance to empty into a natural, circular opening in the surface of the ground. From deep in the bottom of this natural well the water falling from the rim could be heard splashing upon the surface of the water far below. It was dark down there – dark and mysterious, but the bearded ruffians gave no heed either to the beauty or the mystery of the spot.

One huge, fierce-visaged fellow, his countenance disfigured by an ugly scar, confronted a slim girl, who sat upon the turf, her back against a tree, her face buried in her arms.

'You thought me dead, eh?' he exclaimed. 'You thought Bohar the Bloody dead? Well he is not dead. Our boat weathered the storm and passing close to Amiocap we saw the wreck of The Cid's ship lying upon the sand. Knowing that you and the prisoners had been left aboard when we quit the ship, I guessed that perhaps you might be somewhere upon Amiocap; nor was I wrong, Stellara. Bohar the Bloody is seldom wrong.

'We hid close to a village which they call Lar and at the first opportunity we captured one of the villagers – a woman – and from her we learned that you had indeed come ashore, but that you were then in the village of your father and we made the woman guide us there. The rest you know and now be cheerful for at last you are to mate with Bohar the Bloody and return to Korsar.'

'Rather than that I shall die,' cried the girl.

'But how?' laughed Bohar. 'You have no weapons. Perhaps, however, you will choke yourself to death,' and he laughed uproariously at his own joke.

'There is a way,' cried the girl, and before he could guess what she intended, or stay here, she dodged quickly around him and ran toward the natural well that lay a few hundred feet away.

'Quick!' shouted Bohar. 'Stop her!' And instantly the entire twenty sprang in pursuit. But Stellara was swift and there was likelihood that they would not overtake her in the short distance that lay before her and the edge of the abyss.

Fortune, however, was with Bohar the Bloody that day and almost at her goal Stellara's foot caught in a tangle of grasses and she stumbled forward upon her face. Before she could recover her feet the nearest Korsar had seized her, and then Bohar the Bloody ran to her side and, taking her from the grasp of the other Korsar, shook her violently.

'You she tarag!' he cried. 'For this I shall fix you so that never again will you run away. When we reach the sea I shall cut off one of your feet and then I shall know that you will not run away from me again,' and he continued to shake her violently.

Breaking suddenly and unexpectedly from the dense jungle into the opening of the glade a warrior came upon the scene being enacted at the edge of the well. At the moment he thought that Stellara was being killed and he went mad with rage; nor was his rage any the less when he recognized Bohar the Bloody as the author of the assault.

With an angry shout he leaped forward, his heavy spear ready in his hand. What mattered it that twenty men with firearms opposed him? He saw only Stellara in the cruel grip of the bestial Bohar.

At the sound of his voice the Korsar looked up and instantly Bohar recognized the Sarian.

'Look, Stellara,' he said, with a sneer. 'Your lover has come. It is well, for with no lover and only one foot you will have no reason at all for running away.'

A dozen harquebuses had already been raised in readiness and the men stood looking toward Bohar.

Tanar had reached the opposite edge of the well, only a few yards distant, when Bohar nodded and there was a roar of musketry and a flash of flame accompanied by so dense a pall of black smoke that for an instant the figure of the Sarian was entirely obliterated from view.

Stellara, wide-eyed and trembling with pain and horror, tried to penetrate the smoke cloud with her frightened eyes. Quickly it lifted, revealing no sign of Tanar.

'Well done,' cried Bohar to his men. 'Either you blew him all to pieces, or his body fell into the hole,' and going to the edge of the opening he looked down, but it was very dark there and he saw nothing. 'Wherever he is, at least he is dead,' said Bohar. 'I should like to have crushed his life out with my own hands, but at least he is dead by my command and the blow that he struck me is wiped out, as Bohar wipes out the blows of all his enemies.'

As the Korsars resumed the march toward the ocean, Stellara walked among them with bent head and moist, unseeing eyes. Often she stumbled and each time she was jerked roughly to her feet and shaken, at the same time being admonished in hoarse tones to watch her footing.

By the time they reached the seashore Stellara was sick with a high fever and she lay in the camp of the Korsars for what may have been a day or a month, too sick to move, while Bohar and his men felled timbers, hewed planks and constructed a boat to carry them to the distant shores of Korsar.

Rushing forward to rescue Stellara from the clutches of Bohar, Tanar's mind and eyes had been fixed on nothing but the figure of the girl. He had not seen the opening in the ground and at the instant that the Korsars fired their harquebuses he had stepped unwittingly into the opening and plunged to the water far below.

The fall had not hurt him. It had not even stunned him and when he came to the surface he saw before him a quiet stream moving gently through an opening in the limestone wall about him. Beyond the opening was a luminous cavern and into this Tanar swam, clambering to its rocky floor the moment that he had found a low place in the bank of the stream. Looking about him he found himself in a large cavern, the walls of which shone luminously, so considerable was their content of phosphorus.

There was a great deal of rubbish on the floor of the cave – the bones of animals and men, broken weapons, bits of hide. It might have been the dumping ground of some gruesome charnel house.

The Sarian walked back to the opening through which the little stream had borne him into the grotto, but a careful investigation revealed no avenue of escape in this direction, although he reentered the stream and swam into the bottom of the well where he found the walls worn so smooth by the long continued action of falling water that they gave no slightest indication of handhold or foothold.

Then slowly he made a circuit of the outer walls of the grotto, but only where the stream passed out at its far end was there any opening – a rough archway that rose some six feet above the surface of the underground stream.

Along one side was a narrow ledge and looking through the opening he saw a dim corridor leading away into the distance and obscurity.

There being no other way in which to search for freedom Tanar passed along the narrow ledge beneath the archway to find himself in a tunnel that followed the windings of the stream.

Only here and there small patches of the rock that formed the walls and ceiling of the corridor threw out a luminosity that barely relieved the inky darkness of the place, yet relieve it it did so that at least one might be sure of his footing, though at points where the corridor widened its walls were often lost in darkness.

For what distance he followed the tunnel Tanar did not know, but presently he came to a low and narrow opening through which he could pass only upon his hands and knees. Beyond there seemed to be a much lighter chamber and as Tanar came into this, still upon all fours, a heavy body dropped upon his back from above and then another at each side of him and he felt cold, clammy claws seizing his arms and legs, and arms encircled his neck – arms that felt against his flesh like the arms of a corpse.

He struggled but there were too many for him and in a moment he was disarmed and his ankles and wrists securely bound with tough thongs of rawhide. Then he was rolled over on his side and lay looking up into the horrid faces of Coripies, the Buried People of Amiocap.

The blank faces, the corpse-like skin, the bulging protuberances where the eyes would have been, the hairless bodies, the claw-like hands combined to produce such a hideous aspect in the monsters as to make the stoutest of hearts quail.

And when they spoke! The mumbled mouthing revealing yellow fangs withered the heart in the breast of the Sarian. Here, indeed, was a hideous end, for he knew that it was the end, since never in all the many tales the Amiocapians had told him of the Buried People was there any record of a human being escaping from their clutches.

Now they were addressing him and presently, in their hollow mewing, he discerned words. 'How did you get into the land of the Coripies?' demanded one.

'I fell into a hole in the ground,' replied Tanar. 'I did not seek to come here. Take me out and I will reward you.'

'What have you to give the Coripies more than your flesh?' demanded another.

'Do not think to get out for you never shall,' said a third.

Now two of them lifted him lightly and placed him upon the back of one of their companions. So easily the creature carried him that Tanar wondered that he had ever overcome the Coripi that he had met upon the surface of the ground.

Through long corridors, some very dark and others partially lighted by outcroppings of phosphorescent rock, the creature bore him. At times they passed through large grottoes, beautifully wrought in intricate designs by nature, or climbed long stairways carved in the limestone, probably by the Coripies themselves, only presently to descend other stairways and follow winding tunnels that seemed interminable.

But at last the journey ended in a huge cavern, the ceiling of which rose at least two hundred feet above them. This stupendous grotto was more brilliantly lighted than any other section of the subterranean world that Tanar had passed through. Into its limestone walls were cut pathways that zigzagged back and forth upward toward the ceiling, and the entire surface of the surrounding walls was pierced by holes several feet in diameter that appeared to be the mouths of caves.

Squatting about on the floor of the cavern were hundreds of Coripies of all ages and both sexes.

At one end of the grotto, in a large opening, a few feet above the floor, squatted a single, large Coripi. His skin was mottled with a purplish hue that suggested a corpse in which mortification had progressed to a considerable degree. The protuberances that suggested huge eyeballs beneath the skin protruded much further and were much larger than those in any other of the Coripies that Tanar had examined. The creature was, by far, the most repulsive of all the repulsive horde.

On the floor of the grotto, directly before this creature, were gathered a number of male Coripies and toward this congregation Tanar's captors bore him.

Scarcely had they entered the grotto when it became apparent to Tanar that these creatures could see, a thing that he had commenced to suspect shortly after his capture, for now, at sight of him, they commenced to scream and make strange, whistling sounds, and from the openings of many of the high flung caves within the walls heads protruded and the hideous, eyeless faces seemed to be bending eyes upon him.

One cry seemed to rise above all others as he was borne across the grotto towards the creature sitting in the niche. It was 'Flesh! Flesh!' and it sounded gruesome and horrible in its suggestiveness.

Flesh! Yes, he knew that they ate human flesh and it seemed now that they were but awaiting a signal to leap upon him and devour him alive, tearing pieces from him with their heavy claws. But when one did rush upon him there came a scream from the creature in the niche and the fellow desisted, even as one of his captors had turned to defend him.

The cavern crossed at last, Tanar was deposited upon his feet in front of the creature squatting in the niche. Tanar could see the great eyeballs revolving beneath the pulsing skin of the protuberances and though he could see no eyes, he knew that he was being examined coldly and calculatingly.

'Where did you get it?' finally demanded the creature, addressing Tanar's captors.

'He tumbled into the Well of Sounding Water,' replied one.

'How do you know?'

'He told us so.'

'Do you believe him?'

'There was no other way in which he could enter the land of the Coripies,' replied one of the captors.

'Perhaps he was leading a party in to slay us,' said the creature in the niche. 'Go, many of you, and search the corridors and the tunnels about the Well of Sounding Water.' Then the creature turned to Tanar's captors. 'Take this and put it with the others; we have not yet enough.'

Tanar was now again placed upon the back of a Coripi, who carried him across the grotto and up one of the pathways cut into the face of the limestone wall. Ascending this pathway a short distance the creature turned into one of the cave openings, and Tanar found himself again in a narrow, dark, winding tunnel.

The tunnels and corridors through which he had already been conducted had impressed upon Tanar the great antiquity of this underground labyrinthian world, since there was every evidence that the majority of these tunnels had been hewn from the limestone rock or natural passageways enlarged to accommodate the Coripies, and as these creatures appeared to have no implements other than their heavy, three-toed claws the construction of the tunnels must have represented the labor of countless thousands of individuals over a period of many ages.

Tanar, of course, had only a hazy conception of what we describe as the measurable aspect of duration. His consideration of the subject concerned itself with the countless millions of times that these creatures must have slept and eaten during the course of their stupendous labors.

But the mind of the captive was also occupied with other matters as the Coripi bore him through the long tunnel. He thought of the statement of the creature in the niche, as he had ordered Tanar taken into confinement, to the effect that there were not yet enough. What did he mean? Enough of what? Enough prisoners? And when there were enough to what purpose would, they be devoted?

But perhaps, to a far greater extent, his mind was occupied with thoughts of Stellara; with fears for her safety and with vain regret that he had been unable to accomplish her rescue.

From the moment that he had been so unexpectedly precipitated into the underground world of the Buried People, his dominant thought, of course, had been that of escape; but the further into the bowels of the earth he was carried the more hopeless appeared the outcome of any venture in this direction, yet he never for once abandoned it though he realized that he must wait until they had reached the place of his final confinement before he could intelligently consider any plan at all.

How far the tireless Coripi bore Tanar the Sarian could not guess, but presently they emerged into a dimly lighted grotto, before the narrow entrance to which squatted a dozen Coripies. Within the chamber were a score more and one human being – a man with sandy hair, close-set eyes and a certain mean, crafty expression of countenance that repelled the Sarian immediately.

'Here is another,' said the Coripi who had carried Tanar to the cavern, and with that he dumped the Sarian unceremoniously upon the stone floor at the feet of the dozen Coripies who stood guard at the entrance.

With teeth and claws they severed the bonds that secured his wrists and ankles.

'They come slowly,' grumbled one of the guards. 'How much longer must we wait?'

'Old Xax wishes to have the greatest number that has ever been collected,' remarked another of the Coripies.

'But we grow impatient,' said the first speaker. 'If he makes us wait much longer he may be one of the number here himself.'

'Be careful,' cautioned one of his fellows. 'If Xax heard that you had said such a thing as that the number of our prisoners would be increased by one.'

As Tanar arose to his feet, after his bonds were severed, he was pushed roughly toward the other inmates of the room, who he soon was to discover were prisoners, like himself, and quite naturally the first to approach him was the other human captive.

'Another,' said the stranger. 'Our numbers increase but slowly, yet each one brings us closer to our inevitable doom and so I do not know whether I am sorry to see you here or glad because of the human company that I shall now have. I have eaten and slept many times since I was thrown into this accursed place and always nothing but these hideous, mumbling things for company. God, how I hate and loathe them, yet they are in the same predicament as we for they, too, are doomed to the same fate.'

'And what may that be?' asked Tanar.

'You do not know?'

'I may only guess,' replied the Sarian.

'These creatures seldom get flesh with warm blood in it. They subsist mostly upon the fish in their underground rivers and upon the toads and lizards that inhabit their caves. Their expeditions to the surface ordinarily yield nothing more than the carcasses of dead beasts, yet they crave flesh and warm blood. Heretofore they had killed their condemned prisoners one by one as they were available, but this plan gave only a mouthful of flesh to a very few Coripies. Recently Xax hit upon the plan of preserving his own condemned and the prisoners from the outer world until he had accumulated a sufficient number to feast the entire population of the cavern of which he is chief. I do not know how many that will be, but steadily the numbers grow and perhaps it will not be long now before there are enough of us to fill the bellies of Xax's tribe.'

'Xax!' repeated Tanar. 'Was he the creature sitting in the niche in the great cavern to which I was first taken?'

'That was Xax. He is ruler of that cavern. In the underground world of the Buried People there are many tribes, each of which occupies a large cavern similar to that in which you saw Xax. These tribes are not always friendly and the most of the prisoners that you see in this cavern are members of other tribes, though there are a few from the tribe of Xax who have been condemned to death for one reason or another.'

'And there is no escape?' asked Tanar.

'None,' replied the other. 'Absolutely none; but tell me who are you and from what country? I cannot believe that you are a native of Amiocap, for what Amiocapian is there who would need ask questions about the Buried People?'

'I am not of Amiocap,' replied Tanar. 'I am from Sari, upon the far distant mainland.'

'Sari! I never heard of such a country,' said the other. 'What is your name?'

'Tanar, and yours?'

'I am Jude of Hime,' replied the man. 'Hime is an island not far from Amiocap. Perhaps you have heard of it.'

'No,' said Tanar.

'I was fishing in my canoe, off the coast of Hime,' continued Jude, 'when a great storm arose which blew me across the waters and hurled me upon the coast of Amiocap. I had gone into the forest to hunt for food when three of these creatures fell upon me and dragged me into their underworld.'

'And you think that there is no escape?' demanded Tanar.

'None – absolutely none,' replied Jude.

8

Mow

Imprisonment in the dark, ill-lighted, poorly ventilated cavern weighed heavily upon Tanar of Pellucidar, and he knew that it was long for he had eaten and slept many times and though other Coripi prisoners were brought from time to time there seemed not to be enough to satisfy Xax's bloody craving for flesh.

Tanar had been glad of the companionship of Jude, though he never thoroughly understood the man, whose sour and unhappy disposition was so unlike his own. Jude apparently hated and mistrusted everyone, for even in speaking of the people of his own island he mentioned no one except in terms of bitterness and hatred, but this attitude Tanar generously attributed to the effect upon the mind of the Himean of his long and terrible incarceration among the creatures of the underworld, an experience which he was fully convinced might easily affect and unbalance a weak mind.

Even in the breasts of some of the Coripi prisoners Tanar managed to arouse sentiments somewhat analogous to friendship.

Among the latter was a young Coripi named Mow from the grotto of Ictl, who hated all the Coripies from the grotto of Xax and seemed suspicious of those from other grottoes.

Though the creatures seemed endowed with few human attributes or characteristics, yet it was apparent to Tanar that they set a certain value upon companionship, and being denied this among the creatures of his own kind Mow gradually turned to Tanar, whose courageous and happy spirit had not been entirely dampened by his lot.

Jude would have nothing to do with Mow or any other of the Coripies and he reproached Tanar for treating them in a friendly manner.

'We are all prisoners together,' Tanar reminded him, 'and they will suffer the same fate as we. It will neither lessen our danger nor add to our peace of mind to quarrel with our fellow prisoners, and I, for my part, find it interesting to talk with them about this strange world which they inhabit.'

And, indeed, Tanar had learned many interesting things about the Coripies. Through his association with Mow he had discovered that the creatures were color blind, seeing everything in blacks and whites and grays through the skin that covered their great eyeballs. He learned also that owing to the restricted amount of food at their command it had been necessary to restrict their number, and to this end it had become customary to destroy women who gave birth to too many children, the third child being equivalent to a death sentence for the mother.

He learned also that among these unhappy Coripies there were no diversions and no aim in life other than eating. So eager and unvaried was their diet of fish and toads and lizards that the promise of warm flesh was the only great event in the tiresome monotony of their deadly existence.

Although Mow had no words for love and no conception of its significance, Tanar was able to gather from his remarks that this sentiment did not exist among the Buried People. A mother looked upon each child as a threat to her existence and a prophecy of death, with the result that she loathed children from birth; nor is this strange when the fact is considered that the men chose as the mothers of their children the women whom they particularly loathed and hated, since the custom of destroying a woman who had borne three children deterred them from mating with any female for whom they might have entertained any degree of liking.

When not hunting or fishing the creatures squatted around upon their haunches staring stupidly and sullenly at the floor of their cavern.

'I should think,' said Tanar to Mow, 'that, confronted by such a life, you would welcome death in any form.'

The Coripi shook his head. 'I do not want to die,' he said.

'Why?' demanded Tanar.

'I do not know,' replied Mow. 'I simply wish to live.'

'Then I take it that you would like to escape from this cavern, if you could,' suggested Tanar.

'Of course I should like to escape,' said Mow, 'but if I try to escape and they catch me they will kill me.'

'They are going to kill you anyway,' Tanar reminded him.

'Yes, I never thought of that,' said Mow. 'That is quite true; they are going to kill me anyhow.'

'Could you escape?' asked Tanar.

'I could if I had someone to help me,' said Mow.

'This cavern is filled with men who will help you,' said Tanar.

'The Coripies from the grotto of Xax will not help me,' said Mow, 'because if they escape there is no place where they may go in safety. If Xax recaptures them they will be killed, and the same is true if the ruler of any other grotto captures them.'

'But there are men from other grottoes here,' insisted Tanar, 'and there are Jude and I.'

Mow shook his head. 'I would not save any of the Coripies. I hate them. They are all enemies from other grottoes.'

'But you do not hate me,' said Tanar, 'and I will help you, and so will Jude.'

'I need but one,' said Mow, 'but he must be very strong, stronger than you, stronger than Jude.'

'How strong?' asked Tanar.

'He must be able to lift my weight,' replied the Coripi.

'Look then,' said Tanar, and seizing Mow he held him high above his head.

When he had set him down upon the floor again the Coripi gazed at Tanar for some time. 'You are, indeed, strong,' he said.

'Then let us make our plans for escape,' said Tanar.

'Just you and I,' said the Coripi.

'We must take Jude with us,' insisted Tanar.

Mow shrugged his shoulders. 'It is all the same to me,' he said. 'He is not a Coripi, and if we become hungry and cannot find other food we can eat him.'

Tanar made no reply as he felt that it would be unwise to voice his disgust at this proposal and he was sure that he and Jude together could prevent the Coripi from succumbing to his lust for flesh.

'You have noticed at the far end of the cavern, where the shadows are so dense, that one may scarcely see a figure moving there?' asked Mow.

'Yes,' said Tanar.

'There the dim shadows hide the rough, rocky walls and the ceiling there is lost in total darkness, but in the ceiling is an opening that leads through a narrow shaft into a dark tunnel.'

'How do you know this?' asked Tanar.

'I discovered it once when I was hunting. I came upon a strange tunnel leading from that along which I was making my way to the upper world. I followed it to see where it led and I came at last to the opening in the ceiling of this cavern, from whence one may see all that takes place below without being himself seen. When I was brought here as a prisoner I recognized the spot immediately. That is how I know that one may escape if he has proper help.'

'Explain,' said Tanar.

'The wall beneath the opening is, as I have discovered, inclined backward from the floor to a considerable height and so rough that it can easily be scaled to a little ledge beneath the opening in the ceiling, but just so far beneath that one may not reach it unaided. If, however, I could lift you into the opening you could, in turn, reach down and help me up.'

'But how may we hope to climb the wall without being seen by the guards?' demanded Tanar.

'That is the only chance of capture that we shall have to take,' replied

Mow. 'It is very dark there and if we wait until another prisoner is brought and their attention is diverted we may be able to succeed in reaching the opening in the ceiling before we are discovered, and once there they cannot capture us.'

Tanar discussed the plan with Jude, who was so elated at the prospect of escape that he almost revealed a suggestion of happiness.

And now commenced an interminable wait for the moment when a new prisoner might be brought into the cavern. The three conspirators made it a practice to spend most of their time in the shadows at the far end of the cavern so that the guards might become accustomed to seeing them there, and as no one other than themselves was aware of the opening in the ceiling at this point no suspicions were aroused, as the spot where they elected to be was at the opposite end of the cavern from the entrance, which was, in so far as the guards knew, the only opening into the cavern.

Tanar, Jude and Mow ate and slept several times until it began to appear that no more prisoners ever would be brought to the cavern; but if no prisoners came, news trickled in and one item filled them with such alarm that they determined to risk all upon the hazard of a bold dash for freedom.

Some Coripies coming to relieve a part of the guard reported that it had been with difficulty that Xax had been able to suppress an uprising among his infuriated tribesmen, many of whom had conceived the conviction that Xax was saving all of the prisoners for himself.

The result had been that a demand had been made upon Xax for an immediate feast of flesh. Perhaps already other Coripies were on their way to conduct the unfortunate prisoners to the great cavern of Xax, where they would be torn limb from limb by the fierce, hunger-mad throng.

And, true enough, there had been time for but one hunger before the party arrived to conduct them back to the main grotto of the tribe.

'Now is the time,' whispered Tanar to Mow and Jude, seeing that the guard was engaged in conversation with the newcomers, and in accordance with their previously made plan the three started without an instant's hesitation to scale the far wall of the cavern.

Upon a little ledge, twenty-five feet from the floor, Tanar halted, and an instant later Mow and Jude stood upon either side of him. Without a word the Coripi lifted Tanar to his shoulders and in the darkness above Tanar groped for a handhold.

He soon found the opening into the shaft leading into the tunnel above, and, too, he found splendid handholds there so that an instant later he had drawn himself up into the opening and was sitting upon a small ledge that entirely encircled it.

Bracing himself, he reached down and seized the hand of Jude, who was standing upon Mow's shoulders, and drew the Himean to the ledge beside him.

At that instant a great shouting arose below them, and glancing down Tanar saw that one of the guards had discovered them and that now a general rush of both guards and prisoners was being made in their direction.

Even as Tanar reached down to aid Mow to the safety of the shaft's mouth, some of the Coripies were already scaling the wall below them. Mow hesitated and turned to look at the enemies clambering rapidly toward him.

The ledge upon which Mow stood was narrow and the footing precarious. The surprise and shock of their discovery may have unnerved him, or, in turning to look downward he may have lost his balance, but whatever it was Tanar saw him reel, topple and then lunge downward upon the ascending Coripies, scraping three of them from the wall in his descent as he crashed to the stone floor below, where he lay motionless.

Tanar turned to Jude. 'We cannot help him,' he said. 'Come, we had better get out of this as quickly as possible.'

Feeling for each new handhold and foothold the two climbed slowly up the short shaft and presently found themselves in the tunnel, which Mow had described. Darkness was absolute.

'Do you know the way to the surface?' asked Jude.

'No,' said Tanar. 'I was depending upon Mow to lead us.'

'Then we might as well be back in the cavern,' said Jude.

'Not I,' said Tanar, 'for at least I am satisfied now that the Coripies will not eat me alive, if they eat me at all.'

Groping his way through the darkness and followed closely by Jude, Tanar crept slowly through the Stygian darkness. The tunnel seemed interminable. They became very hungry and there was no food, though they would have relished even the filthy fragments of decayed fish that the Coripies had hurled them while they were prisoners.

'Almost,' said Tanar, 'could I eat a toad.'

They became exhausted and slept, and then again they crawled and stumbled onward. There seemed no end to the interminable, inky corridor.

For long distances the floor of the tunnel was quite level, but then again it would pitch downward, sometimes so steeply that they had difficulty in clinging to the sloping floor. It turned and twisted as though its original excavators had been seldom of the same mind as to the direction in which they wished to proceed.

On and on the two went; again they slept, but whether that meant that they had covered a great distance, or that they were becoming weak from hunger, neither knew.

When they awoke they went on again for a long time in silence, but the sleep did not seem to have refreshed them much, and Jude especially was soon exhausted again.

'I cannot go much further,' he said. 'Why did you lure me into this crazy escapade?'

'You need not have come,' Tanar reminded him, 'and if you had not you would by now be out of your misery since doubtless all the prisoners have long since been torn to pieces and devoured by the Coripies of the grotto of Xax.'

Jude shuddered. 'I should not mind being dead,' he said, 'but I should hate to be torn to pieces by those horrible creatures.'

'This is a much nicer death,' said Tanar, 'for when we are sufficiently exhausted we shall simply sleep and awake no more.'

'I do not wish to die,' wailed Jude.

'You have never seemed very happy,' said Tanar. 'I should think one as unhappy as you would be glad to die.'

'I enjoy being unhappy,' said Jude. 'I know that I should be most miserable were I happy and anyway I should much rather be alive and unhappy than dead and unable to know that I was unhappy.'

'Take heart,' said Tanar. 'It cannot be much further to the end of this long corridor. Mow came through it and he did not say that it was so great a length that he became either exhausted or hungry and he not only traversed it from end to end in one direction, but he had to turn around and retrace his steps after he reached the opening into the cavern which we left.'

'The Coripies do not eat much; they are accustomed to starving,' said Jude, 'and they sleep less than we.'

'Perhaps you are right,' said Tanar, 'but I am sure that we are nearing the end.'

'I am,' said Jude, 'but not the end that I had wished.'

Even as they discussed the matter they were moving slowly along, when far ahead Tanar discerned a slight luminosity.

'Look,' he said, 'there is light. We are nearing the end.'

The discovery instilled new strength into both the men and with quickened steps they hastened along the tunnel in the direction of the promised escape. As they advanced, the light became more apparent until finally they came to the point where the tunnel they had been traversing opened into a large corridor, which was filled with a subdued light from occasional patches of phosphorescent rock in walls and ceiling, but neither to the right nor the left could they see any sign of daylight.

'Which way now?' demanded Jude.

Tanar shook his head. 'I do not know,' he said.

'At least I shall not die in that awful blackness,' wailed Jude, and perhaps that factor of their seemingly inevitable doom had weighed most heavily upon the two Pellucidarians, for, living as these people do beneath the brilliant rays of a perpetual noonday sun, darkness is a hideous and abhorrent thing to them, so unaccustomed are they to it.

'In this light, however slight it may be,' said Tanar, 'I can no longer be depressed. I am sure that we shall escape.'

'But in which direction?' again demanded Jude.

'I shall turn to the right,' said Tanar.

Jude shook his head. 'That probably is the wrong direction,' he said.

'If you know that the right direction lies to the left,' said Tanar, 'let us go to the left.'

'I do not know,' said Jude; 'doubtless either direction is wrong.'

'All right,' said Tanar, with a laugh. 'We shall go to the right,' and, turning, he set off at a brisk walk along the larger corridor.

'Do you notice anything, Jude?' asked Tanar.

'No. Why do you ask?' demanded the Himean.

'I smell fresh air from the upper world,' said Tanar, 'and if I am right we must be near the mouth of the tunnel.'

Tanar was almost running now; exhaustion was forgotten in the unexpected hope of immediate deliverance. To be out in the fresh air and the light of day! To be free from the hideous darkness and the constant menace of recapture by the hideous monsters of the underworld! And across that bright hope, like a sinister shadow, came the numbing fear of disappointment.

What, if, after all, the breath of air which was now clear and fresh in their nostrils should prove to be entering the corridor through some unscalable shaft, such as the Well of Sounding Water into which he had fallen upon his entrance into the country of the Buried People, or what, if, at the moment of escape, they should meet a party of the Coripies?

So heavily did these thoughts weigh upon Tanar's mind that he slackened his speed until once again he moved in a slow walk.

'What is the matter?' demanded Jude. 'A moment ago you were running and now you are barely crawling along. Do not tell me that you were mistaken and that, after all, we are not approaching the mouth of the corridor.'

'I do not know,' said Tanar. 'We may be about to meet a terrible disappointment and if that is true I wish to delay it as long as possible. It would be a terrible thing to have hope crushed within our breasts now.'

'I suppose it would,' said Jude, 'but that is precisely what I have been expecting.'

'You, I presume, would derive some satisfaction from disappointment,' said Tanar.

'Yes,' said Jude, 'I suppose I would. It is my nature.'

'Then prepare to be unhappy,' cried Tanar, suddenly, 'for here indeed is the mouth of the tunnel.'

He had spoken just as he had rounded a turn in the corridor, and when Jude came to his side the latter saw daylight creeping into the corridor through an opening just in front of them – an opening beyond which he saw the foliage of growing things and the blue sky of Pellucidar.

Emerging again to the light of the sun after their long incarceration in the bowels of the earth, the two men were compelled to cover their eyes with their hands, while they slowly accustomed themselves again to the brilliant light of the noonday sun of Pellucidar.

When he was able to uncover his eyes and look about him, Tanar saw that the mouth of the tunnel was high upon the precipitous side of a lofty mountain. Below them wooded ravines ran down to a mighty forest, just beyond which lay the sparkling waters of a great ocean that, curving upward, merged in the haze of the distance.

Faintly discernible in the mid-distance an island raised its bulk out of the waters of the ocean.

'That,' said Jude, pointing, 'is the island of Hime.'

'Ah, if I, too, could but see my home from here,' sighed Tanar, 'my happiness would be almost complete. I envy you, Jude.'

'It gives me no happiness to see Hime,' said Jude. 'I hate the place.'

'Then you are not going to try to go back to it?' demanded Tanar.

'Certainly, I shall,' said Jude.

'But, why?' asked Tanar.

'There is no other place where I may go,' grumbled Jude. 'At least in Hime they will not kill me for no reason at all as strangers would do if I went elsewhere.'

Jude's attention was suddenly attracted by something below them in a little glade that lay at the upper end of the ravine, which started a little distance below the mouth of the tunnel.

'Look,' he cried, 'there are people.'

Tanar looked in the direction in which Jude was pointing, and when his eyes found the figures far below they first went wide with incredulity and then narrowed with rage.

'God!' he exclaimed, and as he voiced that single exclamation he leaped swiftly downward in the direction of the figures in the glade.

9

Love and Treachery

Stellara, lying upon a pallet of grasses beneath the shade of a large tree, above the beach where the Korsars were completing the boat in which they hoped to embark for Korsar, knew that the fever had left her and that her strength was rapidly returning, but having discovered that illness, whether real or feigned, protected her from the attentions of Bohar, she continued to permit the Korsars to believe that she was quite ill. In her mind there constantly revolved various plans for escape, but she wished to delay the attempt as long as possible, not only that she might have time to store up a great amount of reserve strength, but also because she realized that if she waited until the Korsar boat was completed it would be unlikely that the majority of the men would brook delay in departure for the purpose of gratifying any desire that Bohar might express to pursue and recapture her.

Again, it was necessary to choose a time when none of the Korsars was in camp and as one of the two, who were detailed to prepare food and stand guard, was invariably on duty it appeared possible that she might never have the opportunity she hoped for, though she had determined that this fact would not prevent her from making an attempt at escape.

All of her hopes in this direction were centered upon one contingency, which her knowledge of nautical matters made to appear almost a certainty of the near future, and this was the fact that the launching of the boat would require the united efforts and strength of the entire party.

She knew from the discussions and conversations that she had overheard that it was Bohar's intention to launch the boat the moment that the hull was completed and to finish the balance of the work upon it while it floated in the little cove upon the beach of which it was being constructed.

This work would require no great amount of time or effort, since the mast, spars, rigging and sail were ready and at hand; bladders and gourds already prepared to receive fresh water, and food provisions for the trip, accumulated by the hunters detailed for this purpose, were neatly sewn up in hides and stored away in a cool, earth-covered dugout.

And so from her couch of grasses beneath the great tree Stellara watched the work progressing upon the hull of the boat that was to carry Bohar and his men to Korsar, and, as she watched, she planned her method of escape.

Above the camp rose the forested slopes of the hills which she must cross in her return to Paraht. For some distance the trees were scattered and then commenced the dense forest. If she could reach this unobserved she felt that she might entertain high hope of successful escape, for once in the denser growth she could take advantage of the skill and experience she had acquired under Tanar's tutorage and prosecute her flight along the leafy pathways of the branches, leaving no spoor that Bohar might follow and at the same time safeguarding herself from the attacks of the larger and more dangerous beasts of the forest, for, though few, there were still dangerous beasts upon Amiocap. Perhaps the most fearsome was the tarag, the giant, saber-toothed tiger that once roamed the hills of the outer crust. For the tandor she felt less concern since they seldom attack an individual unless molested; but in the hills which she must cross the greatest danger lay in the presence of the tarag and the ryth, the gigantic cave bear or Ursus Stelaeus, long since extinct upon the outer crust. Of the men of Amiocap whom she might possibly encounter she entertained little fear, even though they might be members of tribes other than hers, though she shuddered at the thought that she might fall into the hands of the Coripies, as these grotesque monsters engendered within her far greater fear than any of the other dangers that might possibly beset her way.

The exhilaration of contemplated flight and the high hopes produced within her at prospects of successfully returning to her father and her friends were dampened by the realization that Tanar would not be there to greet her. The supposed death of the Sarian had cast a blight upon her happiness that naught ever could remove and her sorrow was the deeper, perhaps, because no words of love had passed between them, and, therefore, she had not the consolation of happy memories to relieve the gnawing anguish of her grief.

The work upon the hull of the boat was at last completed and the men, coming to camp to eat, spoke hopefully of early departure for Korsar. Bohar approached Stellara's couch and stood glaring down upon her, his repulsive face darkened by a malignant scowl.

'How much longer do you intend to lie here entirely useless to me?' he demanded. 'You eat and sleep and the flush of fever has left your skin. I believe that you are feigning illness in order to escape fulfilling your duties as my mate and if that is true, you shall suffer for it. Get up!'

'I am too weak,' said Stellara. 'I cannot rise.'

'That can be remedied,' growled Bohar, and seizing her roughly by the hair, he dragged her from her couch and lifted her to her feet.

As Bohar released his hold upon her, Stellara staggered, her legs trembled, her knees gave beneath her and she fell back upon her couch, and so realistic was the manner in which she carried out the deception that even Bohar was fooled.

'She is sick and dying,' growled one of the Korsars. 'Why should we take her along in an overcrowded boat to eat the food and drink the water that some of us may be dying for before we reach Korsar?'

'Right,' cried another. 'Leave her behind.'

'Stick a knife into her,' said a third. 'She is good for nothing.'

'Shut up!' cried Bohar. 'She is going to be my mate and she is going with us.' He drew his two huge pistols. 'Whoever objects will stay here with a bullet in his guts. Eat now, you filthy hounds, and be quick about it for I shall need all hands and all your strength to launch the hull when you have eaten.'

So they were going to launch the hull! Stellara trembled with excitement as the moment for her break for liberty drew near. With impatience she watched the Korsars as they bolted their food like a pack of hungry wolf-dogs. She saw some of them throw themselves down to sleep after they had eaten, but Bohar the Bloody kicked them into wakefulness, and, at the point of his pistol, herded them to the beach, taking every available man and leaving Stellara alone and unguarded for the first time since he had seized her in the village of Fedol the chief.

She watched them as they descended to the hull and she waited until they seemed to be wholly engrossed in their efforts to shove the heavy boat into the sea; then she rose from her pallet and scurried like a frightened rabbit toward the forest on the slopes above the camp.

The hazards of fate, while beyond our control, are the factors in life which oftentimes make for the success or failure of our most important ventures. Upon them hang the fruition of our most cherished hope. They are, in truth, in the lap of the gods, where lies our future, and it was only by the merest hazard that Bohar the Bloody chanced to glance back toward the camp at the very moment that Stellara rose from her couch to make her bid for freedom.

With an oath he abandoned the work of launching the hull, and, calling his men to follow him, ran hurriedly up the steep slope in pursuit.

His fellows took in the situation at a glance and hesitated. 'Let him chase his own woman,' growled one. 'What have we to do with it? Our business is to launch the boat and get her ready, to sail to Korsar.'

'Right,' said another, 'and if he is not back by the time that we are ready we shall sail without him.'

'Good,' cried a third. 'Let us make haste then in the hope that we may be prepared to sail before he returns.'

And so Bohar the Bloody, unaccompanied by his men, pursued Stellara alone. Perhaps it was as well for the girl that this was true for there were many fleeter among the Korsars than the beefy Bohar.

The girl was instantly aware that her attempt to escape had been discovered, for Bohar was shouting in stentorian tones demanding that she halt, but his words only made her run the faster until presently she had darted into the forest and was lost to his view.

Here she took to the trees, hoping thereby to elude him even though she knew that her speed would be reduced. She heard the sound of his advance as he crashed through the underbrush and she knew that he was gaining rapidly upon her, but this did not unnerve her since she was confident that he could have no suspicion that she was in the branches of the trees and just so long as she kept among thick foliage he might pass directly beneath her without being aware of her close presence, and that is precisely what he did, cursing and puffing as he made his bull-like way up the steep slope of the hillside.

Stellara heard him pass and go crashing on in pursuit, and then she resumed her flight, turning to the right away from the direction of Bohar's advance until presently the noise of his passing was lost in the distance; then she turned upward again toward the height she must cross on her journey to Paraht.

Bohar sweated upward until finally almost utter exhaustion forced him to rest. He found himself in a little glade and here he lay down beneath a shrub that not only protected him from the rays of the sun, but hid him from sight as well, for in savage Pellucidar it is always well to seek rest in concealment.

Bohar's mind was filled with angry thoughts. He cursed himself for leaving the girl alone in camp and he cursed the girl for escaping, and he cursed the fate that had forced him to clamber up this steep hillside upon his futile mission, and most of all he cursed his absent followers whom he now realized had failed to accompany him. He knew that he had lost the girl and that it would be like looking for a particular minnow in the ocean to continue his search for her, and so, having rested, he was determined to hasten back to his camp when his attention was suddenly attracted by a noise at the lower end of the glade. Instinctively he reached for one of his pistols and to his dismay he found that both were gone, evidently having slipped from his sash or been scraped from it as he wallowed upward through the underbrush.

Bohar, despite his bluster and braggadocio, was far from courageous. Without his weapons he was an errant coward and so now he cringed in his concealment as he strained his eyes to discover the author of the noise he had heard, and as he watched a cunning leer of triumph curled his hideous mouth, for before him, at the far end of the glade, he saw Stellara drop from the lower branches of a tree and come upward across the glade toward him.

As the girl came abreast of his hiding place, Bohar the Bloody leaped to his feet and confronted her. With a stifled exclamation of dismay Stellara turned and sought to escape, but the Korsar was too close and too quick and reaching forth he seized her roughly by the hair.

'Will you never learn that you cannot escape Bohar the Bloody?' he demanded. 'You are mine and for this I shall cut off both your feet at the ankles when I get you into the boat, so that there will be no chance whatever that you may again run away from me. But come, mate willingly with me and it will go less hard with you,' and he drew her slim figure into his embrace.

'Never,' cried Stellara, and she struck him in the face with her two clenched fists.

With an oath Bohar seized the girl by the throat and shook her. 'You sheryth,' he cried, 'if I did not want you so badly I should kill you, and by the god of Korsar if ever you strike me again I shall kill you.'

'Then kill me,' cried Stellara, 'for I should rather die than mate with you,' and again she struck him with all her strength full in the face.

Bohar frothed with rage as he closed his fingers more tightly upon the girl's soft neck. 'Die, then, you—'

The words died upon his lips and he wheeled about as there fell upon his ears a man's loud voice raised in anger.

As he stood there hesitating and looking in the direction of the sound, the underbrush at the upper end of the glade parted and a warrior, leaping into the clearing, ran swiftly toward him.

Bohar blanched as though he had seen a ghost, and then, hurling the girl roughly to the ground, he faced the lone warrior.

Bohar would have fled had he not realized the futility of flight, for what chance had he in a race with this lithe man, who leaped toward him with the grace and speed of a deer.

'Go away,' shouted Bohar. 'Go away and leave us alone. This is my mate.'

'You lie,' growled Tanar of Pellucidar as he leaped upon the Korsar.

Down went the two men, the Sarian on top, and as they fell each sought a hold upon the other's throat, and, failing to secure it, they struck blindly at one another's face.

Tanar was mad with rage. He fought like a wild beast, forgetting all that David Innes had taught him. His one thought was to kill; it mattered not how just so long as he killed, and Bohar, on the defensive fighting for his life, battled like a cornered rat. To his advantage were his great weight and his longer reach, but in strength and agility as well as courage Tanar was his superior.

Stellara slowly opened her eyes as she recovered from the swoon into which she had passed beneath the choking fingers of Bohar the Bloody. At first she did not recognize Tanar, seeing only two warriors battling to the death on the sward of the glade and guessing that she would be the prey of him who was victorious. But presently, in the course of the duel, the face of the Sarian was turned toward her.

'Tanar!' she cried. 'God is merciful. I thought you were dead and He has given you back to me.'

At her words the Sarian redoubled his efforts to overcome his antagonist, but Bohar succeeded in getting his fingers upon Tanar's throat.

Horrified, Stellara looked about her for a rock or a stick with which to come to the succor of her champion, but before she had found one she realized that he needed no outside assistance. With a single Herculean movement he tore himself loose from Bohar and leaped to his feet.

Instantly the Korsar sprang to an upright position and lowering his head he charged the Sarian – charged like a mad bull.

Now Tanar was fighting with cool calculation. The blood-madness of the first moment following the sight of Stellara in the choking murderous fingers of the Korsar had passed. He awaited Bohar's rush, and as they came together he clamped an arm around the Korsar's head, and, turning swiftly, hurled the man over his shoulder and heavily to the ground. Then he waited.

Once more Bohar, shaking his head, staggered to his feet. Once more he rushed the Sarian, and once more that deadly arm was locked about his head, and once more he was hurled heavily to the ground.

This time he did not arise so quickly nor so easily. He came up staggering and feeling of his head and neck.

'Prepare to die,' growled Tanar. 'For the suffering you have inflicted upon Stellara you are about to die.'

With a shriek of mingled rage and fright Bohar, gone mad, charged the Sarian again, and for the third time his great body flew through the air, to alight heavily upon the hard ground, but this time it did not arise; it did not stir, for Bohar the Bloody lay dead with a broken neck.

For a moment Tanar of Pellucidar stood ready over the body of his fallen foe, but when he realized that Bohar was dead he turned away with a sneer of disgust.

Before him stood Stellara, her beautiful eyes filled with incredulity and with happiness.

'Tanar!' It was only a whisper, but it carried to him a world of meaning that sent thrill after thrill through his body.

'Stellara!' he cried, as he took the girl in his arms. 'Stellara, I love you.'

Her soft arms stole around his neck and drew his face to hers. His mouth covered her mouth in a long kiss, and, as he raised his face to look down into hers, from her parted lips burst a single exclamation, 'Oh, God!' and from the depth of her half-closed eyes burned a love beyond all understanding.

'My mate,' he cried, as he pressed her form to him.

'My mate,' breathed Stellara, 'while life remains in my body and after life, throughout death, forever!'

Suddenly she looked up and drew away.

'Who is that, Tanar?' she asked.

As Tanar turned to look in the direction indicated by the girl he saw Jude emerging from the forest at the upper end of the glade. 'It is Jude,' he said to Stellara, 'who escaped with me from the country of the Buried People.'

Jude approached them, his sullen countenance clouded by its habitual scowl.

'He frightens me,' said Stellara, pressing closer to Tanar.

'You need not fear him,' said the Sarian. 'He is always scowling and un-happy; but he is my friend and even if he were not he is harmless.'

'I do not like him,' whispered Stellara.

Jude approached and stopped before them. His eyes wandered for a moment to the body of Bohar and then came back and fastened themselves in a steady gaze upon Stellara, apprising her from head to foot. There was a crafty boldness in his gaze that disturbed Stellara even more than his sullen scowl.

'Who is the woman?' he demanded, without taking his eyes from her face.

'My mate,' replied Tanar.

'Then she is going with us?' asked Jude.

'Of course,' replied the Sarian.

'And where are we going?' demanded Jude.

'Stellara and I will return to Paraht, where her father, Fedol, is chief,' re-plied Tanar. 'You may come with us if you wish. We will see that you are received as a friend and treated well until you can find the means to return to Hime.'

'Is he from Hime?' asked Stellara, and Tanar felt her shudder.

'I am from Hime,' said Jude, 'but I do not care if I never return there if your people let me live with them.'

'That,' said Tanar, 'is something that must be decided by Fedol and his people, but I can promise you that they will let you remain with them, if not permanently, at least until you can find the means of returning to Hime. And now, before we set out for Paraht, let us renew our strength with food and sleep.'

Without weapons it was not easy to obtain game and they had traveled up the mountain slopes for some distance before the two men were able to bring down a brace of large birds, which they knocked over with well aimed stones. The birds closely resembled wild turkeys, whose prototypes were doubtless the progenitors of the wild turkeys of the outer crust. The hunt had brought them to a wide plateau, just below the summit of the hills. It was a rolling table-land, waist deep in lush grasses, with here and there a giant tree or a group of trees offering shade from the vertical rays of the noonday sun.

Beside a small stream, which rippled gayly downward toward the sea, they halted to eat and sleep.

Jude gathered firewood while Tanar made fire by the primitive method of rapidly revolving a sharpened stick in a tinder-filled hole in a larger piece of dry wood. As these preparations were going forward Stellara prepared the birds and it was not long before the turkeys were roasting over a hot fire.

Their hunger appeased, the urge to sleep took possession of them, and now Jude insisted that he stand the first watch, arguing that he had not been subjected to the fatigue of battle as had Tanar, and so Stellara and the Sarian lay down beneath the shade of the tree while the scowling Himean stood watch.

Even in the comparative safety of Amiocap danger might always be expected to lurk in the form of carnivorous beast or hunting man, but the watcher cast no solicitous glances beyond the camp. Instead, he squatted upon his haunches, devouring Stellara with his eyes. Not once did he remove them from the beautiful figure of the girl except occasionally to glance quickly at Tanar, where the regular rising and falling of his breast denoted undisturbed slumber.

Whatever thoughts the beauty of the sleeping girl engendered in the breast of the Himean, they were reflected only in the unremitting scowl that never lifted itself from the man's dark brows.

Presently he arose noiselessly and gathered a handful of soft grasses, which he rolled into a small ball. Then he crept stealthily to where Stellara lay and kneeled beside her.

Suddenly he leaned over her and grasped her by the throat, at the same time clamping his other hand, in the palm of which lay the ball of grass, over her mouth.

Thus rudely awakened from deep slumber, her first glance revealing the scowling features of the Himean, Stellara opened her mouth to scream for help, and, as she did so, Jude forced the ball of grass between her teeth and far into her mouth, dragged her to her feet, and, throwing her across his shoulder, bore her swiftly downward across the table-land.

Stellara struggled and fought to free herself, but Jude was a powerful man and her efforts were of no avail against his strength. He held her in such a way that both her arms were confined. The ball of grass expanded in her mouth and she could not force it out with her tongue alone. A single scream she knew would awaken Tanar and bring him to her rescue, but she could not scream.

Down across the rolling table-land the Himean carried Stellara to the edge of a steep cliff that overhung the sea at the upper end of a deep cove which cut far into the island at this point. Here Jude lowered Stellara to her feet, but he still clung tightly to one of her wrists.

'Listen, woman,' he growled, 'you are coming to Hime to be the mate of Jude. If you come peaceably, no harm will befall you and if you will promise to make no outcry I shall remove the gag from your mouth. Do you promise?'

Stellara shook her head determinedly in an unquestionable negative and at the same time struggled to free herself from Jude's grasp.

With an ugly growl the man struck her and as she fell unconscious he gathered long grasses and twisted them into a rope and bound her wrists and ankles; then he lifted her again to his shoulder and started down over the edge of the cliff, where a narrow trail now became discernible.

It was evident that Jude had had knowledge of this path since he had come to it so unerringly, and the ease and assurance with which he descended it strengthened this conviction.

The descent was not over a hundred feet to a little ledge almost at the water's edge.

It was here that Stellara gained consciousness, and, as she opened her eyes, she saw before her a water-worn cave that ran far back beneath the cliff.

Into this, along the narrow ledge, Jude carried her to the far end of the cavern, where, upon a narrow, pebbly beach, were drawn up a half dozen dugouts – the light, well-made canoes of the Himeans.

In one of these Jude placed the girl, and, pushing it off into the deep water of the cove, leaped into it himself, seized the paddle and directed its course out toward the open sea.

10

Pursuit

Awakening from a deep and refreshing slumber, Tanar opened his eyes and lay gazing up into the foliage of the tree above him. Happy thoughts filled his mind, a smile touched his lip and then, following the trend of his thoughts, his eyes turned to feast upon the dear figure of his mate.

She was not there, where he had last seen her huddled snugly in her bed of grasses, but still he felt no concern, thinking merely that she had awakened before him and arisen.

Idly his gaze made a circuit of the little camp, and then with a startled exclamation he leaped to his feet for he realized that both Stellara and Jude had disappeared. Again he looked about him, this time extending the field of his enquiring gaze, but nowhere was there any sign of either the man or the woman that he sought.

He called their names aloud, but there was no response, and then he fell to examining the ground about the camp. He saw where Stellara had been sleeping and to his keen eyes were revealed the tracks of the Himean as he had approached her couch. He saw other tracks leading away, the tracks of Jude alone, but in the crushed grasses where the man had gone he read the true story, for they told him that more than the weight of a single man had bent and bruised them thus; they told him that Jude had carried Stellara off, and Tanar knew that it had been done by force.

Swiftly he followed the well marked spoor through the long grass, oblivious of all else save the prosecution of his search for Stellara and the punishment of Jude. And so he was unaware of the sinister figure that crept along the trail behind him.

Down across the table-land they went – the man and the great beast following silently in his tracks. Down to a cliff overhanging the sea the trail led, and here as Tanar paused an instant to look out across the ocean he saw hazily in the distance a canoe and in the canoe were two figures, but who they were he could only guess since they were too far away for him to recognize.

As he stood there thus, stunned for a moment, a slight noise behind him claimed his attention, recalled him momentarily from the obsession of his sorrow and his rage so that he turned a quick, scowling glance in the direction from which the interruption had come, and there, not ten paces from him, loomed the snarling face of a great tarag.

The fangs of the saber-tooth gleamed in the sunlight; the furry snout was wrinkled in a snarl of anger; the lashing tail came suddenly to rest, except for a slight convulsive twitching of its tip; the beast crouched and Tanar knew that it was about to charge.

Unarmed and single-handed as he was, the man seemed easy prey for the carnivore; nor to right nor to left was there any avenue of escape.

All these things passed swiftly through the mind of the Sarian, yet never did they totally obliterate the memory of the two figures in the canoe far out at sea behind him; nor of the cliff overhanging the waters of the cove beneath. And then the tarag charged.

A hideous scream broke from the savage throat as the great beast hurled itself forward with lightning-like rapidity. Two great bounds it took, and in mid-spring of the second Tanar turned and dove head foremost over the edge of the cliff, for the only alternative that remained to him was death beneath the rending fangs and talons of the sabertooth.

For all he knew jagged rocks might lie just beneath the surface of the water, but there was one chance that the water was deep, while no chance for life remained to him upon the cliff top.

The momentum of the great cat's spring, unchecked by the body of his expected prey, carried him over the edge of the cliff also so that man and beast hurtled downward almost side by side to the water far below.

Tanar cut the water cleanly with extended hands and turning quickly upwards came to the surface scarcely a yard from where the great cat had alighted.

The two faced one another and at sight of the man the tarag burst again into hideous screams and struck out swiftly toward him.

Tanar knew that he might outdistance the tarag in the water, but at the moment that they reached the beach he would be at the mercy of the great carnivore. The snarling face was close to his; the great talons were reaching for him as Tanar of Pellucidar dove beneath the beast.

A few, swift strokes brought him up directly behind the cat and an instant later he had reached out and seized the furry hide. The tarag turned swiftly to strike at him, but already the man was upon his shoulders and his weight was carrying the snarling face below the surface.

Choking, struggling, the maddened animal sought to reach the soft flesh of the man with his raking talons, but in the liquid element that filled the sea its usual methods of offense and defense were worthless. Quickly realizing that death stared it in the face, unless it could immediately overcome this handicap, the tarag now strained its every muscle to reach the solid footing of the land, while Tanar on his part sought to prevent it. Now his fingers had crept from their hold upon the furry shoulders down to the white furred throat and like claws of steel they sank into the straining muscles.

No longer did the beast attempt to scream and the man, for his part, fought in silence.

It was a grim duel; a terrible duel; a savage encounter that might be enacted only in a world that was very young and between primitive creatures who never give up the stern battle for life until the scythe of the Grim Reaper has cut them down.

Deep into the gloomy cavern, beneath the cliff the tarag battled for the tiny strip of beach at the far end and grimly the man fought to hold it back and force its head beneath the water. He felt the efforts of the beast weakening and yet they were very close to the beach. At any instant the great claws might strike bottom and Tanar knew that there was still left within that giant carcass enough vitality to rend him to shreds if ever the tarag got four feet on solid ground and his head above the water.

With a last supreme effort he tightened his fingers upon the throat of the tarag and sliding from its back sought to drag it from its course, and the animal upon its part made one, last supreme effort for life. It reared up in the water and wheeling about struck at the man. The raking talons grazed his flesh, and then he was back upon the giant shoulders forcing the head once more beneath the surface of the sea. He felt a spasm pass through the great frame of the beast beneath him; the muscles relaxed and the tarag floated limp.

A moment later Tanar dragged himself to the pebbly beach, where he lay panting from exhaustion.

Recovered, nor did it take him long to recover, so urgent were the demands of the pursuit upon which he was engaged, Tanar rose and looked about him. Before him were canoes, such as he had never seen before, drawn up upon the narrow beach. Paddles lay in each of the canoes as though they but awaited the early return of their owners. Whence they had come and what they were doing here in this lonely cavern, Tanar could not guess. They were unlike the canoes of the Amiocapians, which fact convinced him that they belonged to a people from some other island, or possibly from the mainland itself. But these were questions which did not concern him greatly at the time. Here were canoes. Here was the means of pursuing the two that he had seen far out at sea and whom he was convinced were none other than Jude and Stellara.

Seizing one of the small craft he dragged it to the water's edge and launched it. Then, leaping into it, he paddled swiftly down the cove out towards the sea, and as he paddled he had an opportunity to examine the craft more closely.

It was evidently fashioned from a single log of very light wood and was all of one piece, except a bulkhead at each end of the cockpit, which was large enough to accommodate three men.

Rapping with his paddle upon the surface of the deck and upon the bulkheads convinced him that the log had been entirely hollowed out beneath the deck and as the bulkheads themselves gave every appearance of having been so neatly fitted as to be watertight, Tanar guessed that the canoe was unsinkable.

His attention was next attracted by a well-tanned and well-worn hide lying in the bottom of the cockpit. A rawhide lacing ran around the entire periphery of the hide and as he tried to determine the purpose to which the whole had been put his eyes fell upon a series of cleats extending entirely around the edge of the cockpit, and he guessed that the hide was intended as a covering for it. Examining it more closely he discovered an opening in it about the size of a man's body and immediately its purpose became apparent to him. With the covering in place and laced tightly around the cockpit and also laced around the man's body the canoe could ship no water and might prove a seaworthy craft, even in severe storms.

As the Sarian fully realized his limitations as a seafaring man, he lost no time in availing himself of this added protection against the elements, and when he had adjusted it and laced it tightly about the outside of the cockpit and secured the lacing which ran around the opening in the center of the hide about his own body, he experienced a feeling of security that he had never before felt when he had been forced to surrender himself to the unknown dangers of the sea.

Now he paddled rapidly in the direction in which he had last seen the canoe with its two occupants, and when he had passed out of the cove into the open sea he espied them again, but this time so far out that the craft and its passengers appeared only as a single dot upon the broad waters. But beyond them hazily loomed the bulk of the island that Jude had pointed out as Hime and this tended to crystallize Tanar's assurance that the canoe ahead of him was being guided by Jude toward the island of his own people.

The open seas of Pellucidar present obstacles to the navigation of a small canoe that would seem insurmountable to men of the outer crust, for their waters are ofttimes alive with saurian monsters of a long past geologic epoch and it was encounters with these that the Sarian mountaineer apprehended with more acute concern than consideration of adverse wind or tempest aroused within him.

He had noticed that one end of the long paddle he wielded was tipped with a piece of sharpened ivory from the end of a tandor's tusk, but the thing seemed an utterly futile weapon with which to combat a tandoraz or an azdyryth, two of the mightiest and most fearsome inhabitants of the deep, but as far as he could see ahead the long, oily swells of a calm ocean were unruffled by marine life of any description.

Well aware of his small experience and great deficiency as a paddler, Tanar held no expectation of being able to overhaul the canoe manned by the experienced Jude. The best that he could hope was that he might keep it in view until he could mark the spot upon Hime where it landed. And once upon solid ground again, even though it was an island peopled by enemies, the Sarian felt that he would be able to cope with any emergency that might arise.

Gradually the outlines of Hime took definite shape before him, while those of Amiocap became correspondingly vague behind.

And between him and the island of Hime the little dot upon the surface of the sea told him that his quarry had not as yet made land. The pursuit seemed interminable. Hime seemed to be receding almost as rapidly as he approached it. He became hungry and thirsty, but there was neither food nor water. There was naught but to bend his paddle ceaselessly through the monotonous grind of pursuit, but at length the details of the shore-line grew more distinct. He saw coves and inlets and wooded hills and then he saw the canoe that he was following disappear far ahead of him beyond the entrance of a cove. Tanar marked the spot well in his mind and redoubled his efforts to reach the shore. And then fate arose in her inexorable perversity and confounded all his hopes and plans.

A sudden flurry on the surface of the water far to his right gave him his first warning. And then, like the hand of a giant, the wind caught his frail craft and turned it at right angles to the course he wished to pursue. The waves rolled; the wind shrieked; the storm was upon him in great fury and there was naught to do but turn and flee before it.

Down the coast of Hime he raced, parallel to the shore, further and further from the spot where Jude had landed with Stellara, but all the time Tanar was striving to drive his craft closer and closer to the wooded slopes of Hime.

Ahead of him, and upon his right, he could see what appeared to be the end of the island. Should he be carried past this he realized that all would be lost, for doubtless the storm would carry him on out of sight of land and if it did he knew that he could never reach Hime nor return to Amiocap, since he had no means whatsoever of ascertaining direction once land slipped from view in the haze of the up-curving horizon.

Straining every muscle, continuously risking being capsized, Tanar strove to drive inward toward the shore, and though he saw that he was gaining he knew that it was too late, for already he was almost abreast of the island's extremity, and still he was a hundred yards off shore. But even so he did not despair, or if he did despair he did not cease to struggle for salvation.

He saw the island slip past him, but there was yet a chance for in its lee he saw calm water and if he could reach that he would be saved.

Straining every muscle the Sarian bent to his crude paddle. Suddenly the breeze stopped and he shot out into the smooth water in the lee of the island, but he did not cease his strenuous efforts until the bow of the canoe had touched the sand of Hime.

Tanar leaped out and dragged the craft ashore. That he should ever need it again he doubted, yet he hid it beneath the foliage of nearby bushes, and alone and unarmed set forth to face the dangers of an unknown country in what appeared even to Tanar as an almost hopeless quest for Stellara.

To the Sarian it seemed wisest to follow the coast-line back until he found the spot at which Jude had landed and then trace his trail inland, and this was the plan that he proceeded to follow.

Being in a strange land and, therefore, in a land of enemies, and being unarmed, Tanar was forced to move with great caution; yet constantly he sacrificed caution to speed. Natural obstacles impeded his progress. A great cliff running far out into the sea barred his way and it was with extreme difficulty that he found a path up the face of the frowning escarpment and then only after traveling inland for a considerable distance.

Beyond the summit rolled a broad table-land dotted with trees. A herd of thags grazed quietly in the sunlight or dozed beneath the shadowy foliage of the trees.

At sight of the man passing among them these great horned cattle became restless. An old bull bellowed and pawed the ground, and Tanar measured the distance to the nearest tree. But on he went, avoiding the beasts as best he could and hoping against hope that he could pass them successfully without further arousing their short tempers. But the challenge of the old bull was being taken up by others of his sex until a score of heavy shoul-dered mountains of beef were converging slowly upon the lone man, stop-ping occasionally to paw or gore the ground, while they bellowed forth their displeasure.

There was still a chance that he might pass them in safety. There was an opening among them just ahead of him, and Tanar accelerated his speed, but just at that instant one of the bulls took it into his head to charge and then the whole twenty bore down upon the Sarian like a band of iron loco-motives suddenly endowed with the venom of hornets.

There was naught to do but seek the safety of the nearest tree and towards this Tanar ran at full speed, while from all sides the angry bulls raced to head him off.

With scarcely more than inches to spare Tanar swung himself into the branches of the tree just as the leading bull passed beneath him. A moment later the bellowing herd congregated beneath his sanctuary and while some contented themselves with pawing and bellowing, others placed their heavy heads against the bole of the tree and sought to push it down, but fortunately for Tanar it was a young oak and it withstood their sturdiest efforts.

But now, having treed him, the thags showed no disposition to leave him. For a while they milled around beneath him and then several deliberately lay down beneath the tree as though to prevent his escape.

To one accustomed to the daily recurrence of the darkness of night, fol-lowing the setting of the sun, escape from such a dilemma as that in which Tanar found himself would have seemed merely a matter of waiting for the coming of night, but where the sun does not set and there is no night, and time is immeasurable and unmeasured, and where one may not know whether a lifetime or a second has been encompassed by the duration of such an event, the enforced idleness and delay are maddening.

But in spite of these conditions, or perhaps because of them, the Sarian possessed a certain philosophic outlook upon life that permitted him to accept his fate with marked stoicism and to take advantage of the enforced delay by fashioning a bow, arrows and a spear from the material afforded by the tree in which he was confined.

The tree gave him everything that he needed except the cord for his bow, and this he cut from the rawhide belt that supported his loin cloth – a long, slender strip of rawhide which he inserted in his mouth and chewed thoroughly until it was entirely impregnated with saliva. Then he bent his bow and stretched the wet rawhide from tip to tip. While it dried, he pointed his arrows with his teeth.

In drying the rawhide shrunk, bending the bow still further and tightening the string until it hummed to the slightest touch.

The weapons were finished and yet the great bulls still stood on guard, and while Tanar remained helpless in the tree Jude was taking Stellara toward the interior of the island.

But all things must end. Impatient of delay, Tanar sought some plan whereby he might rid himself of the short tempered beasts beneath him. He hit upon the plan of yelling and throwing dead branches at them and this did have the effect of bringing them all to their feet. A few wandered away to graze with the balance of the herd, but enough remained to keep Tanar securely imprisoned.

A great bull stood directly beneath him. Tanar jumped up and down upon a small branch, making its leafy end whip through the air, and at the same time he hurled bits of wood at the great thags. And then, suddenly, to the surprise and consternation of both man and beast, the branch broke and precipitated Tanar full upon the broad shoulders of the bull. Instantly his fingers clutched its long hair as, with a bellow of surprise and terror, the beast leaped forward.

Instinct took the frightened animal toward the balance of the herd and when they saw him with a man sitting upon his back they, too, became terrified, with the result that a general stampede ensued, the herd attempting to escape their fellow, while the bull raced to be among them.

Stragglers, that had been grazing at a considerable distance from the balance of the herd, were stringing out to the rear and it was the presence of these that made it impossible for Tanar to slip to the ground and make his escape. Knowing that he would be trampled by those behind if he left the back of the bull, there was no alternative but to remain where he was as long as he could.

The thag, now thoroughly frightened because of his inability to dislodge the man-thing from his shoulders, was racing blindly forward, and presently Tanar found himself carried into the very midst of the lunging herd as it thundered across the table-land toward a distant forest.

The Sarian knew that once they reached the forest he would doubtless be scraped from the back of the thag almost immediately by some low hanging limb, and if he were not killed or injured by the blow he would be trampled to death by the thags behind. But as escape seemed hopeless he could only await the final outcome of this strange adventure.

When the leaders of the herd approached the forest hope was rekindled in Tanar's breast, for he saw that the growth was so thick and the trees so close together that it was impossible for the beasts to enter the woods at a rapid gait.

Immediately the leaders reached the edge of the forest their pace was slowed down and those behind them, pushing forward, were stopped by those in front. Some of them attempted to climb up, or were forced up, upon the backs of those ahead. But, for the most part, the herd slowed down and contented itself with pushing steadily onward toward the woods with the result that when the beast that Tanar was astride arrived at the edge of the dark shadows his gait had been reduced to a walk, and as he passed beneath the first tree Tanar swung lightly into its branches.

He had lost his spear, but his bow and arrows that he had strapped to his back remained with him, and as the herd passed beneath him and he saw the last of them disappear in the dark aisles of the forest, he breathed a deep sigh of relief and turned once more toward the far end of the island.

The thags had carried him inland a considerable distance, so now he cut back diagonally toward the coast to gain as much ground as possible.

Tanar had not yet emerged from the forest when he heard the excited growling of some wild beast directly ahead of him.

He thought that he recognized the voice of a codon, and fitting an arrow to his bow he crept warily forward. What wind was blowing came from the beast toward him and presently brought to his nostrils proof of the correctness of his guess, together with another familiar scent – that of man.

Knowing that the beast could not catch his scent from upwind, Tanar had only to be careful to advance silently, but there are few animals on earth that can move more silently than primitive man when he elects to do so, and so Tanar came in sight of the beast without being discovered by it.

It was, as he had thought, a huge wolf, a pre-historic but gigantic counterpart of our own timber wolf.

No need had the codon to run in packs, for in size, strength, ferocity and courage it was a match for any creature that it sought to bring down, with the possible exception of the mammoth, and this great beast alone it hunted in packs.

The codon stood snarling beneath a great tree, occasionally leaping high against the bole as though, he sought to reach something hidden by the foliage above.

Tanar crept closer and presently he saw the figure of a youth crouching among the lower branches above the codon. It was evident that the boy was terror-stricken, but the thing that puzzled Tanar was that he cast affrighted glances upward into the tree more often than he did downward toward the codon, and presently this fact convinced the Sarian that the youth was menaced by something above him.

Tanar viewed the predicament of the boy and then considered the pitiful inadequacy of his own makeshift bow and arrow, which might only infuriate the beast and turn it upon himself. He doubted that the arrows were heavy enough, or strong enough, to pierce through the savage heart and thus only might he hope to bring down the codon.

Once more he crept to a new position, without attracting the attention either of the codon or the youth, and from this new vantage point he could look further up into the tree in which the boy crouched and then it was that he realized the hopelessness of the boy's position, for only a few feet above him and moving steadily closer appeared the head of a great snake, whose wide, distended jaws revealed formidable fangs.

Tanar's consideration of the boy's plight was influenced by a desire to save him from either of the two creatures that menaced him and also by the hope that if successful he might win sufficient gratitude to enlist the services of the youth as a guide, and especially as a go-between in the event that he should come in contact with natives of the island.

Tanar had now crept to within seven paces of the codon, from the sight of which he was concealed by a low shrub behind which he lay. Had the youth not been so occupied between the wolf and the snake he might have seen the Sarian, but so far he had not seen him.

Fitting an arrow to his crude bow and inserting four others between the fingers of his left hand, Tanar arose quietly and drove a shaft into the back of the codon, between its shoulders.

With a howl of pain and rage the beast wheeled about, only to receive another arrow full in the chest. Then his glaring eyes alighted upon the Sarian and, with a hideous growl, he charged.

With such rapidity do events of this nature transpire that they are over in much less time than it takes to record them, for a wounded wolf, charging its antagonist, can cover seven paces in an incredibly short space of time; yet even in that brief interval three more arrows sank deeply into the white breast of the codon, and the momentum of its last stride sent it rolling against the Sarian's feet – dead.

The youth, freed from the menace of the codon, leaped to the ground and would have fled without a word of thanks had not Tanar covered him with another arrow and commanded him to halt.

The snake, seeing another man and realizing, perhaps, that the odds were now against him, hesitated a moment and then withdrew into the foliage of the tree, as Tanar advanced toward the trembling youth.

'Who are you?' demanded the Sarian.

'My name is Balal,' replied the youth. 'I am the son of Scurv, the chief.'

'Where is your village?' asked Tanar.

'It is not far,' replied Balal.

'Will you take me there?' asked Tanar.

'Yes,' replied Balal.

'Will your father receive me well?' continued the Sarian.

'You saved my life,' said Balal. 'For that he will treat you well, though for the most part we kill strangers who come to Garb.'

'Lead on,' said the Sarian.

11

Gura

Balal led Tanar through the forest until they came at last to the edge of a steep cliff, which the Sarian judged was the opposite side of the promontory that had barred his way along the beach.

Not far from the cliff's edge stood the stump of a great tree that seemed to have been blasted and burned by lightning. It reared its head some ten feet above the ground and from its charred surface protruded the stub end of several broken limbs.

'Follow me,' said Balal, and leaping to the protruding stub, he climbed to the top of the stump and lowered himself into the interior.

Tanar followed and found an opening some three feet in diameter leading down into the bole of the dead tree. Set into the sides of this natural shaft were a series of heavy pegs, which answered the purpose of ladder rungs to the descending Balal.

The noonday sun lighted the interior of the tree for a short distance, but their own shadows, intervening, blotted out everything that lay at a depth greater than six or eight feet.

None too sure that he was not being led into a trap and, therefore, unwilling to permit his guide to get beyond his reach, Tanar hastily entered the hollow stump and followed Balal downward.

The Sarian was aware that the interior of the tree led into a shaft dug in the solid ground and a moment later he felt his feet touch the floor of a dark tunnel.

Along this tunnel Balal led him and presently they emerged into a cave that was dimly lighted through a small opening opposite them and near the floor.

Through this aperture, which was about two feet in diameter and beyond which Tanar could see daylight, Balal crawled, followed closely by the Sarian, who found himself upon a narrow ledge, high up on the face of an almost vertical cliff.

'This,' said Balal, 'is the village of Garb.'

'I see no village nor any people,' said Tanar.

'They are here though,' said Balal. 'Follow me,' and he led the way a short distance along the ledge, which inclined downward and was in places so narrow and so shelving that the two men were compelled to flatten themselves against the side of the cliff and edge their way slowly, inch by inch, sideways.

Presently the ledge ended and here it was much wider so that Balal could lie down upon it, and, lowering his body over the edge, he clung a moment by his hands and then dropped.

Tanar looked over the edge and saw that Balal had alighted upon another narrow ledge about ten feet below. Even to a mountaineer, such as the Sarian was, the feat seemed difficult and fraught with danger, but there was no alternative and so, lying down, he lowered himself slowly over the edge of the ledge, clung an instant with his fingers, and then dropped.

As he alighted beside the youth he was about to remark upon the perilous approach to the village of Garb, but it was so apparent that Balal took it as a matter of course and thought nothing of it that Tanar desisted, realizing, in the instant, that among cliff dwellers, such as these, the little feat that they had just accomplished was as ordinary and everyday an occurrence as walking on level ground was to him.

As Tanar had an opportunity to look about him on this new level, he saw, and not without relief, that the ledge was much wider and that the mouths of several caves opened upon it. In places, and more especially in front of the cave entrances, the ledge widened to as much as six or eight feet, and here Tanar obtained his first view of any considerable number of Himeans.

'Is it not a wonderful village?' asked Balal, and without waiting for an answer, 'Look!' and he pointed downward over the edge of the ledge.

Following the direction indicated by the youth, Tanar saw ledge after ledge scoring the face of a lofty cliff from summit to base, and upon every ledge there were men, women and children.

'Come,' said Balal, 'I will take you to my father,' and forthwith he led the way along the ledge.

As the first people they encountered saw Tanar they leaped to their feet, the men seizing their weapons. 'I am taking him to my father, the chief,' said Balal. 'Do not harm him,' and with sullen looks the warriors let them pass.

A log into which wooden pegs were driven served as an easy means of descent from one ledge to the next, and after descending for a considerable distance to about midway between the summit and the ground Balal halted at the entrance to a cave, before which sat a man, a woman and two children, a girl about Balal's age and a boy much younger.

As had all the other villagers they had passed, these, too, leaped to their feet and seized weapons when they saw Tanar.

'Do not harm him,' repeated Balal. 'I have brought him to you, Scurv, my father, because he saved my life when it was threatened simultaneously by a snake and a wolf and I promised him that you would receive him and treat him well.'

Scurv eyed Tanar suspiciously and there was no softening of the lines upon his sullen countenance even when he heard that the stranger had saved the life of his son. 'Who are you and what are you doing in our country?' he demanded.

'I am looking for one named Jude,' replied Tanar.

'What do you know of Jude?' asked Scurv. 'Is he your friend?'

There was something in the man's tone that made it questionable as to the advisability of claiming Jude as a friend. 'I know him,' he said. 'We were prisoners together among the Coripies on the island of Amiocap.'

'You are an Amiocapian?' demanded Scurv.

'No,' replied Tanar, 'I am a Sarian from a country on a far distant mainland.'

'Then what were you doing on Amiocap?' asked Scurv.

'I was captured by the Korsars and the ship in which they were taking me to their country was wrecked on Amiocap. All that I ask of you is that you give me food and show me where I can find Jude.'

'I do not know where you can find Jude,' said Scurv. 'His people and my people are always at war.'

'Do you not know where their country or village is?' demanded Tanar.

'Yes, of course I know where it is, but I do not know that Jude is there.'

'Are you going to give him food,' asked Balal, 'and treat him well as I promised you would?'

'Yes,' said Scurv, but his tone was sullen and his shifty eyes looked neither at Balal nor Tanar as he replied.

In the center of the ledge, opposite the mouth of the cave, a small fire was burning beneath an earthen bowl, which was supported by three or four small pieces of stone. Squatting close to this was a female, who, in youth, might have been a fine looking girl, but now her face was lined by bitterness and hate as she glared sullenly into the caldron, the contents of which she was stirring with the rib of some large animal.

'Tanar is hungry, Sloo,' said Balal, addressing the woman. 'When will the food be cooked?'

'Have I not enough to do preparing hides and cooking food for all of you without having to cook for every enemy that you see fit to bring to the cave of your father?'

'This is the first time I ever brought any one, mother,' said Balal.

'Let it be the last, then,' snapped the woman.

'Shut up, woman,' snapped Scurv, 'and hasten with the food.'

The woman leaped to her feet, brandishing the rib above her head. 'Don't tell me what to do, Scurv,' she shrilled. 'I have had about enough of you anyway.'

'Hit him, mother!' screamed a lad of about eleven, jumping to his feet and dancing about in evident joy and excitement.

Balal leaped across the cook fire and struck the lad heavily with his open palm across the face, sending him spinning up against the cliff wall. 'Shut up, Dhung,' he cried, 'or I'll pitch you over the edge.'

The remaining member of the family party, a girl, just ripening into womanhood, remained silent where she was seated, leaning against the face of the cliff, her large, dark eyes taking in the scene being enacted before her. Suddenly the woman turned upon her. 'Why don't you do something, Gura?' she demanded. 'You sit there and let them attack me and never raise a hand in my defense.'

'But no one has attacked you, mother,' said the girl, with a sigh.

'But I will,' yelled Scurv, seizing a short club that lay beside him. 'I'll knock her head off if she doesn't keep a still tongue in it and hurry with that food.' At this instant a loud scream attracted the attention of all toward another family group before a cave, a little further along the ledge. Here, a man, grasping a woman by her hair, was beating her with a stick, while several children were throwing pieces of rock, first at their parents and then at one another.

'Hit her again!' yelled Scurv.

'Scratch out his eyes!' screamed Sloo, and for the moment the family of the chief forgot their own differences in the enjoyable spectacle of another family row.

Tanar looked on in consternation and surprise. Never had he witnessed such tumult and turmoil in the villages of the Sarians, and coming, as he just had, from Amiocap, the island of love, the contrast was even more appalling.

'Don't mind them,' said Balal, who was watching the Sarian and had noticed the expression of surprise and disgust upon his face. 'If you stay with us long you will get used to it, for it is always like this. Come on, let's eat, the food is ready,' and drawing his stone knife he fished into the pot and speared a piece of meat.

Tanar, having no knife, had recourse to one of his arrows, which answered the purpose quite as well, and then, one by one, the family gathered around as though nothing unusual had happened, and fell, too, upon the steaming stew with avidity.

During the meal they did not speak other than to call one another vile names, if two chanced to reach into the caldron simultaneously and one interfered with another.

The caldron emptied, Scurv and Sloo crawled into the dark interior of their cave to sleep, where they were presently followed by Balal.

Gura, the daughter, took the caldron and started down the cliff toward the brook to wash out the receptacle and return with it filled with water.

As she made her precarious way down rickety ladders and narrow ledges, little Dhung, her brother, amused himself by hurling stones at her.

'Stop that,' commanded Tanar. 'You might hit her.'

'That is what I am trying to do,' said the little imp. 'Why else should I be throwing stones at her? To miss her?' He hurled another missile and with that Tanar grabbed him by the scruff of the neck.

Instantly Dhung let out a scream that might have been heard in Amiocap – a scream that brought Sloo rushing from the cave.

'He is killing me,' shrieked Dhung, and at that the cave woman turned upon Tanar with flashing eyes and a face distorted with rage.

'Wait,' said Tanar, in a calm voice. 'I was not hurting the child. He was hurling rocks at his sister and I stopped him.'

'What business have you to stop him?' demanded Sloo. 'She is his sister, he has a right to hurl rocks at her if he chooses.'

'But he might have struck her, and if he had she would have fallen to her death below.'

'What if she did? That is none of your business,' snapped Sloo, and grabbing Dhung by his long hair she cuffed his ears and dragged him into the interior of the cave, where for a long time Tanar could hear blows and screams, mingled with the sharp tongue of Sloo and the curses of Scurv.

But finally these died down to silence, permitting the sounds of other domestic brawls from various parts of the cliff village to reach the ears of the disgusted Sarian.

Far below him Tanar saw the girl, Gura, washing the earthenware vessel in a little stream, after which she filled it with fresh water and lifted the heavy burden to her head. He wondered at the ease with which she carried the great weight and was at a loss to know how she intended to scale the precipitous cliff and the rickety, makeshift ladders with her heavy load. Watching her progress with considerable interest he saw her ascend the lowest ladder, apparently with as great ease and agility as though she was unburdened. Up she came, balancing the receptacle with no evident effort.

As he watched her he saw a man ascending also, but several ledges higher than the girl. The fellow came swiftly and noiselessly to the very ledge where Tanar stood. Paying no attention to the Sarian, he slunk cautiously along the ledge to the mouth of the cave next to that of Scurv. Drawing his stone knife from his loin cloth he crept within, and a moment later Tanar heard the sounds of screams and curses and then two men rolled from the mouth of the cave, locked in a deadly embrace. One of them was the fellow whom Tanar had just seen enter the cave. The other was a younger man and smaller and less powerful than his antagonist. They were slashing desperately at one another with their stone knives, but the duel seemed to be resulting in more noise than damage.

At this juncture, a woman came running from the cave. She was armed with the leg bone of a thag and with this she sought to belabor the older man, striking vicious blows at his head and body.

This attack seemed to infuriate the fellow to the point of madness, and, rather than incapacitating him, urged him on to redoubled efforts.

Presently he succeeded in grasping the knife hand of his opponent and an instant later he had driven his own blade into the heart of his opponent.

With a scream of anguish the woman struck again at the older man's head, but she missed her target and her weapon was splintered on the stone of the ledge. The victor leaped to his feet and seizing the body of his opponent hurled it over the cliff, and then grabbing the woman by the hair he dragged her about, shrieking and cursing, as he sought for some missile wherewith to belabor her.

As Tanar stood watching the disgusting spectacle he became aware that someone was standing beside him and, turning, he saw that Gura had returned. She stood there straight as an arrow, balancing the water vessel upon her dead.

'It is terrible,' said Tanar, nodding toward the battling couple.

Gura shrugged indifferently. 'It is nothing,' she said. 'Her mate returned unexpectedly. That is all.'

'You mean,' asked Tanar, 'that this fellow is her mate and that the other was not?'

'Certainly,' said Gura, 'but they all do it. What can you expect where there is nothing but hate,' and walking to the entrance to her father's cave she set the water vessel down within the shadows just inside the entrance. Then she sat down and leaned her back against the cliff, paying no more attention to the matrimonial difficulties of her neighbor.

Tanar, for the first time, noticed the girl particularly. He saw that she had neither the cunning expression that characterized Jude and all of the other Himeans he had seen; nor were there the lines of habitual irritation and malice upon her face; instead it reflected an innate sadness and he guessed that she looked much like her mother might have when she was Gura's age.

Tanar crossed the ledge and sat down beside her. 'Do your people always quarrel thus?' he asked.

'Always,' replied Gura.

'Why?' he asked.

'I do not know,' she replied. 'They take their mates for life and are permitted but one and though both men and women have a choice in the selection of their mates they never seem to be satisfied with one another and are always quarreling, usually because neither one nor the other is faithful. Do the men and women quarrel thus in the land from which you come?'

'No,' replied Tanar. 'They do not. If they did they would be thrown out of the tribe.'

'But suppose that they find that they do not like one another?' insisted the girl.

'Then they do not live together,' replied Tanar. 'They separate and if they care to they find other mates.'

'That is wicked,' said Gura. 'We would kill any of our people who did such a thing.'

Tanar shrugged and laughed.

'At least we are all a very happy people,' he said, 'which is more than you can say for yourselves, and, after all, happiness, it seems to me, is everything.'

The girl thought for some time, seemingly studying an idea that was new to her.

'Perhaps you are right,' she said, presently. 'Nothing could be worse than the life that we live. My mother tells me that it was not thus in her country, but now she is as bad as the rest.'

'Your mother is not a Himean?' asked Tanar.

'No, she is from Amiocap. My father captured her there when she was young.'

'That accounts for the difference,' mused Tanar.

'What difference?' she asked. 'What do you mean?'

'I mean that you are not like the others, Gura,' he replied. 'You neither look like them nor act like them – neither you nor your brother, Balal.'

'Our mother is an Amiocapian,' she replied. 'Perhaps we inherited something from her and then again, and most important, we are young and, as yet, have no mates. When that time comes we shall grow to be like the others, just as our mother has grown to be like them.'

'Do many of your men take their mates from Amiocap?' asked Tanar.

'Many try to, but few succeed for as a rule they are driven away or killed by the Amiocapian warriors. They have a landing place upon the coast of Amiocap in a dark cave beneath a high cliff and of ten Himean warriors who land there scarce one returns, and he not always with an Amiocapian mate. There is a tribe living along our coast that has grown rich by crossing to Amiocap and bringing back the canoes of the warriors, who have crossed for mates and have died at the hands of the Amiocapian warriors.'

For a few moments she was silent, absorbed in thought. 'I should like to go to Amiocap,' she mused, presently.

'Why?' asked Tanar.

'Perhaps I should find there a mate with whom I might be happy,' she said.

Tanar shook his head sadly. 'That is impossible, Gura,' he said.

'Why?' she demanded. 'Am I not beautiful enough for the Amiocapian warriors?'

'Yes,' he replied, 'you are very beautiful, but if you went to Amiocap they would kill you.'

'Why?' she demanded again.

'Because, although your mother is an Amiocapian, your father is not,' explained Tanar.

'That is their law?' asked Gura, sadly.

'Yes,' replied Tanar.

'Well,' she said with a sigh, 'then I suppose I must remain here and seek a mate whom I shall learn to hate and bring children into the world who will hate us both.'

'It is not a pleasant outlook,' said Tanar.

'No,' she said, and then after a pause, 'unless—'

'Unless, what?' asked the Sarian.

'Nothing,' said Gura.

For a time they sat in silence, each occupied with his own thoughts, Tanar's being filled to the exclusion of all else by the face and figure of Stellara.

Presently the girl looked up at him. 'What are you going to do after you find Jude?' she asked.

'I am going to kill him,' replied Tanar.

'And then?' she queried.

'I do not know,' said the Sarian. 'If I find the one whom I believe to be with Jude we shall try to return to Amiocap.'

'Why do you not remain here?' asked Gura. 'I wish that you would.'

Tanar shuddered. 'I would rather die,' he said.

'I do not blame you much,' said the girl, 'but I believe there is a way in which you might be happy even in Hime.'

'How?' asked Tanar.

Gura did not answer and he saw tears come to her eyes. Then she arose hurriedly and entered the cave.

Tanar thought that Scurv would never be done with his sleep. He wanted to talk to him and arrange for a guide to the village of. Jude, but it was Sloo who first emerged from the cave.

She eyed him sullenly. 'You still here?' she demanded.

'I am waiting for Scurv to send a guide to direct me to the village of Jude,' replied the Sarian. 'I shall not remain here an instant longer than is necessary.'

'That will be too long,' growled Sloo, and turning on her heels she reentered the cave.

Presently Balal emerged, rubbing his eyes. 'When will Scurv send me on my way?' demanded Tanar.

'I do not know,' replied the youth. 'He has just awakened. When he comes out you should speak to him about it. He has just sent me to fetch the skin of the codon you killed. He was very angry to think that I left it lying in the forest.'

After Balal departed, Tanar sat with his own thoughts for a long while.

Presently Gura came from the cave. She appeared frightened and excited. She came close to Tanar and, kneeling, placed her lips close to his ear. 'You must escape at once,' she said, in a low whisper. 'Scurv is going to kill you. That is why he sent Balal away.'

'But why does he want to kill me?' demanded Tanar. 'I saved the life of his son and I have only asked that he direct me to the village of Jude.'

'He thinks Sloo is in love with you,' explained Gura, 'for when he awakened she was not in the cave. She was out here upon the ledge with you.'

Tanar laughed. 'Sloo made it very plain to me that she did not like me,' he said, 'and wanted me to be gone.'

'I believe you,' said Gura, 'but Scurv, filled with suspicion and hatred and a guilty conscience, is anxious to believe anything bad that he can of Sloo, and as he does not wish to be convinced that he is wrong it stands to reason that nothing can convince him, so that your only hope is in flight.'

'Thank you, Gura,' said Tanar. 'I shall go at once.'

'No, that will not do,' said the girl. 'Scurv is coming out here immediately.

He would miss you, possibly before you could get out of sight, and in a moment he could muster a hundred warriors to pursue you, and furthermore you have no proper weapons with which to start out in search of Jude.'

'Perhaps you have a better plan, then,' said Tanar.

'I have,' said the girl. 'Listen! Do you see where the stream enters the jungle,' and she pointed across the clearing at the foot of the cliff toward the edge of a dark forest.

'Yes,' said Tanar, 'I see.'

'I shall descend now and hide there in a large tree beside the stream. When Scurv comes out, tell him that you saw a deer there and ask him to loan you weapons, so that you may go and kill it. Meat is always welcome and he will postpone his attack upon you until you have returned with the carcass of your kill, but you will not return. When you enter the forest I shall be there to direct you to the village of Jude.'

'Why are you doing this, Gura?' demanded Tanar.

'Never mind about that,' said the girl. 'Only do as I say. There is no time to lose as Scurv may come out from the cave at any moment,' and without further words she commenced the descent of the cliff face.

Tanar watched her as, with the agility and grace of a chamois, the girl, oftentimes disdaining ladders, leaped lightly from ledge to ledge. Almost before he could realize it she was at the bottom of the cliff and moving swiftly toward the forest beyond, the foliage of which had scarcely closed about her when Scurv emerged from the cave. Directly behind him were Sloo and Dhung, and Tanar saw that each carried a club.

'I am glad you came out now,' said Tanar, losing no time, for he sensed that the three were bent upon immediate attack.

'Why?' growled Scurv.

'I just saw a deer at the edge of the forest. If you will let me take weapons, perhaps I can repay your hospitality by bringing you the carcass.'

Scurv hesitated, his stupid mind requiring time to readjust itself and change from one line of thought to another, but Sloo was quick to see the advantage of utilizing the unwelcome guest and she was willing to delay his murder until he had brought back his kill. 'Get weapons,' she said to Dhung, 'and let the stranger fetch the deer.'

Scurv scratched his head, still in a quandary, and before he had made up his mind one way or the other, Dhung reappeared with a lance and a stone knife, which, instead of handing to Tanar, he threw at him, but the Sarian caught the weapons, and, without awaiting further permission, clambered down the ladder to the next ledge and from thence downward to the ground. Several of the villagers, recognizing him as a stranger, sought to interfere with him, but Scurv, standing upon the ledge high above watching his descent, bellowed commands that he be left alone, and presently the Sarian was crossing the open towards the jungle.

Just inside the concealing verdure of the forest he was accosted by Gura, who was perched upon the limb of a tree above him.

'Your warning came just in time, Gura,' said the man, 'for Scurv and Sloo and Dhung came out almost immediately, armed and ready to kill me.'

'I knew that they would,' she said, 'and I am glad that they will be disappointed, especially Dhung – the little beast! He begged to be allowed to torture you.'

'It does not seem possible that he can be your brother,' said Tanar.

'He is just like Scurv's mother,' said the girl. 'I knew her before she was killed. She was a most terrible old woman, and Dhung has inherited all of her venom and none of the kindly blood of the Amiocapians, which flows in the veins of my mother, despite the change that her horrid life has brought over her.'

'And now,' said Tanar, 'point the way to Jude's village and I shall be gone. Never, Gura, can I repay you for your kindness to me – a kindness which I can only explain on the strength of the Amiocapian blood which is in you. I shall never see you again, Gura, but I shall carry the recollection of your image and your kindness always in my heart.'

'I am going with you,' said Gura.

'You cannot do that,' said Tanar.

'How else may I guide you to the village of Jude then?' she demanded.

'You do not have to guide me; only tell me the direction in which it lies and I shall find it,' replied Tanar.

'I am going with you,' said the girl, determinedly. 'There is only hate and misery in the cave of my father. I would rather be with you.'

'But that cannot be, Gura,' said Tanar.

'If I went back now to the cave of Scurv he would suspect me of having aided your escape and they would all beat me. Come, we cannot waste time here for if you do not return quickly, Scurv will become suspicious and set out upon your trail.' She had dropped to the ground beside him and now she started off into the forest.

'Have it as you wish, then, Gura,' said Tanar, 'but I am afraid that you are going to regret your act – I am afraid that we are both going to regret it.'

'At least I shall have a little happiness in life,' said the girl, 'and if I have that I shall be willing to die.'

'Wait,' said Tanar, 'in which direction does the village of Jude lie?' The girl pointed. 'Very well,' said Tanar, 'instead of going on the ground and leaving our spoor plainly marked for Scurv to follow, we shall take to the trees, for after having watched you descend the cliff I know that you must be able to travel as rapidly among the branches as you do upon the ground.'

'I have never done it,' said the girl, 'but wherever you go I shall follow.'

Although Tanar had been loath to permit the girl to accompany him, nevertheless he found that her companionship made what would have been otherwise a lonely adventure far from unpleasant.

12

'I Hate You!'

The companions of Bohar the Bloody had not waited long for him after he had set out in pursuit of Stellara and had not returned. They hastened the work upon their boat to early completion, and, storing provisions and water, sailed out of the cove on the shores of which they had constructed their craft and bore away for Korsar with no regret for Bohar, whom they all cordially hated.

The very storm that had come near to driving Tanar past the island of Hime bore the Korsars down upon the opposite end, carried away their rude sail and finally dashed their craft, a total wreck, upon the rocks at the upper end of Hime.

The loss of their boat, their provisions and one of their number, who was smashed against a rock and drowned, left the remaining Korsars in even a more savage mood than was customary among them, and the fact that the part of the island upon which they were wrecked afforded no timber suitable for the construction of a boat made it necessary for them to cross over land to the opposite shore.

They were faced now with the necessity of entering a land filled with enemies in search of food and material for a new craft, and, to cap the climax of their misfortune, they found themselves with wet powder and forced to defend themselves, if necessity arose, with daggers and cutlasses alone.

The majority of them being old sailors they were well aware of where they were and even knew a great deal concerning the geography of Hime and the manners and customs of its people, for most of them had accompanied raiding parties into the interior on many occasions when the Korsar ships had fallen upon the island to steal furs and hides, in the perfect curing and tanning of which the Himean women were adept with the result that Himean furs and skins brought high prices in Korsar.

A council of the older sailors decided then to set off across country toward a harbor on the far side of the island, where the timber of an adjoining forest would afford them the material for building another craft with the added possibility of the arrival of a Korsar raider.

As these disgruntled men plodded wearily across the island of Hime, Jude led the reluctant Stellara toward his village, and Gura guided Tanar in the same direction.

Jude had been compelled to make wide detours to avoid unfriendly villagers; nor had Stellara's unwilling feet greatly accelerated his pace, for she constantly hung back, and, though he no longer had to carry her, he had found it necessary to make a leather thong fast about her neck and lead her along in this fashion to prevent the numerous, sudden breaks for liberty that she had made before he had devised this scheme.

Often she pulled back, refusing to go further, saying that she was tired and insisting upon lying down to rest, for in her heart she knew that wherever Jude or another took her, Tanar would seek her out.

Already in her mind's eyes she could see him upon the trail behind them and she hoped to delay Jude's march sufficiently so that the Sarian would overtake them before they reached his village and the protection of his tribe.

Gura was happy. Never before in all her life had she been so happy, and she saw in the end of their journey a possible end to this happiness and so she did not lead Tanar in a direct line to Carn, the village of Jude, but led him hither and thither upon various excuses so that she might have him to herself for as long a time as possible. She found in his companionship a gentleness and an understanding that she had never known in all her life before.

It was not love that Gura felt for Tanar, but something that might have easily been translated into love had the Sarian's own passion been aroused toward the girl, but his love for Stellara precluded such a possibility and while he found pleasure in the company of Gura he was yet madly impatient to continue directly upon the trail of Jude that he might rescue Stellara and have her for himself once more.

The village of Carn is not a cliff village, as is Garb, the village of Scurv. It consists of houses built of stone and clay and, entirely surrounded by a high wall, it stands upon the top of a lofty mesa protected upon all sides by steep cliffs, and overlooking upon one hand the forests and hills of Hime, and upon the other the broad expanse of the Korsar Az, or Sea of Korsar.

Up the steep cliffs toward Carn climbed Jude, dragging Stellara behind him. It was a long and arduous climb and when they reached the summit Jude was glad to stop and rest. He also had some planning to do, since in the village upon the mesa Jude had left a mate, and now he was thinking of some plan whereby he might rid himself of her, but the only plan that Jude could devise was to sneak into the city and murder her. But what was he to do with Stellara in the meantime? And then a happy thought occurred to him.

He knew a cave that lay just below the summit of the cliff and not far distant and toward this he took Stellara, and when they had arrived at it he bound her ankles and her wrists.

'I shall not leave you here long,' he said. 'Presently I shall return and take you into the village of Carn as my mate. Do not be afraid. There are few wild beasts upon the mesa, and I shall return long before any one can find you.'

'Do not hurry,' said Stellara. 'I shall welcome the wild beast that reaches me before you return.'

'You will think differently after you have been the mate of Jude for a while,' said the man, and then he left her and hurried toward the walled village of Carn.

Struggling to a sitting posture Stellara could look out across the country that lay at the foot of the cliff and presently, below her, she saw a man and a woman emerge from the forest.

For a moment her heart stood still, for the instant that her eyes alighted upon him she recognized the man as Tanar. A cry of welcome was upon her lips when a new thought stilled her tongue.

Who was the girl with Tanar? Stellara saw how close she walked to him and she saw her look up into his face and though she was too far away to see the girl's eyes or her expression, there was something in the attitude of the slim body that denoted worship, and Stellara turned her face and buried it against the cold wall of the cave and burst into tears.

Gura pointed upward toward the high mesa. 'There,' she said, 'just beyond the summit of that cliff lies Carn, the village where Jude lives, but if we enter it you will be killed and perhaps I, too, if the women get me first.'

Tanar, who was examining the ground at his feet, seemed not to hear the girl's words. 'Someone has passed just ahead of us,' he said; 'a man and a woman. I can see the imprints of their feet. The grasses that were crushed beneath their sandals are still rising slowly – a man and a woman – and one of them was Stellara and the other Jude.'

'Who is Stellara?' asked the girl.

'My mate,' replied Tanar.

The habitual expression of sadness that had marked Gura's face since childhood, but which had been supplanted by a radiant happiness since she had left the village of Garb with Tanar, returned as with tear-filled eyes she choked back a sob, which went unnoticed by the Sarian as he eagerly searched the ground ahead of them. And in the cave above them warm tears bathed the unhappy cheeks of Stellara, but the urge of love soon drew her eyes back to Tanar just at the moment that he turned and called Gura's attention to the well marked spoor he was following.

The eyes of the Sarian noted the despair in the face of his companion and the tears in her eyes.

'Gura!' he cried. 'What is the matter? Why do you cry?' and impulsively he stepped close to her and put a friendly arm about her shoulders, and Gura, unnerved by kindness, buried her face upon his breast and wept. And this was what Stellara saw – this scene was what love and jealousy put their own interpretation upon – and the eyes of the Amiocapian maiden flashed with hurt pride and anger.

'Why do you cry, Gura?' demanded Tanar.

'Do not ask me,' begged the girl. 'It is nothing. Perhaps I am tired; perhaps I am afraid. But now we may not think of either fatigue or fear, for if Jude is taking your mate toward the village of Carn we must hasten to rescue her before it is too late.'

'You are right,' exclaimed Tanar. 'We must not delay,' and, followed by Gura, he ran swiftly toward the base of the cliff, tracing the spoor of Jude and Stellara where it led to the precarious ascent of the cliffside. And as they hastened on, brutal eyes watched them from the edge of the jungle from which they had themselves so recently emerged.

Where the steep ascent topped the summit of the cliff bare rock gave back no clue to the direction that Jude had taken, but twenty yards further on where the soft ground commenced again Tanar picked up the tracks of the man to which he called Gura's attention.

'Jude's footprints are here alone,' he said.

'Perhaps the woman refused to go further and he was forced to carry her,' suggested Gura.

'That is doubtless the fact,' said Tanar, and he hastened onward along the plain trail left by the Himean.

The way led now along a well marked trail, which ran through a considerable area of bushes that grew considerably higher than a man's head, so that nothing was visible upon either side and only for short distances ahead of them and behind them along the winding trail. But Tanar did not slacken his speed, his sole aim being to overhaul the Himean before he reached his village.

As Tanar and Gura had capped the summit of the cliff and disappeared from view, eighteen hairy men came into view from the forest and followed their trail toward the foot of the cliff.

They were bushy whiskered fellows with gay sashes around their waists and equally brilliant cloths about their heads. Huge pistols and knives bristled from their waist cloths, and cutlasses dangled from their hips – fate had brought these survivors of The Cid's ship to the foot of the cliffs below the village of Carn at almost the same moment that Tanar had arrived. With sensations of surprise, not unmingled with awe, they had recognized the

Sarian who had been a prisoner upon the ship and whom they thought they had seen killed by their musket fire at the edge of the natural well upon the island of Amiocap.

The Korsars, prompted by the pernicious stubbornness of ignorance, were moved by a common impulse to recapture Tanar. And with this end in view they waited until Gura and the Sarian had disappeared beyond the summit of the cliff, when they started in pursuit.

The walls of Carn lie no great distance from the edge of the table-land upon which it stands. In timeless Pellucidar events, which are in reality far separated, seem to follow closely, one upon the heels of another, and for this reason one may not say how long Jude was in the village of Carn, or whether he had had time to carry out the horrid purpose which had taken him thither, but the fact remained that as Tanar and Gura reached the edge of the bushes and looked across the clearing toward the walls of Carn they saw Jude sneaking from the city. Could they have seen his face they might have noticed a malicious leer of triumph and could they have known the purpose that had taken him thus stealthily to his native village they might have reconstructed the scenes of the bloody episode which had just been enacted within the house of the Himean. But Tanar only saw that Jude, whom he sought, was coming toward him, and that Stellara was not with him.

The Sarian drew Gura back into the concealment of the bushes that lined the trail which Jude was approaching.

On came the Himean and while Tanar awaited his coming, the Korsars were making their clumsy ascent of the cliff, while Stellara, sick from jealousy and unhappiness, leaned disconsolately against the cold stone of her prison cave.

Jude, unconscious of danger, hastened back toward the spot where he had left Stellara and as he came opposite Tanar, the Sarian leaped upon him.

The Himean reached for his knife, but he was helpless in the grasp of Tanar, whose steel fingers closed about his wrists with such strength that Jude dropped his weapon with a cry of pain as he felt both of his arms crushed beneath the pressure of the Sarian's grip.

'What do you want?' he cried. 'Why do you attack me?'

'Where is Stellara?' demanded Tanar.

'I do not know,' replied Jude. 'I have not seen her.'

'You lie,' said Tanar. 'I have followed her tracks and yours to the summit of the cliff. Where is she?' He drew his knife. 'Tell me, or die.'

'I left her at the edge of the cliff while I went to Carn to arrange to have her received in a friendly manner. I did it all for her protection, Tanar. She wanted to go back to Korsar and I was but helping her.'

'Again you lie,' said the Sarian; 'but lead me to her and we shall hear her version of the story.'

The Himean held back until the point of Tanar's knife pressed against his ribs; then he gave in. 'If I lead you to her will you promise not to kill me?' asked Jude. 'Will you let me return in peace to my village?'

'I shall make no promises until I learn from her own lips how you have treated her,' replied the Sarian.

'She has not been harmed,' said Jude. 'I swear it.'

'Then lead me to her,' insisted Tanar.

Sullenly the Himean guided them back along the path toward the cave where he had left Stellara, while at the other edge of the bushes eighteen Korsars, warned by the noise of their approach, halted, listening, and presently melted silently from view in the surrounding shrubbery.

They saw Jude and Gura and Tanar emerge from the bushes, but they did not attack them; they waited to see for what purpose they had returned. They saw them disappear over the edge of the cliff at a short distance from the summit of the trail that led down into the valley. And then they emerged from their hiding places and followed cautiously after them.

Jude led Tanar and Gura to the cave where Stellara lay and when Tanar saw her, her dear wrists and ankles bound with thongs and her cheeks still wet with tears, he sprang forward and gathered her into his arms.

'Stellara!' he cried. 'My darling!' But the girl turned her face away from him.

'Do not touch me,' she cried. 'I hate you.'

'Stellara!' he exclaimed in amazement. 'What has happened?' But before she could reply they were startled by a hoarse command from behind them, and, turning, found themselves looking into the muzzles of the pistols of eighteen Korsars.

'Surrender, Sarian!' cried the leader of the Korsars.

Gazing into the muzzles of about thirty-six huge pistols, which equally menaced the lives of Stellara and Gura, Tanar saw no immediate alternative but to surrender.

'What do you intend to do with us if we do surrender?' he demanded.

'That we shall decide later,' growled the spokesman for the Korsars.

'Do you expect ever to return to Korsar?' asked Tanar.

'What is that to you, Sarian?' demanded the Korsar.

'It has a considerable bearing upon whether or not we surrender,' replied Tanar. 'You have tried to kill me before and you have found that I am hard to kill. I know something about your weapons and your powder and I know that even at such close quarters I may be able to kill some of you before you can kill me. But if you answer my question fairly and honestly and if your answer is satisfactory I shall surrender.'

At Tanar's mention of his knowledge of their powder the Korsars immediately assumed that he knew that it was wet, whereas he was only alluding to its uniformly poor quality and so the spokesman decided that it would be better to temporize for the time being at least. 'As soon as we can build a boat we shall return to Korsar,' he said, 'unless in the meantime a Korsar ship anchors in the bay of Carn.'

'Good,' commented the Sarian. 'If you will promise to return the daughter of The Cid safe and unharmed to her people in Korsar I will surrender. And you must also promise that no harm shall befall this other girl and that she shall be permitted to go with you in safety to Korsar or to remain here among her own people as she desires.'

'How about the other man?' demanded the Korsar.

'You may kill him when you kill me,' replied Tanar.

Stellara's eyes widened in fearful apprehension as she heard the words of the Sarian and she found that jealousy was no match for true love.

'Very well,' said the Korsar. 'We accept the condition. The women shall return to Korsar with us, and you two men shall die.'

'Oh, no,' begged Jude. 'I do not wish to die. I am a Himean. Carn is my home. You Korsars come there often to trade. Spare me and I shall see that you are furnished with more hides than you can pack in your boat, after you have built it.'

The leader of the band laughed in his face. 'Eighteen of us can take what we choose from the village of Carn,' he said. 'We are not such fools as to spare you that you may go and warn your people.'

'Then take me along as a prisoner,' wailed Jude.

'And have to feed you and watch you all the time? No, you are worth more to us dead than alive.'

As Jude spoke he had edged over into the mouth of the cave, where he stood half behind Stellara as though taking shelter at the expense of the girl.

With a gesture of disgust, Tanar turned toward the Korsars. 'Come,' he said, impatiently. 'If the bargain is satisfactory there is no use in discussing it further. Kill us, and take the women in safety to Korsar. You have given your word.'

At the instant that Tanar concluded his appeal to the Korsars, Jude turned before any one could prevent him and disappeared into the cave behind him. Instantly Korsars leaped in pursuit, while the others awaited impatiently their return with Jude. But when they emerged they were empty handed.

'He escaped us,' said one of those who had gone after the Himean. 'This cave is the mouth of a dark, long tunnel with many branches. We could see nothing and fearful that we should become lost, we returned to the opening. It would be useless to try to find the man within unless one was familiar with the tunnel which honeycombs the cliff beyond this cave. We had better kill this one immediately before he has an opportunity to escape too,' and the fellow raised his pistol and aimed it at Tanar, possibly hoping that his powder had dried since they had set out from the beach upon the opposite side of the island.

'Stop!' cried Stellara, jumping in front of the man. 'As you all know I am the daughter of The Cid. If you return me to him in safety you will be well rewarded. I will see to that. You all knew that The Cid was taking this man to Korsar, but possibly you did not know why.'

'No,' said one of the Korsars, who, being only common sailors, had had no knowledge of the plans of their commander.

'He knows how to make firearms and powder far superior to ours and The Cid was taking him back to Korsar that he might teach the Korsars the secrets of powder making and the manufacture of weapons, that we do not know. If you kill him The Cid will be furious with you, and you all know what it means to anger The Cid. But if you return him, also, to Korsar your reward will be much larger.'

'How do we know that The Cid is alive?' demanded one of the Korsars; 'and if he is not, who is there who will pay reward for your return, or for the return of this man?'

'The Cid is a better sailor than Bohar the Bloody – that you all know. And if Bohar the Bloody brought his boat safely through to Amiocap there is little doubt but that The Cid took his safely to Korsar. But even if he did not, even if The Cid perished, still will you receive your reward if you return me to Korsar.'

'Who will pay it?' demanded one of the sailors.

'Bulf,' replied Stellara.

'Why should Bulf pay a reward for your return?' asked the Korsar.

'Because I am to be his mate. It was The Cid's wish and his.'

By no change of expression did the Sarian reveal the pain that these words inflicted like a knife thrust through his heart. He merely stood with his arms folded, looking straight ahead. Gura's eyes were wide in surprise as she looked, first at Stellara and then at Tanar, for she recalled that the latter had told her that Stellara was his mate, and she had known, with woman's intuition, how much the man loved this woman. Gura was mystified and, too, she was saddened because she guessed the pain that Stellara's words had inflicted upon Tanar, and so her kind heart prompted her to move close to Tanar's side and to lay her hand gently upon his arm in mute expression of sympathy.

For a time the Korsars discussed Stellara's proposition in low whispers and then the spokesman addressed her. 'But if The Cid is dead there will be no one to reward us for returning the Sarian; therefore, we might as well kill him for there will be enough mouths to feed during the long journey to Korsar.'

'You do not know that The Cid is dead,' insisted Stellara; 'but if he is, who is there better fitted to be chief of the Korsars than Bulf? And if he is chief he will reward you for returning this man when I explain to him the purpose for which he was brought back to Korsar.'

'Well,' said the Korsar, scratching his head, 'perhaps you are right. He may be more valuable to us alive than dead. If he will promise to help us work the boat and not try to escape we shall take him with us. But how about the girl here?'

'Keep her until we are ready to sail,' growled one of the other Korsars, 'and then turn her loose.'

'If you wish to receive any reward for my return you will do nothing of the sort,' said Stellara with finality, and then to Gura, 'What do you wish to do?' Her voice was cold and haughty.

'Where Tanar goes there I wish to go,' replied Gura.

Stellara's eyes narrowed and for an instant they flashed fire, but immediately they resumed their natural, kindly expression, though tinged with sadness. 'Very well, then,' she said, turning sadly away, 'the girl must return with us to Korsar.'

The sailors discussed this question at some length and most of them were opposed to it, but when Stellara insisted and assured them of a still greater reward they finally consented, though with much grumbling.

The Korsars marched boldly across the mesa, past the walls of Carn, their harquebuses ready in their hands, knowing full well the fear of them that past raids had implanted in the breasts of the Himeans. But they did not seek to plunder or demand tribute for they still feared that their powder was useless.

As they reached the opposite side of the mesa, where they could look out across the bay of Carn, a hoarse shout of pleasure arose from the throats of the Korsars, for there, at anchor in the bay, lay a Korsar ship. Not knowing how soon the vessel might weigh anchor and depart, the Korsars fairly tumbled down the precipitous trail to the beach, while in their rear the puzzled villagers watched them over the top of the wall of Carn until the last man had disappeared beyond the summit of the cliff.

Rushing to the edge of the water the Korsars tried to discharge their harquebuses to attract attention from the vessel. A few of the charges had dried and the resulting explosion awakened signs of life upon the anchored ship. The sailors on the shore tore off sashes and handkerchiefs, which they waved frantically as signals of distress, and presently they were rewarded by the sight of the lowering of a boat from the vessel.

Within speaking distance of the shore the boat came to a stop and an officer hailed the men on shore.

'Who are you,' he demanded, 'and what do you want?'

'We are part of the crew of the ship of The Cid,' replied the sailors' spokes-man. 'Our ship was wrecked in mid-ocean and we made our way to Amio-cap and then to Hime, but here we lost the boat that we built upon Amiocap.'

Assured that the men were Korsars the officer commanded that the boat move in closer to the shore and finally it was beached close to where the party stood awaiting its coming.

The brief greetings and explanations over, the officer took them all aboard and shortly afterward Tanar of Pellucidar found himself again upon a Korsar ship of war.

The commander of the ship knew Stellara, and after questioning them carefully he approved her plan and agreed to take Tanar and Gura back to Korsar with them.

Following their interview with the officer, Tanar found himself momen-tarily alone with Stellara.

'Stellara!' he said. 'What change has come over you?'

She turned and looked at him coldly. 'In Amiocap you were well enough,' she said, 'but in Korsar you would be only a naked barbarian,' and, turning, she walked away from him without another word.

13

Prisoners

The voyage to Korsar was uneventful and during its entire extent Tanar saw nothing of either Stellara or Gura for, although he was not confined in the dark hold, he was not permitted above the first deck, and although he often looked up at the higher deck at the stern of the ship he never caught a glimpse of either of the girls, from which he concluded that Gura was con-fined in one of the cabins and that Stellara deliberately avoided him or any sight of him.

As they approached the coast of Korsar Tanar saw a level country curv-ing upward into the mist of the distance. He thought that far away he dis-cerned the outlines of hills, but of that he could not be certain. He saw cultivated fields and patches of forest land and a river running down to the sea – a broad, winding river upon the shore of which a city lay, inland a little from the ocean. There was no harbor at this point upon the coast, but the ship made directly for the mouth of the river, up which it sailed toward the city, which, as he approached it, he saw far surpassed in size and the pretentiousness of its buildings any habitation of man that he had ever seen upon the surface of Pellucidar, not even excepting the new capital of the confederated kingdoms of Pellucidar that the Emperor David was building.

Most of the buildings were white with red-tiled roofs, and there were some with lofty minarets and domes of various colors – blue and red and gold, the last shining in the sunlight like the jewels in the diadem of Dian the Empress.

Where the river widened the town had been built and here there rode at anchor a great fleet of ships of war and many lesser craft – fishing boats and river boats and barges. The street along the riverfront was lined with shops and alive with people.

As their ship approached cannon boomed from the deck of the anchored warships, and the salute was returned by their own craft, which finally came to anchor in midstream, opposite the city.

Small boats put out from the shore and were paddled rapidly toward the warship, which also lowered some of her own boats, into one of which Tanar was ordered under charge of an officer and a couple of sailors. As he was taken to shore and marched along the street he excited considerable attention among the crowds through which they passed, for he was immediately recognized as a barbarian captive from some uncivilized quarter of Pellucidar.

During the debarkation Tanar had seen nothing of either Stellara or Gura and now he wondered if he was ever to see them again. His mind was filled with the same sad thoughts that had been his companions during the entire course of the long journey from Hime to Korsar and which had finally convinced him that he had never known the true Stellara until she had avowed herself upon the deck of the ship in the harbor of Carn. Yes, he was all right upon Amiocap, but in Korsar he was only a naked savage, and this fact was borne in upon him now by the convincing evidence of the haughty contempt with which the natives of Korsar stared at him or exchanged rude jokes at his expense.

It hurt the Sarian's pride to think that he had been so deceived by the woman to whom he had given all his love. He would have staked his life upon his belief that here was the sweetest and purest and most loyal of characters, and to learn at last that she was shallow and insincere cut him to the quick and his suffering was lightened by but a single thought – his unquestioned belief in the sweet and enduring friendship of Gura.

It was with such thoughts that his mind was occupied as he was led into a building along the waterfront, which seemed to be in the nature of a guardhouse.

Here he was turned over to an officer in charge, and, after a few brief questions, two soldiers conducted him into another room, raised a heavy trap door in the floor and bade him descend a rude ladder that led downward into darkness below.

No sooner had his head descended below the floor joists than the door was slammed down above him. He heard the grating of a heavy bolt as the soldiers shut it and then the thud of their footsteps as they left the room above.

Descending slowly for about ten feet Tanar came at last to the surface of a stone floor. His eyes becoming accustomed to the change, he realized that the apartment into which he had descended was not in total darkness, but that daylight filtered into it from a small, barred window near the ceiling. Looking about him he saw that he was the only occupant of the room.

In the wall, opposite the window, he discerned a doorway and crossing to it he saw that it opened into a narrow corridor, running parallel with the length of the room. Looking up and down the corridor he discerned faint patches of light, as though other open doorways lined one side of the hallway.

He was about to enter upon a tour of investigation when the noise of something scurrying along the floor of the corridor attracted his attention, and looking back to his left he saw a dark form creeping toward him. It stood about a foot in height and was, perhaps, three feet long, but in the shadows of the corridor it loomed too indistinctly for him to recognize its details. But presently he saw that it had two shining eyes that seemed to be directed upon him.

As it came boldly forward Tanar stepped back into the room he was about to quit, preferring to meet the thing in the lesser darkness of the apartment rather than in the gloomy corridor, if it was the creature's intent to attack him.

On the thing came and turning into the doorway it stopped and surveyed the Sarian. In his native country Tanar had been familiar with a species of wood rat, which the Sarian considered large, but never in all his life had he dreamed that a rat could grow to the enormous proportions of the hideous thing that confronted him with its bold, gleaming, beady eyes.

Tanar had been disarmed when he had been taken aboard the Korsar ship, but even so he, had no fear of a rodent, even if the thing should elect to attack him, which he doubted. But the ferocious appearance of the rat gave him pause as he thought what the result might be if a number of them should attack a man simultaneously.

Presently the rat, still standing facing him, squealed. For a time there was silence and then the thing squealed again and, as from a great distance, Tanar heard an answering squeal, and then another and another, and presently they grew louder and greater in volume, and he knew that the rat of the

Korsar dungeon was calling its fellows to the attack and the feast.

He looked about him for some weapon of defense, but there was nothing but the bare stone of the floor and the walls. He heard the rat pack coming, and still the scout that had discovered him stood in the doorway, waiting.

But why should he, the man, wait? If he must die, he would die fighting and if he could take the rats as they came, one by one, he might make them pay for their meal and pay dearly. And so, with the agility of a tiger, the man leaped for the rodent, and so sudden and unexpected was his spring that one hand fell upon the loathsome creature before it could escape. With loud squeals it sought to fasten its fangs in his flesh, but the Sarian was too quick and too powerful. His fingers closed once upon the creature's neck. He swung its body around a few times until the neck broke and then he hurled the corpse toward the advancing pack that he could already see in the distance through the dim light in the corridor, in the center of which Tanar now stood awaiting his inevitable doom, but he was prepared to fight until he was dragged down by the creatures.

As he waited he heard a noise behind him and he thought that another pack was taking him in the rear, but as he glanced over his shoulder he saw the figure of a man, standing in front of a doorway further down the corridor.

'Come!' shouted the stranger. 'You will find safety here.' Nor did Tanar lose any time in racing down the corridor to where the man stood, the rats close at his heels.

'Quick, in here,' cried his savior, and seizing Tanar by the arm he dragged him through the doorway into a large room in which there were a dozen or more men.

At the doorway the rat pack stopped, glaring in, but not one of them crossed the threshold.

The room in which he found himself was lighted by two larger windows than that in the room which he had just quitted and in the better light he had an opportunity to examine the man who had rescued him. The fellow was a copper-colored giant with fine features.

As the man turned his face a little more toward the light of the windows, Tanar gave an exclamation of surprise and delight. 'Ja!' he cried, and before Ja could reply to the salutation, another man sprang forward from the far end of the room.

'Tanar!' exclaimed the second man. 'Tanar, the son of Ghak!' As the Sarian wheeled he found himself standing face to face with David Innes, Emperor of Pellucidar.

'Ja of Anoroc and the Emperor!' cried Tanar. 'What has happened? What brought you here?'

'It is well that we were here,' said Ja, 'and that I heard the rat pack squeal-ing just when I did. These other fellows,' and he nodded toward the remain-ing prisoners, 'haven't brains enough to try to save the newcomers that are incarcerated here. David and I have been trying to pound it into their stupid heads that the more of us there are the safer we shall be from the attacks of the rats, but all they think of is that they are safe now, and so they do not care what becomes of the other poor devils that are shoved down here; nor have they brains enough to look into the future and realize that when some of us are taken out or die there may not be enough left to repel the attacks of the hungry beasts. But tell us, Tanar, where you have been and how you came here at last.'

'It is a long story,' replied the Sarian, 'and first I would hear the story of my Emperor.'

'There is little of interest in the adventures that befell us,' said David, 'but there may be points of great value to us in what I have managed to learn from the Korsars concerning a number of problems that have been puzzling me.

'When we saw the Korsars' fleet sail away with you and others of our people, prisoners aboard them, we were filled with dismay and as we stood upon the shore of the great sea above The Land of Awful Shadow, we were depressed by the hopelessness of ever effecting your rescue. It was then that I determined to risk the venture which is responsible for our being here in the dungeon of the capital of Korsar.

'From all those who volunteered to accompany me I selected Ja, and we took with us to be our pilot a Korsar prisoner named Fitt. Our boat was one of those abandoned by the Korsars in their flight and in it we pursued our course toward Korsar without incident until we were overwhelmed by the most terrific storm that I have ever witnessed.'

'Doubtless the same storm that wrecked the Korsars' fleet that was bear-ing us away,' said Tanar.

'Unquestionably,' said David, 'as you will know in a moment. The storm carried away all our rigging, snapping the mast short off at the deck, and left us helpless except for two pairs of oars.

'As you may know, these great sweeps are so heavy that, as a rule, two or three men handle a single oar, and as there were only three of us we could do little more than paddle slowly along with one man paddling on either side while the third relieved first one and then the other at intervals, and even this could be accomplished only after we had cut the great sweeps down to a size that one man might handle without undue fatigue.

'Fitt had laid a course which my compass showed me to be almost due north and this we followed with little or no deviation after the storm had subsided.

'We slept and ate many times before Fitt announced that we were not far from the island of Amiocap, which he says is half way between the point at which we had embarked and the land of Korsar. We still had ample water and provisions to last us the balance of our journey if we had been equipped with a sail, but the slow progress of paddling threatened to find us facing starvation, or death by thirst, long before we could hope to reach Korsar. With this fate staring us in the face we decided to land on Amiocap and refit our craft, but before we could do so we were overtaken by a Korsar ship and being unable either to escape or defend ourselves, we were taken prisoners.

'The vessel was one of those that had formed the armada of The Cid, and was, as far as they knew, the only one that had survived the storm. Shortly before they had found us they had picked up a boat-load of the survivors of The Cid's ship, including The Cid himself, and from The Cid we learned that you and the other prisoners had doubtless been lost with his vessel, which he said was in a sinking condition at the time that he abandoned it. To my surprise I learned that The Cid had also abandoned his own daughter to her fate and I believe that this cowardly act weighed heavily upon his mind, for he was always taciturn and moody, avoiding the companionship of even his own officers.

'She did not die,' said Tanar. 'We escaped together, the sole survivors, as far as we knew, of The Cid's ship, though later we were captured by the members of another boat crew that had also made the island of Amiocap and with them we were brought to Korsar.'

'In my conversation with The Cid and also with the officers and men of the Korsar ship I sought to sound them on their knowledge of the extent of this sea, which is known as the Korsar Az. Among other things I learned that they possess compasses and are conversant with their use and they told me that to the west they had never sailed to the extreme limits of the Korsar Az, which they state reaches on, a vast body of water, for countless leagues beyond the knowledge of man. But to the east they have followed the shore-line from Korsar southward almost to the shore upon which they landed to attack the empire of Pellucidar.

'Now this suggests, in fact almost proves, that Korsar lies upon the same great continent as the empire of Pellucidar and if we can escape from prison, we may be able to make our way by land back to our own country.'

'But there is that "if,"' said Ja. 'We have eaten and slept many times since they threw us into this dark hole, yet we are no nearer escape now than we were at the moment that they put us here; nor do we even know what fate lies in store for us.'

'These other prisoners tell us,' resumed David, 'that the fact that we were not immediately killed, which is the customary fate of prisoners of war among the Korsars, indicates that they are saving us for some purpose; but what that purpose is I cannot conceive.'

'I can,' said Tanar. 'In fact I am quite sure that I know.'

'And what is it?' demanded Ja.

'They wish us to teach them how to make firearms and powder such as ours,' replied the Sarian. 'But where do you suppose they ever got firearms and powder in the first place?'

'Or the great ships they sail,' added Ja; 'ships that are even larger than those which we build? These things were unknown in Pellucidar before David and Perry came to us, yet the Korsars appear to have known of them and used them always.'

'I have an idea,' said David; 'yet it is such a mad idea that I have almost hesitated to entertain it, much less to express it.'

'What is it?' asked Tanar.

'It was suggested to me in my conversations with the Korsars themselves,' replied the Emperor. 'Without exception they have all assured me that their ancestors came from another world – a world above which the sun did not stand perpetually at zenith, but crossed the heavens regularly, leaving the world in darkness half the time. They say that a part of this world is very cold and that their ancestors, who were seafaring men, became caught with their ships in the frozen waters; that their compasses turned in all directions and became useless to them and that when finally they broke through the ice and sailed away in the direction that they thought was south, they came into Pellucidar, which they found inhabited only by naked savages and wild beasts. And here they set up their city and built new ships, their numbers being augmented from time to time by other seafaring men from this world from which they say they originally came.

'They intermarried with the natives, which in this part of Pellucidar seemed to have been of a very low order.' David paused.

'Well,' asked Tanar, 'what does it all mean?'

'It means,' said David, 'that if their legend is true, or based upon fact, that their ancestors came from the same outer world from which Perry and I came, but by what avenue? – that is the astounding enigma.'

Many times during their incarceration the three men discussed this subject, but never were they able to arrive at any definite solution of the mystery. Food was brought them many times and several times they slept before Korsar soldiers came and took them from the dungeon.

They were led to the palace of The Cid, the architecture of which but tended to increase the mystery of the origin of this strange race in the mind of David Innes, for the building seemed to show indisputable proof of Moorish influence.

Within the palace they were conducted to a large room, comfortably filled with bewhiskered Korsars decked out in their gaudiest raiment, which far surpassed in brilliancy of coloring and ornamentation the comparatively mean clothes they had worn aboard ship. Upon a dais, at one end of the room, a man was seated upon a large, ornately carved chair. It was The Cid, and as David's eyes fell upon him his mind suddenly grasped, for the first time, a significant suggestion in the title of the ruler of the Korsars.

Previously the name had been only a name to David. He had not considered it as a title; nor had it by association awakened any particular train of thought, but now, coupled with the Moorish palace and the carved throne, it did.

The Cid! Rodrigo Diaz de Bivar – El Campeandor – a national hero of eleventh century Spain. What did it mean? His thoughts reverted to the ships of the Korsars – their motley crews with harquebuses and cutlasses – and he recalled the thrilling stories he had read as a boy of the pirates of the Spanish Main. Could it be merely coincidence? Could a nation of people have grown up within the inner world, who so closely resembled the buccaneers of the seventeenth century, or had their forebears in truth found their way hither from the outer crust? David Innes did not know. He was frankly puzzled. But now he was being led to the foot of The Cid's throne and there was no further opportunity for the delightful speculation that had absorbed his mind momentarily.

The cruel, cunning eyes of The Cid looked down upon the three prisoners from out his brutal face. 'The Emperor of Pellucidar!' he sneered. 'The King of Anoroc! The son of the King of Sari!' and then he laughed uproariously. He extended his hand, his fingers parted and curled in a clutching gesture. 'Emperor! King! Prince!' he sneered again, 'and yet here you all are in the clutches of The Cid. Emperor – bah! I, The Cid, am the Emperor of all Pellucidar! You and your naked savages!' He turned on David. 'Who are you to take the title of Emperor? I could crush you all,' and he closed his fingers in a gesture of rough cruelty. 'But I shall not. The Cid is generous and he is grateful, too. You shall have your freedom for a small price that you may easily pay.' He paused as though he expected them to question him, but no one of the three spoke. Suddenly he turned upon David. 'Where did you get your firearms and your powder? Who made them for you?'

'We made them ourselves,' replied David.

'Who taught you to make them?' insisted The Cid. 'But never mind; it is enough that you know and we would know. You may win your liberty by teaching us.'

David could make gunpowder, but whether he could make any better gunpowder than the Korsars he did not know. He had left that to Perry and his apprentices in The Empire, and he knew perfectly well that he could not reconstruct a modern rifle such as was being turned out in the arsenals at

Sari, for he had neither the drawings to make the rifles, nor the machinery, nor the drawings to make the machinery, nor the shops in which to make steel. But nevertheless here was one opportunity for possible freedom that might pave the way to escape and he could not throw it away, either for himself or his companions, by admitting their inability to manufacture modern firearms or improve the powder of the Korsars.

'Well,' demanded The Cid, impatiently, 'what is your answer?'

'We cannot make powder and rifles while a man eats,' replied David; 'nor can we make them from the air or from conversation. We must have materials; we must have factories; we must have trained men. You will sleep many times before we are able to accomplish all this. Are you willing to wait?'

'How many times shall we sleep before you have taught our people to make these things?' demanded The Cid.

David shrugged. 'I do not know,' he said. 'In the first place I must find the proper materials.'

'We have all the materials,' said The Cid. 'We have iron and we have the ingredients for making powder. All that you have to do is to put them together in a better way than we have been able to.'

'You may have the materials, but it is possible that they are not of sufficiently good quality to make the things that will alone satisfy the subjects of the Emperor of Pellucidar. Perhaps your niter is low grade; there may be impurities in your sulphur; or even the charcoal may not be properly prepared; and there are even more important matters to consider in the selection of material and its manufacture into steel suitable for making the firearms of the Pellucidarians.'

'You shall not be hurried,' said The Cid. He turned to a man standing near him. 'See that an officer accompanies these men always,' he said. 'Let them go where they please and do what they please in the prosecution of my orders. Furnish them with laborers if they desire them, but do not let them delay and do not let them escape, upon pain of death.' And thus ended their interview with The Cid of Korsar.

As it chanced, the man to be detailed to watch them was Fitt, the fellow whom David had chosen to accompany him and Ja in their pursuit of the Korsar fleet, and Fitt, having become well acquainted with David and Ja and having experienced nothing but considerate treatment from them, was far from unfriendly, though, like the majority of all other Korsars, he was inclined to be savage and cruel.

As they were passing out of the palace they caught a glimpse of a girl in a chamber that opened onto the corridor in which they were. Fitt, big with the importance of his new position and feeling somewhat like a showman revealing and explaining his wonders to the ignorant and uninitiated, had been describing the various objects of interest that they had passed as well as the personages of importance, and now he nodded in the direction of the room in which they had seen the girl, although they had gone along the corridor so far by this time that they could no longer see her. 'That,' he said, 'is The Cid's daughter.' Tanar stopped in his tracks and turned to Fitt.

'May I speak to her?' he asked.

'You!' cried Fitt. 'You speak to the daughter of The Cid!'

'I know her,' said Tanar. 'We two were left alone on the abandoned ship when it was deserted by its officers and crew. Go and ask her if she will speak to me.'

Fitt hesitated. 'The Cid might not approve,' he said.

'He gave you no orders other than to accompany us,' said David. 'How are we to carry on our work if we are to be prevented from speaking to anyone whom we choose? At least you will be safe in leading us to The Cid's daughter. If she wishes to speak to Tanar the responsibility will not be yours.'

'Perhaps you are right,' said Fitt. 'I will ask her.' He stepped to the doorway of the apartment in which were Stellara and Gura, and now, for the first time, he saw that a man was with them. It was Bulf. The three looked up as he entered.

'There is one here who wishes to speak to The Cid's daughter,' he said, addressing Stellara.

'Who is he?' demanded Bulf.

'He is Tanar, a prisoner of war from Sari.'

'Tell him,' said Stellara, 'that The Cid's daughter does not recall him and cannot grant him an interview.'

As Fitt turned and quit the chamber, Gura's ordinarily sad eyes flashed a look of angry surprise at Stellara.

14

Two Suns

David, Ja, and Tanar were quartered in barracks inside the palace wall and immediately set to work to carry out a plan that David had suggested and which included an inspection, not only of the Korsars' powder factory and the arsenals in which their firearms were manufactured, but also visits to the niter beds, sulphur deposits, charcoal pits and iron mines.

These various excursions for the purpose of inspecting the sources of supply and the methods of obtaining it aroused no suspicion in the mind of the Korsar, though their true purpose was anything other than it appeared to be.

In the first place David had not the slightest intention of teaching the Korsars how to improve their powder, thereby transforming them into a far greater menace to the peace of his empire than they could ever become while handicapped by an inferior grade of gunpowder that failed to explode quite as often as it exploded. These tours of inspection, however, which often took them considerable distances from the city of Korsar, afforded an excuse for delaying the lesson in powder making, while David and his companions sought to concoct some plan of escape that might contain at least the seed of success. Also they gave the three men a better knowledge of the surrounding country, familiarized them with the various trails and acquainted them with the manners and customs of the primitive tribes that carried on the agriculture of Korsar and all of the labor of the mines, niter beds and charcoal burning.

It was not long before they had learned that all the Korsars lived in the city of Korsar and that they numbered about five hundred thousand souls, and, as all labor was performed by slaves, every male Korsar above the age of fifteen was free for military service, while those between ten and fifteen were virtually so since this included the period of their training, during which time they learned all that could be taught them of seamanship and the art of piracy and raiding. David soon came to realize that the ferocity of the Korsars, rather than their number, rendered them a menace to the peace of Pellucidar, but he was positive that with an equal number of ships and men he could overcome them and he was glad that he had taken upon himself this dangerous mission, for the longer the three reconnoitered the environs of Korsar the more convinced they became that escape was possible.

The primitive savages from whom the Korsars had wrested their country and whom they had forced into virtual slavery were of such a low order of intelligence that David felt confident that they could never be successfully utilized as soldiers or fighting men by the Korsars, whom they outnumbered ten to one; their villages, according to his Korsar informant, stretching away into the vast hinterland, to the farthest extremities of which no man had ever penetrated.

The natives themselves spoke of a cold country to the north, in the barren and desolate wastes of which no man could live, and of mountains and forests and plains stretching away into the east and southeast to, as they put it, 'the very shores of Molop Az' – the flaming sea of Pellucidarian legend upon which the land of Pellucidar floats.

This belief of the natives of the uninterrupted extent of the land mass to the south and southeast corroborated David's belief that Korsar lay upon the same continent as Sari, and this belief was further carried out by the distinct sense of perfect orientation which the three men experienced the moment they set foot upon the shores of Korsar; or rather which the born Pellucidarians, Ja and Tanar, experienced, since David did not possess this inborn homing instinct. Had there been an ocean of any considerable extent separating them from the land of their birth, the two Pellucidarians felt confident that they could not have been so certain as to the direction of Sari as they now were.

As their excursions to various points outside the city of Korsar increased in number the watchfulness of Fitt relaxed, so that the three men occasionally found themselves alone together in some remote part of the back country.

Tanar, wounded by the repeated rebuffs of Stellara, sought to convince himself that he did not love her. He tried to make himself believe that she was cruel and hard and unfaithful, but all that he succeeded in accomplishing was to make himself more unhappy, though he hid this from his companions and devoted himself as assiduously as they to planning their escape. It filled his heart with agony to think of going away forever from the vicinity of the woman he loved, even though there was little or no hope that he might see her should he remain, for gossip of the approaching nuptials of Stellara and Bulf was current in the barracks where he was quartered.

The window of the room to which he had been assigned overlooked a portion of the garden of The Cid – a spot of great natural beauty in which trees and flowers and shrubs bordered gravelled pathways and a miniature lake and streamlet sparkled in the sunlight.

Tanar was seldom in his apartment and when he was he ordinarily gave no more than casual attention to the garden beyond the wall, but upon one occasion, after returning from an inspection of an iron mine, he had been left alone with his own sad thoughts, and, seating himself upon the sill of the window, he was gazing down upon the lovely scene below when his attention was attracted by the figure of a girl as she came into view almost directly before him along one of the gravelled paths. She was looking up toward his window and their eyes met simultaneously. It was Gura.

Placing her finger to her lips, cautioning him to silence, she came quickly forward until she reached a point as close to his window as it was possible for her to come.

'There is a gate in the garden wall at the far end of your barracks,' she said in a low whisper attuned to reach his ears. 'Come to it at once.'

Tanar stopped to ask no questions. The girl's tone had been peremptory. Her whole manner bespoke urgency. Descending the stairway to the ground floor Tanar left the building and walked slowly toward its far end. Korsars were all about him, but they had been accustomed to seeing him, and now he held himself to a slow and careless pace that aroused no suspicion. Just beyond the end of the barracks he came to a small, heavily planked door set in the garden wall and as he arrived opposite this, it swung open and he stepped quickly within the garden, Gura instantly closing the gate behind him.

'At last I have succeeded,' cried the girl, 'but I thought that I never should. I have tried so hard to see you ever since Fitt took you from The Cid's palace. I learned from one of the slaves where your quarters were in the barracks and whenever I have been free I have been always beneath your window. Twice before I saw you, but I could not attract your attention and now that I have succeeded, perhaps it is too late.'

'Too late! What do you mean? Too late for what?' demanded Tanar.

'Too late to save Stellara,' said the girl.

'She is in danger?' asked Tanar.

'The preparations for her marriage to Bulf are complete. She cannot delay it much longer.'

'Why should she wish to delay it?' demanded the Sarian. 'Is she not content with the man she has chosen?'

'Like all men, you are a fool in matters pertaining to a woman's heart,' cried Gura.

'I know what she told me,' said Tanar.

'After all that you had been through together; after all that she had been to you, how could you have believed that she loved another?' demanded Gura.

'You mean that she does not love Bulf?' asked Tanar.

'Of course she does not love him. He is a horrid beast.'

'And she still loves me?'

'She has never loved anyone else,' replied the girl.

'Then why did she treat me as she did? Why did she say the things that she said?'

'She was jealous.'

'Jealous! Jealous of whom?'

'Of me,' said Gura, dropping her eyes.

The Sarian stood looking dumbly at the dark-haired Himean girl standing before him. He noted her slim body, her drooping shoulders, her attitude of dejection. 'Gura,' he asked, 'did I ever speak words of love to you? Did I ever give Stellara or another the right to believe that I loved you?'

She shook her head. 'No,' she said, 'and I told Stellara that when I found out what she thought. I told her that you did not love me and finally she was convinced and asked me to find you and tell you that she still loves you. But

I have another message for you from myself. I know you, Sarian. I know that you are not planning to remain here contentedly a prisoner of the Korsars. I know that you will try to escape and I have come to beg you to take Stellara with you, for she will kill herself before she will become the mate of Bulf.'

'Escape,' mused Tanar. 'How may it be accomplished from the heart of The Cid's palace?'

'That is the man's work,' said Gura. 'It is for you to plan the way.'

'And you?' asked Tanar. 'You wish to come away with us?'

'Do not think of me,' said Gura. 'If you and Stellara can escape, I do not matter.'

'But you do matter,' said the man, 'and I am sure that you do not wish to stay in Korsar.'

'No, I do not wish to remain in Korsar,' replied the girl, 'and particularly so now that The Cid seems to have taken a fancy to me.'

'You wish to return to Hime?' asked Tanar.

'After the brief taste of happiness I have had,' replied the girl, 'I could not return to the quarrels, the hatred and the constant unhappiness that constitute life within the cave of Scurv and which would be but continued in some other cave were I to take a mate in Hime.'

'Then come with us,' said the Sarian.

'Oh, if I only might!' exclaimed Gura.

'Then that is settled,' exclaimed Tanar. 'You shall come with us and if we reach Sari I know that you can find peace and happiness for yourself always.'

'It sounds like a dream,' said the girl, wistfully, 'from which I shall awaken in the cave of Scurv.'

'We shall make the dream come true,' said the Sarian, 'and now let us plan on how best we can get you and Stellara out of the palace of The Cid.'

'That will not be so easy,' said Gura.

'No, it is the most difficult part of our escape,' agreed the Sarian; 'but it must be done and I believe that the bolder the plan the greater its assurance of success.'

'And it must be done at once,' said Gura, 'for the wedding arrangements are completed and Bulf is impatient for his mate.'

For a moment Tanar stood in thought, seeking to formulate some plan that might contain at least a semblance of feasibility. 'Can you bring Stellara to this gate at once?' he asked Gura.

'If she is alone, yes,' replied the girl.

'Then go and fetch her and wait here with her until I return. My signal will be a low whistle. When you hear it, unlatch the gate.'

'I shall return as quickly as possible,' said Gura, and, as Tanar stepped through the doorway into the barrack yards, he closed and latched the gate behind him.

The Sarian looked about him and was delighted to note that apparently no one had seen him emerge from the garden. Instead of returning along the front of the barracks the way he had come, he turned in the opposite direction and made his way directly to one of the main gates of the palace. And this strategy was prompted also by another motive – he wished to ascertain if he could pass the guard at the main gate without being challenged.

Tanar had not adopted the garments of his captors and was still conspicuous by the scant attire and simple ornaments of a savage warrior and already his comings and goings had made him a familiar figure around the palace yard and in the Korsar streets beyond. But he had never passed through a palace gate alone before; nor without the ever present Fitt.

As he neared the gate he neither hastened nor loitered, but maintained a steady pace and an unconcerned demeanor. Others were passing in and out and as the former naturally received much closer scrutiny by the guards than the latter, Tanar soon found himself in a Korsar street outside the palace of The Cid.

Before him were the usual sights now grown familiar – the narrow, dusty street, the small open shops or bazaars lining the opposite side, the swaggering Korsars in their brilliant kerchiefs and sashes, and the slaves bearing great burdens to and fro – garden truck and the fruits of the chase coming in from the back country, while bales of tanned hides, salt and other commodities, craved by the simple tastes of the aborigines, were being borne out of the city toward the interior. Some of the bales were of considerable size and weight, requiring the services of four carriers, and were supported on two long poles, the ends of which rested on the shoulders of the men.

There were lines of slaves carrying provisions and ammunition to a fleet of ships that was outfitting for a new raid, and another line bearing plunder from the hold of another ship that had but recently come to anchor in the river before the city.

All this activity presented a scene of apparent confusion, which was increased by the voices of the merchants hawking their wares and the shrill bickering of prospective purchasers.

Through the motley throng the Sarian shouldered his way back toward another gate that gave entrance to the palace ground close to the far end of the long, rambling barracks. As this was the gate through which he passed most often he was accorded no more than a glance as he passed through, and once within he hastened immediately to the quarters assigned to David.

Here he found both David and Ja, to whom he immediately unfolded a plan that he had been perfecting since he left the garden of The Cid.

'And now,' he said, 'before you have agreed to my plan, let me make it plain that I do not expect you to accompany me if you feel that the chances of success are too slight. It is my duty, as well as my desire, to save Stellara and Gura. But I cannot ask you to place your plans for escape in jeopardy.'

'Your plan is a good one,' replied David, 'and even if it were not it is the best that has been suggested yet. And as for our deserting either you or Stellara or Gura, that, of course, is not even a question for discussion. We shall go with you and I know that I speak for Ja as well as myself.'

'I knew that you would say that,' said the Sarian, 'and now let us start at once to put the plan to test.'

'Good,' said David. 'You make your purchases and return to the garden and Ja and I will proceed at once to carry out our part.'

The three proceeded at once toward the palace gate at the far end of the barracks, and as they were passing through the Korsar in charge stopped them.

'Where now?' he demanded.

'We are going into the city to make purchases for a long expedition that we are about to make in search of new iron deposits in the back country, further than we have ever been before.'

'And where is Fitt?' demanded the captain of the gate.

'The Cid sent for him, and while he is gone we are making the necessary preparations.'

'All right,' said the man, apparently satisfied. 'You may pass.'

'We shall return presently with porters,' said David, 'for some of our personal belongings and then go out again to collect the balance of our outfit. Will you leave word that we are to be passed in the event that you are not here?'

'I shall be here,' said the man. 'But what are you going to carry into the back country?'

'We expect that we may have to travel even beyond the furthest boundaries of Korsar, where the natives know little or nothing of The Cid and his authority, and for this reason it is necessary for us to carry provisions and articles of trade that we may barter with them for what we want, since we shall not have sufficient numbers in our party to take these things by force.'

'I see,' said the man; 'but it seems funny that The Cid does not send muskets and pistols to take what he wants rather than spoil these savages by trading with them.'

'Yes,' said David, 'it does seem strange,' and the three passed out into the street of Korsar.

Beyond the gate David and Ja turned to the right toward the market place, while Tanar crossed immediately to one of the shops on the opposite side of the street. Here he purchased two large bags, made of well tanned hide, with which he returned immediately to the palace grounds and presently he was before the garden gate where he voiced a low whistle that was to be the signal by which the girls were to know that he arrived.

Almost immediately the gate swung open and Tanar stepped quickly within. As Gura closed the gate behind him, Tanar found himself standing face to face with Stellara. Her eyes were moist with tears, her lips were trembling with suppressed emotion as the Sarian opened his arms and pressed her to him.

The market place of the city of Korsar is a large, open square where the natives from the interior barter their agricultural produce, raw hides and the flesh of the animals they have taken in the chase, for the simple necessities which they wish to take back to their homes with them.

The farmers bring in their vegetables in large hampers made of reed bound together with grasses. These hampers are ordinarily about four feet in each dimension and are borne on a single pole by two men if lightly loaded, or upon two poles and by four carriers if the load is heavy.

David and Ja approached a group of men whose hampers were empty and who were evidently preparing to depart from the market, and after questioning several of the group they found two who were returning to the same village, which lay at a considerable distance almost due north of Korsar.

By the order of The Cid, Fitt had furnished his three prisoners with ample funds in the money of Korsar that they might make necessary purchases in the prosecution of their investigations and their experiments.

The money, which consisted of gold coins of various sizes and weights, was crudely stamped upon one side with what purported to be a likeness of The Cid, and upon the other with a Korsar ship. For so long a time had gold coin been the medium of exchange in Korsar and the surrounding country that it was accepted by the natives of even remote villages and tribes, so that David had little difficulty in engaging the services of eight carriers and their two hampers to carry equipment at least as far as their village, which in reality was much further than David had any intention of utilizing the services of the natives.

Having concluded his arrangements with the men, David and Ja led the way back to the palace gate, where the officer passed them through with a nod.

As they proceeded along the front of the barracks toward its opposite end their only fear was that Fitt might have returned from his interview with The Cid. If he had and if he saw and questioned them, all was lost. They scarcely breathed as they approached the entrance to their quarters, which were also the quarters of Fitt. But they saw nothing of him as they passed the doorway and hastened on to the door in the garden wall. Here they halted, directing the bearers to place the baskets close to the doorway. David Innes whistled. The door swung in, and at a word from Tanar the eight carriers entered, picked up two bundles just inside the gate and deposited one of them in each of the hampers waiting beyond the wall. The lids were closed. The slaves resumed their burden, and the party turned about to retrace its steps to the palace gate through which the carriers had just entered with their empty hampers.

Once again apprehension had chilled the heart of David Innes for fear that Fitt might have returned, but they passed the barracks and reached the gate without seeing him, and here they were halted by the Korsar in charge.

'It did not take you long,' he said. 'What have you in the hampers?' and he raised the cover of one of them.

'Only our personal belongings,' said David. 'When we return again we shall have our full equipment. Would you like to inspect it all at the same time?'

The Korsar, looking down at the skin bag lying at the bottom of the hamper, hesitated for a moment before replying. 'Very well,' he said, 'I will do it all at the same time,' and he let the cover drop back into place.

The hearts of the three men had stood still, but David Innes's voice betrayed no unwonted emotion as he addressed the captain of the gate. 'When Fitt returns,' he said, 'tell him that I am anxious to see him and ask him if he will wait in our quarters until we return.'

The Korsar nodded a surly assent and motioned for them to pass on through the gate.

Turning to the right, David led the party down the narrow street toward the market place. There he turned abruptly to the left, through a winding alleyway and double-backed to the north upon another street that paralleled that upon which the palace fronted. Here were poorer shops and less traffic and the carriers were able to make good time until presently the party passed out of the city of Korsar into the open country beyond. And then, by dint of threats and promises of additional pieces of gold, the three men urged the carriers to accelerate their speed to a swinging trot, which they maintained until they were forced to stop from exhaustion. A brief rest with food and they were off again; nor did they slacken their pace until they reached the rolling, wooded country at the foothills of the mountains, far north of Korsar.

Here, well within the shelter of the woods, the carriers set down their burdens and threw themselves upon the ground to rest, while Tanar and David swung back the covers of the hampers and untying the stout thongs that closed the mouths of the bags revealed their contents. Half smothered and almost unable to move their cramped limbs, Stellara and Gura were lifted from the baskets and revealed to the gaze of the astounded carriers.

Tanar turned upon the men. 'Do you know who this woman is?' he demanded.

'No,' said one of their number.

'It is Stellara, the daughter of The Cid,' said the Sarian. 'You have helped to steal her from the palace of her father. Do you know what that will mean if you are caught?'

The men trembled in evident terror. 'We did not know she was in the basket,' said one of them. 'We had nothing to do with it. It is you who stole her.'

'Will the Korsars believe you when we tell them of the great quantities of gold we paid you if we are captured?' asked Tanar. 'No, they will not believe you and I do not have to tell you what your fate will be. But there is safety for you if you will do what I tell you to do.'

'What is that?' demanded one of the natives.

'Take up your hampers and hasten on to your village and tell no one, as long as you live, what you have done, not even your mates. If you do not tell, no one will know for we shall not tell.'

'We will never tell,' cried the men in chorus.

'Do not even talk about it among yourselves,' cautioned David, 'for even the trees have ears, and if the Korsars come to your village and question you tell them that you saw three men and two women traveling toward the east just beyond the borders of the city of Korsar. Tell them that they were too far away for you to recognize them, but that they may have been The Cid's daughter and her companion with the three men who abducted them.'

'We will do as you say,' replied the carriers.

'Then be gone,' demanded David, and the eight men hurriedly gathered up their hampers and disappeared into the forest toward the north.

When the two girls were sufficiently revived and rested to continue the journey, the party set out again, making their way to the east for a short distance and then turning north again, for it had been Tanar's plan to throw the Korsars off the trail by traveling north, rather than east or south. Later they would turn to the east, far north of the area which the Korsars might be expected to comb in search of them, and then again, after many marches, they would change their direction once more to the south. It was a circuitous route, but it seemed the safest.

The forest changed to pine and cedar and there were windswept wastes dotted with gnarled and stunted trees. The air was cooler than they had ever known it in their native land, and when the wind blew from the north they shivered around roaring camp fires. The animals they met were scarcer and bore heavier fur, and nowhere was there sign of man.

Upon one occasion when they stopped to camp Tanar pointed at the ground before him. 'Look!' he cried to David. 'My shadow is no longer beneath me,' and then, looking up, 'the sun is not above us.'

'I have noticed that,' replied David, 'and I am trying to understand the reason for it, and perhaps I shall with the aid of the legends of the Korsars.'

As they proceeded their shadows grew longer and longer and the light and heat of the sun diminished until they traveled in a semi-twilight that was always cold.

Long since they had been forced to fashion warmer garments from the pelts of the beasts they had killed. Tanar and Ja wanted to turn back toward the southeast, for their strange homing instinct drew them in that direction toward their own country, but David asked them to accompany him yet a little further for his mind had evolved a strange and wonderful theory and he wished to press on yet a little further to obtain still stronger proof of its correctness.

When they slept they rested beside roaring fires and once, when they awoke, they were covered by a light mantle of a cold, white substance that frightened the Pellucidarians, but that David knew was snow. And the air was full of whirling particles and the wind bit those portions of their faces that were exposed, for now they wore fur caps and hoods and their hands were covered with warm mittens.

'We cannot go much further in this direction,' said Ja, 'or we shall all perish.'

'Perhaps you are right,' said David. 'You four turn back to the southeast and I will go yet a little further to the north and overtake you when I have satisfied myself that a thing that I believe is true.'

'No,' cried Tanar, 'we shall remain together. Where you go we shall go.'

'Yes,' said Ja, 'we shall not abandon you.'

'Just a little further north, then,' said David, 'and I shall be ready to turn back with you,' and so they forged ahead over snow covered ground into the deepening gloom that filled the souls of the Pellucidarians with terror. But after a while the wind changed and blew from the south and the snow melted and the air became balmy again, and still further on the twilight slowly lifted and the light increased, though the midday sun of Pellucidar was now scarcely visible behind them.

'I cannot understand it,' said Ja. 'Why should it become lighter again, although the sun is ever further away behind us?'

'I do not know,' said Tanar. 'Ask David.'

'I can only guess,' said David, 'and my guess seems so preposterous that I dare not voice it.'

'Look!' cried Stellara, pointing ahead. 'It is the sea.'

'Yes,' said Gura, 'a gray sea; it does not look like water.'

'And what is that?' cried Tanar. 'There is a great fire upon the sea.'

'And the sea does not curve upward in the distance,' cried Stellara. 'Everything is wrong in this country and I am afraid.'

David had stopped in his tracks and was staring at the deep red glow ahead. The others gathered around him and watched it, too. 'What is it?' demanded Ja.

'As there is a God in heaven it can be but one thing,' replied David; 'and yet I know that it cannot be that thing. The very idea is ridiculous. It is impossible and outlandish.'

'But what might it be?' demanded Stellara.

'The sun,' replied David.

'But the sun is almost out of sight behind us,' Gura reminded him.

'I do not mean the sun of Pellucidar,' replied David; 'but the sun of the outer world, the world from which I came.'

The others stood in silent awe, watching the edge of a blood red disc that seemed to be floating upon a gray ocean across whose reddened surface a brilliant pathway of red and gold led from the shoreline to the blazing orb, where the sea and sky seemed to meet.

15

Madness

'Now,' said Stellara, 'we can go no further;' nor indeed could they for east and west and north stretched a great, sullen sea and along the shore-line at their feet great ice cakes rose and fell with sullen roars and loud reports as the sea ground the churning mass.

For a long time David Innes, Emperor of Pellucidar, stood staring out across that vast and desolate waste of water. 'What lies beyond?' he murmured to himself, and then, shaking his head, he turned away. 'Come,' he said, 'let us strike back for Sari.'

His companions received his words with shouts of joy. Smiles replaced the half troubled expressions that had marked their drawn faces since the moment that they had discovered that their beloved noonday sun was being left behind them.

With light steps, with laughter and joking, they faced the long, arduous journey that lay ahead of them.

During the second march, after they had turned back from the northern sea, Gura discovered a strange object to the left of their line of march.

'It looks as though it might be some queer sort of native hut,' she said.

'We shall have to investigate it,' said David, and the five made their way to the side of the strange object.

It was a large, heavy, wicker basket that lay inverted upon the barren ground. All about it were the rotted remnants of cordage.

At David's suggestion the men turned the basket over upon its side. Beneath it they found well preserved remnants of oiled silk and a network of fine cord.

'What is it?' asked Stellara.

'It is the basket and all that remains of the gas bag of a balloon,' said David.

'What is a balloon,' asked the girl, 'and how did it get here?'

'I can explain what a balloon is,' said David; 'but if I were positive that I was correct in my conjecture as to how it came here, I would hold the answer to a thousand questions that have puzzled the men of the outer crust for ages.' For a long time he stood silently contemplating the weather-worn basket. His mind submerged in thought was oblivious to all else. 'If I only knew,' he mused. 'If I only knew, and yet how else could it have come here? What else could that red disc upon the horizon of the sea have been other than the midnight sun of the arctic regions.'

'What in the world are you talking about?' demanded Gura.

'The poor devils,' mused David, apparently oblivious of the girl's presence. 'They made a greater discovery than they could have hoped for in their wildest dreams. I wonder if they lived to realize it.' Slowly he removed his fur cap and stood facing the basket with bowed head, and for some unaccountable reason, which they could not explain, his companions bared their heads and followed his example. And after they had resumed their journey it was a long time before David Innes could shake off the effects of that desolate reminder of one of the world's most pathetic tragedies.

So anxious were the members of the party to reach the cheering warmth of the beloved Pellucidar that they knew, that they pressed on toward the south with the briefest of rests; nor were they wholly content until once more their shadows lay directly beneath them.

Sari, lying slightly east of south, their return from the north took them over a different route from that which they had followed up from Korsar. Of course the Pellucidarians did not know these points of compass as north or south, and even David Innes carried them in his mind more in accordance with the Pellucidarian scheme than that with which he had been familiar upon the outer crust.

Naturally, with the sun always at zenith and with no stars and no moon and no planets, the Pellucidarians have been compelled to evolve a different system of indicating direction than that with which we are familiar. By instinct they know the direction in which their own country lies and each Pellucidarian reckons all directions from this base line, and he indicates other directions in a simple and ingenious manner.

Suppose you were from Sari and were traveling from the ice girt sea above Korsar to any point upon Pellucidar, you would set and maintain your course in this manner. Extend the fingers of your right hand and hold it in a horizontal position, palm down, directly in front of your body, your little finger pointing in the direction of Sari – a direction which you know by instinct – and your thumb pointing to the left directly at right angles to the line in which your little finger is pointing. Now spread your left hand in the same way and lower it on top of your right hand, so that the little finger of your left hand exactly covers the little finger of your right hand.

You will now see the fingers and thumbs of your two hands cover an arc of one hundred and eighty degrees.

Sari lies southeast of Korsar, while The Land of Awful Shadow lies due south. Therefore a Sarian pointing in the direction toward The Land of Awful Shadow would say that he was traveling two left fingers from Sari, since the middle finger of the left hand would be pointing about due south toward The Land of Awful Shadow. If he were going in the opposite direction, or north, he would merely add the word 'back,' saying that he was traveling two left fingers back from Sari, so that by this plan every point of compass is roughly covered, and with sufficient accuracy for all the requirements of the primitive Pellucidarians. The fact that when one is traveling to the right of his established base line and indicates it by mentioning the fingers of his left hand might, at first, be deemed confusing, but, of course, having followed this system for ages, it is perfectly intelligible to the Pellucidarians.

When they reached a point at which the city of Korsar lay three right fingers back from Sari, they were, in reality, due east of the Korsar city. They were now in fertile, semi-tropical land teeming with animal life. The men were armed with pistols as well as spears, bows and arrows and knives; while Stellara and Gura carried light spears and knives, and seldom was there a march that did not witness an encounter with one or more of the savage beasts of the primeval forests, verdure clad hills or rolling plains across which their journey led them.

They long since had abandoned any apprehension of pursuit or capture by the Korsars and while they had skirted the distant hinterland claimed by Korsar and had encountered some of the natives upon one or two occasions, they had seen no member of the ruling class with the result that for the first time since they had fallen into the clutches of the enemy they felt a sense of unquestioned freedom. And though the other dangers that beset their way might appear appalling to one of the outer world, they had no such effect upon any one of the five, whose experiences of life had tended to make them wholly self-reliant, and, while constantly alert and watchful, unoppressed by the possibility of future calamity. When danger suddenly confronted them, they were ready to meet it. After it had passed they did not depress their spirits by anticipating the next encounter.

Ja and David were anxious to return to their mates, but Tanar and Stellara were supremely happy because they were together, and Gura was content merely to be near Tanar. Sometimes she recalled Balal, her brother, for he had been kind to her, but Scurv and Sloo and Dhung she tried to forget.

Thus they were proceeding, a happy and contented party, when, with the suddenness and unexpectedness of lightning out of a clear sky, disaster overwhelmed them.

They had been passing through a range of low, rocky hills and were descending a narrow gorge on the Sari side of the range when, turning the shoulder of a hill, they came face to face with a large party of Korsars, fully a hundred strong. The leaders saw and recognized them instantly and a shout of savage triumph that broke from their lips was taken up by all their fellows.

David, who was in the lead, saw that resistance would be futile and in the instant his plan was formed. 'We must separate,' he said. 'Tanar, you and Stellara go together. Ja, take Gura with you, and I shall go in a different direction, for we must not all be captured. One, at least, must escape to return to Sari. If it is not I, then let the one who wins through take this message to Ghak and Perry. Tell Perry that I am positive that I have discovered that there is a polar opening in the outer crust leading into Pellucidar and that if he ever gets in radio communication with the outer world, he must inform them of this fact. Tell Ghak to rush his forces by sea on Korsar, as well as by land. And now, good-bye, and each for himself.'

Turning in their tracks the five fled up the gorge and being far more active and agile than the Korsars, they outdistanced them, and though the rattle of musketry followed them and bits of iron and stone fell about them, or whizzed past them, no one was struck.

Tanar and Stellara found and followed a steep ravine that led upward to the right, and almost at the same time Ja and Gura diverged to the left up the course of a dry waterway, while David continued on back up the main gorge.

Almost at the summit and within the reach of safety, Tanar and Stellara found their way blocked by a sheer cliff, which, while not more than fifteen feet in height, was absolutely unscalable; nor could they find footing upon the steep ravine sides to the right or left, and as they stood there in this cul-de-sac, their backs to the wall, a party of twenty or thirty Korsars, toiling laboriously up the ravine, cut off their retreat; nor was there any place in which they might hide, but instead were compelled to stand there in full view of the first of the enemy that came within sight of them, and thus with freedom already within their grasp they fell again into the hands of the Korsars. And Tanar had been compelled to surrender without resistance because he did not dare risk Stellara's life by drawing the fire of the enemy.

Many of the Korsars were for dispatching Tanar immediately, but the officer in command forbade them for it was The Cid's orders that any of the prisoners that might be recaptured were to be returned alive. 'And furthermore,' he added, 'Bulf is particularly anxious to get this Sarian back alive.'

During the long march back to Korsar, Tanar and Stellara learned that this was one of several parties that The Cid had dispatched in search of them with orders never to return until they had rescued his daughter and captured her abductors. They also had impressed upon them the fact that the only reason for The Cid's insistence that the prisoners be returned alive was because he and Bulf desired to mete out to them a death commensurate with their crime.

During the long march back to Korsar, Tanar and Stellara were kept apart as a rule, though on several occasions they were able to exchange a few words.

'My poor Sarian,' said Stellara upon one of these. 'I wish to God that you had never met me for only sorrow and pain and death can come of it.'

'I do not care,' replied Tanar, 'if I die tomorrow, or if they torture me forever, for no price is too high to pay for the happiness that I have had with you, Stellara.'

'Ah, but they will torture you – that is what wrings my heart,' cried the girl. 'Take your life yourself, Tanar. Do not let them get you. I know them and I know their methods and I would rather kill you with my own hands than see you fall into their clutches. The Cid is a beast, and Bulf is worse than Bohar the Bloody. I shall never be his mate; of that you may be sure, and if you die by your own hand I shall follow you shortly. And if there is a life after this, as the ancestors of the Korsars taught them, then we shall meet again where all is peace and beauty and love.'

The Sarian shook his head. 'I know what is here in this life,' he said, 'and I do not know what is there in the other. I shall cling to this, and you must cling to it until some other hand than ours takes it from us.'

'But they will torture you so horribly,' she moaned.

'No torture can kill the happiness of our love, Stellara,' said the man, and then guards separated them and they plodded on across the weary, interminable miles. How different the country looked through eyes of despair and sorrow from the sunlit paradise that they had seen when they journeyed through it, hand in hand with freedom and love.

But at last the long, cruel journey was over, a fitting prelude to its cruel ending, for at the palace gate Stellara and Tanar were separated. She was escorted to her quarters by female attendants whom she recognized as being virtually her guards and keepers, while Tanar was conducted directly into the presence of The Cid.

As he entered the room he saw the glowering face of the Korsar chieftain, and standing below the dais, just in front of him, was Bulf, whom he had seen but once before, but whose face no man could ever forget. But there was another there whose presence brought a look of greater horror to Tanar's face than did the brutal countenances of The Cid or Bulf, for standing directly before the dais, toward which he was being led, the Sarian saw David I, Emperor of Pellucidar. Of all the calamities that could have befallen, this was the worst.

As the Sarian was led to David's side he tried to speak to him, but was roughly silenced by the Korsar guards; nor were they ever again to be allowed to communicate with one another.

The Cid eyed them savagely, as did Bulf. 'For you, who betrayed my confidence and abducted my daughter, there is no punishment that can fit your crime; there is no death so terrible that its dying will expiate your sin. It is not within me to conceive of any form of torture the infliction of which upon you would give me adequate pleasure. I shall have to look for suggestions outside of my own mind,' and his eyes ran questioningly among his officers surrounding him.

'Let me have that one,' roared Bulf, pointing at Tanar, 'and I can promise you that you will witness such tortures as the eyes of man never before beheld; nor the body of man ever before endured.'

'Will it result in death?' asked a tall Korsar with a cadaverous face.

'Of course,' said Bulf, 'but not too soon.'

'Death is a welcome and longed for deliverance from torture,' continued the other. 'Would you give either one of these the satisfaction and pleasure of enjoying even death?'

'But what else is there?' demanded The Cid.

'There is a living death that is worse than death,' said the cadaverous one.

'And if you can name a torture worse than that which I had in mind,' exclaimed Bulf, 'I shall gladly relinquish all my claims upon this Sarian.'

'Explain,' commanded The Cid.

'It is this,' said the cadaverous one. 'These men are accustomed to sunlight, to freedom, to cleanliness, to fresh air, to companionship. There are beneath this palace dark, damp dungeons into which no ray of light ever filters, whose thick walls are impervious to sound. The denizens of these horrid places, as you know, would have an effect opposite to that of human companionship and the only danger, the only weak spot in my plan, lies in the fact that their constant presence might deprive these criminals of their reason and thus defeat the very purpose to which I conceive their presence necessary. A lifetime of hideous loneliness and torture in silence and in darkness! What death, what torture, what punishment can you mete out to these men that would compare in hideousness with that which I have suggested?'

After he had ceased speaking the others remained in silent contemplation of his proposition for some time. It was The Cid who broke the silence.

'Bulf,' he said, 'I believe that he is right, for I know that as much as I love life I would rather die than be left alone in one of the palace dungeons.'

Bulf nodded his Head slowly. 'I hate to give up my plan,' he said, 'for I should like to inflict that torture upon this Sarian myself. But,' and he turned to the cadaverous one, 'you are right. You have named a torture infinitely worse than any that I could conceive.'

'Thus is it ordered,' said The Cid, 'to separate palace dungeons for life.'

In utter silence, unbroken by the Korsar assemblage, Tanar and David were blindfolded; Tanar felt himself being stripped of all his ornaments and of what meager raiment it was his custom to wear, with the exception of his loin cloth. Then he was pushed and dragged roughly along, first this way and then that. He knew when they were passing through narrow corridors by the muffled echoes and there was a different reverberation of the footsteps of his guards as they crossed large apartments. He was hustled down flights of stone steps and through other corridors and at last he felt himself lowered into an opening, a guard seizing him under each arm. The air felt damp and it smelled of mold and must and of something else that was disgusting, but unrecognizable to his nostrils. And then they let go of him and he dropped a short distance and landed upon a stone flagging that felt damp and slippery to his bare feet. He heard a sound above his head – a grating sound as though a stone slab had been pushed across a stone floor to close the trap through which he had been lowered. Then Tanar snatched the bandage from his eyes, but he might as well have left it there for he found himself surrounded by utter darkness. He listened intently, but there was no sound, not even the sounds of the retreating footsteps of his guards – darkness and silence – they had chosen the most terrible torture that they could inflict upon a Sarian – silence, darkness and solitude.

For a long time he stood there motionless and then, slowly, he commenced to grope his way forward. Four steps he took before he touched the wall and this he followed two steps to the end, and there he turned and took six steps to cross before he reached the wall on the opposite side, and thus he made the circuit of his dungeon and found that it was four by six paces – perhaps not small for a dungeon, but narrower than the grave for Tanar of Pellucidar.

He tried to think – to think how he could occupy his time until death released him. Death! Could he not hasten it? But how? Six paces was the length of his prison cell. Could he not dash at full speed from one end to the other, crushing his brains out by the impact? And then he recalled his promise to Stellara, even in the face of her appeal to him to take his own life – 'I shall not die of my own hand.'

Again he made the circuit of his dungeon. He wondered how they would feed him, for he knew that they would feed him because they wished him to live as long as possible, as only thus might they encompass his torture. He thought of the bright sun shining down upon the table-lands of Sari. He thought of the young men and the maidens there free and happy. He thought of Stellara, so close, up there above him somewhere, and yet so infinitely far away. If he were dead, they would be closer. 'Not by my own hand,' he muttered.

He tried to plan for the future – the blank, dark, silent future – the eternity of loneliness that confronted him, and he found that through the despair of utter hopelessness his own unconquerable spirit could still discern hope, for no matter what his plans they all looked forward to a day of freedom and he realized that nothing short of death ever could rob him of this solace, and so his plan finally developed.

He must in some way keep his mind from dwelling constantly upon the present. He must erase from it all consideration of the darkness, the silence and the solitude that surrounded him. And he must keep fit, mentally and physically, for the moment of release or escape. And so he planned to walk and to exercise his arms and the other muscles of his body systematically to the end that he might keep in good condition and at the same time induce sufficient fatigue to enable him to sleep as much as possible, and when he rested preparatory to sleep he concentrated his mind entirely upon pleasant memories. And when he put the plan into practice he found that it was all that he had hoped that it would be. He exercised until he was thoroughly fatigued and then he lay down to pleasant day dreams until sleep claimed him. Being accustomed from childhood to sleeping upon hard ground, the stone flagging gave him no particular discomfort and he was asleep in the midst of pleasant memories of happy hours with Stellara.

But his awakening! As consciousness slowly returned it was accompanied by a sense of horror, the cause of which gradually filtered to his awakening sensibilities. A cold, slimy body was crawling across his chest. Instinctively his hand seized it to thrust it away and his fingers closed upon a scaly thing that wriggled and writhed and struggled.

Tanar leaped to his feet, cold sweat bursting from every pore. He could feel the hairs upon his head rising in horror. He stepped back and his foot touched another of those horrid things. He slipped and fell, and, falling, his body encountered others – cold, clammy, wriggling. Scrambling to his feet he retreated to the opposite end of his dungeon, but everywhere the floor was covered with writhing, scaly bodies. And now the silence became a pandemonium of seething sounds, a black cauldron of venomous hisses.

Long bodies curled themselves about his legs and writhed and wriggled upward toward his face. No sooner did he tear one from him and hurl it aside than another took its place.

This was no dream as he had at first hoped, but stark, horrible reality. These hideous serpents that filled his cell were but a part of his torture, but they would defeat their purpose. They would drive him mad. Already he felt his mind tottering and then into it crept the cunning scheme of a madman. With their own weapons he would defeat their ends. He would rob them quickly of the power to torture him further, and he burst into a shrill, mirthless laugh as he tore a snake from around his body and held it before him.

The reptile writhed and struggled and very slowly Tanar of Pellucidar worked his hand upward to its throat. It was not a large snake for Pellucidar, measuring perhaps five feet in length with a body about six inches in diameter.

Grasping the reptile about a foot below its head with one hand, Tanar slapped it repeatedly in the face with the other and then held it close to his breast. Laughing and screaming, he struck and struck again, and at last the snake struck back, burying its fangs deep in the flesh of the Sarian.

With a cry of triumph Tanar hurled the thing from him, and then slowly sank to the floor upon the writhing, wriggling forms that carpeted it.

'With your own weapons I have robbed you of your revenge,' he shrieked, and then he lapsed into unconsciousness.

Who may say how long he lay thus in the darkness and silence of that buried dungeon in a timeless world. But at length he stirred; slowly his eyes opened and as consciousness returned he felt about him. The stone flagging was bare. He sat up. He was not dead and to his surprise he discovered that he had suffered neither pain nor swelling from the strike of the serpent.

He arose and moved cautiously about the dungeon. The snakes were gone. Sleep had restored his mental equilibrium, but he shuddered as he realized how close he had been to madness, and he smiled somewhat shamefacedly, as he reflected upon the futility of his needless terror. For the first time in his life Tanar of Pellucidar had understood the meaning of the word fear.

As he paced slowly around his dungeon one foot came in contact with something lying on the floor in a corner – something which had not been there before the snakes came. He stooped and felt cautiously with his hand and found an iron bowl fitted with a heavy cover. He lifted the cover. Here was food and without questioning what it was or whence it came, he ate.

16

The Darkness Beyond

The deadly monotony of his incarceration dragged on. He exercised; he ate; he slept. He never knew how the food was brought to his cell, nor when, and after a while he ceased to care.

The snakes came usually while he slept, but since that first experience they no longer filled him with horror. And after a dozen repetitions of their visit they not only ceased to annoy him, but he came to look forward to their coming as a break in the deadly monotony of his solitude. He found that by stroking them and talking to them in low tones he could quiet their restless writhing. And after repeated recurrences of their visits he was confident that one of them had become almost a pet.

Of course in the darkness he could not differentiate one snake from another, but always he was awakened by the nose of one pounding gently upon his chest, and when he took it in his hands and stroked it, it made no effort to escape; not ever again did one of them strike him with its fangs after that first orgy of madness, during which he had thought and hoped that the reptiles were venomous.

It took him a long time to find the opening through which the reptiles found ingress to his cell, but at length, after diligent search, he discovered an aperture about eight inches in diameter, some three feet above the floor. Its sides were worn smooth by the countless passings of scaly bodies. He inserted his hand in the opening and feeling around discovered that the wall at this point was about a foot in thickness, and when he inserted his arm to the shoulder he could feel nothing in any direction beyond the wall. Perhaps there was another chamber there – another dell like his – or possibly the aperture opened into a deep pit that was filled with snakes. He thought of many explanations and the more he thought the more anxious he became to solve the riddle of the mysterious space beyond his cell. Thus did his mind occupy itself with trivial things, and the loneliness and the darkness and the silence exaggerated the importance of the matter beyond all reason until it became an obsession with him. During all his waking hours he thought about that hole in the wall and what lay beyond in the Stygian darkness which his eyes could not penetrate. He questioned the snake that rapped upon his chest, but it did not answer him and then he went to the hole in the wall and asked the hole. And he was on the point of becoming angry when it did not reply when his mind suddenly caught itself, and with a shudder he turned away, realizing that this way led to madness and that he must, above all else, remain master of his mind.

But still he did not abandon his speculation; only now he conducted it with reason and sanity, and at last he hit upon a shrewd plan.

When next his food was brought and he had devoured it he took the iron cover from the iron pot, which had contained it, and hurled it to the stone flagging of his cell, where it broke into several pieces. One of these was long and slender and had a sharp point, which was what he had hoped he would find in the debris of the broken cover. This piece he kept; the others he put back into the pot and then he went to the aperture in the wall and commenced to scratch, slowly, slowly, slowly at the hard mortar in which the stones around the hole were set.

He ate and slept many times before his labor was rewarded by the loosening of a single stone next to the hole. And again he ate and slept many times before a second stone was removed.

How long he worked at this he did not know, but the time passed more quickly now and his mind was so engrossed with his labors that he was almost happy.

During this time he did not neglect his exercising, but he slept less often. When the snakes came he had to stop his work, for they were continually passing in and out through the hole.

He wished that he knew how the food was brought to his cell, that he might know if there was danger that those who brought it could hear him scraping at the mortar in the wall, but as he never heard the food brought he hoped that those who brought it could not hear him and he was quite sure that they could not see him.

And so he worked on unceasingly until at last he had scratched away an opening large enough to admit his body, and then for a long time he sat before it, waiting, seeking to assure himself that he was master of his mind, for in this eternal night of solitude that had been his existence for how long he could not even guess, he realized that this adventure which he was facing had assumed such momentous proportions that once more he felt himself upon the brink of madness. And now he wanted to make sure that no matter what lay beyond that aperture he could meet it with calm nerves and a serene and sane mind, for he could not help but realize that keen disappointment might be lying in wait for him, since during all the long periods of his scratching and scraping since he had discovered the hole through which the snakes came into his cell he had realized that a hope of escape was the foundation of the desire that prompted him to prosecute the work. And though he expected to be disappointed he knew how cruel would be the blow when it fell.

With a touch that was almost a caress he let his fingers run slowly over the rough edges of the enlarged aperture. He inserted his head and shoulders into it and reached far out upon the other side, groping with a hand that found nothing, searching with eyes that saw nothing, and then he drew himself back into his dungeon and walked to its far end and sat down upon the floor and leaned back against the wall and waited – waited because he did not dare to pass that aperture to face some new discouragement.

It took him a long time to master himself, and then he waited again. But this time, after reasoned consideration of the matter that filled his mind.

He would wait until they brought his food and had taken away the empty receptacle – that he might be given a longer interval before possible discovery of his absence, in the event he did not return to his cell. And though he went often to the corner where the food was ordinarily deposited, it seemed an eternity before he found it there. And after he had eaten it, another eternity before the receptacle was taken away; but at last it was removed. And once again he crossed his cell and stood before the opening that led he knew not where.

This time he did not hesitate. He was master of his mind and nerves.

One after the other he put his feet through the aperture until he sat with his legs both upon the far side of the wall. Then, turning on his stomach, he started to lower himself, because he did not know where the floor might be, but he found it immediately, on the same level as his own. And an instant later he stood erect and if not free, at least no longer a prisoner within his own cell.

Cautiously he groped about him in the darkness, feeling his way a few inches at a time. This cell, he discovered, was much narrower than his own, but it was very long. By extending his hands in both directions he could touch both walls, and thus he advanced, placing a foot cautiously to feel each step before he took it.

He had brought with him from his cell the iron sliver that he had broken from the cover of the pot and with which he had scratched himself thus far toward freedom. And the possession of this bit of iron imparted to him a certain sense of security, since it meant that he was not entirely unarmed.

Presently, as he advanced, he became convinced that he was in a long corridor. One foot came in contact with a rough substance directly in the center of the tunnel. He took his hands from the walls and groped in front of him.

It was a rough-coated cylinder about eight inches in diameter that rose directly upward from the center of the tunnel, and his fingers quickly told him that it was the trunk of a tree with the bark still on, though worn off in patches.

Passing this column, which he guessed to be a support for a weak section of the roof of the tunnel, he continued on, but he had taken but a couple of steps when he came to a blank wall – the tunnel had come to an abrupt end.

Tanar's heart sank within him. His hopes had been rising with each forward step and now they were suddenly dashed to despair. Again and again his fingers ran over the cold wall that had halted his advance toward hoped for freedom, but there was no sign of break or crevice, and slowly he turned back toward his cell, passing the wooden column and retracing his steps in utter dejection. But as he moved sadly along he mustered all his spiritual forces, determined not to let his expected disappointment crush him. He would go back to his cell, but he would still continue to use the tunnel. It would be a respite from the monotony of his own four walls. It would extend the distance that he might walk and after all he would make it worth the effort that had been necessary to gain ingress to it.

Back in his own cell again he lay down to sleep, for he had denied himself sleep a great deal of late that he might prosecute the work upon which he had been engaged. When he awoke the snakes were with him again and his friend was tapping gently on his chest, and once again he took up the dull monotony of his existence, altered only by regular excursions into his new found domain, the black interior of which he came to know as well as he did his own cell, so that he walked briskly from the hole he had made to the wooden column at the far end of the tunnel, passed around it and walked back again at a brisk gait and with as much assurance as though he could see plainly, for he had counted the paces from one end to the other so many times that he knew to an instant when he had covered the distance from one extremity to the other.

He ate; he slept; he exercised; he played with his slimy, reptilian companion; and he paced the narrow tunnel of his discovery. And often when he passed around the wooden column at its far end, he speculated upon the real purpose of it.

Once he went to sleep in his own cell thinking about it, and when he awoke to the gentle tapping of the snake's snout upon his breast he sat up so suddenly that the reptile fell hissing to the flagging, for clear and sharp upon the threshold of his awakening mind stood an idea – a wonderful idea – why had he not thought of it before?

Excitedly he hastened to the opening leading into the tunnel. Snakes were passing through it, but he fought for precedence with the reptilian horde and tumbled through head first upon a bed of hissing snakes. Scrambling to his feet he almost ran the length of the corridor until his outstretched hands came in contact with the rough bole of the tree. There he stood quite some time, trembling like a leaf, and then, encircling the column with his arms and legs, he started to climb slowly and deliberately aloft. This was the idea that had seized him in its compelling grip upon his awakening.

Upward through the darkness he went, and pausing now and then to grope about with his hands, he found that the tree trunk ran up the center of a narrow, circular shaft.

He climbed slowly upward and at a distance of about thirty feet above the floor of the tunnel, his head struck stone. Feeling upward with one hand he discovered that the tree was set in mortar in the ceiling above him.

This could not be the end! What reason could there be for a tunnel and a shaft that led nowhere? He groped through the darkness in all directions with his hand and he was rewarded by finding an opening in the side of the shaft about six feet below the ceiling. Quitting the bole of the tree he climbed into the opening in the wall of the shaft, and here he found himself in another tunnel, lower and narrower than that at the base of the shaft. It was still dark, so that he was compelled to advance as slowly and with as great caution as he had upon that occasion when he first explored his tunnel below.

He advanced but a short distance when the tunnel turned abruptly to the right, and ahead of him, beyond the turn, he saw a ray of light!

A condemned man snatched from the jaws of death could not have greeted salvation with more joyousness than Tanar of Pellucidar greeted this first slender ray of daylight that he had seen for a seeming eternity. It shone dimly through a tiny crevice, but it was light, the light of heaven that he had never expected to again behold.

Enraptured, he walked slowly toward it, and as he reached it his hand came in contact with rough, unpainted boards that blocked his way. It was through a tiny crack between two of these boards that the light was filtering.

As dim as the light was it hurt his eyes, so long unaccustomed to light of any kind. But by turning them away so that the light did not shine directly into them, he finally became accustomed to it, and when he did he discovered that as small as the aperture was through which the light came it let in sufficient to dispel the utter darkness of the interior of the tunnel and he also discovered that he could discern objects. He could see the stone walls on either side of the tunnel, and by looking closely he could see the boards that formed the obstacle that barred his further progress. And as he examined them he discovered that at one side there was something that resembled a latch, an invention of which he had been entirely ignorant before he had come aboard the Korsar ship upon which he had been made prisoner, for in Sari there are no locks nor latches.

But he knew the thing for what it was and it told him that the boards before him formed a door, which opened into light and toward liberty, but what lay immediately beyond?

He clinched his ear to the door and listened, but he heard no sound. Then very carefully he examined the latch, experimenting with it until he discovered how to operate it. Steadying his nerves, he pushed gently upon the rough planks. As they swung away from him slowly a flood of light rushed into the first narrow crack, and Tanar covered his eyes with his hands and turned away, realizing that he must become accustomed to this light slowly and gradually, or he might be permanently blinded.

With closed eyes he listened at the crack, but could hear nothing. And then with utmost care he started to accustom his eyes to the light, but it was long before he could stand the full glare that came through even this tiny crack.

When he could stand the light without pain he opened the door a little further and looked out. Just beyond the door lay a fairly large room, in which wicker hampers, iron and earthen receptacles and bundles sewed up in hides littered the floor and were piled high against the walls. Everything seemed covered with dust and cobwebs and there was no sign of a human being about.

Pushing the door open still further Tanar stepped from the tunnel into the apartment and looked about him. Everywhere the room was a litter of bundles and packages with articles of clothing strewn about, together with various fittings for ships, bales of hide and numerous weapons.

The thick coating of dust upon everything suggested to the Sarian that the room had not been visited lately.

For a moment he stood with his hand still on the open door and as he started to step into the room his hand stuck for an instant where he had grasped the rough boards. Looking at his fingers to ascertain the cause he discovered that they were covered with sticky pitch. It was his left hand and when he tried to rub the pitch from it he found that it was almost impossible to do so.

As he moved around the room examining the contents everything that he touched with his left hand stuck to it – it was annoying, but unavoidable.

An inspection of the room revealed several windows along one side and a door at one end.

The door was equipped with a latch similar to that through which he had just passed and which was made to open from the outside with a key, but which could be operated by hand from the inside. It was a very crude and simple affair, and for that Tanar would have been grateful had he known how intricate locks may be made.

Lifting the catch Tanar pushed the door slightly ajar and before him he saw a long corridor, lighted by windows upon one side and with doors opening from it upon the other. As he looked a Korsar came from one of the doorways and, turning, walked down the corridor away from him and a moment later a woman emerged from another doorway, and then he saw other people at the far end of the corridor. Quickly Tanar of Pellucidar closed and latched the door.

Here was no avenue of escape. Were he back in his dark cell he could not have been cut off more effectually from the outer world than he was in this apartment at the far end of a corridor constantly used by Korsars; for with his smooth face and his naked body, he would be recognized and seized the instant that he stepped from the room. But Tanar was far from being overwhelmed by discouragement. Already he had come much further on the road to escape than he had previously dreamed could be possible and not only this thought heartened him, but even more the effect of daylight, which had for so long been denied him. He had felt his spirit and his courage expand beneath the beneficent influence of the light of the noonday sun, so that he felt ready for any emergency that might confront him.

Turning back once more into the room he searched it carefully for some other avenue of escape. He went to the windows and found that they overlooked the garden of The Cid, but there were many people there, too, in that part of the garden close to the palace. The trees cut off his view of the far end from which he had helped Stellara and Gura to escape, but he guessed that there were few, if any, people there, though to reach it would be a difficult procedure from the windows of this storeroom.

To his left, near the opposite side of the garden, he could see that the trees grew closely together and extended thus apparently the full length of the enclosure.

If those trees had been upon this side of the garden he guessed that he might have found a way to escape; at least as far as the gate in the garden wall close to the barracks, but they were not and so he must abandon thought of them.

There seemed, therefore, no other avenue of escape than the corridor into which he had just looked; nor could he remain indefinitely in this chamber where there was neither food nor water and with a steadily increasing danger that his absence from the dungeon would be discovered when they found that he did not consume the food they brought him.

Seating himself upon a bale of hide Tanar gave himself over to contemplation of his predicament and as he studied the matter his eyes fell upon some of the loose clothing strewn about the room. There he saw the shorts and shirts of Korsar, the gay sashes and head handkerchiefs, the wide topped boots, and with a half smile upon his lips he gathered such of them as he required, shook the dust from them and clothed himself after the manner of a Korsar. He needed no mirror though to know that his smooth face would betray him.

He selected pistols, a dirk and a cutlass, but he could find neither powder nor balls for his firearms.

Thus arrayed and armed he surveyed himself as best he might without a mirror. 'If I could keep my back toward all Korsar,' he mused, 'I might escape with ease for I warrant I look as much a Korsar as any of them from the rear, but unless I can grow bushy whiskers I shall not deceive anyone.'

As he sat musing thus he became aware suddenly of voices raised in altercation just outside the door of the storeroom. One was a man's voice; the other a woman's.

'And if you won't have me,' growled the man, 'I'll take you.'

Tanar could not hear the woman's reply, though he heard her speak and knew from her voice that it was a woman.

'What do I care for The Cid?' cried the man. 'I am as powerful in Korsar as he. I could take the throne and be Cid myself, if I chose.'

Again Tanar heard the woman speak.

'If you do I'll choke the wind out of you,' threatened the man. 'Come in here where we can talk better. Then you can yell all you want for no one can hear you.'

Tanar heard the man insert a key in the lock and as he did so the Pellucidarian sought a hiding place behind a pile of wicker hampers.

'And after you get out of this room,' continued the man, 'there will be nothing left for you to yell about.'

'I have told you right along,' said the woman, 'that I would rather kill myself than mate with you, but if you take me by force I shall still kill myself, but I shall kill you first.'

The heart of Tanar of Pellucidar leaped in his breast when he heard that voice. His fingers closed upon the hilt of the cutlass at his side, and as Bulf voiced a sneering laugh in answer to the girl's threat, the Sarian leaped from his concealment, a naked blade shining in his right hand.

At the sound behind him Bulf wheeled about and for an instant he did not recognize the Sarian in the Korsar garb, but Stellara did and she voiced a cry of mingled surprise and joy.

'Tanar!' she cried. 'My Tanar!'

As the Sarian rushed him Bulf fell back, drawing his cutlass as he retreated. Tanar saw that he was making for the door leading into the corridor and he rushed at the man to engage him before he could escape, so that Bulf was forced to stand and defend himself.

'Stand back,' cried Bulf, 'or you shall die for this,' but Tanar of Pellucidar only laughed in his face, as he swung a wicked blow at the man's head, which Bulf but barely parried, and then they were at one another like two wild beasts.

Tanar drew first blood from a slight gash in Bulf's shoulder and then the fellow yelled for help.

'You said that no one could hear Stellara's cries for help from this apartment,' taunted Tanar, 'so why do you think that they can hear yours?'

'Let me out of here,' cried Bulf. 'Let me out and I will give you your freedom.' But Tanar rushed him into a corner and the sharp edge of his cutlass sheared an ear from Bulf's head.

'Help!' shrieked the Korsar. 'Help! it is Bulf. The Sarian is killing me.'

Fearful that his loud cries might reach the corridor beyond and attract attention, Tanar increased the fury of his assault. He beat down the Korsar's guard. He swung his cutlass in one terrible circle that clove Bulf's ugly skull to the bridge of his nose, and with a gurgling gasp the great brute lunged forward upon his face. And Tanar of Pellucidar turned and took Stellara in his arms.

'Thank God,' he said, 'that I was in time.'

'It must have been God Himself who led you to this room,' said the girl. 'I thought you dead. They told me that you were dead.'

'No,' said Tanar. 'They put me in a dark dungeon beneath the palace, where I was condemned to remain for life.'

'And you have been so near me all this time,' said Stellara, 'and I thought that you were dead.'

'For a long time I thought that I was worse than dead,' replied the man. 'Darkness, solitude and silence – God! That is worse than death.'

'And yet you escaped!' The girl's voice was filled with awe.

'It was because of you that I escaped,' said Tanar. 'Thoughts of you kept me from going mad – thought and hope urged me on to seek some avenue of escape. Never again as long as life is in me shall I feel that there can be any situation that is entirely hopeless after what I have passed through.'

Stellara shook her head. 'Your hope will have to be strong, dear heart, against the discouragement that you must face in seeking a way out of the palace of The Cid and the city of Korsar.'

'I have come this far,' replied Tanar. 'Already have I achieved the impossible. Why should I doubt my ability to wrest freedom for you and for me from whatever fate holds in store for us?'

'You cannot pass them with that smooth face, Tanar,' said the girl, sadly. 'Ah, if you only had Bulf's whiskers,' and she glanced down at the corpse of the fallen man.

Tanar turned, too, and looked down at Bulf, where he lay in a pool of blood upon the floor. And then quickly he faced Stellara. 'Why not?' he cried. 'Why not?'

17

Down to the Sea

'What do you mean?' demanded Stellara.

'Wait and you shall see,' replied Tanar, and drawing his dirk he stooped and turned Bulf over upon his back. Then with the razor-sharp blade of his weapon he commenced to hack off the bushy, black beard of the dead Korsar, while Stellara looked on in questioning wonder.

Spreading Bulf's headcloth flat upon the floor, Tanar deposited upon it the hair that he cut from the man's face, and when he had completed his gruesome tonsorial effort he folded the hair into the handkerchief, and, rising, motioned for Stellara to follow him.

Going to the door that led into the tunnel through which he had escaped from the dungeon, Tanar opened it, and, smearing his fingers with the pitch that exuded from the boards upon the inside of the door, he smeared some of it upon the side of his face and then turned to Stellara.

'Put this hair upon my face in as natural a way as you can. You have lived among them all your life, so you should know well how a Korsar's beard should look.'

Horrible as the plan seemed and though she shrank from touching the hair of the dead man, Stellara steeled herself and did as Tanar bid. Little by little, patch by patch, Tanar applied pitch to his face and Stellara placed the hair upon it until presently only the eyes and nose of the Sarian remained exposed. The expression of the former were altered by increasing the size and bushiness of the eyebrows with shreds of Bulf's beard that had been left over, and then Tanar smeared his nose with some of Bulf's blood, for many of the Korsars had large, red noses. Then Stellara stood away and surveyed him critically. 'Your own mother would not know you,' she said.

'Do you think I can pass as a Korsar?' he asked.

'No one will suspect, unless they question you closely as you leave the palace.'

'We are going together,' said Tanar.

'But how?' asked Stellara.

'I have been thinking of another plan,' he said. 'I noticed when I was living in the barracks that sailors going toward the river had no difficulty in passing through the gate leaving the palace. In fact, it is always much easier to leave the palace than to enter it. On many occasions I have heard them say merely that they were going to their ships. We can do the same.'

'Do I look like a Korsar sailor?' demanded Stellara.

'You will when I get through with you,' said Tanar, with a grin.

'What do you mean?'

'There is Korsar clothing here,' said Tanar; 'enough to outfit a dozen and there is still plenty of hair on Bulf's head.'

The girl drew back with a shudder. 'Oh, Tanar! You cannot mean that.'

'What other way is there?' he demanded. 'If we can escape together is it not worth any price that we might have to pay?'

'You are right,' she said. 'I will do it.'

When Tanar completed his work upon her, Stellara had been transformed into a bearded Korsar, but the best that he could do in the way of disguise failed to entirely hide the contours of her hips and breasts.

'I am afraid they will suspect,' he said. 'Your figure is too feminine for shorts and a shirt to hide it.'

'Wait,' exclaimed Stellara. 'Sometimes the sailors, when they are going on long voyages, wear cloaks, which they use to sleep in if the nights are cool. Let us see if we can find such a one here.'

'Yes, I saw one,' replied Tanar, and crossing the room he returned with a cloak made of wide striped goods. 'That will give you greater height,' he said. But when they draped it about her, her hips were still too much in evidence.

'Build out my shoulders,' suggested Stellara, and with scarfs and handkerchiefs the Sarian built the girl's shoulders out so that the cloak hung straight and she resembled a short, stocky man, more than a slender, well-formed girl.

'Now we are ready,' said the Sarian. Stellara pointed to the body of Bulf.

'We cannot leave that lying there,' she said. 'Someone may come to this room and discover it and when they do every man in the palace – yes, even in the entire city – will be arrested and questioned.'

Tanar looked about the room and then he seized the corpse of Bulf and dragged it into a far corner, after which he piled bundles of hides and baskets upon it until it was entirely concealed, and over the blood stains upon the floor he dragged other bales and baskets until all signs of the duel had been erased or hidden.

'And now,' he said, 'is as good a time as another to put our disguises to the test.' Together they approached the door. 'You know the least frequented passages to the garden,' said Tanar. 'Let us make our way from the palace through the garden to the gate that gave us escape before.'

'Then follow me,' replied Stellara, as Tanar opened the door and the two stepped out into the corridor beyond. It was empty. Tanar closed the door behind him, and Stellara led the way down the passage.

They had proceeded but a short distance when they heard a man's voice in an apartment to the left.

'Where is she?' he demanded.

'I do not know,' replied a woman's voice. 'She was here but a moment ago and Bulf was with her.'

'Find them and lose no time about it,' commanded the man, sternly. And he stepped from the apartment just as Tanar and Stellara were approaching.

It was The Cid. Stellara's heart stopped beating as the Korsar ruler looked into the faces of Tanar and herself.

'Who are you?' demanded The Cid.

'We are sailors,' said Tanar, quickly, before Stellara could reply.

'What are you doing here in my palace?' demanded the Korsar ruler.

'We were sent here with packages to the storeroom,' replied Tanar, 'and we are but now returning to our ship.'

'Well, be quick about it. I do not like your looks,' growled The Cid as he stamped off down the corridor ahead of them.

Tanar saw Stellara sway and he stepped to her side and supported her, but she quickly gained possession of herself, and an instant later turned to the right and led Tanar through a doorway into the garden.

'God!' whispered the man, as they walked side by side after quitting the building. 'If The Cid did not know you, then your disguise must be perfect.'

Stellara shook her head for even as yet she could not control her voice to speak, following the terror induced by her encounter with The Cid.

There were a number of men and women in the garden close to the palace. Some of these scrutinized them casually, but they passed by in safety and a moment later the gravel walk they were following wound through dense shrubbery that hid them from view and then they were at the doorway in the garden wall.

Again fortune favored them here and they passed out into the barracks yards without being noticed.

Electing to try the main gate because of the greater number of people who passed to and fro through it, Tanar turned to the right, passed along the full length of the barracks past a dozen men and approached the gate with Stellara at his side.

They were almost through when a stupid looking Korsar soldier stopped them. 'Who are you,' he demanded, 'and what business takes you from the palace?'

'We are sailors,' replied Tanar. 'We are going to our ship.'

'What were you doing in the palace?' demanded the man.

'We took packages there from the captain of the ship to The Cid's storeroom,' explained the Sarian.

'I do not like the looks of you,' said the man. 'I have never seen either one of you before.'

'We have been away upon a long cruise,' replied Tanar.

'Wait here until the captain of the gate returns,' said the man. 'He will wish to question you.'

The Sarian's heart sank. 'If we are late in returning to our ship, we shall be punished,' said he.

'That is nothing to me,' replied the soldier.

Stellara reached inside her cloak and beneath the man's shorts that covered her own apparel and searched until she found a pouch that was attached to her girdle. From this she drew something which she slipped into Tanar's hands. He understood immediately, and stepping close to the soldier he pressed two pieces of gold into the fellow's palm. 'It will go very hard with us if we are late,' he said.

The man felt the cool gold within his palm. 'Very well,' he said, gruffly, 'go on about your business, and be quick about it.'

Without waiting for a second invitation Tanar and Stellara merged with the crowd upon the Korsar street. Nor did either speak, and it is possible that Stellara did not even breathe until they had left the palace gate well behind.

'And where now?' she asked at last.

'We are going to sea,' replied the man.

'In a Korsar ship?' she demanded.

'In a Korsar boat,' he replied. 'We are going fishing.'

Along the banks of the river were moored many craft, but when Tanar saw how many men were on or around them he realized that the plan he had chosen, which contemplated stealing a fishing boat, most probably would end disastrously, and he explained his doubts to Stellara.

'We could never do it,' she said. 'Stealing a boat is considered the most heinous crime that one can commit in Korsar, and if the owner of a boat is not aboard it you may rest assured that some of his friends are watching it for him, even though there is little likelihood that anyone will attempt to steal it since the penalty is death.'

Tanar shook his head. 'Then we shall have to risk passing through the entire city of Korsar,' he said, 'and going out into the open country without any reasonable excuse in the event that we are questioned.'

'We might buy a boat,' suggested Stellara.

'I have no money,' said Tanar.

'I have,' replied the girl. 'The Cid has always kept me well supplied with gold.' Once more she reached into her pouch and drew forth a handful of gold pieces. 'Here,' she said, 'take these. If they are not enough you can ask me for more, but I think that you can buy a boat for half that sum.'

Questioning the first man that he approached at the river side, Tanar learned that there was a small fishing boat for sale a short way down the river, and it was not long before they had found its owner and consummated the purchase.

As they pushed off into the current and floated down stream, Tanar became conscious of a sudden conviction that his escape from Korsar had been effected too easily; that there must be something wrong, that either he was dreaming or else disaster and recapture lay just ahead.

Borne down toward the sea by the slow current of the river, Tanar wielded a single oar, paddlewise from the stern, to keep the boat out in the channel and its bow in the right direction, for he did not wish to make sail under the eyes of Korsar sailors and fishermen, as he was well aware that he could not do so without attracting attention by his bungling to his evident inexperience and thus casting suspicion upon them.

Slowly the boat drew away from the city and from the Korsar raiders anchored in mid-stream and then, at last, he felt that it would be safe to hoist the sail and take advantage of the land breeze that was blowing.

With Stellara's assistance the canvas was spread and as it bellied to the wind the craft bore forward with accelerated speed, and then behind them they heard shouts and, turning, saw three boats speeding toward them.

Across the waters came commands for them to lay to.

The pursuing boats, which had set out under sail and had already acquired considerable momentum, appeared to be rapidly overhauling the smaller craft. But presently, as the speed of the latter increased, the distance between them seemed not to vary.

The shouts of the pursuers had attracted the attention of the sailors on board the anchored raiders, and presently Tanar and Stellara heard the deep boom of a cannon and a heavy shot struck the water just off their starboard bow.

Tanar shook his head. 'That is too close,' he said. 'I had better come about.'

'Why?' demanded Stellara.

'I do not mind risking capture,' he said, 'because in that event no harm will befall you when they discover your identity, but I cannot risk the cannon shots for if one of them strikes us, you will be killed.'

'Do not come about,' cried the girl. 'I would rather die here with you than be captured, for capture would mean death for you and then I should not care to live. Keep on, Tanar, we may outdistance them yet. And as for their cannon shots, a small, moving boat like this is a difficult target and their marksmanship is none too good.'

Again the cannon boomed and this time the ball passed over them and struck the water just beyond.

'They are getting our range,' said Tanar.

The girl moved close to his side, where he sat by the tiller. 'Put your arm around me, Tanar,' she said. 'If we must die, let us die together.'

The Sarian encircled her with his free arm and drew her close to him, and an instant later there was a terrific explosion from the direction of the raider that had been firing on them. Turning quickly toward the ship, they saw what had happened – an overcharged cannon had exploded.

'They were too anxious,' said Tanar.

It was some time before another shot was fired and this one fell far astern, but the pursuing boats were clinging tenaciously to their wake.

'They are not gaining,' said Stellara.

'No,' said Tanar, 'and neither are we.'

'But I think we shall after we reach the open sea,' said the girl. 'We shall get more wind there and this boat is lighter and speedier than theirs. Fate smiled upon us when it led us to this boat rather than to a larger one.'

As they approached the sea their pursuers, evidently fearing precisely what Stellara had suggested, opened fire upon them with harquebuses and pistols. Occasionally a missile would come dangerously close, but the range was just a little too great for their primitive weapons and poor powder.

On they sailed out into the open Korsar Az, which stretched onward and upward into the concealing mist of the distance. Upon their left the sea ran inward forming a great bay, while almost directly ahead of them, though at so great a distance that it was barely discernible, rose the dim outlines of a headland, and toward this Tanar held his course.

The chase had settled down into a dogged test of endurance. It was evident that the Korsars had no intention of giving up their prey even though the pursuit led to the opposite shore of the Korsar Az, and it was equally evident that Tanar entertained no thought of surrender.

On and on they sped, the pursued and the pursuers. Slowly the headland took shape before them, and later a great forest was visible to the left of it – a forest that ran down almost to the sea.

'You are making for land?' asked Stellara.

'Yes,' replied the Sarian: 'We have neither food nor water and if we had I am not sufficiently a sailor to risk navigating this craft across the Korsar Az.'

'But if we take to the land, they will be able to trail us,' said the girl.

'You forget the trees, Stellara,' the man reminded her.

'Yes, the trees,' she cried. 'I had forgotten. If we can reach the trees I believe that we shall be safe.'

As they approached the shore inside the headland, they saw great combing rollers breaking among the rocks and the angry, sullen boom of the sea came back to their ears.

'No boat can live in that,' said Stellara.

Tanar glanced up and down the shore-line as far as he could see and then he turned and let his eyes rest sadly upon his companion.

'It looks hopeless,' he said. 'If we had time to make the search we might find a safer landing place, but within sight of us one place seems to be as good as another.'

'Or as bad,' said Stellara.

'It cannot be helped,' said the Sarian. 'To beat back now around that promontory in an attempt to gain the open sea again, would so delay us that we should be overtaken and captured. We must take our chances in the surf, or turn about and give up.'

Behind them their pursuers had come about and were waiting, rising and falling upon the great billows.

'They think that they have us,' said Stellara. 'They believe that we shall tack here and make a run for the open sea around the end of that promontory, and they are ready to head us off.'

Tanar held the boat's nose straight for the shoreline. Beyond the angry surf he could see a sandy beach, but between lay a barrier of rock upon which the waves broke, hurling their spume far into the air.

'Look!' exclaimed Stellara, as the boat raced toward the smother of boiling water. 'Look! There! Right ahead! There may be a way yet!'

'I have been watching that place,' said Tanar. 'I have been holding her straight for it, and if it is a break in the rocky wall we shall soon know it, and if it is not—'

The Sarian glanced back in the direction of the Korsars' boats and saw that they were again in pursuit, for by this time it must have become evident to them that their quarry was throwing itself upon the rocky shore-line in desperation rather than to risk capture by turning again toward the open sea.

Every inch of sail was spread upon the little craft and the taut, bellowing canvas strained upon the cordage until it hummed, as the boat sped straight for the rocks dead ahead.

Tanar and Stellara crouched in the stern, the man's left arm pressing the girl protectingly to his side. With grim fascination they watched the bowsprit rise and fall as it rushed straight toward what seemed must be inevitable disaster.

They were there! The sea lifted them high in the air and launched them forward upon the rocks. To the right a jagged finger of granite broke through the smother of spume. To the left the sleek, water-worn side of a huge boulder revealed itself for an instant as they sped past. The boat grated and rasped upon a sunken rock, slid over and raced toward the sandy beach.

Tanar whipped out his dirk and slashed the halyards, bringing the sail down as the boat's keel touched the sand. Then, seizing Stellara in his arms, he leaped into the shallow water and hastened up the shore.

Pausing, they looked back toward the pursuing Korsars and to their astonishment saw that all three boats were making swiftly toward the rocky shore.

'They dare not go back without us,' said Stellara, 'or they would never risk that surf.'

'The Cid must have guessed our identity, then, when a search failed to reveal you,' said Tanar.

'It may also be that they discovered your absence from the dungeon, and coupling this with the fact that I, too, was missing, someone guessed the identity of the two sailors who sought to pass through the gate and who paid gold for a small boat at the river,' suggested Stellara.

'There goes one of them on the rocks,' cried Tanar, as the leading boat disappeared in a smother of water.

The second boat shared the same fate as its predecessor, but the third rode through the same opening that had carried Tanar and Stellara to the safety of the beach and as it did the two fugitives turned and ran toward the forest.

Behind them raced a dozen Korsars and amidst the crack of pistols and harquebuses Tanar and Stellara disappeared within the dark shadows of the primeval forest.

The story of their long and arduous journey through unknown lands to the kingdom of Sari would be replete with interest, excitement and adventure, but it is no part of this story.

It is enough to say that they arrived at Sari shortly before Ja and Gura made their appearance, the latter having been delayed by adventures that had almost cost them their lives.

The people of Sari welcomed the Amiocapian mate that the son of Ghak had brought back to his own country. And Gura they accepted, too, because she had befriended Tanar, though the young men accepted her for herself and many were the trophies that were laid before the hut of the beautiful Himean maiden. But she repulsed them all for in her heart she held a secret love that she had never divulged, but which, perhaps, Stellara had guessed and which may have accounted for the tender solicitude which the Amiocapian maid revealed for her Himean sister.

CONCLUSION

As Perry neared the end of the story of Tanar of Pellucidar, the sending became weaker and weaker until it died out entirely, and Jason Gridley could hear no more.

He turned to me. 'I think Perry had something more to say,' he said. 'He was trying to tell us something. He was trying to ask something.'

'Jason,' I said, reproachfully, 'didn't you tell me that the story of the inner world is perfectly ridiculous; that there could be no such place peopled by strange reptiles and men of the stone age? Didn't you insist that there is no Emperor of Pellucidar?'

'Tut-tut,' he said. 'I apologize. I am sorry. But that is past. The question now is what can we do.'

'About what?' I asked.

'Do you not realize that David Innes lies a prisoner in a dark dungeon beneath the palace of The Cid of Korsar?' he demanded with more excitement than I have ever known Jason Gridley to exhibit.

'Well, what of it?' I demanded. 'I am sorry, of course; but what in the world can we do to help him?'

'We can do a lot,' said Jason Gridley, determinedly.

I must confess that as I looked at him I felt considerable solicitude for the state of his mind for he was evidently laboring under great excitement.

'Think of it!' he cried. 'Think of that poor devil buried there in utter darkness, silence, solitude – and with those snakes! God!' he shuddered. 'Snakes crawling all over him, winding about his arms and his legs and his body, creeping across his face as he sleeps, and nothing else to break the monotony – no human voice, the song of no bird, no ray of sunlight. Something must be done. He must be saved.'

'But who is going to do it?' I asked.

'I am!' replied Jason Gridley.

If you've enjoyed these books and would
like to read more, you'll find literally thousands
of classic Science Fiction & Fantasy titles
through the **SF Gateway**

✳

For the new home of
Science Fiction & Fantasy . . .

✳

For the most comprehensive collection
of classic SF on the internet . . .

✳

Visit the SF Gateway

www.sfgateway.com

Edgar Rice Burroughs (1875 – 1950)

Edgar Rice Burroughs was a prolific American author of the 'pulp' era. The son of a Civil War veteran, he saw brief military service with the 7th U.S. Cavalry before he was diagnosed with a heart problem and discharged. After working for five years in his father's business, Burroughs left for a string of disparate and short-lived jobs, and was working as a pencil sharpener wholesaler when he decided to try his hand at writing. He found almost instant success when his story 'Under the Moons of Mars' was serialised in *All-Story Magazine* in 1912, earning him the then-princely sum of $400.

Burroughs went on to have tremendous success as a writer, his wide-ranging imagination taking in other planets (John Carter of Mars and Carson of Venus), a hollow earth (Pellucidar), a lost world, westerns, historicals and adventure stories. Although he wrote in many genres, Burroughs is best known for his creation of the archetypal jungle hero, Tarzan. Edgar Rice Burroughs died in 1950.